L.M. RANSOM

fine the magic in everyday life ♡

WICKED WHALE PUBLISHING

L.M. Ransom

First Edition: March 2019

Cover Design: Cape Cod Scribe
Editor: Kat Szmit, OneWickedWordsmith.com

Library of Congress Cataloging-in-Publication Data

Ransom, L.M..

TILT/ by L.M. Ransom – First Edition.

    Pages: 394

    Summary: Sixteen-year-old Charlotte Flynn must search for the missing, magical carousel horses and find them before the forces of darkness track them down first.

Wicked Whale Publishing

P.O. Box 264,

Sagamore Beach, MA 02562

www.WickedWhalePublishing.com

ISBN: 978-1-7320588-2-8

Published in the United States of America

Dedication

To all the horses I've known over the many years of riding, but specifically to Misty, Promise, Dipper, Crescendo (who belonged to my Aunt Lorraine but was loved like one of my own), Romeo, Billy, and especially BJ, my current riding partner. You all taught me well. You were, and are, the best horses a girl could ever have. I see each of you in the Flying Ponies.

"*Horses are predictably unpredictable.*"

— Loretta Gage

There are 33 horses on the Flying Ponies Grand Carousel, and each one of them is based on a real carousel horse. Some of them are in museums now, such as the Daniel Muller Cavalry Horse (the only "haunted" carousel horse in existence), who lives at the Frontier Museum at Cedar Point Amusement Park in Ohio and is my model for Dreadful. Others, including the Charles Looff dapple grey that I used as my model for Penumbra, belong to private owners.

And then there are the ones who still reside on carousels, where people can ride them and experience the magic of bygone years. The 1928 Spillman carousel at the Grand Rapids Public Museum in Grand Rapids, MI, owns five of the horses I used as models. Contessa, Czarina, Memento, Oriflamme, and Phantasm (my names for them, of course) are available along with several other horses and animals for daily rides at the museum. The Spillman carousel is beautiful, and a testament to the craftsmanship and dedication of the men who created them.

I encourage all my readers to visit the Grand Rapids Public Museum and ride the carousel, located in its own unique glass enclosure. Tell the Flying Ponies there I said hi.

This was crazy. Completely nuts! Why had she agreed to this? Charlotte Flynn's stomach dropped as the bay carousel horse she was riding dove toward a line of pine trees. She squeezed her eyes shut. *You won't yell at him. You won't yell at him...*"Dreadful!" His name ripped from her throat. With a loud whinny that sounded suspiciously like a laugh, the stallion bucked and climbed high into the cold October air.

"Not funny," Charlotte muttered. Dreadful tossed his head.

"Dreadful thinks it's funny," he retorted.

She was sure he did. He'd only tried knocking her off four times already. Bending her face close to his shiny wooden neck, she wondered how much further they had to go. The world below them was starting to wake up; she could make out vehicles along the roads that twisted their way through the Michigan terrain. *I hope Dreadful knows where to go.* She hadn't thought of that before climbing on his back. When she had thought of it, the horse told her he knew where to go. How, she had no idea. But he was full of powerful magic. Besides, she had other things to consider.

Things like our family owning an antique magical carousel. Things like people who haven't aged in decades. Things like boys who make me crazy. She flushed with the last thought.

What boys? Dreadful's voice cut through her mind. It was dry like the rustle of wind through dune grass, and it made Charlotte think of the beach Uncle Baron had taken her and her five siblings to during the hot summer months.

Her stomach clenched and anger flooded through her. Her uncle had taken them in after the death of their father and taken care of them, until the last few weeks. Then he'd turned on them and taken off with Penumbra, the lead horse on the Flying Ponies Grand Carousel. *My carousel.* Well, technically, the *family* carousel, but it was hard for her to distinguish the difference anymore.

WHAT BOYS? Dreadful's voice thundered in her mind, and she flinched.

"Black, I mean Sullivan, and Dante," she muttered, leaning down close to his ear. The horse snorted, making her frown. Why was she having this discussion with a wooden horse? What did he care?

Dreadful likes Sullivan.

"Not Dante?" Now she was curious. Dreadful tossed his head and suddenly dove. Charlotte squeaked and wrapped her arms around his neck. The wind gusted past them, but she was warm. Did his magic protect her from the elements? She would've asked him, but as it was she was barely hanging on. He leveled out just above a farmhouse, and she glanced down, seeing a yellow school bus slowing to a stop in front of the house. Two children, about Danny's age, probably, raced down the driveway to it.

Dreadful let out a loud neigh, and the kids jerked to a stop and looked up. Charlotte caught a glimpse of them with their mouths hanging open before her mount shifted directions and took off to the north. *They could see us – the magic is getting a lot stronger.*

Dreadful doesn't trust Dante. The words murmured through Charlotte's mind as the stallion raced across the sky, the wind now at their back.

She couldn't blame him. Dante Romano didn't give off the stable vibes that Sullivan "Black" Midnight did. Her stomach fluttered. Black had kissed her right before she'd taken off into the sky. Wishing he'd been able to come with her, and thinking it was probably a good thing he hadn't considering the way Dreadful was acting, she hoped he'd be back at the house in the woods soon. She couldn't wait to see him again.

An hour later the house came into view, but Dreadful flew over it. "Wait, go back," Charlotte urged, tugging on his mane. The stallion gave a hard buck, almost knocking her off. "Dreadful!" she yelled. "Go back!"

The cavalry horse landed near the carousel instead. Instantly Charlotte could sense the animosity radiating from the dapple-grey stallion that jumped off the carousel's platform to meet them.

3

Penumbra struck the ground with his front left leg, sending splashes of dazzling green up from the ground. "You are not welcome here, Dreadful," he called. His voice was loud and commanding.

Dreadful pinned his ears and sidestepped, almost dumping Charlotte again. "Off," he ordered, and she hurried to obey. He whirled and kicked out at her as she jumped away from him. Turning to face Penumbra again, the bay horse said, "This is Dreadful's carousel."

"Ha," Penumbra snorted. His dark eyes glittered in the low light of the morning. "The Flying Ponies are mine, you crazy nag." He gave a sharp whinny, and Charlotte heard the clatter of hooves as the other carousel horses left the platform and joined their leader on the ground.

Charlotte's heart was hammering. Did she try to intervene between the two of them? She hadn't expected the two stallions to meet this early. And if Penumbra was here, did that mean Uncle Baron was, too? She looked toward the empty carousel. No one was coming up from the center of it, where Black and his grandfather, Mr. Coal, kept a tiny apartment. It was just her and the small herd of brightly-painted wooden horses.

Penumbra looked at her. "You are not welcome here, Charlotte," he said. When she opened her mouth, Warpaint, the chestnut pinto stallion wearing a blue bridle and saddle stepped up next to the dapple grey.

"He *said* you are not welcome," Warpaint told her. A thin ray of sunlight highlighted the carved pistol that hung on the front of his saddle.

Charlotte put a hand on her hip and pointed at the two horses. "I'm the Capall. It might not mean that much to you, but there it is. I'm not afraid of you." Truth be told, she was trying hard not to let them see her shake.

Penumbra gave a snorting horse laugh. "Yes you are," he said. He lifted his right front hoof and jabbed it toward Dreadful. The bay stallion bared his teeth. "You're frightened, so you brought him back," Penumbra added.

Well, that was true. Charlotte's stomach growled. *Oh, for Pete's sake. Not now!* How could she possibly be hungry now, when there was a carousel horse rumble about to go down? She frowned and said, "Why are you working with my uncle? You know he's going to use your magic for evil!" How could these magnificent horses turn against humanity?

"It's best if you go." The quiet words came from Flint-lock, the husky palomino mare. She moved to stand on Penumbra's other side.

"Don't do this," Charlotte said. "You don't have to listen to Uncle Baron!"

"Nor do we need to listen to you." Penumbra suddenly lunged at her. Charlotte stumbled back, her blue-grey eyes widening in fear. Dreadful raced in from her right side and met the grey stallion. Penumbra drew up short and tossed his head.

"Go, before I hurt you," he ordered the bay.

"You can't hurt Dreadful," the cavalry pony said, shaking his head. His thick black mane tumbled about his neck, small flecks of sunlight catching in it. "You are afraid of him."

Charlotte saw the other Flying Ponies starting to move, forming a circle around the two stallions. This wasn't good. She doubted Dreadful could take them all on by himself, and she didn't want any of them to get hurt. Even though they'd chosen to follow her uncle, they were still important to her. They were important to her whole family, in fact. She took a step toward the bay horse.

"Dreadful, come on," she said, her voice low. She caught movement from the corner of her eye, and saw Sirocco, the elegant palomino mare, edging toward her. Beside her was Chimerical, the cornflower-blue mare, her ears flattened back against her skull. "Dreadful, *come on*," Charlotte said between gritted teeth. There was no way this would end well for him.

The cavalry horse glanced at her, and she could see an orangish glow in his dark eye. Something inside her chest twisted. He was going to fight. "No!" she said and grabbed his mane. "We're leaving!" Dreadful snapped his teeth at her, but she wasn't giving in. She couldn't afford for him to get hurt. Grabbing a bigger handful of his mane she tugged hard. Dreadful squealed at her, but she only pulled harder. "Come on," she urged. The other carousel ponies were pressing in around them; she saw Penumbra's dark eyes glittering, and the horses began to stomp their hooves in unison. A strange hum began building in the space around them.

"Dreadful!" Charlotte stepped quickly to his side as she

said his name. She stepped into the stirrup and mounted. He danced sideways but she held on. "We have to get out of here," she told him. Fear pooled in her veins. Bits of color flashed in the air around them and the atmosphere was heavy.

Dreadful suddenly reared and lunged forward. Penumbra, directly in his path, jumped to the side, and the bay horse rushed past him. Charlotte cried out, afraid he was running to the carousel, but he leapt upward into the cold air. She gulped and chanced a look downward. The other Flying Ponies were staring up at them, and she made eye contact for a split-second with Penumbra.

Fury brightened his dark eyes.

We go home now?

Yes, Dreadful. We go home. Charlotte put her cheek against the smooth silk of his wooden coat and closed her eyes.

2

They landed a few minutes later in the yard, and Charlotte slid off his back. She took a deep breath and looked up at the old house. Weathered and huge, it hadn't been at all what she'd expected when Uncle Baron had told her and her siblings they were moving into a mansion in the woods. Still, it was home now, for better or worse. She started up the stairs to the wrap-around porch. "Come on," she said over her shoulder to the horse.

"No."

She stopped and turned to face him. He showed her his teeth, but she ignored the show of aggression. "Why not?"

He pawed at the ground. "Bad magic."

His words gave Charlotte pause. She knew how bad the house could be. "I'll be with you. It's okay," she told him. "I won't let it hurt you."

He looked at her, and she smiled. And waited. Finally,

he bobbed his head and walked up to the steps. "Good boy," she coached, and turned to the door. It was unlocked, and she cautiously stepped in, reaching to her left to turn the lights on. What if Uncle Baron or Mr. Coal were here? "Hello?" she called out. No one answered, and she breathed a sigh of relief. Pushing the door open wider, she beckoned to the stallion. "It's safe," she said.

Dreadful stepped into the house. A roar of wind gusted through the foyer, tangling Charlotte's russet hair and blowing the horse's mane about his neck. He snorted. The chandelier above them swayed in the breeze, throwing weird shadows on the walls.

A chill crawled down Charlotte's back. What if the house didn't like Dreadful being here? What would it do? She put her hand on his neck. The door slammed shut behind them, and then the wind abruptly died. The dancing shadows on the walls disappeared. "See? Nothing to worry about," Charlotte murmured, rubbing Dreadful's neck.

He rolled his eye at her. "Bad magic," he said.

"It's *fine*," she told him. Her stomach growled. "Come with me." She headed down the hall toward the kitchen, and could hear his clattering hoof beats on the marble floor behind her. It gave her a strange sense of protection.

After making a chicken sandwich and offering Dreadful an apple, to which he said carousel horses didn't eat, *ever*, she led him to the large living room off the left of the foyer. She plopped down on one of the couches. Dreadful stood in the doorway for several moments, looking the place over, before finally coming in. He sniffed the TV and game console on the floor next to it, and then sat down on his haunches on the other couch.

Charlotte stared at him, and he looked down his nose at her. "What?" he said.

"Why are you sitting like that? You look like a giant dog," she said, and a small giggle rolled up her throat. Dreadful's answering snort sounded like a chuckle. It felt good to laugh, even it was for just a second. Something stormed across the floor over their heads, causing them both to look up at the ceiling.

"The house hates Dreadful," the horse said, his voice low.

"It doesn't," she assured him. "Hey, can you stop referring to yourself in the third, um, horse?" she asked. "That's getting annoying."

He scrunched his nose at her. "Dreadful prefers it that way."

"Yeah but I don't," she retorted. "So stop." It would annoy the daylights out of her siblings, too. *Speaking of siblings, I wonder where the boys are. How long before they get home?* Her three youngest siblings, Gavin, Marta and Danny, were at Uncle Baron's townhouse in Smoke City, staying with Mrs. Trudeau, Baron's trustworthy housekeeper. She hoped Baron hadn't been there. He probably wouldn't harm them, but after he'd betrayed her and turned the carousel horses against her, she couldn't be completely sure.

They sat in relative quiet for the next ten minutes or so, in which Dreadful kept looking up at the ceiling and she kept pulling her phone out of her pocket and checking the time. She wasn't exactly sure how it was her phone had service; as far she knew, no towers had ever been installed way out here. *Must be the magic,* she mused. So much of her life was infused with it now. Her mind wandered back to the city. How were her friends doing? Did they miss her? She put her head back against the couch and closed her eyes. She missed the city sometimes. Things were less complicated there.

Dreadful rapped a hoof on the wooden floor. Charlotte opened her eyes and sat up. "What is it?" she asked him.

"Something comes," he said. The wind rushed against the house, pummeling it, and she heard a scratching noise at one of the windows. Dreadful leapt off the couch and spun toward the window. "Monster comes," he said.

Charlotte got to her feet and looked at the window. It was gloomy out, the sun's rays just touching the ground here and there. Something moved into view. She choked back a cry. A Desolate stood at the window, its hollow vacant eyes staring in at them. Dreadful shuddered, the movement racing through his sleek wooden body. Black had told her there would be more of the creatures in the woods now that the magic was returning in full-strength. It tapped the glass, pressing closer to it. Dreadful reared, slashing at the air with his sharp hooves.

"Easy, boy," Charlotte murmured. "It can't hurt us." But if it were to try and get in, could it? Would the house protect them? She wished Black was here, and her brothers. And even Dante, though she thought he might be more amused with the monster than anything.

"Bad, bad monster," the stallion said, dropping to all fours again. "Dreadful hates it."

She didn't hate it. It had once been human, but magic had turned it into this creature. Black said they still had a small amount of their humanity left. Looking at the thing, she wasn't sure about that. It tapped the window again with its long slender fingers, making a drumming sound on the glass. She turned away.

"Let's go somewhere else," she said and left the room. After a few moments, Dreadful followed. The house screeched, the noise like nails on a chalkboard, and he whinnied. Charlotte turned to him in time to see an orange glow emanating from him. Little bits of twinkling orange floated around him like a mist, and she could feel the magic wrapping around her. "Dreadful, stop," she said, but her voice was weak. "What are you doing?"

He didn't speak. The magic glistened all around them and her vision blurred. She tried to talk to him again, but her voice wasn't working, and the air was too heavy, too solid to breathe, and then—

"Charlotte." Someone was shaking her shoulder, and she blinked, a hazy film filling her eyes. "Charlotte, wake up."

"Jared?" she asked and dragged a hand across her face.

"Yes. Are you okay? What happened?" Her older brother's voice was sharp and she winced. He put his arm around her shoulders and helped her sit up. She blinked hard and found herself looking at Rory, her younger brother by one year.

"Hey," he said. "You look terrible." He smirked when Jared reached out and cuffed him. "You okay?" Concern filtered into Rory's voice.

"I-I think so." She swallowed. "Where's Dreadful?"

"He's here. Black and Dante are with him." Jared's voice was dark. "Did he hurt you?"

"No." At least, she didn't think so. "I think he was trying to scare the house or something. He had all this orange magic around him." It hurt to think too hard. A headache was sharpening itself behind her eyes.

Rory took her hands and gave them a gentle squeeze before pulling her up. She wobbled for a second, feeling Jared's hand on her back. "Okay?" Rory asked before letting go of her.

"How long have you been here?" she asked, looking between the two of them.

"About ten minutes." Jared's voice was clipped. "We walked in and that horse was standing over you." He sighed. "It didn't look like he was hurting you, but you were lying on the floor. I just assumed things."

Suspicion flared to life. "What did you do to him?" she asked, her eyes narrowing when he looked at the floor.

"Let's just say Dreadful might be scared of him now," Rory told her, shrugging. "Black and Dante figured it was better to separate them."

"Jared," Charlotte said, shaking her head. "He's helping us. He won't hurt me."

Jared met her gaze. "You sure about that?" He jerked a nod toward the living room. "They say he's crazy. Maybe we shouldn't trust him."

"We have to." Charlotte winced as a hot pain stroked across her forehead. "I have a headache."

"I'll get you something. Rory, stay with her." Jared took off down the hall. Rory rolled his eyes.

"I think you're okay," he said. Charlotte didn't bother to respond. She wanted to see Black and ask him about Dreadful's orange magic. Did each pony have its own color like that? And, if she could be honest, she just wanted to see him. There was so much between them, and his gentle kiss had solidified her feelings for him. They needed some time to talk.

Jared tromped back down the hall and gave her a Motrin and a glass of water. She swallowed down the pill gratefully and drank the water. Handing the glass back to him, she headed toward the living room. Jared grabbed her arm. "It's fine," she insisted. "He might be crazy but he's not mean," she added.

He gave her a look. "We'll see," he said and moved toward the room ahead of her. Rory scoffed.

"I'm pretty sure Black wouldn't let that horse near her if he thought she'd get hurt," he said.

Charlotte ducked her head. They had all witnessed Black kissing her; it would give Rory enough ammo to tease her for months. When she stepped into the living room, her eyes were immediately drawn to the umber-haired boy standing next to the bay stallion. Black returned her gaze, a small smile quirking the corner of his mouth. He hurried over to her.

Giving her a quick but firm hug, he stepped back and looked her up and down. "Are you all right?"

She noted that he didn't assume Dreadful had harmed her like Jared did. "I'm fine," she said, nodding. She glanced at the horse. "I think maybe the house scared him. He had all this orange magic around him." When Black said nothing, she looked up at him.

"You're sure you're okay? Dreadful's magic, when concentrated like that, is powerful," he said. Worry filled his blue eyes.

"She looks fine," Dante said, strolling over. He winked at Charlotte when she glanced at him. She frowned at him. "Darling, I only tell the truth. You *are* fine," he added.

Black scowled at him. "Stop it." He put his hand on Charlotte's shoulder, bringing her attention back to him. "Dreadful said there was a monster outside. I'm assuming it was a Desolate?"

"Yes," she said, nodding. "It was at that window." She pointed and added, "It was tapping on the glass." Trepidation at the memory trickled through her. She was happy the boys were here, in case it came back. She and Dreadful could handle it but backup was nice.

"There will be more of them now, with the magic

gaining strength," Black said. He looked at Jared and Rory. "You should be careful whenever you leave the house. Maybe take something with you."

"Like what?" Jared asked.

"We've got baseball bats," Rory added.

"Are you good with them?" Black asked, raising an eyebrow.

Rory snorted. "Good with them? Please. Jared played varsity all four years, and I made varsity my freshman year." He affected a cocky smile. "Yeah, we're *good* with them."

Charlotte wished he wasn't so arrogant. She hated the thought of her brothers having to fight the creatures. "Don't be overconfident," she warned. Rory made a face at her.

"You're the one who needs protecting, not us," he told her.

"Rory." Jared's voice was cold. "Don't tease her." He gestured toward Dreadful. "So now that we have him, what do we do? Do we try to take the other horses back from Uncle Baron?"

"We went to the carousel," Charlotte said. The four boys locked their gazes on her. She glanced at Dreadful; the stallion was once again sitting on the couch, looking up at the ceiling. A tiny smile touched her lips.

"Why did you go there? Why didn't you wait for us?" Jared asked. "Was Uncle Baron around?"

"No." She shook her head. "I didn't have a choice. Dreadful took me to it." She glanced at the horse again, but he wasn't listening. "Penumbra and the other ponies confronted us. I thought he and Dreadful were going to fight." The fear she'd felt in the meadow returned, causing a slight rise in her voice. "He wouldn't have been able to beat all of them."

"I'm not sure the others would've fought," Black said, shaking his head. "If Penumbra had told them to, maybe." His eyes were full of concern, and he added, "I'm assuming you stopped it?"

"I did, but barely." Charlotte twisted her hands together. "You said Penumbra is afraid of him, but he didn't seem to be."

"They haven't seen each other in decades. Perhaps Penumbra forgot how formidable he is," Dante speculated. "It would've been a great fight."

Black frowned. "Maybe, but we're not ready for that yet. We need to find the other missing horses before Baron does. That way, if there is a big fight, Dreadful will have backup too."

"Can he find the missing ones, though?" Rory asked.

"We'll see," Black said. He turned toward the bay. "Dreadful, can you find the missing ponies?"

The stallion got up off the couch and shook himself. When he walked over to them, his hooves beat a staccato rhythm on the floor. "Dreadful can do anything Penumbra can," he said.

Rory laughed. "Does he always do that?"

"Yes," Charlotte said, sighing. "It's annoying but he won't stop."

Dreadful sidled closer to Rory, and without warning bit his arm.

"Ow!" Rory yelled and clamped a hand over the injured spot. "Stupid horse!"

"Enough," Dante ordered. He reached out and slapped Dreadful on the nose. The stallion squealed and snaked out his neck, his teeth snapping. Dante danced backward out of reach.

"This is getting us nowhere," Jared said. Disgust filled his voice. "We need to come up with a plan. Otherwise Uncle Baron is going to win."

"We won't let him," Black said. He glanced at his watch. "It's getting late. We should all get some sleep."

"Should we lock him up?" Jared asked, waving at the horse.

"Duh, what do you think? *Yes,*" Rory told him, shooting a vicious glare at Dreadful.

"I concur with Rory," Dante said. He moved close to Charlotte and put his arm around her shoulders. "I'll walk Charlotte to her room."

Jared's dark blue eyes turned icy. "I'll do that, thanks." He gestured toward the door to the foyer. "Come on."

Charlotte stepped out from Dante's embrace. She wanted Black to go with her but knew it wasn't going to happen. Despite knowing that Black was honorable, Jared wasn't letting down his protective shield just yet.

"I'll take first watch," Black said. "We'll sleep in shifts, in case Baron shows up, or a Desolate tries to get in."

"I'll take the next one," Jared told him. He gave Char-lotte an impatient look. "Let's go."

She nodded and cast a quick look at Black, trying to convey how much she wished it was him going with her. He offered her a small smile, and she smiled back. Jared made an annoyed sound in his throat. Frowning, she hustled to his side and they left the room.

"He's not going to try anything," she muttered as they started up the massive staircase on the left side of the foyer.

"He seems like a good guy, but we don't know him that well."

"Even if you did, you'd probably still act like this." Her petulant tone caused him to chuckle. "That's funny?" She shot him a dark look.

"It is," he said, nodding. "I'm your big brother. It's my job to protect you."

She knew that, and she knew how seriously he took it. When she'd been a freshman, and Jared a junior, one of his baseball teammates had gotten handsy with her after school, when she'd been waiting for Jared to drive her home. She'd tried to get away, but the boy had barricaded her against the lockers. He had teased her, telling her she should be grateful a guy like him was giving her attention, since she was just a geek. Before he'd been able to do too much, Jared had come around the corner, grabbed the boy's shoulder and knocked him to the floor. The boy had stayed down.

Jared glanced at her. "I know you get tired of me some-times, but I do it because I don't want you to get hurt."

"I know. And I appreciate it." Even now, remembering that scene caused her heart to beat harder. He nudged her with his elbow and she looked at him. Immediately he stopped. "I'm okay," she assured him. "I was just thinking about when Tommy corralled me after school." Her voice dropped. She didn't like thinking about it.

"That's why I'm protective," Jared said, his voice gentle. "I'm sure Black is a good guy, but I want you to be careful, okay?" They resumed walking, and she knew he didn't expect an answer.

Once he'd left her in her fanciful carousel horse room, Charlotte collapsed on the bed. So much was going on, swirling through her mind that she didn't think sleep would come. They had Dreadful now, but they had no idea where the missing horses were. She sighed and sat up. No use dwelling on it. After she changed into blue flannel pajamas and took care of her night routine, she climbed back into bed and snuggled down into the thick blankets.

She replayed the scene at the carousel again. Penumbra had been so fierce, and with all the other horses to back him, Dreadful would've lost the fight if it had come to that. She rolled over and squeezed her eyes shut. Thinking about the what-ifs wasn't helping. Instead, she turned her thoughts to Black, and a warm fuzziness filled her chest. She wanted to kiss him again. *I doubt we'll get any alone time, though. And if Rory saw us kiss again I'd never ever hear the end of it.* She groaned into her fluffy pillow. Brothers. *Oy.*

That led her to thinking about her other siblings, and she decided she'd ask Jared if they could go visit them. She missed them, even though they weren't into the Flying Ponies like she was. *But we're a family, and even though Uncle Baron abandoned us, we still have each other. That's enough.* Her thoughts grew foggier, and finally, she drifted into slumber.

3

*B*lack pulled the double doors to Baron's study shut and turned to face Dante. "That will hold him," Black said, confident Dreadful wouldn't escape.

"If you say so. You remember how wild he can be," Dante said, shrugging. They walked across the foyer and back into the living room. "You sure you want the first watch?"

"I'm sure." Black walked over to the windows and peered out. It was pitch-dark outside, and a low wind purred around the house. He wondered if the carousel was all right, if his grandfather was there keeping watch over it.

"All right, then I'm headed back to Whimsies."

Black turned to him. "Why? I assumed you'd be staying here."

Dante shook his head. The solemn look in his eyes made Black uneasy. "I want to make sure things are in order. And I need to contact Orrick."

The uneasiness swamped Black's stomach. "I don't think that's a good idea. You know we can't let him have any say in the carousel."

Dante shoved his hands in the pockets of his dark trousers. "That's not for us to decide, now is it? That decision is Charlotte's."

Agitation hummed through Black, and he tried to shove it down. He wasn't going to wake her now, when she'd probably just fallen asleep. But he wasn't okaying the decision to let the Tyranny have any control over what happened with the Flying Ponies Grand Carousel, either. "She's not going to let them make decisions," he finally said.

Dante's eyes narrowed a titch. "Speaking for the lady now, are we, Sully? Sure that's not just you carrying a grudge toward them?"

"A grudge?" Black's hands balled into fists. "They *stole* horses from the carousel, Romano. They're not any more trustworthy than Baron is and you know it." Anger surged through the words, but he didn't care. How could Dante be so casual about all this? He knew what the Tyranny was capable of.

Shrugging, Dante turned to go. "Charlotte was going to say yes, and we're going to need their help. We'll have access to the ponies they stole."

"Romano." Black's voice cut like a whip. "You can't call them. That's not your decision to make."

Dante stopped. His shoulders were rigid. "Don't let your misplaced feelings for the girl blind you to what has to be done," he said. He shot Black a cutting look and left the room. Seconds later, Black heard the front door open and slam shut, and then the Cadillac start up.

Black muttered unbecoming things and watched the taillights of the SUV disappear from the yard. He cursed again and turned away from the window. There was nothing else he could've done, save for beating Dante up to keep him here. A smirk touched Black's mouth. That might've been enjoyable. Particularly since Romano had made fun of his feelings for Charlotte. *Misplaced. I'd like to misplace **him**.* He knew what he felt for Charlotte ran deep, deeper than he'd allowed himself to feel for a long time.

Shaking his head, he padded out to the foyer. It was silent throughout the house now. The Flynns had retired to bed, and Dreadful was behaving himself for once. Black headed to the kitchen. He could use a sandwich or some-thing. As he stepped into the dining room, though, a crash echoed somewhere above his head. He heard yelling and sprinted back down the hallway and up the staircase on the right.

Reaching the top of the stairs, he moved into the hall-way. There was another crash. This was one directly above him. Someone screamed. "Charlotte!" he yelled and spun in a circle. Where was the next set of stairs? How did he reach the third floor? He ran down the hallway to the left, looking frantically for another staircase. Around him, the house moaned and he heard Dreadful whinny down below.

There were no stairs leading up or down. He stopped in his tracks at the far end of the hallway. His heart pounded against his ribcage. How did he get to her? He remembered, in a moment of sharp clarity, reading about the Winchester House in California, with its never-ending mazes of odd hallways and staircases that led nowhere. Was this mansion built similarly? His breath coming hard, he tried to rationalize what was going on. Charlotte was somewhere above him. There had to be a way to reach her.

He turned and ran back down the hallway to the staircase he'd used. Racing across the foyer, he pounded up the staircase to the left. Halfway up, his eyes caught on an old picture hanging on the wall. He paused, his momentum carrying him a step past it. Bracing a hand on the wall, he peered closely at the framed photo. With a jolt he realized it was the Flying Ponies in the picture. The house murmured, and something nudged his hand closer to the left bottom corner of the frame. Frowning, he felt around it, and suddenly the wall slid backward with a small groan.

Black stepped through the opening and saw another staircase. Climbing it as fast as he could, two stairs at a time, he found himself in another hallway. A nightlight was plugged in half-way down the darkened hall, and he stole down it, his steps cushioned by the thick burgundy carpet. There was another door at the end of the hallway, and he stopped in front of it, wondering if it belonged to Charlotte. He hadn't heard any other noises, but he couldn't calm the thrashing of his heart. That had been her scream – he was positive.

The door had silver inlays, and he had a hunch it was hers. He reached out for the doorknob.

Someone hit him from behind, thrusting him into the door. Black pushed back and turned to face his attacker. Jared's face was inches from his, a steel glower in his eyes. He didn't relent even after a flash of recognition crossed his face, and Black shoved him backward.

"What are you doing?" he demanded.

"What are *you* doing? Why are you going into Charlotte's room?" Hostility flared through Jared's voice, and he took a step closer to Black. "And how did you know about the third floor?"

"I heard her scream, and I came looking for her. She wasn't on the second floor, so obviously there's a third one," Black said. Irritation lined his face. "I'm checking on her."

"I didn't hear her," Jared said. His eyes narrowed. "Why should I believe you?"

"Really? After everything we've been through, you don't trust me?" Black glared at him and turned to the door.

As he reached for the doorknob, it twisted and he barely had time to step back before Charlotte shoved it open. Her eyes were blurry with sleep, and Black inhaled a sharp breath of relief. She looked perfectly fine.

"What's going on? What are you guys doing?" she asked, her voice husky with confusion. "Black? Are you okay?" The instant concern for him made his face flush and a surge of warmth flooded his body.

"Hey, what are you guys doing?" Rory said, walking up to them while rubbing at his eyes.

"I heard Charlotte scream, so I came to check on her,"

Black explained, watching her carefully. She looked at him, her cheeks turning pink.

"I didn't scream…did I?" She sounded even more confused.

"I didn't hear you." Jared's voice was dark with concealed accusations. Black turned his head to look at him and met Jared's antagonistic look with iron confidence. He knew what he'd heard.

"I heard you scream from the second floor," he said, facing her. It might not have been wise to turn his back to her brothers, but he wasn't afraid of them. He was more afraid of Charlotte being hurt. "Maybe it was a dream?" he suggested.

"Maybe," she said. She didn't sound confident though, and now she looked spooked.

Black cursed in his mind. He hadn't meant to upset or scare her. Those were the last things he'd ever want to do. Knowing his every move was being scrutinized by the other two, particularly Jared, he reached out and cupped her chin. Charlotte's eyes darted to his. He smiled and said, his voice gentle, "It was probably a nightmare. I wouldn't worry about it."

"Maybe it was the house playing tricks on you," Rory said. Black stiffened and dropped his hand before looking at the other two. Rory met his eyes and shrugged. "It's possible. It makes noise all the time." He leaned against the wall. "How did you know how to get up here, anyway?"

Black considered. "I saw the carousel picture. I just figured it out." He wasn't telling them that something had nudged his hand to the corner of the frame. "Maybe it was just the house."

"You're right," Charlotte offered. Her voice was quiet and Black knew she was exhausted by the lilt of it.

"Go back to sleep," Jared told her.

"Okay." She yawned and hid it behind her hand. Black watched her go and heard Jared clear his throat.

"I'm going," Black said. He pushed past Jared, making sure his shoulder hit contact with Jared's. Rory stepped back out of his way. At least one brother had some common sense. Why on earth would he ever want to hurt Charlotte? He didn't wait to see if the brothers hung around or went back into their rooms.

Once back on the main floor, he opened a door to Baron's study. Dreadful was standing at the far end, staring out a window. The horse didn't acknowledge him, and Black shut the door. He headed back to the kitchen, his stomach growling now. After making a ham sandwich he sat at the dining room table and stretched out his long legs.

Why would Jared think I'd do something to Charlotte? I haven't been anything but protective of her. Agitation filled him as he tore into his food. Charlotte meant more to him than he could admit to anyone. She was royalty, at least in the world of magical carousel horses. He was nothing more than their caretaker. *And not even that, now.* He'd quit when Baron had turned the Flying Ponies against Charlotte. There was nothing he could offer her, except protection against her crazy uncle. *Desolates, too, I guess.* He knew how to use a ratchet in more than one way.

Finished eating and feeling sick to his stomach, he went to the living room and sat on one of the two couches. The TV held little interest and the game console even less. There were just some things about this thoroughly modern world that he didn't get. Everyone's obsession with their phones boggled him. Why would anyone want to stare at a tiny screen all day long?

He put his head back and closed his eyes. Jared had said he'd take the next watch, but Black wasn't sure he wanted to wake him again. If the house stayed quiet, maybe he'd just let everyone else sleep. Dante would probably be back in the morning. A small groan escaped his lips. How could they explain to Charlotte that the Tyranny was now invested in the Flying Ponies? That was not a conversation he wanted to have.

He fell asleep at some point, his dreams crammed with raging wooden horses, a girl he wanted to protect but failed, and a man with wild black hair and shining blue eyes who spewed dark magic from his mouth whenever he spoke. They were disturbing and when he finally awoke around six, he was no more rested than he'd been when he succumbed to sleep.

The front door opened and shut. Black launched himself off the couch and hurried into the foyer. Dante was standing there, a cardboard carrier laden with coffees hanging from one hand. His other hand grasped a leather bridle. "Good morning, Sully," he said, grinning.

"You have the bridle." Black's voice was low. "How did

you get it? And more importantly, how did you get into the apartment?"

"I stopped in at the carousel, and used my key of course."

Of course. Like it was no big deal. Black frowned. "Was my grandfather there? Or Baron?" He wouldn't ask about the key. Dante had all sorts of magical phenomena at his shop. Of *course* he had a magical key to unlock the center of the carousel.

Dante set the cup carrier down on a small table that sat next to the door. "No, neither of them. Penumbra wasn't happy to see me, though." He paused and met Black's eyes. "It's going to be war for us." He nodded his head toward the ceiling. "For them." He handed Black a cup and held the bridle in both hands. "I thought maybe Charlotte could try putting this on Dreadful. We'll see if he takes it."

Black sipped his coffee, contemplating. *If* the bridle still possessed any magic, it would be worth trying it. But what if the magic just drove the cavalry horse crazier? He voiced this opinion, making Dante scowl.

"Well, we won't know until we try," Dante told him. He glanced up the stairs. "We should wake them soon. We need to get ahead of Baron, if we can."

"What did Orrick say?" Black didn't want to ask, but knew he had to. If Orrick had been brought in, then he wanted to soften the blow for Charlotte, if he could.

Dante drank from his own cup. "He wants to hear it from Charlotte," he said. He smirked. "She's going to say yes. She has to. We need his help."

"We don't." Black stalked past him toward the stairs. If anyone was going to wake the Flynns up, it would be him, not Romano. "Go check on Dreadful," he called over his shoulder.

"If he hurts me you'll feel bad," Dante told him.

Black just grinned as he walked up the stairs.

4

*A*n hour later, the group sat around the dining room table. Charlotte was playing with the bridle, her eyes darting to Black every few moments. Dreadful was still in Baron's study; Dante had felt it was best to keep him separated. It was gloomy outside again, with ominous grey clouds blanketing the sun.

"What's the first step?" Jared asked. He focused on Dante. "Should Charlotte talk to Orrick?"

"No," Black said. He was sitting forward in his chair, his hands clasped in front of him.

"We need the Tyranny," Dante said, shrugging. "It's that simple."

"No, we need the ponies they stole," Black argued. "That's not the same thing." He cast a quick glance at Charlotte. Her heart beat a little harder.

She'd hoped to spend a little time with him alone, but her brothers and Dante had stuck like glue to her since she'd come downstairs. It was annoying. Jared acted like he needed to protect her at any second, and she didn't know why. Yes, she and Black liked one another. Yes, they had kissed. Once. *It's not like he's going to hurt me. All he's ever been is protective.*

"Orrick's not going to give us his horses," Dante said, shaking his head. "He'll need some show of faith on our part."

"They're not *his* horses," Charlotte retorted. She pulled her thoughts away from Black. "They belong to the carousel. To the Flynn family. And I'm not letting him have any say over them."

Dante leaned back in his chair and crossed his arms over his chest. "What's your plan then, sweetheart?" His eyes were sharp. "You must have one, to be so confident that we don't need the Tyranny."

She didn't. There was no plan. They couldn't work with Orrick though, not if he wanted some control over the carousel. Giving in to him would be akin to letting Baron have his way. That wasn't going to happen, not on her watch. Lightning flashed in the windows and thunder roared across the sky.

"So there is no plan," Dante said a few moments later. He looked around the table. "Am I the only one who thinks that's bad?" The agitation in his voice grated on Charlotte.

"You brought the bridle here. I can try it on Dreadful," she said.

"That's not much, but at least it's something," Dante said, and took a sip from his coffee cup.

"Only if it works, though, right?" Jared asked. "What if he won't wear it?"

"It's possible it doesn't have magic anymore, anyway," Black told him. He looked at Charlotte and gave her a quiet smile. "It's worth checking out though." Getting to his feet, he added, "I'll go get him."

Charlotte watched him leave the room, admiring the pull of his shoulders beneath the faded blue flannel shirt he was wearing. Jared cleared his throat, and she dropped her gaze to the table. Rory snickered something. Jared smacked him on the back of the head. This made her smile, it was so normal. She'd almost forgotten what that was.

A door slammed and Jared jumped up. "That was the front door," he said before racing from the room. The rest of them quickly followed, Charlotte tripping over the green rug on the floor in her haste. Dante caught her elbow and steadied her. They heard Dreadful whinny and a swirl of arctic air flowed around them as they ran down the hallway to the foyer.

Baron was standing by the door. He wore a blue pinstriped suit and a dark orange tie. His gloves matched it. His eyes found Charlotte as she skittered to a stop. Her heart banged unsteadily in her chest.

"Hello, darling," Baron said. He glanced toward the study, where Dreadful was standing in the doorway, next to Black. "I see you managed to talk Dreadful into coming here. Nicely done."

"What are you doing here?" Rory asked. He stood next to Charlotte, his fists clenched at his sides.

Baron cocked his head to the side. "This is my home."

"It's not," Charlotte blurted, drawing her uncle's attention. His blue eyes pierced through her and she faltered. "It's not," she said, shaking her head. "You're not welcome here anymore."

"Is that right," he said. A wicked grin crossed his mouth. "I might have something to say about that." Before anyone could move, he clapped his hands once. Though the sound was muffled by his gloves, it filled the entire foyer with a loud thudding noise. Beneath their feet, the floors shook in undulating waves, and Charlotte grabbed Dante's arm to stay upright. The air turned into a dark miasma around them, glittering with bits of onyx. Charlotte coughed when she breathed it in – it stuck in her throat, sharp and cold.

"Stop!" Black's voice rang out seconds before Dreadful burst from the doorway. His eyes, a rich caramel color, flashed with orange flecks, and a bloom of orange magic rose around him. "Dreadful, no!" Black yelled.

The cavalry horse lashed out toward Baron, his teeth a bold flash of white in the dark air. Baron stumbled back against the door, his eyes widening. But there was no fear in them. Instead, Charlotte was alarmed to see only desire. Dreadful reared, his black front legs flailing inches from her uncle's face. Baron never flinched.

"You *are* mad," he said. Admiration colored his tone. He reached a hand out to the stallion. Dreadful dropped to all fours and shied away from him, shaking his head.

"I am Dreadful!" the horse shouted. His voice rumbled through the room.

"Yes you are," Baron said, nodding. He threw a look at Charlotte that made her cringe. "He is magnificent, isn't he?" Baron's eyes roved over the carousel horse. "He's too much for you." He took a step toward the stallion. "Why don't you come with me, Dreadful? I know what you are. I know what you can do." His voice was soft and musical, and suddenly, Dreadful was still. His orange magic wafted around him, a ginger mist of magical proportions. "Yes, yes, that's a good boy," Baron whispered.

"No!" Charlotte lunged away from Rory and Dante and dashed to the bay. She wrapped her left arm around his neck. "He's mine!" she yelled at her uncle. "Get out of our house!"

Baron laughed. "You sweet silly little girl," he chided. He tapped his chin with a slender finger. His gaze locked on her. "You are no match for me. None of you are."

"You heard her – get out," Jared ordered. He was standing by the doors to the study. Black stood next to him, hands balled at his waist.

Baron made a tsking sound. "You realize this house belongs to me, dear boy," he said. "You are merely guests that I've allowed to stay." He flexed one of his hands. The lights in the chandelier above him flickered. "Don't make me regret it."

Charlotte forced herself to look away from him. *Dreadful, are you all right? Why aren't you doing anything?*

The horse remained silent. She summoned up a swell of courage and stared at her uncle, meeting his haughty gaze. "I want you to get out," she told him. "You've taken the Flying Ponies from us. You're a traitor to the Flynn family. The least you can do is let us stay here." She hated that she sounded weak. She hated that she was considering begging. Where else could they go? There was no way she was taking Dreadful to the city, to the townhouse. They couldn't risk that.

Something changed in her uncle's eyes at the same time the dark air turned red and smothering. Her eyes watered and she inhaled, pulling the thick red magic into her lungs. She immediately coughed as it choked her. She could hear the boys coughing and hacking too, and she tried to talk but couldn't. Her arm was still around Dreadful's neck and she felt a surge of power race through his muscular wooden body.

Seconds later he seemed to explode. He leapt off the floor, all four legs stretched out, and his orange magic shot out in all directions. It crashed through Baron's red magic. Baron cried out and fell back against the door. Charlotte dropped to the floor, gasping and wheezing. The red and orange magic swirled around each other, and she swore the orange magic was *growling*.

Dreadful landed in front of Baron and bit him on the shoulder. Baron jerked back and tried to hit him. The stallion struck out with a hoof and hit the door. "You will **get out**," he ordered. When Baron didn't move, the horse slammed his hoof into the door near his knees. This time Baron reacted. He pushed off the door, turned and yanked it open. Thrusting himself through it, he barely missed getting bit again. He slammed the door shut and it shook the whole wall.

"Gone," Dreadful announced and promptly trotted back into the study.

Charlotte dragged herself into a sitting position. The magic was slowly clearing. Some of it fell to the marble floor, where it coalesced in shiny pools and then disappeared. She coughed, leaning over her drawn-up knees. *Was Uncle Baron trying to kill us with that? Why didn't it affect him?* She rubbed her eyes, which were heavy with grit from the red magic.

Black dropped down into a crouch beside her. He touched her cheek. "You okay?" he asked, his voice gruff from coughing. A delicate shiver twitched between her shoulder blades. That tone worked for him. She looked away. "Charlotte?"

"I'm okay," she said, nodding. Her voice was raspy too, but she was sure it didn't sound as nice as his did. "Are you?"

"Yeah." He got to his feet and helped her up. She looked at her brothers; Jared was running his hands through his hair and she watched particles of red fall from it. He caught her eye and frowned.

"How did he do that?" he asked, walking over to them. Rory and Dante were sitting on the bottom step of the giant staircase, talking in low tones.

"He can access the magic," Black said. "I didn't know he was that strong, though. Doing what he did, that takes time to learn, and excellent concentration, which Dreadful managed to interrupt."

"Took him long enough," Jared said, scowling.

Charlotte coughed, and a bit of red magic floated free. She grimaced, grossed out by it, and hoping the boys hadn't noticed. She glanced at them. They hadn't. They were frowning at one another, and she made an irritated noise, drawing their attention.

"What now?" she asked. "How can we fight him if he's that tough? He has fifteen Flying Ponies to back him up, and with *his* magic that strong, how are we going to win?"

Black's face softened and he said, "Don't lose hope. We have Dreadful, and he ran Baron off all on his own. That counts for something."

Dante strolled over with Rory in tow. "And, sweetie, you've got something up your sleeve, too," Dante told her, grinning.

"Dante." Black's voice was frosty with warning. "Don't."

"Don't what?" Jared asked, looking between the two of them.

Dante's chocolate-brown eyes narrowed. "We need to tell her."

"Tell me what?" Charlotte asked. Neither of them said anything. They just kept glaring at one another. "Black," she snapped. He jerked and his eyes flew to her. "What is going on?"

He shook his head. "Nothing you need to worry about." But his tone was all wrong, and her stomach filled with skittering spiders.

Dante sniffed and ran a hand over his face. "Tell her, Sully, or I will."

Black muttered beneath his breath. "This isn't the right time."

"Her uncle nearly smothered us with dark magic, and you don't think it's the *right time?*" Dante swore and reached out to take Charlotte's hands. His were warm and strong compared to her icy delicate ones. She looked up at him, apprehension flooding through her. "Sweetheart, your uncle is an archimage, a powerful magician." His eyes were deep with truth. "Oliver, your great-great-grandfather, was also one. Certain people in certain families can access the magic; the really powerful ones can manipulate it to do anything they want, just like your uncle. Just like —"

"No." Black's voice cut through Dante's like an ax. "Stop."

Charlotte looked at him. He was breathing hard, like he couldn't get enough oxygen, and there was pain in his blue eyes. "Black? What's wrong? What don't you want me to hear?" she asked. Dante's hands tightened around hers, as if he knew she was thinking about moving closer to Black.

"You." Dante breathed the word and let go of her hands.

Black growled and shoved him in the chest. "I didn't want her to know!" he snarled. "She isn't ready!"

Dante poked Black in the chest. "She'll never be ready if we don't help her prepare." His words were flat and heavy. "You and I both know she'll need all the help she can get." He tossed a hand toward Jared and Rory. "None of the others have the ability. She needs to hone hers."

"Wait, what?" Jared's voice was tentative. "Uncle Baron is a magician, and you're saying Charlotte is, too?" He looked at her, and she saw unease in his eyes.

"And we're not?" Rory sounded angry. "How unfair is *that?*"

"Rory." Jared's voice was harsh. He jabbed a finger toward Dante and Black. "How long have you two known?"

They looked at one another. Black finally drew back his shoulders and said, "For a while now." His eyes sought out Charlotte. "I didn't recognize it at first. I knew Baron was of course. He almost pulses with it."

"Why didn't you tell me?" she asked, her voice soft.

Sadness touched his eyes. "Because it can hurt you. You've seen what it's done to Baron, how it's twisted him. You've seen the Desolates."

"They're archimages?" Rory asked. Gone was the mock-anger.

"Not all of them," Dante said, cutting in. "Some of them just tangled with the magic one too many times, and it consumed them. But not everyone who can access magic is an archimage." He pointed to himself. "I can access the magic, but I'm not nearly strong enough to be one."

"Got it." Rory nodded. He looked at Charlotte, and she saw fear in that look. Fear for her. Fear for himself, and their siblings. Her stomach turned over.

"So what does this mean for us now, with her being an archimage?" Jared directed his question to Black. "Can she make the Flying Ponies listen to her?"

"No." Black shook his head. "She isn't as strong with magic as Baron is. She couldn't go against him yet." His gaze flickered to Charlotte. "Remember that." His voice was terse. "Baron must sense it in you too," he added. He frowned and turned to Dante. "But if so, why wouldn't he try and force her to his side? Why would he just run off with the ponies?"

Dante shrugged. "I'm not sure. That surprised me, too. My guess is that because she didn't know what she was, he knew he couldn't use her."

Charlotte swallowed hard. This was getting to be too much. They had a crazy carousel horse in the study, her uncle had basically tried to smother all of them, and now Black and Dante were saying she was a powerful magician that could manipulate magic. Her vision swam a little, and she tottered.

"Charlotte." Jared instantly reached for her.

"I'm okay," she muttered even as her vision blurred again. Her knees buckled and she heard Black say her name but she was falling down into darkness and then—

5

*B*lack paced in front of the windows in the living room. After Charlotte had collapsed, Jared had carried her in and set her down carefully on one of the couches. He was pacing, too, on the opposite side of the room. Dante had stepped out to make a phone call, and Rory was sitting on the other couch, staring at the blank TV screen.

Dante had no right to tell her. She wasn't ready. Anger fueled Black's thoughts, propelling his hard strides up and down the floor. Dante hadn't even seemed that alarmed, which only made Black's anger burn hotter. *He doesn't care about her like I do.* Though Dante flirted with Charlotte, that's all it was. There was nothing deeper beneath all his pet names and flattering words. At least, he didn't think so. His stomach tightened. The thought of Romano courting Charlotte made him sick.

Charlotte moaned and Black instantly moved to kneel beside her. Jared came around to lean over the back of the couch and Rory sat at her feet. "Charlotte," Black murmured. He brushed the back of his hand against her cheek. Her lashes fluttered and she opened her eyes. "Hey," Black whispered. He wanted to take her into his arms and tuck her in tight against his chest.

"Hey," she mumbled. Her eyes were glassy and unfocused, and Black frowned. What had caused her collapse? Had it been the knowledge she was an archimage, or had Baron's red magic adversely affected her?

"How do you feel?" he asked, his voice soft.

She blinked up at him, and he saw she wasn't quite coherent yet. Something twinged in his chest. Her wavy hair framed her wan face, and he swept it back behind her ear, his hand gentle. Jared shifted, looming over the back of the couch, and Black pushed down his irritation. He could respect Jared's tenacity in protecting his sister, but it wasn't necessary at the moment.

Dreadful pranced into the room and over to the couch. He stretched out his neck and sniffed Charlotte's leg. Pulling away and showing his teeth, he said, "She is sick."

"Sick?" Rory turned his head to look at the horse. "With what?"

"Bad magic." Dreadful tapped a hoof on the floor, and his eyes burned into Black's. "Bad magic, tainted magic, sick," he announced. He then whirled around and cantered out of the room. They heard Dante yell at him to watch where he was going.

Black turned back to Charlotte. She was staring at him, and now he could see a tiny red fleck in her blue-grey eyes. *Bad magic,* his mind whispered. He swallowed and took her hand in both of his and rubbed it. It was ice-cold.

"What does he mean *bad* magic?" Rory asked, bewildered. "She doesn't have bad magic."

"Black?" Jared was leaning further over the couch, and Black had no choice but to look at him. "What did he mean?"

He didn't want to tell them. Charlotte coughed and her eyes widened and he saw tiny bits of red float from her mouth. She struggled to sit up, and he eased his arm around her slender shoulders and helped her. Trying to talk, all she could do was gasp and choke.

"Rory, get some water," Jared ordered and Rory ran from the room.

"Easy," Black murmured. "You're okay." He rubbed her back, wishing he could do something more for her. At the moment, though, this had to be enough. She finally got her breath and relaxed into his hold.

"I-I'm fine," she wheezed. Rory came back in with a glass of water and sat on the edge of the couch. He held it to her lips, his expression pained as he watched her drink. When she stopped, he set the glass on the floor and turned his attention to her.

"How do you feel?" he asked. Gone was the usual snarky brother; in his place was a younger brother who was worried about his older sister. The truth of that was in his eyes and voice.

She started to talk, thought better of it, and tried to reach the glass. Black snatched it and handed it to her. She wrapped both hands around it and drank deep. Black exchanged a look with Jared, seeing his concern mirrored in her older brother's eyes. When she was done, Rory took it from her and set it back down. She swallowed several times, and then ventured, "Feel weird." It came out croaky and she turned pink in embarrassment.

"Weird like sick?" Jared asked. She pursed her lips and shook her head.

"Not myself," she said. Her throat was starting to clear, though she still didn't look like she felt well. She turned her head to look at Black, and his lungs tightened at the fear in her eyes. "Could the red magic change me?" she asked.

He knew what she asking. He didn't know, and though he wanted to comfort her, he didn't want to lie. "I don't know," he said. "I'm sorry." The words stuck in his throat.

Her eyes widened and she ducked her head away from him. Jared reached down and put his hand on her shoulder. "It'll be all right," he said. The grimace on his face belied what he said, however. None of them could assure she'd be all right.

Dante walked into the room and stopped. "What is going on?" he demanded. He stalked closer. "What happened?"

"She's sick," Rory said. "That's what Dreadful said."

"Sick?" Dante moved so he could sit on the end of the

couch. He frowned as he observed Charlotte. "What do you mean by that?"

"She appears to have inhaled a lot of that red magic," Black told him. His body tensed as he saw Dante stiffen.

"That can't be good," Dante murmured. "But we all breathed some of it in. How do the rest of you feel?" His eyes were sharp as he glanced at them all.

"Fine," Rory said.

"Same," Jared told him.

Dante looked to Black. "You, Sully? I don't feel anything myself."

"No, I'm good," Black said. But he winced when he saw Charlotte hunch in on herself. Regretting his words, he struggled to find something that would put her at ease, but nothing came.

"Is she going to change into a Desolate?" Rory's quiet question hung in the air between them all. When Charlotte made a small sound, Black squeezed her hand, trying to offer what little comfort he could in the moment.

"I don't think so," Dante said. His voice didn't carry nearly the conviction the words warranted. "It seems like she would've started changing by now." He got to his feet. "Baron would've known the magic would affect her if she got some of it into her system," he added.

"He's trying to force her into using *her* magic," Black said. He drew in a deep breath and met his old friend's eyes. "What now? Any suggestions?"

"We talk to Orrick." Dante held up a hand when Black

started to protest. "I know you distrust him. But he's got plenty of experience with magic and archimages, and I think we need him. Plus, he has the majority of the Flying Ponies." Tipping his head to the side and considering Black, he said, "I know you don't want to work with him, but this is our best shot, Midnight."

Charlotte squeezed Black's hand and he dropped his eyes to her. "We need help," she whispered. There was growing fear in her, and he would do whatever he could to ease it. He slowly nodded.

"Call him again. Tell him we need help," he said, glancing at Dante.

"Good." Dante got to his feet and left the room.

Charlotte straightened and leaned against the back of the couch. "I want to see our sibs," she said, looking at Jared as he came around the couch to sit next to her.

"They won't want to come back," he said. His voice was gentle. "It's probably for the best they're far away from all this."

She laced her fingers together in her lap. "I know, but I want to make sure they're okay. And we might need them, too." The pleading tone was enough to cause Black's heart to pound harder. He was pretty sure he'd drive back to Smoke City right now to get the younger three Flynns if she asked. She looked at Jared. "What if Uncle Baron does something? He tried to hurt us. Why wouldn't he do the same to them?"

"Mrs. Trudeau wouldn't allow it," Rory told her. He reached out and put his hand over hers. "Trust me on that.

You know how she is." His eyes twinkled. He was back to his normal self now that his sister wasn't coughing and choking on dark magic.

Charlotte offered a thin smile. "I know. But I miss them." The longing in her voice made Jared sit straighter.

"We don't have a way to get there," he pointed out. "And if Mrs. Trudeau sent them back to school, we can't just bring them back here."

She eyed him, and Jared frowned. "You're the oldest," she said. "You're supposed to protect all of us."

"Ouch," he told her. He glanced at Rory and back to her. "It's not that easy, Char. You know that." He shoved a hand through his raven hair, causing it to stick up. "They wouldn't be that safe here, anyway. Uncle Baron can come and go as he pleases." His voice was firm.

"He's afraid of Dreadful now, though," Rory said. He shrugged when Jared glared at him. "I'm just saying."

Dante came back in. "We need to meet Orrick at Whimsies in twenty minutes. Let's go." Gone was his joviality. He stopped in front of Charlotte and held his hands out to her. She took them and let him ease her to her feet.

Irritation crept through Black. Why was it Romano had to be so familiar with Charlotte? His heart wasn't in it. It never had been, with any woman, as far as Black knew. Dante had had plenty of female companionship during their Coney Island days, but none of the women had ever meant anything. They were just there to swoon and sigh and look pretty. *Charlotte is nothing like those girls.* And that was one reason he had fallen for her, despite his best attempts at keeping her at bay.

A hand in his face roused him from his thoughts. He looked up at Charlotte and saw worry in her eyes. "You okay?" she asked.

"Yes," he said, nodding. He had the feeling he'd missed something. Dante huffed out a chuckle, and the irritation bubbling in Black's veins leapt.

"I'm going with you," he said, getting to his feet.

"That's what she just asked you," Jared said, and Black saw the ire in his eyes.

"Who's babysitting Dreadful?" Rory asked. The bay horse clattered into the room and stopped near the couch, his neck arched.

"You two," Black said, nodding to the brothers. The annoyance in Jared's eyes grew, but Black wasn't being dissuaded. He wanted some time alone with Charlotte, and Dante would be distracted once they got back to his shop. If the brothers were mad, so be it. Plus, he wasn't about to leave Charlotte alone with Dante.

"Shall we then?" Dante led Charlotte from the room, keeping hold of her hand. Black made to follow, but Jared stepped into his way. Black stopped, his eyes narrowing.

"Watch him with her," Jared said, his voice low.

"So you've decided you can trust me?" *About time.*

"More than I trust *him*," Jared said. His gaze had gone steely, and even though Black was still agitated with the situation, he could appreciate where her brother was coming from. Charlotte glanced back at them, and he moved past Jared, already forgetting about both brothers. She was the one who mattered.

He wasn't sure about leaving the brothers with Dreadful; the stallion was as crazy as he'd remembered, but hopefully they could hold their own if he freaked out. They got into the Cadillac and Dante drove down the narrow trail that led out to the main road. Charlotte looked back at Black once, and he saw apprehension mingled with fear in her eyes. He leaned forward and put his hand on her shoulder.

"It will be okay," he murmured. She reached up and covered his hand with hers, and again he wished he could just take her into his arms and hold her. But this wasn't the place or time, and he tried to shove those feelings down where he couldn't access them. It didn't work.

They were quiet the rest of the ride to Whimsies. When they arrived, Dante pulled around back and they got out. He hurried into the store, and Black took the moment to take Charlotte's hand and stop her. She looked up at him, and he swallowed. His feelings for her were reflections of what she was feeling for him, and that made it all the harder to not kiss her.

"Don't be afraid of Orrick," he said. "Even if he threatens you, or the ponies, remember: I've got your back. Dante does too." He couldn't resist reaching up and pushing a lock of her wavy hair back behind her ear. She tilted her head into his touch, and his heartbeat kicked up a notch. He gently cupped her cheek, rubbing his thumb along her jawline. She made a soft sound, and he started to drop his head closer. Charlotte looked up through her lashes, and he knew he wasn't going to stop himself from kissing her. His mouth dipped down to hers, and she tipped her head back, meeting him.

The back door banged open. "Are you two – oh good grief." Dante's exasperated voice shattered the moment and Black took a big step back, dropping his hands to his sides. "Honestly, Sully. We don't have time for your misguided feelings!" Dante snagged Charlotte's hand and dragged her into the store.

Black growled something unbecoming beneath his breath and followed them in. The air in the store was dry and heavy with the weight of the magical things Dante had been collecting for decades. Black walked down the short hallway that led out into the main room of the store. Charlotte was standing near the poster of Dante and Penumbra at Coney Island. She was twisting her hands together, and he stopped beside her and reached out to still them.

"Relax," he said, his voice calm. The door to the store opened, the chimes went off, and Orrick Fowler, head man of the Tyranny, stepped in.

His eyes swept around the store before coming to light on Charlotte. Black felt her tense and squeezed her hands. He took a step so he was just ahead of her, a shield against the wickedness he saw in the older man's eyes. Dante strode past them, bumping into Black as he went by, and sparks jumped in Black's eyes.

"Orrick, old chap, it's good to see you," Dante said,

putting out his hand. He waited, and dropped his hand when the other man didn't take it.

"Let's drop the pleasantries," Orrick said. He moved past Dante toward the other two and Black straightened. He was as tall as Orrick, though his frame wasn't as heavy. He took another step in front of Charlotte. This was a dangerous man, no matter how harmless he looked in his overcoat and old fedora. *And I will **not** let him hurt her.*

"Miss Flynn, are you ready to get to work?" Orrick asked, stopping a foot away from Black.

She stepped out from behind Black, and he saw a tremble race across her shoulders. But she held her head high, and when she spoke, her voice was firm. "Are you ready to strike a fair deal?" One hand dropped to her hip, and she looked defiant.

Orrick smiled, and the ferocity of it made Black's eyes twitch. "I will be the one setting the parameters of our deal, dear child." His smug voice was cloying in the small space between them. He glanced at Black. "Mr. Midnight, I can assure you I am not going to harm the girl, so please drop the bodyguard act."

"What do you want?" Charlotte asked. The dim lights from the wall sconces made her hair look darker than it really was, and Black saw that some of it had swung forward into her face. His fingers itched to push it back.

"I want a controlling interest in the Flying Ponies," Orrick told her.

"No." Her refusal was immediate. "That's not going to happen."

Orrick grunted and turned his head to look at Dante, who walked up next to him, looking perturbed. "You told me she was willing to work with us, Romano. What is the problem?" A growl wove through Orrick's voice, and Dante swallowed.

"She is, she is," he cajoled. He frowned at Charlotte and said, "Sweetie, we've talked about this. We need their help to beat Baron."

"Not if they want to have any say in the carousel, we don't," she retorted. Her shoulders were square, and Black couldn't have been more proud of her right then. He looked at Dante, and the sight of his old friend looking so uncomfortable almost made him laugh. It wasn't often that Dante didn't get his way. Charlotte fixed her gaze on Orrick. "You should want to help us because you told me my uncle is going to ruin the world with the Flying Ponies. You should want to help me because it's the right thing to do." Her voice was level and firm and Black saw Orrick's eyes tighten.

"That's a nice idea, Miss Flynn, but that's not how this is going to work," he told her. He pulled on the lapels of his coat. "You're going to let us have a say in what happens to the carousel after this is over. Where you keep it, what you do with it, etcetera. Are we clear?"

"No." Charlotte shook her head. Dante's eyes widened a little, and he gestured to Orrick.

"Sweetheart, you have to agree to this. There's no way we can beat your uncle without the ponies the Tyranny has," Dante said. There was a tinge of desperation to his words.

Charlotte balled her fists at her sides. "This doesn't concern you, Dante, so stay out of it."

Orrick chuckled. "You certainly have your great-great-grandfather's spirit," he said, nodding. "It's nice to see that. But what *isn't* nice," and here his demeanor got cold and hostile, "is arguing with me about this. Mr. Romano is right. You cannot beat Baron and Penumbra without our help. And if you keep refusing to work with us, you will see the world end in bitter, magical destruction, and know that you could've saved it." He stared at her for several moments. "This is your last chance."

Dante was practically shaking with agitation, and Black couldn't help but wonder why. What did it matter to Romano if Charlotte turned Orrick down? Suspicion crept into his thoughts, but he kept them to himself.

"Good day, Miss Flynn." Orrick turned to go and Dante grabbed his arm. Orrick's eyes fell to where his hand was, and Dante let go and shoved a hand through his hair.

"You can't leave," Dante said, shaking his head. He looked at Charlotte, and that same desperation was flashing in his eyes. "Please, Charlotte. You've got to work with them!"

"Why?" Her voice was soft but filled with determination. "What does it matter to you?"

Orrick chuckled. "It would seem, Mr. Romano, that you made a hasty deal." The ice in his voice chilled Black's blood. "I will send Ignace over this afternoon to collect."

"Wait, what?" Charlotte stepped forward. "What is he talking about, Dante?"

Orrick left the store and Dante, now physically shaking, had to lower himself to the floor. Charlotte knelt down beside him, and Black's gut churned. Just what had Romano gotten himself into now?

6

"*D*ante? What's going on? What did he mean, Ignace would collect?" Charlotte asked, settling a hand on his knee. Ignace Marseau, the redhead in the Tyranny, was no one she would want to deal with. Neither was Roswald Dengler, the third member. They were both menacing.

Dante put his head in his hands. He didn't speak, and she cast a frightened look at Black, who quickly came to kneel at Dante's feet.

"Romano. Pull yourself together," he ordered. "Tell us what Orrick meant."

Dante took a shuddering breath and lifted his head to meet Black's sharp gaze. "I did something foolish, it would seem," he said. He rubbed his face with both hands. "I can't believe this is happening."

"Tell us," Black demanded.

Charlotte suddenly inhaled as Dante grabbed her

forearm and twisted it. She cried out and tried to jerk away, but he held fast. "You stupid, simple little girl!" he snarled. "You were supposed to *take the deal*! I'm losing everything because of you!" He thrust his face close to hers and she dodged back as far as she could.

"Let her go!" Black lunged forward, grabbing Dante's arm. "Romano! Let her go!"

Dante growled and shoved Charlotte away from him. She teetered and fell back on her elbows, bruising them on the hardwood floor. Black grabbed Dante by the collar, hauled him upright and shook him. "Get off me!" Dante howled and pulled back a fist. Black ducked the punch and came back with his own, snapping Dante's head backward. Black took Charlotte's arm, tugged her up to her feet, and eased her behind him.

"What did you do, Romano?" he grated out between his teeth. "Sell yourself to Orrick?"

Dante wiped his mouth where a spot of blood had formed. He looked at the red liquid and then at Black, who stood his ground, arms over his chest. "Something like that, yes," Dante snarled. He jabbed a finger at Charlotte, who was peeking at him from around Black's shoulder. "You were supposed to take the deal, *sweetie*," he sneered. "Why couldn't you do that? Why do you have to make this so complicated?"

"Don't put this on her!" Black thundered, making her jump. He took a step toward Dante. "This is *your* fault! You know you can't trust the Tyranny!"

"Just get out." Dante pointed to the hallway behind them. "Go."

But Charlotte could see he was hurting behind the anger, and sympathy swept through her. She didn't trust him like she did Black, and he *had* just hurt her, but she couldn't turn her back on him. He was as much a part of this whole thing with the Flying Ponies as the rest of them were. "Dante." She stepped out from behind Black, who put his arm out to shield her. "It's okay," she murmured, looking up at him. He frowned, but slowly lowered his arm.

"Just go," Dante told her again. "There's nothing you can do now."

"Are you sure?" She kept her voice soft. "What exactly do you owe Orrick?" If she could help him, she would. But she wasn't selling the Flying Ponies out. Not to anyone.

He smiled but there was only despair in it. "Everything."

"What do mean?" Black asked, his voice hard.

"I mean *everything*, Sully." Dante met his eyes. "I've basically sold my soul to those devils."

"Why? Why would you do that!" Charlotte was aghast. "You seriously bet that I would let them control the Flying Ponies?" What had he been thinking? He should've known her better than that!

He scrubbed a hand through his sleek hair. "It wasn't the smartest move, I'll give you that." Dropping his hand to his side, he nailed her with a harsh glare. "You know you're going to lose to your uncle, don't you? And now that you've turned Orrick away, you're dead to him." His voice matched his eyes, and Charlotte resisted the urge to shiver. She was done cowering in the face of a threat.

"I didn't force you to sign your life away," she shot back. Dante's eyes hardened.

"Just go," he ordered. "You've already wrecked me. Get out."

Before she could retort, Black latched onto her elbow. "He's wrong. He's made this mess. He has to clean it up," he said. His voice wasn't cold, just matter-of-fact. "Let's go."

Charlotte wanted to say something else. She wanted to offer some kind of hope to Dante, but what could she give? The Flying Ponies were out of the question. Dante turned away, and she followed Black from the store. Once outside, she stopped and took a deep breath. "We have to do something."

"No." Black shook his head. He was staring off toward the Cadillac. "He did it to himself. He should've known you'd never give Orrick any clout over the carousel. Come on." He started for the SUV. Her shoulders sagging, she trailed after him.

Black was silent as they drove back toward the mansion. Charlotte, her chin in her hand, watched out the window. It was cold today, and black clouds scudded across what little bit of sun peeked out. A few homes along the old highway had Halloween decorations up. *Our house would be a great place for a party. I bet the twins and Danny would love to decorate it.* She wanted to go see them, to make sure they were really all right.

"It's not your fault." Black's voice was firm. "He did this to himself."

"Why would he place so much on me taking their deal?" she asked. "He should've known better, don't you think?"

"Yeah." His grip on the steering wheel tightened. "This isn't your fault, so don't think that, okay?" He glanced at her, and in that look she saw how serious he was. "He did this to himself."

"I know." But he was part of their group now, part of their crew. How could they just turn their backs on him? The drive didn't take long, and soon they were pulling up to the house. It was still standing, which she thought was good, considering who was inside. She hurried up the stairs and the door swung open. Rory was scowling, arms over his chest.

"Next time you two want to be alone, don't make us babysit that monster," he said. "He was a nightmare!"

"Dreadful?" Charlotte pushed past him into the house, Black right behind her. The horse trotted down the hallway from the kitchen toward them, tossing his head. "Were you bad?" she asked him.

He stopped and tipped his head to the side. "Dreadful was bored."

"Right. Bored." Rory snorted behind them. "He's a jerk."

"Where's Jared?" Charlotte asked, turning to her younger brother.

He mimicked making a phone call. "He wanted to check on the kids."

"Kids?" Black coughed to cover a chuckle. "The twins are fourteen."

"Whatever." Rory nodded toward the living room. "I'm gonna go play something. You two can deal with crazy horse!" He stalked from the room, and Charlotte turned her attention to the carousel pony.

"You misbehaved, huh?" she asked, reaching out to touch his nose. He nipped at her.

"Bored," he repeated.

Jared stepped out of Baron's study and said, "Bored, bad, same difference apparently." He took a deep breath. "He wasn't terrible, just really loud and demanding."

"How are the others?" Charlotte asked, pointing at the cell phone he was holding.

"I talked to Mrs. Trudeau. They went to school today. I guess the superintendent came by."

"Why? Uncle Baron said we were moving."

Jared shrugged. "I don't know. Maybe they thought he was lying? Anyway, there's paperwork at the house I have to sign for college, so I'm going to the city today." He cocked his head. "You want to go? Get out of here for a while? We'll stay long enough so we can see the kids."

Her stomach rolled. "Right, I keep forgetting you're going to State in January," she murmured. How was she going to live in this creepy old house without her big brother?

His face softened, and he said, "It's still a ways off." He shifted his gaze to Black. "Could you handle watching the house and the pony for the afternoon?"

"Sure." Black's voice was firm. "You can take the Caddy – it belongs to your uncle anyway."

"Great." Jared reached out and ran a hand down Dreadful's neck. The horse didn't shy away or try to bite him, and Charlotte wondered why. Had the bay decided he liked one of them? "We'll leave in five minutes or so, then." Jared walked across the foyer and headed up the staircase on the left.

Dreadful pranced over to the living room and stuck his head in. Rory told him to get out. The stallion half-reared. "You do not tell Dreadful what to do!" he said. His voice was a dry crackle and sounded ominous when he raised it.

"Dreadful, leave him alone," Black said, frowning. The horse ignored him and went into the living room anyway. Black sighed. "He's every bit as mad as I remember him," he said.

"Will you be okay here?" Charlotte asked. "When we go to the city?"

"Yes," he told her. "It will be good for you to see the others. I'm sure they miss you."

"Yeah," she said. She wondered if it had been their decision to go back to school, or Mrs. Trudeau's. Baron was supposed to get tutors for them out here, and obviously that wasn't going to happen now. Rory could care less, but she wanted to graduate.

Jared came back down stairs. "Ready?"

"Um, sure," she said. "Dreadful is driving Rory nuts, so he'll want to go."

63

Rory came out of the living room. "Ugh, let's go. That horse is annoying."

"Okay." Jared nodded to Black. "We'll be back tonight. Thanks for watching the place and the pony."

"No problem." Black tossed the Cadillac's keys to Jared. "Be careful." He smiled at Charlotte, which made her heart flip, and then went into the living room and started talking to the stallion.

The three siblings got their coats and shoes on and headed out to the SUV. "You remember how to get back to Smoke City?" Rory asked as he climbed in the shot gun seat.

Jared held up his phone. "I'm pretty sure, and I've got navigation."

They pulled out of the yard, and Charlotte turned to look out the back window. Black was nowhere to be seen; she supposed he was in the house with the horse, but she wished he'd come out to the porch to see them off. It was odd to be apart from him. *He was going to kiss me again at Dante's.* The memory of his fingers gentle on her face made her flush red, and she tried to force the memory away. Rory didn't need more fodder than what he already had.

They drove for two hours, and Jared had no problem getting back to the townhouse. It sat on a tree-lined street filled with other houses just like it. Theirs sat at the very end on the left, at the top of a slight hill. Jared hit the remote and the garage door went up. Uncle Baron's black and yellow 1938 BMW 327 was sitting on the right; Jared inched in beside it.

As they got out of the vehicle, the door that led into the kitchen opened, and Mrs. Trudeau stood there waiting for them. She was fifty-five with stern hazel eyes and steel-grey hair that was always in a severe bun at the nape of her long neck. She stood six feet, wore sensible oxfords, and never put up with shenanigans.

"Welcome home," she said as they hurried up the steps. She stood back and let them in, and looked them over after shutting the door. Making tsking sounds, she finally said, "You all look like you've lost weight. We'll have to remedy that." She patted Jared on the cheek, ran a hand through Rory's hair, and tapped Charlotte on the nose. "It's good to have you back," she added.

They all grinned at one another. Mrs. Trudeau had been a much-needed harbor in the aftermath of their father's accident. She'd fussed over them, cooked them anything they wanted, and even allowed them to stay up late on Sunday nights to watch classic horror movies with Uncle Baron.

"Mrs. Trudeau, Jared said the superintendent of the school stopped by," Charlotte said. "Why? Uncle Baron told him we were moving, so why would he care?"

"He informed me that your uncle had never said a word about the family leaving the school district," she said, shaking her head. She pulled fixings for sandwiches from the huge chrome fridge. Shutting the door, she eyed the three of them. "He insisted your brothers and sister return at once to school, so they did." She turned away and started to pull bread from the box on the counter. "Has your uncle hired tutors yet?"

They all looked at one another. Didn't she realize what was going on? Hadn't the younger three told her? Jared cleared his throat. "Well," he started.

She pointed a butter knife at him. Her expression was serious. "Let me stop you," she said. "I know what's been going on. Gavin, Marta and Danny have been very up front about this whole magical carousel business." She waited to see if they said anything. "Nothing to add? All right. I'm assuming Baron hasn't taken your education seriously then. He hasn't gotten you tutors yet."

"He hasn't, no," Jared told her. He went to the counter and peered at the food. "This looks great."

"Danny said the food at the new house was good," Mrs. Trudeau said.

"Not as good as *yours*," Rory said, stealing a slice of cheese and stuffing it into his mouth.

"Pish posh, I'm sure it was," she said through a smile. "Now, let's have ourselves some lunch, and you can tell me everything that's been happening."

7

*B*lack turned the TV off and got to his feet. The Flynns had been gone for two hours; it annoyed him that he knew that. He'd never been one to live by the clock, but he missed Charlotte. Walking out of the room, he scanned the foyer. Dreadful was nowhere to be seen. Black made an impatient noise and headed across to the study. Its doors were open, and sure enough, the bay cavalry horse was at one of the huge windows. He glanced at Black.

"What are you doing?" he asked the horse.

"Watching."

"Watching what?"

Dreadful nosed the window. "Monsters."

"Really?" Black frowned and came to stand beside him. "Where?"

"Out there."

Black sighed. He'd figured the Desolates would be drawn more to the house now that the carousel horse was here. Gazing out the window around the yard, he noticed that the bark on the closest tree had a golden sheen to it. He took a breath. *It has to be the magic. I wonder what else the magic is changing.* The wind came rushing up against the house, banging around the eves, and Dreadful rolled his eyes and backed away from the window.

"Dreadful doesn't like this," he muttered.

"It's all right," Black assured him. "It's just the wind. Remember when it would get windy at Coney Island?" The breeze off the Atlantic was always welcoming, particularly on weekends, when the crowds would reach a million strong.

"I remember," Dreadful said, his voice soft.

"Hey, you didn't say your name."

The horse gave him a sideways look and made a noise like a chuckle. "I don't always have to use it," he said. "It annoys people."

Black rolled his eyes. The horse was too crazy and smart for his own good. "I'm going to get some food. You want to come?"

"No. I will watch for monsters." The horse put his nose to the window.

Black left the study and wandered down to the kitchen. Pulling open the fridge door, he bent down to peruse the interior. As he was taking out a plate of leftover chicken, he heard a door open and slam shut. Setting the plate back in the fridge, he hurried through the dining room and down the hall.

Mr. Coal stood inside the foyer. He took his hat off and held it in his hands. "Grandfather? What are you doing here?" Black asked. He was glad to see him, but cautious. After all, Cornelius had thrown in all the way with Baron.

"I'm happy to see you, too," Cornelius said, frowning. "I was looking for Charlotte. Is she here?"

"No." A subtle growl wove through Black's voice and he tensed.

"Defensive, are we?" Cornelius looked around the room.

"Can you blame me? You sided with Baron!"

A clatter of hooves announced Dreadful, who trotted over to stand next to Black. He looked the old man up and down, and bared his teeth.

"Nice to see you, too," Cornelius said, bowing his head with a smirk.

"What do you want, Grandfather?" Black put his hand on the horse's neck, hoping he wouldn't do anything wild. "Why do you want to see Charlotte?"

Cornelius headed toward the study. "Let's go sit down, my boy."

Black didn't want to, but followed. Dreadful walked behind him, and Black jumped when the horse nipped his shirt. His grandfather sat down behind Baron's big desk, so Black sat in one of the leather armchairs. He crossed his arms over his chest. Dreadful went back to the windows.

Cornelius took something out of his inside coat pocket and set it on the desk. Black saw that it was the black leather book Charlotte had noticed at their apartment a couple of weeks ago. "What is this?" he asked, frowning.

"This, grandson, is all of Oliver's information on the Flying Ponies," Cornelius said, tapping a long finger on its cover. When Black's jaw dropped, he chuckled. "I know. You had no idea what was sitting on that little bookshelf all these years."

Black didn't know what to ask first. He tried to collect his thoughts. "Why didn't you tell me about this?" he finally asked.

Cornelius sat back in the chair and tucked his hands on his stomach. "It wasn't anything you needed to know at the time. Oliver entrusted me with it years and years ago, before he went away."

"Died you mean."

Cornelius didn't answer, and Black's eyebrows shot up. "Grandfather, he's dead. We went to his funeral on the Island!" His pulse tingled and raced as he waited for Cornelius to confirm this. "He's not alive!" *He can't be – I saw him in that coffin!*

Dreadful turned from the window and watched them. Cornelius took his time answering; he picked the book up and rifled through its pages before looking at his grandson. Black could barely breathe; it seemed like all the air in the room had been sucked out.

"That's not true." Cornelius set the book down. "He's an

archimage, just like his great-grandson and great-great-granddaughter." He waited a few seconds for this to register. "You already knew, didn't you, about Charlotte? You sensed it within her."

His head was pounding, and Black took a long deep breath. His world was tilting, falling to one side of its axis. Oliver was alive? "How long have you known? About Oliver?" he asked instead of answering Cornelius's question. "We saw his body at the funeral."

"You saw what he wanted you to see," Cornelius corrected. He pursed his lips. "Oliver was growing tired of everything, and wanted to get away. He no longer wanted the burden of the carousel, so he left, after having that staged memorial at Coney. I was in charge of the Flying Ponies, until someone else in the family took it. Neither of Oliver and Adara's twins wanted it, and neither did their children. But Baron and Baxter, sons of Keegan, now *they* were *interested*." He smiled, showing off his spectacularly white teeth. "But Baxter fell in love with Cordelia, had six children, and had no time for running a magical carousel. Baron, on the other hand…"

"He wanted it." Black's voice was hard. "If you knew he was going to go rogue with it, though, why did you help him so much?" He remembered a young Baron coming to play on the carousel during his school vacations; the lanky youth with the wild black hair and flashing blue eyes was constantly grinning and scheming. He loved running the merry-go-round and riding Penumbra around and around the platform. Back when Baron was a child, the carousel had been only that – just something to ride and play on. Black's chest hurt. He and Baron had been great friends once the young man got old enough to hang out, but Baron had kept aging, and Black had not, stuck with the same seventeen-year-old body he'd had when he first started working with the machine.

He frowned and eyed his grandfather. "Why didn't you try to stop him?"

Cornelius sighed. "What was I going to do against an archimage? We know how strong they are with magic. And there was no telling that Baron was going to do something like this, either. Oliver never had that wicked streak."

Black scowled. "He had his own issues, Grandfather. Let's not forget that."

Cornelius chuckled. "Yes, he does, but not that malevolent spirit." He leaned forward and pushed the journal toward Black. "You're going to need this, son."

It didn't go unnoticed by Black that his grandfather used *does* and not *did* to describe Oliver, and he tried to imagine his old boss being alive. "Where is Oliver now?"

"Can't say. He sends me a quick note every once in a while, but I haven't heard from him in, oh, going on two months now." Cornelius pressed his lips together. "Charlotte needs help, Sullivan. You're one of the few who can help her." He let the weight of that settle in on top of Black, and then added, "I wouldn't trust Dante with her, or the Flying Ponies."

"Not to worry there," Black said, his scowl deepening.

"He bet that Charlotte would let the Tyranny have some say in the carousel, and when she didn't, he basically lost everything to Orrick. Idiot."

"Well, that's unfortunate. Even though I don't trust Romano, he *can* be an asset at times." Cornelius gave the journal another little push with his fingertip. "Baron knows Charlotte is an archimage." His tone was grave. "He hasn't tried to harm her yet, probably because she is not yet aware of her own powers, but—"

"Actually, she knows. Baron attacked us here, using his magic. She breathed quite a bit in, and it affected her. I'm not sure yet how much, but it did. We told her what she is." Black's voice was heavy. "I didn't want to, but Dante did anyway." He touched the journal. The leather was rough beneath his fingertips. What secrets about the Flying Ponies were written inside it? "I won't let Baron hurt her," he said, looking at his grandfather. His voice reflected the steel resolve in his light blue eyes.

"I know you won't," Cornelius said.

"Why the change of heart? I mean, I thought for sure you were on Baron's side," Black said.

The old man slumped in his seat. "Well, at first I thought what he wanted wasn't so bad, so evil. He talked to me about using the magic to change things, to better the world for everyone. But then once he and Penumbra turned, I knew. It wasn't about helping anyone but himself. I knew I had to do something, and soon. This journal contains all of Oliver's notes about each pony, the carousel itself, and archimages. You're going to need that information."

"Do you think Oliver would help us, if we could find him?" Black's voice was low and tense. Having the man who'd first given life to the Flying Ponies on their side would give them a tremendous advantage.

"I don't know. I honestly don't. He was ready to be done with the carousel when he left." Cornelius shrugged. "If you could find him, it wouldn't hurt to talk to him. But I have no idea where he would be."

"This will have to be enough, then." Black picked up the journal and ran his thumb down its rough pages. "Thank you, Grandfather." A thought occurred to him, and he added, "Won't Baron know you've turned against him, though? I don't want him to hurt you."

"I can handle myself, son. Your responsibility is to Charlotte, both keeping her safe and finding the stolen ponies. There's nothing in here about who stole the missing ponies, unfortunately. I know the Tyranny still has some of them, and of course you got Dreadful back, whom the mob stole from Oliver that time."

"That's right," Black said, nodding. "Do you think they took any of the others?" Oliver had told them Orrick had taken Dreadful, but they'd known better. Their boss was in deep with the mob; Dreadful had merely been payment when he couldn't keep his end of a deal.

"If they did, they might be lost to us. I wouldn't have any idea who's running the old families in Brooklyn now." Cornelius hunched his shoulders, almost folding in on himself, and for the first time, perhaps ever, Black realized how old his grandfather really was.

"Well, then we'll have to hope the missing ponies were all taken by Orrick," Black said.

"Wait." Cornelius suddenly straightened. "There *is* someone who might know." His eyes locked with Black's, and for a second, Black had no idea who he meant. But then his eyes narrowed even as his heart twinged.

"No, Grandfather. Absolutely not. I'm not dealing with her."

Cornelius smiled. "She could be a great advantage for you. You have to consider asking her."

"I have no idea where she is."

"I do. She and I have kept in touch. She's been in touch with Dante, too. In fact, he might turn to her for help with his newfound circumstances." Cornelius glanced at Dreadful. "Perhaps the mob only took Dreadful, but I doubt it. There were plenty of times Oliver came up short with them."

Black's gut churned. His heart started to pound. He hadn't thought about the Songbird in years. Symphony Cantata was blonde and svelte and had piercing pine-green eyes that could stop a man in his tracks at a hundred yards. But it hadn't been her looks that had drawn so many crowds at Coney Island – it had been her voice. Strong and sweet and melodious, no one had been immune to it, not even himself. Black's cheeks grew warm just thinking about her.

"I know that look," Cornelius said, a smile in his voice.

"But you'll have to keep your head about you if you do ask for her help."

Black frowned. "She doesn't mean anything to me, Grandfather. Not anymore."

"I remember." His grandfather's voice fell. "She was too magical for anyone to cage."

Even Oliver. The dark thought wasn't welcome, and he tried to push it away. "I guess it wouldn't hurt to speak with her."

"No, it would not." Cornelius reached over for a pen near Baron's computer and put his hand out for the journal. Black handed it to him, and his grandfather wrote a quick note in the back before handing it back. "I would contact her soon, son. Baron is already fifteen ponies strong, and his own magic defies definition. Charlotte's going to need all the help she can get."

They both got to their feet, and Black glanced at Dreadful. The bay stallion had been suspiciously quiet the entire time, and he wondered what was going through his wooden head, if anything.

"I'm noticing bits of magic here and there," Black said as he followed Cornelius out to the front door.

"Yes, it's coming back strong now. It was caged away behind that barrier for so long, that now it's infinitely more powerful." Cornelius turned to face him, and there was something sad in his vivid green eyes. "I'm proud of you, Sullivan, prouder than any grandparent has ever been. I know you'll do what's needed to defeat Baron." He pulled Black into a hug; stunned, Black couldn't bring his arms up around the old man. Cornelius gave him a squeeze and stepped back. "One last thing to remember: even Penumbra answers to someone." He turned to the door and opened it. "Goodbye." He stepped out and closed the door behind him.

8

"So that's what's been going on," Charlotte said and sat back in her chair. The three of them had been catching Mrs. Trudeau up; Charlotte had just finished telling her and her brothers about Dante selling himself to the Tyranny. She wasn't sure how much the housekeeper believed.

Mrs. Trudeau nodded and got to her feet. "I've always known there was something different about the Flynn family."

"Dante really did that?" Rory asked, shaking his head. "Now he has to work for Orrick?"

"As far as I can tell," Charlotte told him. She crossed her arms over her chest. "The only ally we have now is Black."

"You're forgetting someone." Mrs. Trudeau looked down at the three of them. "I have no intentions of letting you continue on this adventure without me."

Jared frowned. "Do you really believe any of this?"

"All of it, dear boy." She smiled. "Magic is what drew me to this home."

"How? No one was supposed to be able to see it." Rory echoed his siblings' growing confusion.

Her smile grew. "And what makes you think I couldn't see it? It's been difficult, yes, but it's been returning."

The three of them could say nothing. All they could do was stare at her. She laughed, a great booming sound, and clapped her hands together. "Oh my, the look on your faces! Precious!"

"But…" Jared just shook his head.

"How?" Rory asked.

"Why didn't you tell us you could see magic?" Charlotte asked.

"I didn't tell you because I never wanted your uncle to know. He's a, well, *complicated* man, and I didn't trust him enough for that." Her hazel eyes twinkled. "I've been waiting for Penumbra to choose someone and lift the barrier. Charlotte, dear, I'm so happy it's you!"

Charlotte couldn't speak. Her vision was narrowing in on itself, and she swallowed. How could Mrs. Trudeau see the magic? How had she known about it? She couldn't reconcile this happy woman with the demanding one who had been taking care of the family for so long. *What if she was on the Island? What if she knows Black and Mr. Coal and Dante?* "Were you at the Island?" she asked, her voice faint.

Mrs. Trudeau's giddiness faded as abruptly as it had come on. "Yes, I was. I knew your great-great-grandparents. I knew Dante and Sullivan and Cornelius."

Charlotte wasn't sure, but she thought maybe there'd been a tiny catch in the older woman's voice when she mentioned Mr. Coal. "Did you work with them?"

"No. I was the governess of a young singer who worked on the Island at the time. Her stage name was the Songbird, and she was as lovely as a rainbow." Mrs. Trudeau's voice took on a faraway note. "Her voice could tame the wildest beast. She had many admirers, including Dante and Sullivan. They were quite taken with her." She gave a small sigh. "We spent a great deal of time at the carousel, and thus absorbed enough of its magic to stop the aging process."

The blood drained from Charlotte's face, and she saw Rory open his mouth. She slid down in her chair and kicked out, catching him in the leg. He glared at her and she put a finger to her lips. She did not need Mrs. Trudeau to know she liked Black and had kissed him.

"But that was a long time ago, and Symphony has moved on since then, like so many of us did."

"Symphony?" Jared asked.

"Symphony Cantata," Mrs. Trudeau said. "That isn't her real name, of course. I never did know what it was, but it didn't matter. Symph was what we all called her, those of us in the inner circle."

"Do you miss her?" Rory asked, shooting another glare at Charlotte.

"I do. But we've stayed in touch. She was always a darling girl." She glanced at the clock. "Dear me, the time has gotten away. The children will be home in minutes." She bustled around the kitchen, pulling the milk jug from the fridge and piling homemade chocolate chip cookies on a plate.

"This is weird," Jared whispered, leaning toward Charlotte. "I mean, our world *is* weird now. I get that. But her, too? At the Island? I don't know."

"I believe her," Rory whispered, shrugging.

"Me too," Charlotte added, even though she was still reeling from the news that Black had liked a girl who called herself *Symphony*. How was she supposed to compete with that? She was plain and had no singing skills whatsoever.

The front door opened and soon their younger three siblings walked into the kitchen. They stopped short at the sight of the older three, and then Danny said, "Bring us a Flying Pony?" and laughed.

"You wish, squirt," Rory said and got to his feet. He gave Danny a scrub across the top of his head, fist-bumped Gavin and hugged Marta close. She sank into it, leaning against him for several long seconds before stepping back.

"What are you guys doing here?" Gavin asked, setting his backpack down.

"I have some paperwork for State to fill out, and we wanted to see you guys," Jared told him. He hugged all three of them, giving Danny a hard squeeze when he tried to wriggle free. "How was school?"

"It sucks," Danny said and walked to the counter. Grabbing a cookie, he stuffed it in his mouth.

"How are the ponies?" Gavin asked, looking at Charlotte.

"Um, they've sided with Uncle Baron," she said, swallowing. "He's decided he wants to rule the world with magic, and Penumbra is helping him." The words were like daggers in her throat.

The younger three went still. Marta's eyes were wide behind her glasses and she looked up at Jared. "That can't be good for anyone," she said, her voice quiet.

"It's not," he assured her. "But we have Dreadful. He's a cavalry horse, and he's supposed to be super powerful. Penumbra is scared of him."

"Well, we think he is, anyway," Charlotte amended. "He didn't seem that frightened when Dreadful and I went to the carousel." She told the younger three everything that happened, catching them up. When she was finished, she glanced at Mrs. Trudeau. Was she going to join in, and tell them all about her?

"Well what are we waiting for?" Danny asked, swallowing down his food. "We should be looking for the missing horses, right?"

"Since when are you excited about this?" Jared asked, frowning at him. "You three were never that into the carousel."

"Well not then, but if we get to save the world, then count me in!" Danny told him, grinning.

Jared heaved an older brother sigh. "I think the best thing is for you three to stay in school and stay here."

"Rory and Charlotte aren't in school," Danny was quick to point out.

"Yeah, but we've got the world to save," Rory argued.

"It's dangerous," Jared cut in, his voice sharp. "I don't even like Charlotte and Rory being a part of it, okay? I can't watch over all of you."

"No one asked you to," Gavin said. He was solemn. "You were right, when you told us that this was a family matter. The carousel belongs to all of us. Uncle Baron is going to use it for evil. We *all* need to help stop him." The quiet defiance in his voice just begged Jared to dispute him.

"I think Gavin is quite right," Mrs. Trudeau said, her tone overriding any dissension from the other siblings. "In fact, I think we all should go back to the mansion and figure out how to proceed."

"You too? But why?" Marta asked. There was a little frown line across her forehead. "Don't you have to stay here and take care of the house?"

Mrs. Trudeau laughed, the sound filling the room. The three younger siblings stared wide-eyed at her. "I suppose I should tell you who I used to be, shouldn't I, dear ones?" And she told them her story of being Symphony Cantata's governess on Coney Island, and how she knew Oliver and Adara Flynn, Dante Romano, and Cornelius and Sullivan Midnight.

"Wow!" Danny said, his eyes shining. "That is so cool!"

She laughed again. "Yes, I'm glad you think so." She looked at her watch, which Charlotte had always loved. The band was delicate gold link chain, and the face was surrounded by intertwining rose-gold roses and leaves. She'd always figured it was an antique; now she wondered if Mrs. Trudeau had bought it new in New York City during her time on the Island.

"I think everyone should pack, I will call the school, and we should be on our way," Mrs. Trudeau said, her voice cheery. "We don't want to keep Sullivan waiting too long, and I'm anxious to see Dreadful again."

"Wait, what? You're *really* going with us?" Jared's brows were drawn together. "But — "

"But nothing, young man," she interrupted. "Shoo, go on. I'll call the superintendent and let him know we are leaving the school district post haste." The excitement in her voice seemed to rally the younger three, and they fled the kitchen. Charlotte could hear their shoes pounding up the staircase to the second floor.

She exchanged a bewildered look with Jared. Was this actually going to happen? Their strict housekeeper was truly going with them to the house in the woods and helping them beat their uncle? Rory was too busy eating cookies to offer any insights, and she followed Jared from the kitchen and into the hallway. He took a deep breath.

"Did I hear all of that right? She's from the Island and she's coming with us?"

"That's what I heard," Charlotte confirmed. A sudden woozy feeling came over her and she grabbed for his arm to keep from falling. Jared took hold of her shoulder and steadied her.

"You okay? What's wrong?" he asked. His instant concern was welcome, but she wasn't sure what was happening. Another wave came over her, and she blinked hard, seeing red spots dancing in her eyes. She gave her head a shake to clear it. "Char? What's going on?"

"I-I don't know," she mumbled. Her body was tingling, and her lungs suddenly didn't work. She gasped, struggling to breathe, and felt Jared's arms as he scooped her up.

"Mrs. Trudeau!" he yelled as he shoved open the swinging kitchen door and stepped through.

"My goodness. Set her down," the housekeeper demanded. "She can't breathe if you've got her all scrunched up."

Jared mumbled an apology and quickly set Charlotte on her feet. He put his arm around her back, giving her support. "What's wrong with her? She was fine a minute ago."

"Yes, yes, but you did tell me she inhaled a lot of Baron's magic," Mrs. Trudeau said, tsking. She took hold of Charlotte's chin and tipped her head back and side to side. Her gaze darkened. "It's as I suspected. His magic is warring with hers."

"Well, what do we do?" he asked, desperation in his deep voice. "She isn't breathing!"

"Give her to me." Mrs. Trudeau didn't wait for Jared's compliance – she merely pulled Charlotte from him, bent her over, and whacked her on the back. Jared cried out just as Charlotte choked and hacked and particles of red magic floated free from her throat. Another whack, and another coughing fit. "There, you see, she's fine, for now." She straightened Charlotte, who tottered but didn't go down.

"Charlotte," Jared said and put his hand on her shoulder. "Are you okay?" There were still desperate overtones to his voice, but he didn't look as panicky.

She sucked in air and finally nodded. Rory strode over and said, "So how come she's rejecting Uncle Baron's magic?" He settled a hand on her opposite shoulder and gave it a gentle squeeze, and she could see the concern in his eyes.

"Every archimage has their magic," Mrs. Trudeau said. "Baron was trying to overtake Charlotte's, to force her into becoming like him. Her magic is repelling it." She tipped Charlotte's chin up so she could see her eyes. "You're likely to have more of these fits, my girl, until your magic has gotten rid of his."

All Charlotte could do was nod. Her lungs felt seared, and she couldn't think past drawing in clean air to clear them. Both brothers stayed at her side, even after Mrs. Trudeau moved away to call the school.

"You okay?" Jared finally asked, his voice low.

"I think so," Charlotte said. Her breathing was settling out, but she was glad for their support. "I hope she's wrong, and I don't have any more." Choking and coughing was not fun. And the whole concept of magic warring within her body was just plain odd. She'd read the *Harry Potter* series and the *Lunar Chronicles*, and the magic in those books wasn't nearly as bizarre as this kind was. This kind made no sense; it had no rhyme or reason to it.

"Here, sit," Jared said and led her over to the table. He pulled out a chair for her and she eased down into it.

"That's that," Mrs. Trudeau said, walking over to them.

She planted her fists on her hips and surveyed the three of them. "We will work on tutors after this war with your uncle is over."

"War?" Rory looked puzzled.

She gave a sharp nod. "Yes, war. I know your uncle. He's stubborn. He's going to do everything he can to win. So we must do likewise, and find the missing horses and unite the Flying Ponies. Only then do we stand a chance. So let's get your siblings and get going."

"Aren't you going to pack?" Rory asked, a baffled look on his face.

"Oh my dear, I packed while the younger three were at school. I knew something was coming."

"What about your paperwork?" Charlotte asked, glancing at Jared.

"We'll bring it with us." Mrs. Trudeau marched over to the counter and grabbed a manila envelope off it. "Now let's get moving."

"Wait." Jared's voice was strident. "Should we stay here instead? Uncle Baron might keep coming back to the other house."

Mrs. Trudeau's eyes sharpened. "Let him come. The house's magic is strong, and we need to be in the thick of things. We're too out of the loop here." She waved toward the door. "Move out."

9

*H*is mind was spinning. How could his grandfather have dropped so much knowledge in his lap and then left like that? Black stared at the TV screen, where some inane cop drama was playing. Dreadful was sitting on the other couch, cocking his head from side to side, as if he was trying to make sense of the show.

Symphony. Why does it have to be her? Was it even possible that she'd help him? He wasn't sure, since they hadn't parted on the best of terms. He groaned. This was getting much more complicated than he'd dreamed it would.

The house started moaning and he sat upright. Dreadful jumped to his hooves. They clacked on the floor. A breeze blew through the room, the hairs on the back of Black's neck standing to attention. His face stern with concentration, he made his way to the door. Looking into the foyer, he swallowed. The front door was open.

Dreadful nipped his shirt and Black reached back to swat at his nose. His pulse drumming in his ears, he stepped out into the foyer, scanning for an immediate threat. "Monster," Dreadful said in his dry throaty voice.

"Shh," Black warned. If a Desolate had somehow gotten in, he wanted an advantage. His ratchet was in his coat, which was hanging up in the closet across the room. He walked steadily over to it and reached to open the door.

"Why, Sullivan. You're still in my house." Baron's voice was deep and dark, and Black straightened his shoulders before turning to face him. "Why?"

"Guarding it," Black told him. He reached back, searching for the heavy wool of his pea coat. He watched as Baron turned his head to look at Dreadful. The stallion pawed at the floor, and the lights from the chandelier glinted in his caramel eyes.

"Not very well, you aren't. I'm not sure what my niece sees in you." Baron moved toward Dreadful. "You on the other hand, I can see the draw," he added. He held his hand out to the horse. Dreadful backed away from him.

"Leave him alone," Black said. "He's not going with you."

"I think we'll leave that up to him," Baron told him. "You want to be with the herd, don't you?" he asked Dreadful. The carousel pony snorted and tossed his head.

"Dreadful doesn't like you," he said.

Baron laughed. "You don't have to like me, you miserable wretch. You just have to work with me and Penumbra." His voice had a sing-song lilt to it, and Black scowled.

"He's not stupid, Baron. He knows why you want him," he said. His fingers finally found the pocket of his coat, and gripped the cool steel of his ratchet. He slid it out and shoved it into the back pocket of his faded jeans.

Baron turned to face Black, and there was a sinister gleam in his eyes. "Where is my darling niece, Mr. Midnight? Are you hiding her from me?"

Black scowled. "She's not here."

"Really." Baron glanced up at the ceiling. Around them, the old house creaked and shuddered, and he smiled. "Perhaps I'll stay and wait for her."

"You should leave. No one wants you here," Black told him. A chiming sound echoed through the mansion, and an idea drifted through his mind. "The house doesn't like you much, does it?"

Baron chuckled. "The house is its own entity. If it chooses not to like me, well," he lifted a hand in the air and a dark array of black and red magic sprung from it, slicking the air, "it has that right, just as I have the right to retaliate." His voice dropped to ice on the last word, and the magic whirled itself into a mini cyclone. As it spun faster and faster, the house moaned and screeched, the noise blasting through the foyer. Black covered his hears and cringed. Dreadful reared up and whinnied, and the cyclone burst like a confetti cannon, spewing the spinning magic every which way.

The house roared and shook and Black fell to his knees as the floor buckled and twisted beneath him. He heard Baron laughing. Black reached back for his ratchet; he would harm Baron if needed to make him leave. But then the front door slammed, the house went still, and Black pushed himself to his feet. Dreadful was standing with his head lowered, but he looked okay.

Why did Baron do that? Just to prove a point? To show that he's got powerful magic? He walked over to Dreadful and touched the horse's neck. "You okay?" he asked, his voice quiet.

"I won't help him," the stallion said.

"Me either." Black startled when the door opened again. Jared walked in, followed by the rest of his siblings and—

"Helen?" Black's jaw went slack. He hadn't seen Helen Trudeau since that last morning he'd spent on the Island, decades ago. She looked exactly like he remembered. "What are *you* doing here?"

She smiled and walked over, taking him by the shoulders and hugging him. "It's so *good* to see you, Sullivan!" She stepped back. "I'm the housekeeper."

"You? But..." He looked at the siblings and then back at her. "I knew *a* Mrs. Trudeau was Baron's housekeeper, but I never imagined it was you!"

A laugh burbled up out of her and she clapped her hands. "Believe it, dear boy!" Her hazel eyes, sharp as tacks, went past him and she said, "Why Dreadful. I wasn't sure I'd ever see you again!"

The bay horse had backed into the living room until only his head was showing. He almost looked like he was frowning. Helen put a hand out to him, and he sniffed it, then snorted and pranced forward to meet her. She threw her arms around him and squeezed tight. "It's so wonderful to see you, old boy," she said.

He sidestepped away and she let go of him. "Happy to see you," he said, bobbing his head. He focused on the other newcomers then, and Danny held his hand out.

"Be careful," Jared warned, eying the bay stallion with a grimace.

"Nah, he's fine," Danny said. Dreadful bumped his hand with his nose and recoiled.

"More Flynns," he said.

"More Flynns," Rory agreed. "Danny, Marta and Gavin, this is Dreadful. He's supposed to be powerful enough to take down Penumbra and Uncle Baron."

Black glanced at Charlotte, and was perturbed by her downtrodden expression. He walked over to her and touched her arm. She looked up at him. "You okay?" he whispered.

"It's time for dinner," Helen announced. "Everyone wash your hands and meet me in the dining room in ten minutes." She rubbed her hands together and smiled. "Let's see what the house and I can cook up!"

"You and the house?" Marta asked, frowning. "What do you mean?"

"I mean that you don't think I cleaned that massive townhouse all by my lonesome, do you?" Helen's eyes twinkled. "No sir. I know how to access just enough magic to make it do my bidding. Now go on – scoot!" She whirled around and headed down the hallway toward the dining room like she knew precisely where she was going.

"Access the magic?" Marta and Gavin looked at each other. Rory slung an arm over their shoulders.

"I'll explain it," he said cheerily. They went down the hallway toward the first floor bathroom, leaving Jared, Danny, Charlotte and Black with Dreadful.

"Your uncle was here not more than fifteen minutes ago," Black finally said. "He asked where Charlotte was and tried talking Dreadful into leaving."

"What happened?" Jared asked.

"He used some magic on the house after I realized the house didn't want him here. It was making a lot of noise, like it was unhappy with him." Black shook his head. "He's in control of a lot of magic. It's going to take a lot to beat him."

"It's too bad Uncle B has to be such a jerk." Danny's good mood had vanished, and there was a sulky tone to his voice. "I mean, he was always so cool."

"Not now, he's not." Jared ruffled Danny's hair, and the younger Flynn shoved his hand away. "Come on, I'm starving. Let's get washed up and see what Mrs. Trudeau is making."

The two brothers wandered down the hallway, and Black refocused on Charlotte. He touched her cheek. "What is it? Something's wrong," he murmured, sure of himself.

She swallowed and said, "I had another choking fit. Its Uncle Baron's magic. Mrs. Trudeau said his magic is warring with mine." Her voice was dispirited.

"I'm sorry," he said and reached around her, drawing

her in close to him. She nestled her head against his shoulder, and a sudden urge to take her away from all this overwhelmed him. She hadn't asked for any of this, and yet had been thrust into a war for the whole world. Anger ignited throughout him. How could Baron turn on her? How could he turn on his entire family?

She pushed back from him and tried to smile. "It's okay. We should go eat."

"Charlotte." He was free now to call her by name; their brief kiss at the amusement park had sealed that deal for him. "We're going to get through this," he said, his voice gentle. "My grandfather gave me that journal that you saw at our apartment. He said it has all of Oliver's notes about the Flying Ponies in it."

Her eyes widened. "Is Mr. Coal helping us now, then? I thought he was working with my uncle."

"He said he was, when he thought Baron wasn't crazy. But he says he knows now that Baron only has bad intentions," Black told her. "The journal might have information we can use."

"That's great." This time her smile was genuine. It faded fast though. "Did you tell him about Dante?"

"I did. He said that was unfortunate." But maybe it wasn't completely. Black had never totally trusted his old coworker and friend. "There's more I need to tell you, but I think everyone should hear it at the same time."

"Good thinking." They started down the hall toward the dining room, Dreadful walking behind them. "Has he been behaving?" Charlotte whispered, glancing over her shoulder at the stallion.

"Yeah, as much as he normally does." This was said with humor; Black remembered full well the bay horse jumping down off the carousel after hours on the Island and running around. He loved chasing the seagulls that flocked in from the ocean to snatch stray pieces of popcorn off the street. It was always amusing, until someone had to coerce the stallion to get back on the carousel.

Mrs. Trudeau was bringing out a platter of fried chicken when they entered the dining room. She smiled and told them to sit. Dreadful stood in the doorway, watching everything with interest, but then turned and trotted back down the hallway. Black sat down across from Charlotte and next to Marta, who gave him an awkward smile.

"Hello," he said, trying to put her at ease. She mumbled a hello back and then looked away. Frowning, Black wondered if he'd said or done something to put her off, but then he saw Charlotte shaking her head. Perhaps Marta wasn't that friendly.

"Rory, say grace, please," Mrs. Trudeau said after sitting down at the head of the table.

Rory turned red but complied, his blessing muttered and short. When he finished, he reached for the chicken. Mrs. Trudeau reached out and smacked his hand.

"Ladies first," she said. Her tone was stern, but Black noticed that Gavin and Danny snickered, probably more from their older brother getting chastised than from her voice.

"Right," Rory said. He caught Danny smirking and cuffed him. Mrs. Trudeau cleared her throat, and the two boys straightened up.

"This is really good," Jared said a few minutes later after having cleaned his plate. "Thank you."

"You're welcome," Mrs. Trudeau said, smiling. "I'm glad to see all that junk food your uncle lets you eat hasn't spoiled you for wholesome food."

"He made us real food," Danny contradicted. Then, considering, he added, "Well, the house made the food, I guess. He wasn't around enough to do it."

Mrs. Trudeau harrumphed and said, "That sounds exactly like him."

The siblings were quiet after that, and Black wondered if Baron had been around much for them after they'd come to live with him. He knew their father hadn't died that long ago. His eyes went to Charlotte, wondering how she was holding up. She was wearing a periwinkle sweatshirt that set off her eyes. His heart beat harder and he dropped his gaze, afraid to draw too much attention if he turned red – which he knew he was.

"Hey." Danny's voice was sharp.

Black jerked his head up and looked at him. "What?"

Danny pointed his fork at him. "I saw that. Better watch yourself."

"Saw what?" Rory asked, glancing between the two of them.

"He's watching Charlotte," Danny said, frowning.

"Danny, behave yourself," Charlotte chastised, sending a furtive look at Black.

Jared set his glass of milk down with a hard thunk, drawing Black's attention. Black swallowed. "Danny's right. Watch yourself," Jared rebuked.

"Really?" Charlotte shot her older brother a dark look. "We like each other, okay? Leave him alone!"

"*Children*." Mrs. Trudeau's voice shot through the room. "Enough. Eat your dinner and leave Sullivan and Charlotte be." She resumed eating, but her penetrating eyes swept the table. There was no need for that, however – everyone went back to staring at their plates.

Black couldn't hide a quick smirk. It was good to know that Helen still had that fire he remembered from the Island. Symphony could be hard to handle, but Helen always made it look easy. His smirk fell away. *I guess I'd better call Symph tonight and ask her to help us.* He jolted a little; her nickname came back so easily, even though he hadn't called her that in decades. Now heat was rising through him, but not because of the sweet young woman sitting across from him. Unbidden thoughts of the golden-haired singing beauty flooded his mind, and he found it hard to concentrate on his food.

The house let out a screech, hauling Black out of his treasury of memories. Everyone was staring at one another, while around them the mansion began to rumble and moan. Black shot to his feet; if the noises were any kind of indication, Baron could well be inside with them.

They heard Dreadful shriek, and Black and Jared bolted for the doorway, Black reaching it first and nudging Jared out of the way with his shoulder. Racing down the hallway, they found the bay stallion standing in a defensive position. His head was lowered, like he might charge, and his four black legs were spread wide. Black's eyes jumped to the front door. There was no one there.

"What is it?" he asked, walking up next to the horse.

Dreadful snapped his teeth. "Monsters," he said.

Black went to the windows on the side of the door, peered out, and sucked in a breath. Six Desolates were outside in the yard, and as he watched, one of them lumbered up onto the porch and struck the door. He jumped back, though the creature couldn't hurt him from out there.

"What is it?" Jared asked. The others ran into the room, and Black turned to face Charlotte. She saw the look on his face and paled.

"Desolates?" she guessed.

"Yes," he said, nodding. "Six of them."

Jared and Rory moved to look out the windows and Jared grimaced. "Nasty looking," he observed.

"And dangerous," Black told him. "Everyone, go back to the dining room."

"What are you going to do?" Gavin asked.

"Nothing," Black told him. "I'm just going to watch. That's too many for me to drive off." When they all looked ready to argue, he added, "Go. If they somehow manage to break in, you guys can escape out the back door from the kitchen." In his mind, this was a solid plan. But the Flynns were nothing if not stubborn – the whole lot of them.

"No way," Rory told him. He smacked a fist into the palm of his other hand. "If they do break in, we're going to fight them."

"That's right," Jared added. "This is our home. We're not letting those creatures take it."

The Desolate at the door pounded on it again, making everyone jump. Black looked at Helen. "Take the girls, Gavin, and Danny back to the dining room," he said.

Helen smiled. "And miss all the fun? I think not. Arm yourselves, children," she ordered.

"Arm themselves? Are you crazy?" Irritation wove through Black's voice. "I'm trying to keep everyone safe!"

"Yes, and doing a fair job of it," Helen told him. She walked over to the umbrella stand in the corner near the closet and pulled out a black umbrella. Examining it, she nodded once. "This will do."

The four boys raced off up the staircase to the left of the room. Black heard their pounding feet overhead and glanced at Charlotte.

"They're getting their baseball bats," she told him, shrugging.

Black huffed out a sigh. "You and Marta should at least go to the dining room," he said, trying not to sound annoyed.

Charlotte put her hands on her hips. "No. I want to see what happens. Besides, with you and Dreadful here, what can go wrong?" She said this with a small smile, but it didn't make Black feel any better. With Helen standing there holding an umbrella like a samurai warrior, though, he knew he wasn't winning the battle of making the girls leave the room.

By the time the boys came back, each gripping a solid ash bat, three more Desolates had joined the first on the porch. They were pummeling the house with their fists. Black slid his ratchet from his back pocket and held it loose in his right hand. He really didn't think the creatures would break in, but it didn't hurt to be prepared, either.

Dreadful had placed himself between the women and the door, and Black stood next to him, tense and watchful. The creatures were now roaming up and down the porch, occasionally striking the house with a fist. With each passing moment, Black wondered when they would attack the house outright, but they seemed almost distracted now, and after another ten minutes, they all left the porch, and then the yard. Black exhaled a long slow breath, but he was curious: what had made them leave?

"I'm going to go look around," he announced and started to open the door.

"Are you serious?" Jared asked. There was disbelief in his eyes. "Right now, right after they just left?"

"Yes," Black said, giving an emphatic nod, "because I want to know what was strong enough to draw them off. They're pulled to this house because of the magic, so what other magic is out there drawing them away?"

"The carousel?" Gavin suggested.

"Only if the horses were there," Black told him. "And

maybe they are, but if so, why weren't all the creatures there, then?" He turned to the door. "Stay inside," he ordered as he stepped outside. But the door opened behind him as soon as he shut it; glancing back, expecting to see Jared, he found Charlotte instead, a grim set to her lips.

"Don't," she warned him. "I want to go with you." She walked past him and down the steps, and knowing she wouldn't listen, he stepped down the stairs after her.

That was one of the qualities that had drawn him to her; she was sixteen and had no true idea of what she was up against, but she was brave anyway. Tightening his grip on the ratchet, he followed her as she walked after the creatures.

10

*I*t wasn't so much bravery that drove Charlotte out onto the porch; it was wanting some time alone with Black that did it. As much as she loved and adored her family, there were times they were just too much to take. Jared had taken one look at her face and stepped aside when she hustled after Black. It wasn't like she wouldn't be safe; Black was protective and wouldn't let anything harm her.

She glanced at her companion. He was focused on the woods around them, the ratchet gleaming in his hand. Wanting to talk to him but feeling like he was too much in the moment, she stayed silent as they tracked the Desolates. The ground was littered with fallen leaves, and they crunched as she walked over them.

"Hold up." Black stopped, his gaze on something she couldn't see. "It looks like they went that way." He started walking again, and she stayed at his side, still wanting to talk but not sure how welcome it would be. Plus, tracking magical monsters probably wasn't the best time for conversation. Sherlock and Watson never spoke a lot when they were tracking, either. *But it's nice just being with him.*

"Stop." He took hold of her hand and tugged her to a halt. "I'm going to get closer, but I want you to stay right here." His eyes met hers. "Okay?"

She frowned. "I want to see what they're up to."

He frowned back at her. "And I want to protect you, so stay here, yeah?"

It was the *yeah* that did it. She'd probably never tell him that, but it was an adorable quirk, and got her good every time he used it. "Okay, fine," she said, making sure it sounded like a grumble. He grinned and took off, stalking toward where he thought the creatures were. Charlotte rubbed her arms. It was chilly, of course, and she hadn't grabbed her coat. The trees were almost naked now, and the breeze rattled through their empty branches, creating a ghostly concerto. She watched Black disappear into a thicket of high bushes and fought the urge to go after him. He could handle himself.

A few spatters of rain kissed her face, and she looked up. A gasp erupted from her. The clouds above were dark grey but edged with bright orange and hot pink. As she stared, streaks of cerulean blue shot through, streaking toward earth. The rain came harder, and as she watched it fall, it glittered in the low sunlight. Holding her hand palm up, she let some of it collect, and swallowed hard.

The rain not only glittered, it was vibrant green, like the jungle trees of the Amazon. She held it in her palm until it began to run down her hand, and let it splash to the ground. *It's beautiful,* she thought, *like something out of a fantasy novel.* A noise behind her interrupted her thoughts, and she turned, her heart suddenly hammering. *Uncle Baron!*

He sat astride Penumbra. The magnificent dapple-grey stallion stood with his head lifted proudly. "So nice to see you, darling," Baron said. Condescension rolled through his deep voice.

"Uncle." Charlotte spat the word. She tried to control the beating of her heart. It wasn't like she was alone; if she yelled, Black would come.

Baron grinned. "I really am pleased to see you," he said. "How have you been feeling?"

Her eyes flashed. "I think you know," she told him. "Your magic is trying to do something to me." All around them, the green rain continued to slick the air.

"My magic is trying to help unlock your own," Baron said. He swung down off Penumbra and put a hand on the grey's neck. "Once that happens, you'll see my side of things and help me." The smug self-assurance in his voice made Charlotte want to vomit.

"No, I won't," she retorted. "And anyway, my body is rejecting your magic."

"Is it now." Baron tapped his chin. His gloves were peacock blue today, and garish against the black rain coat he wore. "We need to change that." His smile turned devious.

Charlotte resisted the desire to back away from him. "I'm not afraid of you."

"Good." He stepped away from Penumbra and rubbed his hands together. Bits of red magic floated out from between his gloves, and this time, Charlotte couldn't help but shuffle back a step or two. The motion caught Baron's eyes and he smiled. "Don't leave yet," he told her.

"I'm not," she said, her voice frosty. "I don't want any of your magic, Uncle Baron. Keep it to yourself."

Penumbra snorted. "His magic far overpowers yours."

Charlotte pointed at the horse. "You be quiet," she ordered. "This doesn't involve you."

"Oh, but it does," Baron said. "It involves them all." His tone dropped down into creepy uncle range, and a shiver ranged across her shoulders. It was only then that she noticed the other Flying Ponies stepping out into view, tossing their heads, their eyes gleaming. She counted them: fifteen, including Penumbra, which meant he hadn't found any of the missing ones. Or if he had, he was hiding them.

"You can't resist all of us," Warpaint said. The chestnut pinto stallion stopped next to Penumbra. His voice was rough and dusty, like he'd just come off a trail.

"He is right," Sirocco added. The palomino mare spoke softly. "Please don't try."

Charlotte's heart twinged. "Sirocco, don't do this. You don't have to listen to them!"

"We *choose* to listen," Chimerical, the pale blue mare, told her. She spoke with a haughty tone that matched the way she looked down her nose at Charlotte. "Your magic is weak, Capall. Join us."

"Yes, Charlotte, please do join us," Baron said. He was smiling, but it didn't reach his blue eyes. They were frigid. "I have so much to teach you."

"I don't want to learn anything from you," she said, shaking her head. "Besides, how powerful can you really be? You can't make Dreadful listen to you!" At that, she noticed the other horses murmuring amongst themselves, and added, "That's right – Dreadful doesn't bow down to him or Penumbra, so why should all of you?"

"Careful now, darling," Baron warned. He moved toward her, and red magic trailed after him, turning the air around him crimson. Charlotte took another step back. She knew what his magic felt like and wanted nothing to do with it. "I really don't want to hurt you," Baron added, "but you must be taught." He threw up his left hand. A wall of magic sizzled against the blowing rain.

Charlotte ducked and yelled, "Black!" The red magic washed over her like a wave, and inside, deep within her body, she felt a corresponding swell. Something cold and wild writhed and twisted, rising through her until she could feel it trying to take control.

"Yes," Baron said, his voice loud. "Yes, that's it, let it flow!"

The magic inside her rolled and crashed, and she dropped to her knees, her chest feeling like it would burst. Around her, soaking the air with its weight, was purple magic. It spun and danced in the chilly breeze, and she struggled to her feet. She held her hands out in front of her, and saw the magic pooling in her palms, only to drift away with each passing swirl of air.

"Magnificent," Baron declared. He clapped his hands together, and his magic collected at his feet, a blood-red puddle of power. "Now, my dear, we really must be on our way," he said. "Choose a pony."

"What?" Charlotte glanced up at him, startled by how close he was. "I'm not leaving with you." She pushed her soaked hair away from her face.

"The others don't understand you," he told her. "I do. I can show you how to use your magic. After all, you're an archimage. You and I, seated upon Flying Ponies, will be unstoppable!"

Perhaps if he hadn't said it that way, or spoken in such a devilish manner, Charlotte might've gone with him. But her mind cleared, and she clenched her fists and said, "No. I will **never** side with you!"

The Flying Ponies began to stomp their hooves and mutter, and Penumbra walked up next to Baron. "Foolish child," he chastised. "You have no idea what you could accomplish with us. Come, Baron. We're better off without her." The grey stallion tossed his head with disdain. "She is not fit to be our Capall any longer." He nudged Baron's arm with his nose. "I choose *you*, Baron Flynn, as the new Capall of the Flying Ponies!"

At his words, the carousel horses rose onto their hind legs and whinnied, the sound reverberating off the trees. Charlotte watched her uncle's eyes widen with pleasure, and the smile that stretched his face could only be called maniacal. Her breathing grew ragged; somehow, in the last few seconds, things had gone wrong, more wrong than they'd been before.

"Charlotte!" Black's cry reached her seconds before he did. He pushed her behind him, but the damage was done. She moved to stand beside him, and he reached out and took her hand. "What happened?" he asked, his voice low.

"*What happened?*" Baron threw back his head and laughed. "What happened is now I have all the power of the Flying Ponies! And that means," he focused his gaze on Charlotte, locking eyes with her, "that each of them must yield to me. Even your precious Dreadful, darling." He moved closer to her, and she tensed even as Black stepped in front of her. "I have no more use for you, Charlotte, now that I'm the Capall. Absolutely *no use* at all."

The red magic cascaded over them at the same moment Black turned and yanked her against him, protecting her as best he could from the magical onslaught. But this time, she was not unarmed: her purple magic battled back against the red, creating chaotic mini hurricanes all around them, and turning the air dark and dangerous. She lifted her head from its safe position against Black's chest, and saw the horses racing by, a herd of living wood flowing all around them.

"You should've joined us," Flintlock said close to them. Charlotte pulled as far away from Black as he'd let her. The dark palomino mare's eyes glinted with power, and she looked ominous.

"*You* should've sided with *me*," Charlotte told her. She struggled to keep the tears from her voice. Flintlock had stood with her against the Tyranny; how could she succumb to Baron's equally mad plans now? Lucida and Crescendo, two of the grey mares, plunged to a halt on either side of Flintlock, their eyes brimming with malice.

"Don't talk to her," Lucida snapped. "We are not yours to command!"

"Let's go," Crescendo added, her sing-song voice like sandpaper on Charlotte's nerves. The three mares bolted after the others, and Black snagged Charlotte's wrist when she tried to run after them.

"Let go of me," she ordered.

"Don't," Black said, pulling her back to his side. "It's not worth it. They're gone."

She sagged and felt his hand on her back. "Why? Why did Penumbra do that?"

"I'm surprised he hadn't already thought of it, to be honest," Black said. "Come on. There's a lot of residual magic floating around here. It'll draw the Desolates." He started to walk, but Charlotte refused. He turned to face her, and his eyes went soft. "It's horrible, but don't give up. We have Dreadful. If we can find the other ponies, we can stop your uncle."

"Being the Capall isn't really that big of a deal, though, right? I mean, it didn't do much for me," she said. "Why would my uncle get that excited over it?"

He sighed. "It depends on who it is," he said. "As strong with magic as Baron is, it means something more to him, and to the Flying Ponies. You had the title, but not the strength to back it up." He held his hand out to her. "We really should get back to the house."

Anger swept through her. "So, because I didn't have access to my magic when I was the Capall, the ponies didn't have to respect me?"

"That's right."

"But I do now," she argued. "All that purple magic floating around? That's *mine*, Black."

"That's all well and good, but Penumbra already bestowed the title upon your uncle." He gave his hand a shake. "Come on. The rain isn't going to let up, and if those Desolates come this way, I won't be able to hold them all off." The slight edge of desperation in his voice broke her, and she grudgingly nodded. But she ignored his hand; she wasn't in the mood for that sort of thing. Anger roiled and boiled throughout her at the turn in events.

It wasn't fair that when she'd been the Capall, it hadn't meant much. But now that Uncle Baron held the title, *he* got the respect of the Flying Ponies? *Ooh! I wish I could just scream!* It would come off as juvenile, though, and she was trying not to seem that way with Black walking next to her.

"It's okay to be upset," Black murmured a moment later. He glanced at her. "He didn't hurt you, did he?"

"No." No, her uncle had just annihilated her pride, that was all. *Stupid title, anyway. I shouldn't let it get to me. That's what he wants.* "He can't really command Dreadful now, though, can he? That's what he told me." This was something to worry about; without the cavalry pony, they'd have nothing.

Black was quiet for a few paces. "I know that when your great-great-grandmother was the Capall, they all listened to her," he finally said.

"Was she an archimage too?"

"No, not at all. She didn't even command any magic," Black said. "But Oliver was an archimage. They respected him enough that they extended it to her."

"Wouldn't that have been nice," she sniped, and immediately turned red. Black stopped walking and turned to face her. "I'm sorry," she muttered. She knew she was being a brat.

"Don't let Baron get to you," he said. He took her hands in his and squeezed. "Dreadful is plenty strong enough to repel him. At least, he has so far. And the house doesn't like your uncle, either. We'll find the horses the Tyranny has. I know someone who can help, an old friend of mine from the Island."

Charlotte's stomach knotted. "I don't suppose you're talking about Dante." When Black shook his head, she let out a breath. "Is it Symphony Cantata?"

His eyes went wide. "How did you know?"

"Mrs. Trudeau told us she was Symphony's governess." She studied Black, the way his cheeks had turned pink and the way his breathing hitched. "Were you guys good friends?"

"You could say that," he said, nodding. "My grandfather has kept in contact with her and gave me her information."

Before she could say anything, a pair of Desolates walked into view. She jumped, and Black swung around to face them. "Head for the house, that way," he ordered.

"You too! You can't fight them both," she retorted. She'd had to leave Uncle Baron alone with the creatures once before, and she wasn't about to do that with the boy she'd fallen for. "We can outrun them."

"Go!" They raced off toward the house, Charlotte deferring to his lead. The creatures let out a wail and started chasing them. The shimmering green rain raced down from the sky, the breeze blowing it into her face. Behind her she could hear the Desolates gaining ground and quickened her strides. The house came into view.

Almost there! Keep running! The door flew open and her brothers ran onto the porch, all four of them clutching their bats.

"Charlotte! Look out!" Jared yelled just as she tripped over a fallen tree limb. She crashed to the ground, stunned for a brief second. It was enough for one of the creatures to reach her.

11

"Charlotte!" Black was instantly there, throwing himself in between her and the Desolate. It roared and swung its ashy hands at him, clawing the air. Charlotte scrambled back, and Black took a second to make sure she was clear before he yanked his ratchet from his pocket and went after the creature. He drove into it, catching it upside the head and forcing it to stumble backward. Jared and Rory were there in moments, holding their bats with death grips and taunting it.

"Is Charlotte safe?" Black demanded, cracking the Desolate across the jaw.

"She is. She's with Gav and Danny," Jared told him. He turned to hit the second creature. "Man, these things are ugly!"

Black had no reply as he threw himself out of reach of the Desolate's long arm. Rory cut in, whacking it in the back of the knees with his bat. It pitched backward with a high keen, and Black lunged in close enough to hit it hard across the chest. It stumbled and fell, landing on its back in the mud. Black leaned in and hit it solidly across the neck, and its body ceased moving.

"Dude," Rory muttered but Black was already moving in on the second one. He was tired of the creatures, tired of having to drive them away only for them to return. Somewhere in his subconscious, his brain was panicking at how close Charlotte had been to getting touched. He would have to deal with that later – for now, he just wanted them down.

"Hit it harder," he ordered Jared, who was only putting in glancing blows.

"But they're people, right?" Jared asked, jerking backward out of harm's way as Black got in front of him.

"Once, but not anymore." Black couldn't let old memories get in his way. He thumped the creature hard in the gut, and it doubled over. A second blow, this time across the left side of its face, took it down, and he struck it across the back of the head. It too fell silent.

Breathing hard, he backed away and motioned to the boys. "Go inside and make sure Charlotte's all right. I'll make sure these don't get up." When they just stared at him, he barked, "Go!"

"All right, all right," Rory said, glaring at him. "We heard you the first time!" He turned for the porch, where Gavin and Danny were standing watch. Jared watched him go, and then turned to face Black.

"Was this really necessary?" he asked, his voice low.

"Necessary?" Black choked out a sharp laugh. "If they had touched your skin, you would already be changing into one of them. Once that happens, it can't be reversed. Yes, it was *necessary*," he growled.

Jared reeled back at his tone and said, his own cautious, "Did you know someone who turned into a Desolate?"

Black closed his eyes. Why hadn't Jared just gone back to the house? Why did he have to hang around and ask questions that Black didn't want to answer? Jared wasn't leaving, though, and Black said, "Yeah. Yeah, I knew someone." He opened his eyes and looked at Jared, meeting his inquisitive gaze. "My grandmother, actually. Greta Midnight." The words tasted like bile and his heart turned heavy. "My grandparents took me in. My parents didn't want to be saddled with me, so they dropped me off one day at Coney Island and told me to go find my grandfather, that he'd take care of me for a while." Black lifted his head and looked up at the sky. The rain was green; funny how he hadn't noticed it before this. "But they never came back." He lowered his gaze to Jared's again, and saw the shock and empathy in his blue eyes. Black shrugged. "So now you know." He heaved a weighty breath and shoved the ratchet into his back pocket. "I promised myself that I would never let another person get turned into a Desolate, so long as I could help it."

Jared worked his jaw for several seconds before saying, "I'm sorry. That's horrible." He looked down at the two fallen creatures. "No wonder you threw yourself in front of

Charlotte like that. I wasn't fast enough. Neither was Rory." He swallowed a couple of times and met Black's eyes. Holding Black's gaze, he said, "I'm sorry I misjudged you. Charlotte's never had a boyfriend before, and, well, you know." He reached up and rubbed the back of his neck, his face flushing red.

"And I'm decades older than she is," Black said, nodding. He had figured that's what Jared's biggest problem with him was. "You know how I feel toward her." Now it was his turn to go red in the face. "I promise that I'll do my best to protect her."

"We all will," Jared told him. They shook hands, and then Jared added, "We better go in. Charlotte will want to know you're okay." They started toward the house.

"She'll want to know the same of you, too," Black told him. As they reached the porch steps, Black stopped. "I ask that you don't tell anyone about my grandmother."

Jared, a step ahead of him, turned back. Frowning, he asked, "Why not? I mean, why is it a secret?"

Black gave a slight shake of his head. "It's not, really, but I'd rather tell people myself. It's personal."

"I get that." Jared nodded. "You've got my word." They hurried up the steps and into the house, where Charlotte was indeed waiting for them. She cast a quick look at Jared, who smiled. "I'm okay," he told her. "Black did most of the work."

She moved to Black and looked up at him. "Are you really okay? You were awfully close to that first one," she murmured.

Though he knew he hadn't needed Jared's blessing, it did make it easier to reach out and touch her cheek, his fingertips gentle. "I was," he agreed, his voice soft. "But I wasn't letting it harm you."

She tipped her head against his hand. "Thank you," she whispered.

"You're welcome." He ran his thumb along her jawline and then let his hand drop, not wanting to draw too much attention and embarrass her. She gave him another smile before turning away.

"We saw Uncle Baron," she announced, and her smile bled away. Black could hear the irritation in her voice now. "Penumbra renounced me as Capall and gave the title to our uncle."

"What does that matter? The Capall doesn't have any power," Rory said, shrugging. He was holding his bat across his shoulders.

"The Capall does if he's an archimage," Black said. He shoved his hands into his front jeans pockets. "As he gets stronger, the more the horses will have to listen to him."

"That's stupid," Danny said, scowling. "I mean, the ponies are supposed to be super powerful, but they must not be if they have to listen to Uncle Baron."

"Where's Dreadful?" Charlotte asked.

"Upstairs with Marta and Mrs. Trudeau," Gavin said. "We wanted them to be safe."

"Good idea," Black said, giving his approval. "We'll have to be careful with Dreadful now. I don't think he'll have to listen to Baron, but I really don't know that for sure."

"Uh, sis, what is *that?*" Danny's voice was full of awe. "Is that magic?"

Charlotte gave herself a cursory glance. "Yes, my magic," she confirmed. Bits of purple drifted in the air around her. "Uncle Baron attacked me with his, and then all this purple magic started swirling around and fighting with his red magic." She shrugged. "The rain is green, by the way." At her brothers' disbelieving looks, she wrung some of her wet hair out, and collected the drops of rain water in her hand. "See?"

"Dude!" Danny said, eyes as wide as the sky. "That's awesome!"

"The magic is getting stronger," Black told them. "And your ability to see it is, too. Obviously." He waved a hand at the tiny drops of water in Charlotte's hand.

"Is that a good thing?" Gavin asked, sounding dubious.

"Yes," Charlotte said. She twisted her lips together and looked at Black. "Do you think any of them will be able to access the magic?"

"I don't know." Black shrugged. "I guess we'll see as the magic grows stronger."

There was the sound of hoof beats on the stairs, and Dreadful came prancing down. "Monsters are gone?" he asked.

"Monsters are knocked out," Jared told him. Dreadful reached the floor of the foyer and dashed over to Charlotte. She hugged him and then shoved his head away when he squealed at her.

"What's our next step?" Gavin asked. He looked between Black and Charlotte. "I'm assuming you have one."

Black nodded. "I do, and I have things to tell you, but you should all hear them together."

"I'll get Marta and Mrs. Trudeau," Danny said and raced off up the staircase to the left.

Charlotte flung an arm over Dreadful's neck, and the bay stallion stood quietly beside her. It was one of those casual moments, and it caught Black off guard. In a second, he was back on Coney Island, standing around the carousel and trading insults with Dante, while Cornelius and Oliver talked business. Dreadful was misbehaving, of course, but he liked Adara – she was one of the few who could make him mind himself. All Adara had to do was call him over and put her arm over his neck, and it transformed him into a gentleman. Black blinked several times to clear his eyes.

"You all right?" Rory asked him, frowning. "You look like you saw a ghost."

"I did," Black whispered, but not loud enough they could hear him. Danny came back down the stairs with his sister and Helen, and Black said, "Let's go into Baron's study. I have something to show you."

Once they were all settled in, Dreadful included, Black pulled open a drawer on Baron's desk and pulled out the journal his grandfather had given him. "This has all of your great-great-grandfather's notes about the Flying Ponies in it," he said, and set it down on the desk. "My grandfather stopped by while you were all in Smoke City and said it might be able to help us." He spread his hands on the surface and leaned on them. His gaze shifted to Helen. "He also said I should contact Symphony. He said she might know if any of the missing ponies were taken by the mob."

"The mob?" Charlotte said. "*Really?*" Her eyes widened and then narrowed.

"Symphony?" Helen's composure collapsed a little. "You think she would know about the mob?" Her voice dared Black to say it again.

"I do." He held her eyes for several moments before adding, "And you know it, too."

"Wait, wait, time out." Jared folded his arms over his chest. "Why would the mob want carousel horses?"

"Because, my boy, they knew what they were," Helen said. "Oliver was mixed up with several of the crime families, and even had some dealings with Lucky Luciano himself, although he always denied it when asked." She heaved a dramatic sigh. "I suppose Symph could've known what was going down."

"She *did*," Black said, surprising himself with his insistency. "Anyway," he added, looking at the siblings, "Dreadful was taken by one of the crime families when Oliver couldn't pay back a debt. We all knew that's who took him, but Oliver insisted it was the Tyranny. I don't know how Dreadful ended up at that amusement park, but it doesn't matter. If the mob took some of the other horses, then that means that Orrick doesn't know where they are, either. I hope."

"So, if Symphony has some leads, then we can track them down," Jared said, nodding. "What are we waiting for, then?"

"Wait." Charlotte got up and started pacing. She had her hands shoved into the kangaroo pocket of her hoodie, and she was biting her lip. She paced over to the windows and back. "Can we trust her? I mean, if she has mob connections…"

Helen snorted. "Of course we can trust her! I know that girl better than anyone." She shot a discreet look at Black, and it took all his resolve to not say something. There was no need for the Flynns to know how well he knew the Songbird, especially Charlotte.

"Let's go, then," Rory said and got up.

"I have her number," Black said, and reached out to pick up the journal. "Are we all in agreement, then? We ask Symph for help?"

"She won't hurt the ponies, will she?" Marta's quiet voice broke into the assents from Rory, Danny, and Helen. "I mean, the Tyranny said they would help, but then they wanted to control the carousel."

"She has a strong point," Gavin said, giving his twin a little nod.

"Black? Can you guarantee she'll help without wanting anything in return?" Charlotte asked. But that wasn't all that she was asking, and he knew it. Somehow, she knew he'd been more to Symphony than a friend. Perhaps Helen had told her, or perhaps she'd picked up on how he reacted whenever they'd talked about the singer. They were all waiting on him, even Helen, and that probably wasn't a good sign.

"To be honest, I don't know. I haven't spoken to her since the day I left the Island to come here with my grandfather, to help oversee the carousel," he said. That hadn't been a good day. They hadn't parted on good terms. "But we need her help. Orrick is out, and so is Dante, as far as we know." He locked eyes with Charlotte. "Your call."

She drew in a sharp breath, and he could see that he hadn't given her the answer she wanted. Needed. It couldn't be helped, though. He had absolutely no idea how the Songbird was going to react to him reaching out.

"Char?" Jared turned to face her. "I know you want to keep this close to the chest, but Black's right: we need help. I say we call her." His voice was full of determination, and Black saw Charlotte's resolve wavering. She might not listen to him, but she would heed her older brother's advice.

"Okay," she breathed out. "Call her."

He nodded and waited for the others to leave the room. Charlotte lingered for a moment, until Rory took her wrist and tugged her through the door. Once they were gone, and he'd locked the doors, he returned to Baron's desk and took out his cell phone. He still didn't like using it, but it was a necessity in today's world. Punching in the number from the back page of the journal, he waited.

"Hello?" Symphony's lyrical voice hit him hard in the

chest, and he couldn't talk. He couldn't even *breathe*. "Hello? Is anyone there?"

"Hiya, Symph," he said, grateful he didn't sound like he was gasping for air. "How are you?"

There was a long pause, and then, "Sullivan? Is it really you?"

"It is, Songbird," he said, a slow smile rolling over his face. He knew he shouldn't be so happy she recognized his voice, but he was. He was over the *moon*! "Got your number from my grandfather," he added, trying to rein in his emotions.

"Oh, Cornelius," she said, that beautiful voice settling into the delicate Irish lilt he remembered. "How is he?"

Black drew in a deep breath. "He's fine, Symphony. I'm calling about the Flying Ponies. Oliver's great grandson, Baron, along with Penumbra, has taken them over. Baron wants to use their magic to rule the world." It sounded so ridiculous, and yet it was the truth.

"Oh." She sounded surprised. "The magic has been getting stronger, so I wondered what was going on. It's been so long, you know." Her voice was falling into that dangerous lullaby tone that he'd found irresistible back in the day.

And yeah, he knew. *Time to shift gears, Sully.* "It's been so long for a lot of things, Symph," he said, his voice low. "I'm really calling because we need to know if you still have any of those old *family* connections from the Island."

"*Oh.*" She said nothing else, and he wondered if he'd

offended her. She hadn't been offended back on the Island when those connections had doted on her, giving her money and clothes and expensive champagne.

"Symphony. Yes or no?"

"Well, I might be able to help you," she finally admitted. "I suppose you need to know if any of my connections took more of the ponies."

"Yeah." He had to keep this conversation on track, because it would be dangerous if it derailed.

"I'll have to do some talking, but I can get what you need," she said, and when Black's heart rate went up, he wasn't sure she was talking strictly about the carousel. "Give me a couple hours."

"You won't get into trouble, will you?" He hated that he thought about it. She really didn't deserve his concern.

"Worried about me, Sully?" she asked, and that Irish accent was in full force now. "No, I'll be fine. I'll call you soon." There was a pause, then, "Good to hear your voice, Midnight."

He didn't realize he'd been holding his breath until she ended the call. Inhaling sharply, he set his phone down and ran his hands through his hair. *Stupid. I can't let her affect me like this!* What would Charlotte think, if she saw him so worked up over a simple phone call? *Really stupid, Sully. You've got to get yourself together.* He took several deep breaths, pocketed his phone, put the journal back in the drawer, and left the room.

Helen was the only one in the foyer. She lifted an eyebrow, and even before he could speak, she chuckled.

"Still has some of you, doesn't she?" she asked. When he opened his mouth, she waved her hand. "No, don't try to deny it. I see it." She pointed a finger up at the ceiling. "My advice to you is this: decide which one you want, because that young woman upstairs already holds you dear." She set her mouth into a firm line. "I don't want her to get hurt."

"That's the last thing I want," Black argued. "It was the first time I've spoken to Symph since I left. Of course it was going to affect me!" He couldn't hide his anger at her assessment of him, nor did he want to. "I care about Charlotte!"

Helen frowned and tapped her foot on the marble floor. "Enough that you won't go back to Symphony? Charlotte is a smart girl. She's going to notice if you can't work together with Symphony without getting emotional." Her voice was matter-of-fact and chilly.

"What's going on?" Charlotte was walking down the stairs, her eyes pinned to Black. He groaned inwardly. Why did she have to come down now? "Is Symphony going to help us?"

"Yes," Black told her. "She's going to talk to some people, and then call me back." He kept his voice even, barely. He heard Helen give a harrumph but didn't respond to it.

"That's good." Charlotte came down the stairs all the way, and then seemed to notice the mood between them. "Is everything all right?"

Before Black or Helen could say anything, something thumped against the door. Black muttered beneath his breath and crossed to the door to open it. His eyes widened, and he lunged to catch the person leaning on the door before he fell.

"Hello, Sully," Dante muttered before passing out in Black's arms.

"Oh, my word!" Charlotte rushed to Black as he staggered with Dante in his arms. Helen made tsking sounds and yelled for the others to come back down. Black struggled to lift Dante up and then carried him into the living room, where he carefully laid him down on a couch. Charlotte knelt by Dante's head and reached out to touch his forehead.

"What happened to him?" Jared asked as he ran into the room.

"I don't know," Charlotte said, distressed. "But someone hit him. Look," she added, pushing aside his hair so Jared could see the big bruise on Dante's forehead.

"Someone hit him hard," Jared said, scowling. "You think Orrick did this? Or one of the others?" He looked at Black, who had come around to stand behind the couch.

"I don't know. With them, it's a possibility." He sounded

angry. "But he had this coming to him, throwing in with them like that."

"Let me see." Mrs. Trudeau gave Jared a nudge, and he stepped back out of her way. The rest of the siblings had crowded together at the end of the couch. She murmured to herself as she looked Dante over. "He'll be fine. This is nothing worse than what he experienced on the Island."

"Did he fight a lot?" Danny asked.

"Oh, my, yes. He was always getting into a scrap," Mrs. Trudeau said, laughing. "But he could handle himself quite well in a fight." There was fondness in her voice, and Charlotte reached out to touch Dante's shoulder.

"Do you think he'll wake up soon?"

"I'm awake now, thank you," Dante muttered, sounding put out. He opened his eyes and tried to smile. He groaned instead.

"What happened?" Jared asked.

Dante pushed himself upright. "Let's just say Orrick wasn't happy with my decision to back out." He shrugged and looked Charlotte in the eyes. "I couldn't work against you, sweetie. I don't have it in me."

She frowned at him, not swayed by his pretty speech. "Dante, you sold me out. You honestly thought I would just hand the carousel over to them!"

His eyes flashed. "You told me before we went to get Dreadful that you were willing to work with them. What was I supposed to think?"

"Enough." Black's voice cracked like a whip. "She's right, Romano. Why should we trust anything you say now?" He came around to stand behind Charlotte, one hand resting on her shoulder.

Dante said nothing. His eyes danced over the whole group, and suddenly he seemed to see Mrs. Trudeau for the first time. "Helen!" he cried and hugged her.

"Mrs. Trudeau to *you*," Danny told him, a hostile note in his voice.

"Oh, pish posh. Everyone should call me Helen," she said, giving Danny a look. "Even Dante," she added before he could say anything.

"What in the world are you doing here?" Dante asked her, his focus on her.

"I was Baron's housekeeper," she told him. "And now we're all going to take him down and return the Flying Ponies to their rightful owners." She motioned to all the Flynn siblings. "We're waiting to hear if Symphony has some information we can use."

"The Songbird?" Dante's gaze shifted to Black, and Charlotte felt his hand tighten on her shoulder. "*Really*. That's interesting."

"Why?" Rory asked, and when Charlotte looked at her younger brother, she knew he was just egging Dante on. He knew darn well that both Black and Dante had liked the singer. Helen had told them so.

Dante's eyes grew hard. "She and Sully here were a thing," he said. "She would come around the carousel and ask to ride Oriflamme," he added.

"Oriflamme?" Jared asked. "What's that?"

"Not a what, but a who," Dante corrected. "He was an

armored palomino stallion, one of the most popular horses on the carousel when it was at the Island." His gaze darkened. "I thought perhaps the Songbird was flirting with me, but no. She only had eyes for Sullivan Midnight, the mechanic." He tipped his head to the side a little, but his heavy gaze never left Black. "Isn't that right, Sully? She and you were quite the pair."

"That's enough," Black growled. "That's in the past, and it's going to stay there." He loosened his grip on Charlotte's shoulder and rubbed it. She reached up and squeezed his hand, as much to calm her nerves as to settle his. His fingers, calloused and strong, returned the squeeze.

"Yes, keep telling yourself that," Dante taunted. "I know the truth." His eyes narrowed as they went to Charlotte's. "You'd do better to stay away from him, sweetheart."

"Don't call her that," Jared ordered. "She's not dating *you*."

"Oh, so now you two are a thing, eh, Sully?" Dante's voice was full of maliciousness. "How nice."

Helen reached out, quicker than scat, and smacked him on the cheek. "That is quite enough, Mr. Romano," she snapped. "You came to us because you wanted to help, is that it? Well, you've done nothing thus far but stir up the pot! So, either you keep your comments to yourself, or we'll escort you back to Orrick. Your preference." Her voice was as hard as her open-handed slap had been.

Dante had the audacity to look wounded. "I would rather stay here, if it's all the same," he muttered.

"Then behave yourself." Helen stepped back from the

couch. "Now, it's getting late. We all need sleep. Everyone, off to bed!" she ordered.

"Can Dreadful sleep in my room?" Marta asked. She'd been watching the entire exchange with wide eyes, and it was clear to Charlotte that her younger sister didn't trust Dante. She wasn't sure any of them should.

"Yes," Jared told her. "Try to keep him quiet."

"Everyone, go on, shoo," Helen said.

"Aw, we wanna listen to Dante get schooled some more," Rory said, chuckling. But the look he gave Dante was anything but funny.

"Shut up," Dante said, shooting him a glare.

"Make me," Rory challenged.

"Go on," Jared said, giving his younger brothers all a shove when they made no move toward the door. "You heard Helen. We all need sleep if we're going to hunt down missing carousel horses."

"Our life is really weird now," Danny said, laughing. But he too shot Dante a hostile look before leaving the room.

Black muttered something beneath his breath as he watched everyone file from the room. Once they'd gone, Helen included, he said, "If you're going to work with us, then we're establishing some ground rules." He pointed at Dante, whose gaze narrowed in ire. "Don't you *ever* lay a hand on Charlotte again. **Ever**. And no more calling her pet names."

"No?" Dante scowled. "Who's going to back you on that?"

"My brothers," Charlotte told him, matching his scowl.

Dante chortled. "I bet they'd try, sweethe — " He broke off abruptly at the look on Black's face. "Fine, fine. What else?"

"You *do not* talk to the Tyranny. I hear you've been, and I'll take you to task," Black told him. His tone was ice. Charlotte wasn't sure what all Black meant, but it was clear from Dante's reaction that it wouldn't be good. "No more taunts about Symphony and me. That was a long time ago, and it was over the day I left the Island." He took two steps and leaned down into Dante's face. "Is that clear?"

"Yes, fine. Get out of my face," Dante snarled.

Black stepped away. "You listen to us. No rash decision making on your own. And whatever information you have on the Tyranny or anyone else involved with the carousel, you give it to us."

"Anything else?" Dante asked, arching a sleek black brow.

"I'll let you know." Black nodded at him. "You can take the couch. Get some rest so you can help us tomorrow." He didn't wait for any more comments; instead, he took Charlotte's hand gently in his and led her out of the room and across the foyer to the study. After leading her in and shutting the door behind him, he took her face in his hands, tipped it up a bit, and kissed her.

It took her breath away. She knew that was so cliché, but there it was. Not that she had much experience kissing boys; it was limited to the simple kiss they'd shared before she left the amusement park with Dreadful. Her cheeks were hot when he pulled away from her. "W-what was that for?" she whispered, watching his eyes.

"I want you to know where you stand with me," he told her. "I courted Symphony when we were on the Island." He studied her. "I don't want you second-guessing how I feel because of that. You're my girl now, yeah?"

Tingles and butterflies shot through her. "Yeah," she murmured, suddenly shy. He grinned and gave her another soft kiss on the lips.

"Good. Don't forget it." He stepped back. "You should go get some rest. I have the feeling we're going to be busy pony hunting soon."

"All right." She hesitated and whispered, "Good night, Black." Though his real name was Sullivan, it didn't feel right to call him that. Someday she'd have to ask him why he and Cornelius went by different names, but not now. Now all that mattered was that he had chosen her, over all the other girls he must've known through the years. "Sleep tight," she added.

"You too." He kissed her cheek and then opened the doors. She walked across the foyer and up the stairs, passing Helen as she came down.

"Good night, sweet girl," Helen said, giving Charlotte's arm a squeeze as they passed one another. Charlotte wanted to say something back, but her heart was near-bursting, and she rushed up the stairs, through the crack in the wall and hurried upward until she reached her room. Flinging the door shut, she raced up the short set of stairs and flung herself onto her bed.

You're my girl now, yeah? Black's soft-spoken words echoed over and over in her head, and she grabbed a fluffy pillow and gave a girly squeal into it. Rolling over onto her back, she stared up at the lacy canopy over her bed and sighed. *I have to focus. This isn't the time to be a girl right now. We have carousel horses to find and a crazy man to stop.* That sobered her up, and the fuzzy feelings swarming in her chest dissipated. She started getting ready for bed.

Finding the missing Flying Ponies and stopping her uncle's diabolical plans was her mission. As much as she liked Black, was falling for him, she couldn't let those feelings get in her way. She reached over and turned the little Tiffany lamp on and plugged her phone in. Then she picked up her book where she'd laid it the night before. With everything going on, her mind was racing along much too fast for sleep, but immersing herself in a fantasy world she knew so well might help calm it.

An hour later, she was still wide-awake. She kept thinking about her confrontation with her uncle and the ponies. *How could all of them blindly follow him and Penumbra like that? Don't they care that their magic is being used for bad things?* It especially hurt that Flintlock would do it. Charlotte thought she'd bonded with the mare, but apparently that hadn't been the case. *I guess the only one I've really bonded with is crazy pants.* A small smile stole across her face. Dreadful was something else, but she loved him the way he was. His biggest quirk, for her, had been talking about himself in the third person, *um, horse*, but he'd given that up, thank goodness.

She woke up later, not having remembered falling asleep, and checked her phone. It was after eight, and she threw back her blankets. After a quick shower and dressing, she pulled her still-wet hair up in a ponytail and headed downstairs. No one seemed to be around, and puzzled, she went to the dining room, where she found her siblings eating.

"Good morning, sleepyhead," Rory said, pushing back a chair for her.

"Why didn't anyone wake me up?" she asked, sitting down. Helen set a plate of eggs and bacon down in front of her. "Thank you," Charlotte murmured.

"You needed the sleep," Jared told her, shrugging. "We haven't been up long."

"Where's everyone else?"

"Black and Dante took Dreadful for a walk," Gavin said. He poured her some orange juice from the pitcher.

"Thanks," Charlotte said, distracted by what he'd said. "They took him for a *walk*? He's not a dog."

"I think they needed to work some things out," Marta said. "They weren't getting along well."

"They've always had an antagonistic relationship," Helen told them all as she sat down in Baron's place. "Now eat up. We've got work to do."

"What kind of work?" Marta asked. She was eating slowly, her eyes on their former housekeeper.

Helen smiled. "We have ponies to find, my dear. That's not going to be easy." She leaned in closer to the table, a conspiratorial look in her hazel eyes. "In fact, it might even be dangerous." A broad smile filled her face.

Jared coughed and looked at her, and Charlotte could see he wasn't amused. "And you're really okay with all of this?"

"Of course. The Flying Ponies Grand Carousel is your family's legacy, Jared. The horses need to be reunited, and the carousel needs to be protected," Helen said.

"Maybe when we get it all back together, we should put it in a museum or something," Gavin said.

"They don't want to be stuck in a boring old museum," Danny retorted as he shoveled eggs into his mouth. "They'd hate that!"

"Yeah, I'm with him," Rory said, nodding. "I mean, they *fly*. Why would we want to stick them in a place they couldn't do that?"

"To protect them?" Gavin argued. "What if someone else tries to steal them?"

"Dreadful would hate it," Marta said. When her twin looked at her, she shrugged at him. "Well, he would."

It was amazing to Charlotte that her siblings, especially Marta, had rallied around the carousel and its magical horses. She was happy about it, of course. They needed as much help as they could get. A door banged down the hall, and they could hear Dreadful trotting toward them.

"Have a good walk, crazy?" Rory asked the bay stallion as he came into the room.

Dreadful walked over and nipped him in the shoulder.

"Yes," he said. His voice was raspy. Rory shoved him in the chest.

"Don't bite," he chastised.

Black and Dante followed the horse in, and Black took a seat next to Rory at the table. Dante sat beside Marta, who shifted to her right in her chair, the motion slight but enough for Dante to notice.

"I'll behave myself," he promised her with a wink.

"Believe that when I see it," Black muttered. When Dante shot him a dark look, he added, "Oh, come on. It's the truth."

"Boys." Helen's voice rang out. "Eat."

Dreadful proceeded to walk around the table, nosing in on everyone's plate and nipping here and there. Charlotte couldn't help but giggle as she watched him. This would look so bizarre to her friends back home, and yet, she couldn't imagine life as anything but this now. Black caught her eye from across the table, and she smiled, a rush of warmth filling her when he grinned back. She was a little surprised when Jared caught their look and said nothing. Had he finally decided that Black wasn't going to hurt her?

"What's the plan for today?" Jared asked, glancing between Black and Helen.

Black cleared his throat, drawing everyone's attention. He set his fork down. "Symphony called me back last night. She's got information on five more of the ponies." He looked down the table at Helen. "One of them is Oriflamme."

"Oh, her favorite!" Helen said, clapping her hands.

"Better than that," Dante said, "he's also one of the more powerful ones."

"He's the armored horse?" Jared asked. "The palomino?"

"Yes." Black nodded. "Palomino was a favored color of the carousel painters. Anyway, Symph said she knows where the five are." He exhaled a long breath. "It means we have to travel, though. We have to go to New York City."

Everyone was quiet for a moment. How was that going to happen? It would be a long car ride, and not everyone would be able to go. Charlotte was about to voice her concerns when Rory said, "What are we waiting for?"

"How will we get there, though?" she asked. "I mean, we can't all fit in the Cadillac."

Black exchanged a long look with Dante. "We aren't driving," Black said. "We have a direct connection to the Island." He waited for a moment, and then added, "The ponies are being held in an old warehouse on Coney."

Charlotte took a long deep breath. Coney Island? Where this had all started so many years ago? "What do you mean, a direct connection?"

"There are doors in the basement of the house," Black said, his voice low. "Each one leads somewhere different." Around them, the house began to murmur, delicate whispers floating through the air. "One of them goes to Coney Island."

Jared and Charlotte looked at one another, their eyes wide with amazement. "Mr. Coal told us he had a meeting down there," Jared said, looking at Black. "He was really going somewhere, right?"

"Yes," Black said, and held up a hand when Jared's mouth opened. "I don't know where he would've gone. There are several places the doors can take you." He swept his glance around the table. "Symphony said the horses haven't been around people in a long time, and if we all go, we'll frighten them."

"And someone should stay behind to keep the house safe, anyway," Dante added.

"Will we take Dreadful?" Charlotte asked. She automatically assumed she would be going with Black; though no longer the Capall, she might still have some kind of connection with the horses.

"Yes. It will help if he can talk to them," Black confirmed. Dreadful stopped pacing around the table and turned his head to look at Black. The overhead lights glinted on the stallion's shining wooden body.

"Oriflamme?" Dreadful said, and Black nodded. The cavalry horse bobbed his head. "He is a friend," he said.

Black chuckled. "Yes, you two did get along pretty well," he said. "Which is good, because we need him to help us against Penumbra."

The stallion tossed his head. "I'm not afraid of him."

"I know." Black focused on Charlotte. "We should go tonight, after the park is shut down."

"Who goes and who stays?" Rory asked. "Because I'm going."

Black shook his head. "Charlotte, myself, and Dreadful are going. Helen, you'll be in charge of things here."

Charlotte expected Jared to jump right in and disagree with that plan, but instead he simply nodded. "Works for me," he said. "What should we be doing now, though?"

"Dante and I are going to go through all the info he brought with him. We might be able to figure out where some of the Tyranny's horses are," Black said. "No one goes outside, not alone, anyway. The Desolates are hanging around too much."

With that, the group broke up. Helen shooed everyone out of the kitchen, and Charlotte followed her brothers and sister to the huge living room. Dante and Black disappeared into Baron's study. Charlotte tried to engage with her siblings, but was too distracted, and she finally went to the study and knocked on the door. When Black opened it, she bit her lip and asked, "Can I help?"

"Not at the moment," Black said, his tone apologetic. When her face fell, he added, "I'll come get you when you can, yeah?"

"Okay." She swallowed back her disappointment as he shut the door, and wandered back to the living room. Jared patted the cushion next to him on the couch, and she sat down.

"Excited about tonight?" he asked.

She nodded. "You aren't upset that we're going by ourselves?"

"Let's just say we've come to an understanding," Jared said. "You okay?"

"I think so." She really wanted to be in the study with Black and Dante, and didn't understand why she couldn't be. But maybe they were still working things out between them, and in that case, she was all right with not being there.

Rory turned on an old movie about two guys taking a road trip to save the company one of them owned, and she allowed herself to get sucked into it, even though they'd seen it a dozen times. Laughing along with her family made her realize how much she missed this, and how much she missed Uncle Baron.

Maybe he'll go back to being who he was when this is all over. There's a chance, right? There has to be a chance. She couldn't accept that her beloved uncle was truly gone for good. She would do whatever it took to bring him back from the darkness overtaking him.

*D*ante finished laying out the information he had, and Black leaned over the big desk, studying each note, each snapshot. "This all you have?" he asked, glancing up at Dante, who stood on the opposite side of the desk.

"It is."

"You swear to me?" The ice in Black's voice only made Dante scowl.

"You know, you used to be a lot more carefree, Sully. This girl has you in knots, doesn't she?" Dante fired back.

Black let the instant anger wash away for a moment, and then lifted his head to look his old friend in the eyes. Dante stiffened. "*This girl* is important to me," Black said. "And we've already established the fact that you're willing to go against her for your own benefit." Black jabbed a finger at him. "I'll ask again: is this **everything** you have?"

Fury crackled in Dante's eyes, and for several seconds,

Black wasn't sure he'd answer him. The air was oppressive and hot, and the house was dead quiet. "This is everything I have," Dante finally said. "I'll give you a warning, just because we're friends." His voice was low and cold. "The Tyranny is strong, stronger than they've ever been. Even if you find the horses Symphony told you about, it won't be enough. You and I know how unfocused Dreadful can be. He's not a lead horse. He won't be able to command Oriflamme and the others you find. At the end, after Orrick and Baron have torn the world apart, all you're going to have, Sully, is yourself."

Black's gaze narrowed. "Nothing is going to happen to Charlotte and her siblings. I won't let it."

Dante studied him until Black got uncomfortable and shifted on his feet. "You can try to save them, but we both know Baron is powerful, and Orrick isn't going to roll over and let him win. They will destroy everything by the time they're done." Dante shook his head. "You've an admirable constitution, old friend, but even you won't win this."

"So why are you helping me then?" Black's voice was filled with irritation. "If you're so positive Baron will abolish everything good in this world, including the people I care about, then what's in it for *you*?"

A slow grin wended its way over Dante's face. "Why not? What do I have to lose? I'm good with trickery and parsing out black magic on the sly, but I can't go against an archimage or Orrick alone. You know that."

Black crossed his arms over his chest. "You figure you'll go down fighting alongside me and mine, is that it, then?"

143

"Might as well try to right some of the wrongs I've done," Dante said, shrugging. He kept his eyes on Black but reached down to tap the desk. "Are we going over this information or not? It cost me getting it out." He reached his other hand up to rub at his cheek. "Ignace has a mean left cross."

"You had it coming," Black said, his tone wry. Dante sighed.

"Be that as it may, I'm finished with that lot." He suddenly stuck his hand out. "I'll be with you all the way to the last of it, Midnight."

Black surprised himself when he immediately shook on it, but deep down, he knew Romano was a good man. It just took an awful lot of squinting to see it. "To the last," he echoed.

Dante flashed a grin, but it faded fast. He picked up an old photo. "I believe this could be one of our famous Flying Ponies. It's hard to tell from this angle, but this reminds me of Eidolon."

"Great. Another crazy one," Black said, shaking his head.

Dante nodded. "I know, but she and Dreadful did get along. And she's strong, which we'll need."

"Where is this at?"

Dante handed him the photo. "In the country, which I know doesn't help much. My guess is Orrick spread his ponies out, so they'd be harder to find."

"Makes sense." Black studied the picture. It appeared to be the interior of a barn, and in the background of the photo was the hazy outline of a carousel horse. The pose looked like Eidolon; she was a blood bay and white pinto, with her two back feet planted on the ground and her two front ones raised in a semi-rear. If this was Eidolon, it could be difficult to secure her. Perhaps even a touch more mad than Dreadful, she was flighty and wild, and with Charlotte no longer the Capall, Black wasn't sure the mare could be dealt with.

"I don't suppose you have leads on our gentler ponies?" Black asked, setting the photo down.

"We don't need gentle, we need tough."

"I agree, but not with crazy thrown in." Black tapped the photo. "I'm not sure we can handle her."

"We did on the Island."

Black ran a hand through his hair. "Yeah, but we weren't preparing to throw down with an archimage, either. Or the Tyranny, for that matter. We need horses we can depend on, trust. I don't want Charlotte dealing with ones like Eidolon."

Dante smiled. "She's got you pretty good, doesn't she?"

"You just can't resist harassing me, can you?" Black asked. But there was no anger in his voice. "She does," he admitted. "She's different than other girls."

Dante smirked. "You've been holed up here in the woods for too long, old boy. She's not so different."

"She is to *me*, and that's all that matters." Black sorted through the other photos on the big desk. "What else do you have?"

Dante muttered something beneath his breath. "Did Symph tell you who the other four horses are?"

"No." Black picked up another photo and peered closely at it. "Is this Ringmaster?"

"It could be," Dante said, nodding. "He'd be a good one to get back." The buckskin circus horse had been gentle and calm, and a natural favorite of the hordes of children who thronged the Island during the weekends. "Although, he didn't tolerate Dreadful well, did he?"

"Doesn't matter. Ringmaster is easy to handle," Black said. And for him, that was a bonus. The last thing they'd need were wild horses like Eidolon while they were trying to take down Baron.

"Symphony going to meet you there?"

The question came out off-handed, but Black knew it wasn't. He kept looking through the pictures and documents on the desk. When Dante cleared his throat, Black said, "I don't know. I doubt it."

"Oh, I don't know. You really think she'd pass up the chance to see you again? I don't." Dante took a step back from the desk. "I say you get those five back tonight, and we go from there. One thing at a time."

It made sense, and at least going through the information was giving them something to do. Black said nothing. What if Symph did show up? How would Charlotte react? How would Symph react to *her*? Black swiped an arm across his forehead. Dante chuckled.

"Getting nervous thinking about the two women in your life meeting?"

"Shut up." It wasn't making him nervous, but it *was* giving him a headache, which was ridiculous, because he doubted the Songbird would meet them at the warehouse.

There was a polite knock at the door, and both straightened and looked at it. "Charlotte is getting impatient," Dante observed. "You going to let her in?"

He didn't want to, not just yet. "It could be any of the others," he said.

Dante scoffed. "Sure." He moved around the desk toward the doors, and Black held up a hand.

"Not yet. Tell her we're still working."

Dante cast a frown at him. "Really? Why don't you want her to come in?"

Because I need to sort things out in my head, Black thought. But he couldn't say that out loud. Dante would have a field day with that information. "I want us to make some kind of plan, that's why, before we involve all of them."

Dante scowled. "No, Sully, you have to do better than that." He walked to the doors and pulled one open, despite Black telling him not to. Charlotte stood on the other side; she looked uncertain and innocent. "Hello, lo —," Dante broke off, sounding flustered. "Come in."

Charlotte stepped in, her eyes seeking Black. He turned his back on her. "How's it going?" she asked, walking over to stand next to him.

"Fine." He knew he was being short with her, but *confound* it, he wasn't ready to be around her yet. Curse Romano for letting her in.

"Oh." She was quiet then as Dante maneuvered his way

around the desk again to stand opposite them. She reached out and picked up the photo of who they thought might be Eidolon. "Is this one of the ponies?"

"We're not sure," Black told her.

"It might be Eidolon," Dante said, and explained the mare to her.

"She's crazier than Dreadful?" Charlotte sounded suspicious.

"No, not crazy," Black retorted. When she glanced at him, he knew he was hot in the face. He sounded like a jerk. "She's wild," he added, attempting to sound calmer.

"Oh." She set the picture down. "What time are we going tonight?"

"I'm not sure. Not until late." Black shifted a step away from her. He could sense Dante smirking and wished he could tell him off. The language he wanted to use was saucier than he cared to share in front of Charlotte, though, so he kept his mouth shut.

"Okay, well, just let me know what the plan is," she said, sounded a bit crestfallen.

Black waited until she'd left the room before sighing and saying, "Really, Romano? You had to let her in." He added a few choice words.

"I don't know what your problem is," Dante said, waving a hand around. "You obviously like the girl, have told me as much, so why are you shunning her now?"

"I don't have to explain myself to you."

Dante was quiet for all of three seconds. "Oh, oh, I see.

You still have a thing for the Songbird, is that it?" He burst out in laughter. "Oh, that's rich!"

Black shut his eyes and counted down from ten. It didn't work. "Look, I do *not* have a *thing* for Symph, all right? I just don't think Charlotte needs to be in here until we have a direction to move in." He couldn't have a thing for the Songbird. She was part of his past – his distant past.

"Sure, sure." Dante sat down behind the desk and kicked his feet up onto it.

Black grabbed a handful of documents off the desk and retreated to the windows that lined the room. Outside the green rain was letting up, but it pooled and puddled on the sodden ground, drawing his attention. Magic was coming fast now to the modern world; he wondered when ordinary people would start realizing it, start noticing it. Had they already? The Flynns were beginning to see it, so that was something. His mind wanted to analyze his behavior toward Charlotte, speaking of Flynns, so he turned its attention to the papers in his hand instead.

After reading a few lines, he turned his attention back to Dante, who was now reclining in the chair with his eyes closed. "Hey, is this right? This info about the magic items Orrick has?"

Dante opened one eye. "I believe so."

Black muttered beneath his breath. "Impressive list."

"No kidding." Dante kicked his feet down and sat up. "So what *is* your grand plan for the night, if I can ask?"

Black shuffled through the papers. "We take the door,

go to the warehouse, persuade the horses to come with us, and come home."

Dante tipped his head to the side, considering. "Seems simple enough."

"It will be." There shouldn't be anything difficult about getting the stolen ponies back. The hardest part about the whole thing would be convincing them to come with him. But Dreadful had remembered who Black was, so hopefully these others would, too. He came back to the desk and set the papers down. "You think Orrick's used these things on the horses?"

"If not, then Roswald has," Dante said. There was a dark thread in his voice. "That man is certifiably unwell."

"Yeah, I remember." Black leaned on the desk. Roswald was the only one of the Tyranny who creeped him out. Orrick and Ignace were menacing, but not unhinged. Roswald had liked to watch Symphony during her performances, and it had made Black nervous, the way the older man studied her.

"You look a little pale, Sully," Dante said.

"Remembering how he used to watch Symphony."

"Ah." Dante nodded. He tipped his head toward the study doors. "You really should go talk to the poor girl, considering how rude you were to her."

It took Black a second to realize Dante meant Charlotte. He frowned. "I wasn't rude. I wasn't ready to discuss things with her yet." But a swell of remorse went through him. He hadn't exactly been nice, either. And, if he was going to be honest, with himself, at least – yeah, there were some lingering feelings over Symph. He would deal with those, though, if and when he ever saw her again.

He huffed out a breath and went to the doors, hearing Dante's soft chuckling behind him. Maybe he should've left his old friend on the doorstep instead of letting him in. Opening one of the doors, Black peered out into the foyer. No one was there, but he could hear some laughter coming from the living room across the way. Stepping out, he shut the door and walked over.

Dreadful was sitting on one of the couches with Marta, who had a hand settled on his shiny bay neck. She glanced at Black but said nothing. Jared and Danny were playing some absurd video game, and Gavin was reading on the other couch. Rory and Charlotte were nowhere to be seen, and Black was about to step out when he heard Jared clear his throat.

"She's upstairs in her room," he said, and there was a flash of something unpleasant in his eyes when Black met them. Black said nothing and left, heading up the stairs toward the hidden staircase.

He supposed he had that look coming, but it was still irritating. Jared knew he cared for Charlotte. That should be enough. It wasn't, though, and Black couldn't bring himself to be upset with the eldest Flynn as he walked down the hallway to Charlotte's room. He raised his hand to knock on the door when it opened.

*C*harlotte stared up at him, and then stepped out, forcing Black to step backward. "Hi," she murmured.

"Hi," he said. His voice was low, and he looked contrite. "I'm sorry for not letting you in," he said.

"In on the plan? In the room? What *in* are you referring to?" she asked, trying to keep her eyes on his. It wasn't easy; emotions rolled through his eyes like storm waves.

"All of it?" he suggested. He opened his mouth, closed it, and then said, "There's a chance we might see Symphony tonight."

Ah. She'd been worrying that he might still be hung up on the other girl. "And that's a problem for you, isn't it," she said.

He looked miserable right then. "It might be. I don't want it to be. We didn't end on good terms." The words tumbled from his mouth like crackerjacks from an open box. He took a deep breath and ran a hand through his hair. "I'm sorry," he added. "I was a jerk."

The sincerity and sweetness in his voice made her smile, even though she wasn't sure she wanted to. She wasn't one of those girls, anyway, the kind that made their friends or boyfriends suffer after they'd apologized. "You were a jerk," she said, watching his expression. He looked wounded for a moment, and then his eyes softened.

"I know. That's why I apologized," he said, nodding. "I really am over Symphony, but it might be hard for me to see her again."

"Well, if she does show up, I can tell her to leave," Charlotte said. There was a little bit of protectiveness in her voice that made Black grin.

"I don't think she'll come, but thank you, anyway," he told her. "The park will probably shut down at ten, if it's even open that late. We'll go through the door at eleven. That should give the workers time to be on their way."

"Do you know where the warehouse is?"

"I do." He nodded. "And I'm hoping Dreadful might be able to find them, anyway. I know Penumbra can find the other missing horses."

"But isn't that because he's the lead horse on the carousel?" she asked, puzzled. "At least that's what I've been told."

"And that's possibly the truth." Black leaned back against the wall. "But Dreadful is special, so he might be able to pull it off." He seemed to consider something, and added, "You'll like Oriflamme. He's a neat horse. He's one of the chargers."

"How many chargers are there?"

"Just two, Oriflamme and Chevalier," Black told her. "A lot of carousels only have one, but Oliver wanted more than that. He liked the look of their armor."

"Are they both nice horses?"

"Yeah. Oriflamme is a little gentler than Chevalier, but they were both pretty easy to handle," he said. He glanced at his watch. "We won't be going for quite a while yet."

The house started to murmur, swirls of unintelligible whispers wending down the hallway around them. Charlotte closed her eyes. Inside her, the magic was rolling through her system, and she reached for its power. The house chortled and whistled then, and she smiled. *You don't like my uncle, but you like me, don't you?* In response, the mansion gave a great shake, and her eyes flew open. Black was staring at her.

"What were you doing?" he asked. A fine line appeared between his brows.

"Seeing if I could contact my magic. Uncle Baron seems to access his so easily," she said.

An unpleasant look crossed his face. "He's already powerful," he muttered. "You need to be careful," he added, pushing himself from the wall. "The more you use it, the stronger the hold it takes over you."

Unless she used it though, how was she supposed to stop her uncle? They had but one carousel horse, and would hopefully gain five more that night, but they wouldn't be enough to bring Baron down. "I have to use it," she said, shrugging. After all, nothing had ever been gained by shirking one's responsibility. Look at all the trouble the Doctor or Sherlock knowingly walked into.

"Why?"

"How else are we going to beat Baron?"

"With the ponies," Black told her, his voice firm. "You don't need to use your magic any more than absolutely necessary."

"That might be true, but I need to know how to wield it if I need it," she said. She looked down at her hands; purple sparkles were coalescing in them, dripping down and making shiny swirls on the floor. She looked up at Black. He was grimacing. Uncomfortable. "I can do it without losing myself to it," she added. "I have you to help me, and Dante, and the ponies."

He took a deep breath. "It's dangerous, you know." He motioned to the purple magic. "But you're right – you'll need some of it to beat Baron." Glancing at his watch, he said, "Do you want to go watch TV or something? We won't leave for a while yet."

"Sure." They headed down the hallway, and Charlotte's thoughts drifted to her uncle. Was he out looking for the missing ponies? "Did Symphony tell you who the other horses were with Oriflamme?"

"No."

She considered this. "Who was he friends with on the carousel?"

Black glanced at her as he waited for her to step

through the door in the wall that led to the main staircase. "He and Chevalier got along really well. They're both serious, but Chevalier is more stoic, I guess."

"Who are the two stallions my uncle came back with that day? The pinto and the Appaloosa?" *The day we found out how terrible he really was. The day that Penumbra betrayed me.* Her stomach rolled a little.

"Tomahawk and Bathos. Both are strong, dependable. They'll be good fighters for Baron." There was a grumble in Black's voice. "But I know we can beat him, if we can get the other horses."

They reached the living room, and Dreadful got off the couch and trotted over to them. He shoved his nose in Charlotte's stomach, and she scratched his ears. At the least, they had him. "Hi, crazy pants," she murmured.

"Dreadful is not crazy," he told her, rolling his eyes. His lips stretched into what could only be a horsey grin.

She chuckled and pushed his head away. Black was sitting on the arm of a couch, his attention on the TV, where Jared and Rory were playing some zombie game. Charlotte sat on the couch. "You guys didn't get enough action when the Desolates attacked?" she asked, her voice wry.

"Getting in more practice," Rory told her as his character lashed out at a zombie and took its head off.

"Ew," Marta said. She went back to her book.

The house was creaking and shifting, and Charlotte wondered if it knew something they didn't. Why did the house like them and not Baron? He was more powerful than she was. *It did trap me down in the basement that time. Has it just gotten fonder of me, or what?* A gust of wind slammed up against the side of the mansion, and the house bellowed, making them all jump. Black got to his feet and went to the windows.

"Weather's turning bad," he said. Charlotte turned her head to see vibrant yellow rain hitting the windowpanes, and a loud boom resonated overhead. Dreadful went to the window to stand next to Black.

"Not good," the stallion muttered. "Bad things are coming."

A shiver raced through Charlotte, and she saw from the corner of her eye her brothers putting their game controllers down. Marta sat upright on the couch. None of them said a word, though – it was like they were waiting for the bad things to appear.

Dante strolled into the room with Helen, and they both stopped and looked at Black and Dreadful. "What's going on?" Dante asked, walking over to stand on the other side of Dreadful.

"Bad outside," the horse told him, shaking his mane. "Bad, bad."

"I get it," Dante said, frowning. "But why? Desolates or what?"

"Not sure," Black said. "The rain changed colors. Not sure that's a good sign." The rain that fell now was a sickly yellow, the color of stomach bile. "The magic is really returning in full-force."

"That's to be expected, what with the Flying Ponies

getting stronger again," Dante told him. "Maybe you three should head to Coney sooner than later."

The house let out a piercing scream, like a woman in a B-rated horror flick, and everyone, including Dreadful, jumped. "I don't like this," Marta said, her eyes wide behind her glasses.

"It's okay," Jared assured her. "We're inside."

"Yeah, but the house is getting upset," Danny said. He and Gavin had been sitting on the other couch, waiting their turn with the game system. A great belching noise shook through the room. "Ugh. Sounds like it's burping," he added, scowling.

Black turned from the window and looked at Charlotte. "I think Dante's right. We should go now, before things start to get worse."

She got to her feet and nodded. Her stomach tensed, tying itself in knots. She wanted to go to the Island, even though it wouldn't be like it was back then, but now that the time was here, it was nerve-wracking. Dreadful pranced out of the room, and the rest of them followed him, down the hallway to the basement door and then down the narrow steps. Dreadful was stopped in front of the last door and pawed at the floor. "This one," he said.

"I know," Black told him. He turned to Helen. "Stay inside, and keep the doors and windows locked." His gaze traveled over the rest of them. "Be careful. I think the house will be okay, but don't trust it too much." At that, the house let out a great sigh. Black frowned. "I mean it."

"Just go already," Rory said, making a shooing motion. "I want to meet the new ponies."

"Me too," Danny added. Gavin and Marta added their assent.

Jared gave Charlotte a quick hug and shook Black's hand. "You guys stay safe, too," he said.

"We will." Black turned to the door and opened it. A burst of yellow light shot from the door and the air turned shimmery and warm. "Dreadful, go on," Black told him. "Let's go get your friends." He stepped through the doorway after the bay stallion raced through it, and Charlotte gave her older brother a quick smile and stepped through after them.

15

*W*hen Charlotte emerged on the other side of the door, she found herself immersed in air cooled by a drifting breeze coming off the Atlantic Ocean. She smelled popcorn and could see the giant Wonder Wheel slowly turning. "Wow," she breathed.

Black turned back to her, noticing that she had stopped. He grinned. "This is nice, but it's nothing compared to how it was." They both heard Dreadful whinny, and hurried after him.

"Does he know where he's going?" she asked, hurrying to keep up with Black's long strides.

"I guess we'll see." He was looking around, swinging his head from side-to-side, and she wondered, with a flare of jealousy, if he was looking for Symphony. She shouldn't care; he'd been up front about how he felt about them both. Still, the jealousy burned longer than it should have.

The skyline was punctuated here and there with

amusement rides. There were still small knots of people wandering around, many of them not much older than she was. Dreadful was heedless of them, though – he was making a beeline for the entrance gates. Black finally started running to chase him, and so did she, even as she noticed people turning their heads to watch the glossy wooden carousel horse streak by.

What must they think, if they were thinking at all? Did Dreadful seem like some apparition, nothing more than a ghost of a bygone era? No one seemed bothered enough to call out, so Charlotte focused on following Black and the bay. Once they reached the gates, they ran through. The man in the booth barely looked up from his paper. Charlotte guessed he hadn't even seen Dreadful.

They stopped when they came out to the main street going into the Island. Dreadful was gone. Black muttered beneath his breath. "We should've made him stay with us," he said. "The warehouse is down that way. Come on."

Leaving the Island property, they headed toward the building. Charlotte glanced behind them; she wanted to stay there, wanted to ride the Wonder Wheel and the B & B Carousell, the only antique carousel to reside on the Island. After all, she'd never been here, and she wanted to see if the place held any residual magic from its early days. But Black was getting far ahead of her, and with a longing last look, she ran after him.

"We can go back sometime, once this is all done," he told her when she caught up, and she nodded, trying to be satisfied with that. They were close to the old building now, and she wondered why no one had bothered doing away with it. Rusting and rundown, it tarnished the landscape around it.

Black led her around back, where a door sagged in its framework. Dreadful was standing there, pawing at the ground. "Late," he scolded. "You run too slow."

"You should've stayed with us," Black retorted. "Someone could've seen you."

Dreadful made a scoffing noise. "Too afraid of me to make noise," he said.

"Boys." Charlotte took a slow breath and put her hand on the doorknob. "Ready?" she asked. The doorknob seemed stuck, but as she watched, a little purple magic drifted into the air and swarmed over the knob, and when she tried it again, it turned. Delight warmed her, and she started to push the door open.

"Better let me go first," Black said. "They don't know you." He spoke in a kind voice, but it still rankled a little.

"Do you think they'll listen?" she asked. "I'm not even the Capall anymore." A pang jabbed her chest, and she looked away to hide the sudden glint of tears in her eyes.

He nodded and said, his voice softer now, "They will. We have Dreadful, and they'll remember me. I know they will." He turned to the door and twisting the knob, shoved it open. "Stay here," he whispered and moved in, leaving her to stand out in the rapidly-cooling air with Dreadful, who was dancing around and trying to get past her.

"Will you stop?" Charlotte admonished, scowling at him. What was Black seeing? She peeked in, and there were no lights on yet. The building seemed to have swallowed him whole, like the whale gulping down Jonah. It was foreboding and creepy, and she took a hesitant step into the doorway.

Suddenly the interior lit up with overhead fluorescents, and she saw Black hugging the necks of five beautiful, ornate carousel horses standing in the center of the large building. She hurried inside, frowning and muttering as Dreadful raced past her, bumping her with his rear end as he swept by. A joyous whinny from him echoed around the big space.

A bejeweled armored horse immediately broke from the small herd and bolted toward him. Dreadful pulled up short, his head high and nostrils flaring. The armored horse, a palomino stallion, stopped and reached his nose out. Dreadful did the same, and the two horses touched noses for the first time since the twenties. Charlotte watched as they drew back from one another, and she started walking cautiously up to them. The charger, his rose, silver and dark blue armor plating flashing beneath the brilliant overhead lights, looked at her. His dark eyes were intense, and she stopped, breath in her throat.

"I am Oriflamme," the palomino said. His voice was deep and heavy, and he moved toward her, his strides deliberate, his grey hooves hard on the cement floor. Stopping just a foot from her, he raised his head and studied her. "You are a Flynn," he said, and when she nodded, he added, "Then you are a friend to me."

At that, tears filled her eyes, and not able to stop herself,

Charlotte wrapped her arms around the horse's sturdy wooden neck and hugged him hard. The horse made a sound like a chuckle, and she couldn't help but laugh. Drawing back and dropping her arms, she said, "I am so happy to meet you, Oriflamme. My name is Charlotte."

"Charlotte," the stallion said, nodding. He half-turned and jerked his head toward the other four horses standing with Black. "They are also your friends."

She walked with him and Dreadful over to the others. Black grinned and put an arm around the neck of a brown mare with a blue and red desert type bridle and breast collar. Her saddle was orange and gold, and her blanket turquoise and dark red, with some darker blue thrown in. She had a delicate face with a slight dish in her nose, like an Arabian, and Charlotte was instantly drawn to her.

"I am Czarina," the mare said. Her voice was soft and full, and Charlotte reached out to touch her nose.

"This is Charlotte Flynn," Black said to the ponies. "She needs your help. Her uncle Baron and Penumbra have decided to take control of the world, using the magic of the Flying Ponies to do it. We have to stop them." His voice was hard and smooth.

"We will help." This voice belonged to a shiny black stallion with four high white stockings and a white mane and tail. His tack was relatively simple: a brown bridle, saddle in the shape of a bald eagle, and an American flag blanket. "I am Compatriot," he said, bobbing his head.

"We always wondered when this sort of thing would happen," a dapple grey mare said. Her tack was a mixture of reds and greens, and she looked down her nose at Charlotte. "You do realize Penumbra is our leader, don't you?"

"This is Ranee," Black said, giving the mare a rub on the neck.

"I know he is, but he's doing bad things," Charlotte said. "You don't have to listen to him."

The horses were silent, even Dreadful, and she exchanged a look with Black. She wasn't sure what else to say to them. Was a lead horse's rule *that* powerful? The only horse not to have spoken was a light grey stallion with a black and grey roached mane and black tail. His tack was elegant; a blue saddle over a red and gold saddle blanket, and a blue and white bridle and breast collar. He looked like a Trojan war horse, and he seemed to be contemplating something.

He was strong and solid, and reminded Charlotte of Flintlock. A pang shot through her chest. "We can figure it out," she said, her tone imploring. "I only ask that you stand with me, and not with my uncle and Penumbra."

The grey stallion finally said, "You ask a lot of us." He stepped forward and sniffed the hand Charlotte put out. "I am Hawker." He studied Charlotte some more. "I think there is more to you than what you are saying, young one," Hawker added, sounding amused. "You smell of dark magic, the same as Oliver Flynn."

"I am his great-great-granddaughter," Charlotte told him. "And an archimage, like he was."

"Yes," Hawker said, nodding. "I sense it." He lifted his head and looked at the other Flying Ponies. "We need to decide now, friends. Do we stand with this girl or do we give in to Penumbra?"

More silence, until Dreadful spoke up in his dry, dusty voice. "I stand with Charlotte," he said.

"As do I," Oriflamme added, his bass voice rumbling.

Ranee tossed her head, her dark eyes glinting. "Penumbra will be difficult to withstand," she said, and with a great sigh, added, "But I will resist his call." She looked at Charlotte. "I too am with you."

"I as well," Czarina said, bowing her head a little to Charlotte.

"I will fight with you. It's the right thing to do," Compatriot said.

"There you have it," Hawker said. "I will stand with you as well. Six of us against whatever force Penumbra has."

It was a big force, much bigger than what they had, even with the five new horses. Charlotte knew she was no match for Baron when it came to wielding their archimage magic, but she had to be positive. She had Black, Dante, Helen, and her siblings. And they were going to find the other missing horses, the ones the Tyranny had absconded with so many years before.

"We should go," Black said, bringing her out of her momentary reverie. "The others will wonder what's going on."

"You don't think anyone will notice six living carousel horses?" she asked.

"Not if they run fast enough," he told her, a smile on his lips. With that he turned to Ranee and mounted her.

Settling into her saddle and patting her neck, he shrugged. "We'll be gone before anyone can do anything about it."

She supposed that was true. Deciding to ride Dreadful, as she didn't know the others, she was surprised when Hawker moved to her side. "Thank you," Charlotte whispered, and got up on the big solid stallion. They left the warehouse and she saw that twilight had fallen, the sky rich in varied purples and blues. As they were about to cross the street, a high melodious voice cried out to Black, and the herd came to a halt.

Charlotte turned her head slowly, already guessing who was hailing them. A young woman with dark blonde hair was rushing toward them, her green eyes warm and sparkling. Swallowing down the instant jealousy at the sight of the older girl, Charlotte tried to relax.

"Symphony," Black called and jumped down off Ranee. He walked over to the girl and after looking at each other for several seconds, he laughed and pulled her into his arms. "It's so good to see you!" he said, his voice bright.

"You as well, Sullivan," she said. Her voice was musical and as much as Charlotte wanted to hate it – she couldn't. Black turned and waved her over, so she dismounted and made her way to them. Reaching out for her hand, Black drew her to him.

"Symphony Cantata, this is Charlotte Flynn, Oliver's great-great-granddaughter," he said. He squeezed her hand gently. "Penumbra originally named her as the new Capall, but he's since given the title to her Uncle Baron instead."

"I'm pleased to meet you," Symphony said and extended her hand to Charlotte.

"You too," Charlotte said, not sure about the lacy white gloves the other girl wore. "Your governess, Helen Trudeau, has been my uncle's housekeeper." *Not, of course, that she ever offered that information.*

"Oh, yes, Helen has told me all about you and your family," Symphony said. She had a lilt in her voice, and Charlotte guessed it was Irish. Because of *course* the beautiful girl Black had once dated was Irish! Charlotte knew her family hailed from the Emerald Isle way back in her past, too, but she looked nothing like this girl. "She's so enjoyed all of you!"

Black glanced at the horses. "We really need to go, Symph," he told her. "It was good seeing you, but —"

"Oh, no, I'm coming with you!" she said. "I talked with Dante and Helen, and they both said I might be of help in finding the rest of the missing horses. I really want to," she finished, an eager look on her face.

"I'm sure they did," Black said, and Charlotte could hear the skepticism in his voice. "All right, well, let's get going, then."

Symphony gave a radiant smile and practically skipped over to Oriflamme. The armored horse stood for her to hug his neck and whisper to him, and then she mounted. Gracefully, too, like she'd been born riding. Charlotte frowned and got back on Hawker while Black mounted Ranee. They made their way quickly to the entrance to the park. It was still open, and the ponies took flight and soared overhead of the lingering pockets of people.

Charlotte wondered why Dreadful hadn't flown to the warehouse, but figured he'd been too excited to see his old friends to think of it. Hawker was concrete beneath her, steady and stable, and she decided that so far, the light grey stallion was her favorite to ride. They landed near where they'd come through the door, and Charlotte wondered how Black would know where to find it. There was nothing here – the door had disappeared.

Black turned in his saddle to look at her. "I hate to ask, because I don't want you accessing your magic much, but can you find the door? I thought it would show up when the ponies got close to it, but," he waved a hand at the empty space in front of them, "it hasn't."

"Um, sure," Charlotte said. She closed her eyes and tried to grasp the magic coiled inside her. She heard Symphony say something to Black, but tried to ignore her.

"There you go," Black said, and Charlotte's eyes popped open. Purple magic wafted in the cold air between the ponies, and she saw a great looming door painted with old Coney Island poster motifs in front of them. "Great job," Black said and winked at her. She smiled and waited for him to ride Ranee up to it. The door swung open and they rode through. Symphony and Oriflamme went next, and then Dreadful and Czarina.

"Go ahead," Compatriot told Charlotte and Hawker. "I will go last to make sure all is well." The black stallion stood back and waited, and Hawker stepped through the door. Within seconds, they were back inside the basement, and Charlotte slid off the stallion and waited for Compatriot. When he stepped into the room, Rory shut the door.

"Symphony!" Helen looked over the small group and her eyes lit up when she saw the young woman. Symphony slid off Oriflamme and stepped into her former governess's arms, the two of them talking excitedly over one another.

"Wow," Danny breathed. He was standing next to Hawker, and his eyes were glued to the singer. "Is she *pretty!*"

Charlotte bit back her answer as she got off the grey stallion. Everyone was trying to meet the newcomer, and Charlotte wanted to yell at them and tell them it was about the *ponies*, not the new girl. But that would be rude and probably unwise, and so she stayed quiet.

"She looks just as I remember." Dante's soft voice in her ear made her jump, and she glared at him. He chuckled. "Seems everyone is enamored with the Songbird."

"It does."

"Jealousy, sweetheart, doesn't fit you," Dante whispered.

"No pet names," she reminded him.

He shrugged and grinned. "He didn't hear me. What can it hurt? Besides, his eyes are full of her at the moment."

And that was true, much to Charlotte's chagrin. *All* the boys except for Dante were practically drooling over her. Black didn't seem quite as into her as her brothers did, but it still irked her. They hadn't even bothered asking if she was all right.

Hawker bumped his nose into Charlotte's arm. "Your

house is full of secrets," the stallion told her. His voice was quiet and contemplative.

"It's temperamental, too," Charlotte said.

"Hmm, but it likes you," the stallion said.

That was good, but at the moment, she wished the house would make some huge ruckus and break up the welcoming committee attending to Symphony. The blonde laughed and giggled, and Charlotte's good nature drained away. "Come on, Hawker, let's go upstairs," she said. She and the stallion went up the steps, and before she left the basement, she could hear Dante's laughter mingling with that of the others.

"Ugh." Charlotte let the Trojan horse up onto the main floor and then slammed the door shut so she couldn't hear them anymore. Why had Symphony shown up? Did she really want to help, or were there ulterior motives underlying her appearance at the warehouse? She went into the kitchen, the grey stallion following close behind, and her heart warmed to him. At least she had one friend at the moment. *I'm being stupid. I know they're just being nice, because that's how my family is.* She sighed and pulled open the fridge. A plate of chocolate chip cookies caught her eye, and she yanked it out and plunked it down on the counter. Reaching back in, she got the milk out.

Hawker wandered around the kitchen. He paused to look out the window over the sink. "The rain is pretty," he said.

Charlotte walked over and looked out. The rain was no

longer yellow but pale pink, and the sky was a frothy seafoam green. "The magic is pretty," she agreed.

"Coney Island was magical," the stallion told her. He backed away and paced around the kitchen. "Oliver would let us run around after the parks shut down."

Charlotte went to the counter and taking a cookie off the plate, bit into it. "Do you miss it?"

"Oh yes." The fervor in the horse's voice made Charlotte smile. Hawker turned to face her, and his expression was animated. "We were the most magical carousel there, you know." He tossed his short upright mane.

The house abruptly shook, causing Charlotte to grab onto the counter to keep her balance. Overhead, thunder crashed in the sky, and she could see through the window that the rain was now inky blue, leaving great splashes against the pane. Hawker whinnied and half-reared. "Easy boy, it's okay," Charlotte said, trying to sound confident. The back door blew open, and she rushed to close it, throwing herself against it. Wind bellowed into the room, careening and billowing, and Hawker bolted from the room.

"Hawker!" Charlotte locked the door and took off after the horse. The house was wailing and crying, and Charlotte's magic was reacting, her veins, her whole body, shaking with it. Clouds of purple drifted through the air, and this only served to drive the house madder. The floors buckled and bucked beneath her feet as she raced down the hallway to the foyer. Hawker was standing by the door, his neck arched, his nose pressed to the window left of the door.

"Wicked ones," the stallion said, turning his head to look at Charlotte. "Wicked ones are coming!"

Charlotte hurried to look out. A sleek silver car sat in front of the house, and with growing horror, she watched the men of the Tyranny step out of it.

"Charlotte!" Black's voice was frantic as he ran into the foyer, and she turned to him. He drew up short at the look on her face.

"Orrick," she said, and stepped away from the window.

16

*B*lack moved to the door just as it opened and Orrick stepped in. Ignace and Roswald were right behind him. Shaking in protest, the house groaned and screeched.

"That will be enough of that," Orrick said and withdrew a match from his pocket. The house stopped, and silence stretched to take up the void. Orrick smiled at Black, and he held his ground.

"You aren't welcome here," Black told him. He watched the older man's eyes travel to Charlotte, and anger smoldered in his veins. "You have no business here."

"You found the ponies the mob took," Orrick said to Charlotte. "How clever of you. I think you probably had some help, though." He paused and scanned the room. Black turned and saw that everyone else had joined them, the new ponies and Dreadful included. Symphony was standing between Jared and Rory, and Black thought for a second that she looked guilty, but the moment was too fleeting and he couldn't be sure. "Why now, you've invited the Songbird into your home." Orrick's voice grew malicious. "How wonderful."

"Get out!" Charlotte ordered. Her eyes flashed, and she crossed her arms, squeezing them tightly to her body. "I told you I don't want your help!"

"That's amusing," Orrick said, chuckling. He looked at Roswald and Ignace. "She thinks we've come to help her." His voice was icy, and when he turned his gaze back on Charlotte, she glared at him. "The time is past for that, young one." He tipped his head to the side. "There's something different about you, isn't there? Roswald?"

The man with the drooping brown mustache stepped forward. Black took a couple of sliding steps so he was next to Charlotte. Roswald studied her and closed his eyes for a second. "Ah, yes, there it is," he said, opening them. He gestured to her. "Her magic grows, but she has been stripped of the Capall power."

Orrick's eyes widened. "So that's what it is," he murmured. "You no longer hold any sway over the Flying Ponies. This is interesting, isn't it?" he added. His hard eyes swept over the six carousel horses. "They owe you no allegiance, and you can no longer command them." He snapped his fingers, and all the horses spooked.

"Perhaps we should take them off their hands," Ignace suggested, stroking his red beard.

"We won't let you have them," Black told him.

"We'll take them if we want them," Ignace said, smiling.

"We got some baseball bats that say you won't," Rory shot back from behind Charlotte. A grin slipped by Black's face. It was good to see the Flynns all rallying around the horses.

"You were asked to leave." Oriflamme stepped forward, his deep voice menacing. "So do as asked." The lights from the chandelier glinted off his heavy armor.

Dreadful and Compatriot moved forward too, and the sight of the bay cavalry horse had the three men stepping back. Dreadful bared his teeth and lunged, driving Orrick back to the door. "**Get out!**" he thundered, and around them the house went crazy, lights flashing, floors shifting, threads of silvery magic winding their way down the staircases.

Orrick motioned for his men to stand their ground. "You're under the assumption that we take orders from you, Dreadful," he said. He held his hand out, and Ignace handed him a small tarnished silver whistle. The bay stallion's ears went up, and he stood still, eyes locked on the small object. "You remember this, then, don't you?"

Black tried to remember what the whistle did. He knew it was more than what it appeared to be; Orrick had several magical items in his possession, and they all held powers beyond their functions.

"You don't want to be blowing on that," Dante said, strolling forward. He stopped between Oriflamme and Compatriot, and his voice was chilly. "You and I both know what it can do."

Orrick smiled. "Exactly." He looked at Charlotte. "I am

taking command of your six horses, Miss Flynn. Try to stop me, and I will blow this." He held the whistle up, and its short body caught the lights from above, making its old silver glow.

"It's a whistle," Charlotte said, angry.

Orrick's responding smile was patronizing. He shifted his gaze to Dante. "You haven't told her much about our collection, have you, Romano?" He held the whistle out so it could be seen more plainly. "This isn't just a whistle, Miss Flynn. This can disrupt all magic within the hearing distance. If I were to blow it, the magic would be in disarray. I could quite possibly force the horses to follow me, and they could do nothing about it." There was doubt in his voice, though, like he didn't totally believe what he was saying.

Black could feel the air shifting around Charlotte, and looked at her from the corner of his eye. Her eyes were focused on Orrick and bits of purple magic began drifting around her. He wished he could stop her from using it, but Orrick had a lot of power on his side at the moment. The air around Charlotte began to sizzle.

"You know what I think?" she asked. Her voice seemed odd to Black, the cadence of it not quite right. "I think you monologue a lot." She threw up her hands and a swirling cyclone of purple spun away from her and hit Orrick. He stumbled backward, batting at the thick purple air, and the whistle went flying. Charlotte stepped forward, and more magic spun from her and rammed into Ignace and Roswald.

Dante rushed to the door and opened it, and Charlotte drove the three men back, back, until the magic forced them outside. Dante slammed the door and dusted his hands off. "Nicely done, sweetie," he said, grinning.

Black shot him a look and turned to Charlotte. She was breathing heavily, and he put his hand on her back, rubbing it. "Just relax," he coached, his voice low and firm.

"That was impressive," Symphony said, walking over to stand next to Oriflamme. "I didn't realize she was an archimage."

"Impressive or not, I don't want her doing it too much," Black said, disgusted with himself. He should've done something to get rid of Orrick instead of letting Charlotte access her magic. He knew she was strong and independent, and he liked that about her, but he felt it was his duty to protect her as much as he could, too. "Are you all right?" he asked her, concern lacing his words.

"I think so." She looked at him, and he saw tiny bits of her magic floating through her eyes. It turned them more periwinkle than the blue-grey he was familiar with. His stomach clenched. "Where did the whistle go?" she asked.

"Right here." Rory had picked it up. "So... if this disrupts all the magic, wouldn't it do the same to yours, too?" he asked her.

She looked at Dante. "Well?" she prompted.

"I don't know," he said, shrugging. "I know it's a powerful little bugger, but I don't know if it could make an archimage heel to it. The ponies, maybe. Orrick thinks it would cause them to become disoriented and listen to him, but I don't know about that. Magic works in mysterious ways, particularly on other magic." He smiled. "I'd say we just got an edge over your uncle, maybe."

"Maybe?" Jared asked. He came to stand beside Rory and peered at the little trinket.

"Maybe, as in, your uncle is a right dangerous archimage. This little thing might help disturb his power." Dante gestured to the door. "But as we've seen, Charlotte's magic is growing, and that will be advantageous to us as well."

Black didn't like the look in Dante's eyes. He knew that gleam all too well. Though Dante couldn't wield as much magic like others could, he was invested in it. He *loved* it. And he loved anything that was magical *and* strong.

Someone pounded on the door, and Dante looked out. "Well, I have to give the old boys credit. They aren't intimidated."

Black strode to the door and yanked it open. Orrick stood there, fury blazing in his eyes. "This isn't over," he spat.

"Get off our property," Black ordered, "or I'll turn the ponies loose on you."

"We're not afraid of them," Ignace growled from behind Orrick. "So go ahead."

Charlotte shoved her way into the doorway beside Black, and he fought back the urge to push her behind him. She was tough, and he was right next to her in case the men tried anything. "You heard Black. Go. You're not wanted here, and I'm tired of entertaining you." She threw out some magic at them, and the purple sparkles turned into a frenzy as they danced around the three men. They howled and tried to wave the magic-laden air away from them. Charlotte stepped back inside and said, "Close the door, Black."

He did as asked and turned to her. The purple in her eyes was growing, and something cold filled his veins. This wasn't what he wanted for her. He could see the beginnings of the madness Baron had given into. She liked the power, just like he did. "Can I talk to you, alone?" he asked, his voice low.

"Okay." She didn't look like she was too excited about it, but she followed him into Baron's study. He locked the doors and turned to her.

"It's starting to possess you," he said. There was no point in being coy about the situation. "Isn't it?" He kept his voice gentle and even. This wasn't an interrogation – he was genuinely worried about her.

She looked away and walked over to the large windows. For several moments she was silent, but he didn't push her. This was all brand-new for her, and he didn't want to rush what she was feeling.

"It's strong," she finally said, turning to him. "I feel it all the time now."

That's what he'd been afraid of. "You don't have to give in to it."

"I don't know as I can stop it now," she whispered. "And we need it to beat Uncle Baron. You know that. Six ponies aren't enough."

"We'll get the others. I know we will." He put vehemence into his voice, because he needed her to believe him.

"How? Orrick isn't going to be any help. Unless Dreadful or one of the others can track down the ones he has, we're done." The anger in her voice surprised him.

"We haven't put the bridle on Dreadful yet. Maybe that will help," he suggested. He wasn't letting her lose her faith. "Baron's biggest mistake is that he thinks he's untouchable now, what with being the Capall. He's not. And I think we can change Penumbra's mind, too. If we can turn him, we'll gain back the other fifteen horses Baron has."

"You're so certain of that?"

"What's wrong?" he countered. "Why are you so down?"

She looked at him like he was crazy. "*Why*? Do you know what we're up against? I mean, the Tyranny has all these magical items, plus eleven of the Flying Ponies! We have six and a bridle that may or may not still have magic!"

He could see now the panic she'd been forcing down, the horror of having to actually face her uncle in a confrontation that would determine the fate of their world. *I'm so stupid. She's been so brave, and I haven't remembered that she's only sixteen. This is more than even Dante and I should have to take on.* He went to her and put his hands on her shoulders, giving them a gentle squeeze. "Yes, but one of those ponies is crazy and strong and wild, and the other five aren't so shabby, either. And now we have a bridle *and* a whistle." He smiled as he talked, hoping to alleviate some of her worry and panic. "And you have me. And Dante, and everyone else. You won't be doing this alone, Charlotte. I promise."

She settled her forehead against his chest. "I know, but it seems so insurmountable, you know?" The fatigue and despondence in her voice made a little chip in his heart.

"We're going to be all right," he told her, hugging her to him. "I know it doesn't seem like we have much, but the six horses we have are strong, and Dante knows how to manipulate magic. We can try the bridle on Dreadful, too, and see if it does anything. We'll be okay, yeah?"

"Yeah." She eased back so she could see his face. "Thank you. I needed a pep talk." A small smile wound across her face, and he nodded.

"You're welcome." He pushed a strand of her hair back behind her ear, the tips of his fingers just grazing her cheekbone. "I'm always here for you," he added.

"Thank you." She was motionless for a second, and then she bounced on her toes and kissed his cheek.

Someone banged on the doors, and she turned away to unlock them. Black wished there was more he could do for her. Helen stepped into the room and he snapped to attention.

"We need to make a battle plan," Helen told them. "Now that Orrick knows we have the Flying Ponies that the mob stole, he knows we'll be coming for his."

"That's a good idea," Black told her. "But it's getting late – we should probably eat something and get some sleep."

Helen gave him an appraising look. "That makes perfect sense, Sullivan. I'll see what the kitchen feels like making."

She didn't leave immediately, though; she continued to appraise him, and he had to force himself not to fidget. Why didn't she just go? What was she waiting for? He could make an educated guess, he supposed. She finally nodded to herself and turned and left.

Charlotte looked at Black, and he could see the questions in her eyes. "She trusts you, doesn't she?" she asked.

"As far as I know," he said. He figured he knew why Helen had been watching him – she was looking for any signs that Symphony's arrival was putting him off, was making him rethink things with Charlotte. It wasn't. "Come on, let's go get something to eat." He waited for her to leave in front of him, and took a deep fortifying breath. While having Symph around wasn't causing disloyal thoughts about Charlotte, it was going to be a different dynamic, and he hoped the Songbird wouldn't try to start things up with him again. He was done with that.

17

*M*uch later that night Charlotte lay in bed and tried to convince herself to sleep. She needed rest so that she'd be ready for what was to come. Talk around the table had been about a plan of attack for finding the horses the Tyranny had. Her brothers had had plenty of ideas that Black and Dante had batted around, but at the end of dinner, nothing concrete had been decided on.

Rory had suggested they split up into teams and go out looking for the missing horses, but Black had pointed out that they needed to know where to look first. Charlotte had thought it was a bad idea. She didn't like the thought of them all apart, because to her that made them vulnerable to attacks from both their uncle and the Tyranny.

And then we had to deal with Symphony making gaga eyes at Jared. Ugh. She supposed she could appreciate what Jared went through with her and Black now, but that didn't make her feel any better about it. *At least she wasn't talking to Black then, I guess.* She had to be thankful for that.

With a groan she got out of bed. Sleep wasn't coming, and she couldn't just lie there anymore. She turned on the Tiffany lamp and changed back into her jeans and sweatshirt, then switched it off and went down the stairs. She moved quickly down the hall, thankful for the thick carpeting. The house murmured to her, and she put a finger to her lips. She no longer feared the house, although she didn't know why it had attacked her in the basement that time. It was likely a mystery that would remain unsolved, particularly now that there were much more pressing issues to figure out.

She found the six horses in the living room. Oriflamme and Compatriot walked over to her, and she rubbed their necks, loving the feel of the silken wood beneath her palm. "You guys are amazing," she whispered to the two stallions. How was she so lucky that her family was the one with a magical carousel?

"Thank you," Oriflamme said, dipping his head to her. He was stately and grand, just as she pictured a knight's destrier would be, and she ran her hand lightly over the silver armor that covered his neck.

She liked that these new horses were quiet. Dreadful could be when he wanted, but he was often getting into something when he was. He was sitting on one of the couches, watching the TV. The volume was turned low, but he seemed to have no problem hearing it. Hawker and Czarina were in the back of the room, looking out the big windows there, and Ranee stood behind the couch Dreadful sat on, her dark eyes on the TV as well.

How would these six fare in a fight with Baron's ponies? Would they want to fight against their friends? They had said they'd stand with her against Uncle Baron and Penumbra, but when it came down to it, could they? She thought of the whistle and the bridle. Dante had been ecstatic to have them both, but did they hold as much magic as he thought they did?

"You should try to sleep," Compatriot told her. His American-themed tack gleamed in the low lights of the room, and his shiny black coat was a sharp contrast to the vibrant white of his mane, tail, and stockings.

"You may stay here with us, if you wish," Oriflamme said, his voice low and deep. "We will watch over you."

At that, Charlotte smiled and hugged him around the neck. "Thank you," she murmured. "I'll take you up on that." She lay down on the other couch, and Dreadful, using his teeth, tossed her a pillow from his couch. She laughed and put it beneath her head. Oriflamme placed himself at the entrance to the room, Compatriot moved to the windows behind the couch, and Charlotte snuggled down into the cushions. With the horses watching over her, their presence reassuring, she finally drifted off into dreams laced with shimmering spinning lights and glossy wooden horses.

The morning broke gloomy and dark, with spitting black rain that fell from monstrous brown clouds. Charlotte ate in silence, content to listen to the others around her. Symphony was talking animatedly with Jared, who hung on every single word she said. Rory and Danny were equally enamored, and Charlotte caught Helen watching her young charges with speculation and barely-hid amusement. That, at least, made her smile.

She'd slept well after coming downstairs to the ponies, and her heart jumped a little when she thought of them. They were still in the living room; Dreadful was much more content to be out of her company now that he had his old friends at his side. The thought of placing the six of them in any kind of danger made her breathing quicken and her heart hurt. Could she really ask that of them? They were magic, yes, but they were also antiques, and wooden. Surely they could break if something drastic enough happened to them.

"You okay?" Gavin nudged her with his elbow, breaking her out of the dark spiral her thoughts were taking.

"Yeah," she said. He frowned at her. "Okay, maybe not," she amended, whispering. "I'm worried the horses will get hurt."

"Me too," Marta said from her other side. When Charlotte looked at her, Marta said, "I care about them, you know. Maybe I didn't at first, but I do now. I don't want any of them to get hurt, even the ones Uncle Baron has. They're still Flying Ponies, and they belong to the carousel and to us." She spoke in a quiet firm voice.

Charlotte reached around her younger sister's shoulders and gave them a squeeze, a little amazed when Marta didn't pull away. She had never been an affectionate person, not even with their father, Baxter. Uncle Baron had showered the two girls with hugs and kisses on the tops of their heads when they'd first moved in with him, but Marta had always given him a cold shoulder.

"Thank you," Charlotte whispered. "We'll get all the ponies back, and keep them safe." She had no idea how to do that yet, but she had faith that something would happen to give them a chance.

The wind rustled around the eaves, and the black rain turned into sleet, tapping the windows like a million fingernails. Everyone ceased talking; the house muttered and the light above the table, an ornate wrought iron creation, swayed and flickered. Even the mansion hated this weather.

"Well." Dante pushed his plate back, his loud voice getting everyone's attention. "We need to quit fooling around and make a decision. We need to get those horses."

"What's your plan?" Black asked, leaning back in his chair. He sat across from Charlotte, and she couldn't stop from admiring how his blue eyes caught the light.

*Focus! This is **not** the time for romance. Ugh.* She hated that her thoughts so often traveled to romance, because this was serious. This was her family going against their beloved uncle for the fate of the world. *Fate of the world – sounds like something out of Doctor Who!*

"Charlotte." Dante's sharp voice brought her around.

"What?" she said.

"Pay attention," he told her. For once, there was no joking in his tone. "The consensus is we should put the bridle on Dreadful, and see if it has anything left in it. If so, maybe that magical boost will enable him to find the horses the Tyranny has. If not, then we might have to split into groups and go looking."

"Where is the bridle?" she asked. She hadn't seen it since Dante had brought it over from the carousel.

"I'll go get it," Gavin volunteered.

"You have it?" Charlotte asked, frowning.

He shrugged. "It was left in the kitchen, and it's important. I wanted to make sure it was safe, so I put it in my closet. I'll be right back." He took off from the room, and Charlotte decided she needed to pay more attention to what was going around the house and with her siblings. With the entrance of the Flying Ponies into her life, she hadn't been hanging out with the others like she used to.

While they waited for Gavin to return, she watched the sky out the window. The clouds were dark brown with random yellow streaks through them, and the sleet was still black as coal. Charlotte wondered how magic would affect other things, like technology. It would, wouldn't it, since it was affecting the weather and nature? It almost hurt her mind to think of how much things could change now.

"We should try it on Dreadful out in the foyer," Black suggested. "If he starts to go crazy, he shouldn't do as much damage there."

"Crazier than he is?" Rory said, smirking. "I'm not sure that's possible."

Black shot him a look. "We'll see." He got up and the

others started to do the same. Helen came bustling out of the kitchen and stopped, giving them a quizzical look. "We're going to put the bridle on Dreadful," Black explained.

"Oh, I have to see this," she said, smiling. She whipped off the cherry red apron she'd been wearing and set it over the back of a chair. "Jared, Symphony. I'm assuming you're joining us?" she asked, her voice pointed.

Jared jumped in his seat and nodded. "Of course," he said.

"Yeah, *of course,*" Danny echoed, grinning when his eldest brother shot him an angry look.

Symphony smiled and got to her feet. "I'm sorry. I know I'm a distraction. We need to focus on the Flying Ponies."

Yes, we do, Charlotte thought as she followed Black from the dining room. But she hadn't been able to focus on just that, either. Now, though, was go time. This was the Doctor racing to save an alien whale. This was Luke Skywalker in the trench. *Well, okay. Maybe it's not* exactly *that desperate. Still. Romance has nothing to do with this.*

Gavin had gone into the living room to get the bay stallion, and when they came into the foyer, the other five horses followed. Oriflamme took up position next to Symphony, his expression solemn. Compatriot and Hawker stood next to Marta, and the two mares stayed by Charlotte. Black took the bridle from Gavin and walked over to Dreadful.

"You probably don't remember this," Black said, holding

up the worn leather bridle and showing it to the horse. "This is what gave you magic."

Dreadful snorted and rolled his eyes. "I know," he said, his dry voice snarky. "You want me to wear it again."

"I do." Black moved to his left side and held the bit, a western curb, in his hand. "Open up."

"Wait a minute," Charlotte said. "How did Oliver ever fit it to their heads, when some of them were carved with closed mouths? The bit wouldn't fit."

"Good point," Black said, shaking his head. "I don't know. Maybe it's written in his journal." He turned back to the cavalry horse. "All right, Dreadful. Take it."

The horse tossed his head, his inky black mane full of orange sparkles. "I don't want to."

Dante heaved an animated sigh and strolled over to them. "Yes, horse, you have to. If you want to beat Penumbra, you need this."

Dreadful reached out his neck and snapped his teeth at Dante, who slapped his muzzle. "Don't be a baby. Just take the bit," he ordered.

"Hmph," Dreadful snorted. He scowled and then with a giant sigh, opened his mouth. Black warily eased the metal into his mouth, and the stallion snapped his mouth shut. Black muttered and pulled the headstall up over the horse's ears, and then fastened the throat latch.

"Looks good," Dante said, applauding. "Now old boy, do you feel any different?"

They all watched the stallion carefully. Nothing happening, and Dreadful turned his head this way and that, as if adjusting to the feel of it. He gave his head a shake and opened his mouth, but the bit restricted his speech.

"Well, that's one way to keep him quiet," Rory said, chuckling. "So it doesn't work. Can we split into teams now?"

"Give him a minute," Black said, and touched the horse's head. "Concentrate, Dreadful. See if there's any magic in it you can unlock."

"Wait, he has to unlock it? I thought he just had to wear it," Jared said.

"We don't know how it works," Dante reminded him. "We just know it brought them to life."

Marta walked over and examined the bridle, running her fingers down the stitching. She pursed her lips and turned to Charlotte. "Maybe if you helped him it would work," she said. "You're an archimage, right? Use your magic."

Charlotte nodded and walked over. She put her hands on either side of the headstall and closed her eyes. Her magic welled, a tide of power that she only had to touch to stoke it into a tidal wave. She felt a hand on her shoulder, and assumed it was Black's. *Okay. We need help, and if I have to access my magic, so be it.* She took a breath and stretched out her mind, letting the magic swell and grow and fill it. Gasping, she opened her eyes. Purple sparkles filled the air around them, dancing and drifting on invisible eddies of current. Dreadful was still, and the magic swarmed all over the bridle, until it was solid purple. Charlotte let go and dropped her hands to her sides.

"Well?" Rory said.

"Be patient," Dante snapped. He pinched his chin in-between his thumb and forefinger and stared at the cavalry horse.

Dreadful made some noises that sounded like he was trying to talk, and finally gave up on that. Instead he gave his head a violent shake. Black and Dante looked at one another.

"I think whatever magic it had is gone," Black said, disappointed. He unbuckled the throat latch and slid the headstall off. Dreadful spit the bit out.

"Ick," he said, clucking. "Tastes terrible."

Charlotte couldn't help the rise of frustration in her. What were they going to do now? Did they really have to split up and go on blind searches? A thought came to her, and she suggested, "What if we try it on a different horse? Like Oriflamme maybe?"

"That's not a bad idea," Black said, smiling at her. "Oriflamme? Want to give this thing a go?"

The charger walked over and lowered his head. "I will try," he said. He opened his mouth, and Black slipped the bit in, and then pulled the headstall up and over so he could buckle it into place. They waited; no one seemed to be breathing. The palomino stallion stood still for several long moments, and then looked at Charlotte. She knew he wanted it off, and she reached for the throat latch buckle.

"Wait!" Dante's sharp voice rang out, and she stepped back, her eyes widening as she saw sparkles beginning to coalesce in the air around the horse. They were a swirl of rose, blue and silver, matching his armor, and they spun faster and faster until they were a solid blur. Oriflamme remained calm, and his magic suddenly stilled and hung in the air, before dropping down all over him, dusting him until he gleamed with it.

"Wow," Danny whispered. "That is so cool!"

Charlotte wasn't interested in *cool* – she wanted to know if Oriflamme could do anything with the bridle. "Do you feel different?" she asked, her voice lined with caution.

The charger closed his eyes for a moment, and she remembered he couldn't talk with the bit in his mouth. She tried speaking to his mind; it didn't work, and she guessed it was because she was no longer the Capall.

Black took the bridle off, and the charger gave his head a shake. "I believe," he said, looking at Charlotte, "that I may be able to find our missing comrades."

A stupid grin broke out over her face, and she threw her arms around his neck. He laughed, a great guttural sound that filled the room. When Charlotte pulled back, everyone else was laughing and speaking fast and over one another. Black laid a hand on Oriflamme's neck.

"Good job, old boy," he said, grinning. "Well done."

18

*A*n hour later, they were still giddy with excitement. That Oriflamme could sense the missing ponies while wearing the bridle was an unexpected break. Black wasn't sure why he'd only thought Dreadful would be able to do it; each pony had their own magic, and perhaps each one could do something different with it. Maybe Oriflamme's magic could seek lost things. Whatever it was, they would take it.

"I think we should take the bit off," Marta was saying as she stroked Dreadful's neck. They were sitting on one of the couches. The bay stallion seemed quite fond of her, and she of him.

"Would the bridle work, though?" Gavin asked, gesturing to Oriflamme. "I would think it would have to stay intact."

"Maybe not." Dante picked the headstall up and examined it. "We should try it. It would be nice for him to have his speech when he's wearing it." He smiled at Marta. "Good thinking, my dear."

"Hey, no using nicknames," Danny warned him.

"Get off that stupid game system and make me," Dante taunted.

Danny shot him a scowl and set his controller down. "Take it easy," Jared said, shaking his head. "He's just teasing you."

"Yeah, well, he better not call Marta stuff," Danny said. He picked his controller back up but stuck his tongue out at Dante.

"Very mature," he told the youngest Flynn.

"Enough," Helen barked. "We have ponies to save, and we're wasting time sitting here."

"But we still don't know how to do this," Charlotte told her. "I mean, do some of us go out with Oriflamme and walk around to see if he can get a better read on the missing horses?"

"That's exactly what we do," Helen said. "I would suggest that you, Black, Jared and Dante go, and take Oriflamme, Compatriot and Hawker with you."

"Why them?" Marta asked, sitting upright. "I want to go."

Helen gave her a stern look, but it was softened by a twist in her lips. "Indeed, my girl, you will have things to do here. For one, Dreadful likes you, and he needs a handler. Two, you love research. We'll go through the library upstairs. Chances are good that there are books about the Flying Ponies Grand Carousel in it."

"There's at least one," Gavin said, nodding. "But it didn't say much."

"There *are* a lot of books, though," Marta said, shrugging. "There might be more." She shoved Dreadful's muzzle away when he nipped at her.

"Sounds like a plan," Charlotte said. "Let's get going."

"Wait." Black looked at Helen. "Are you sure both Dante and I should go?"

"Yes." Helen made a shooing motion with her hands. "Take the horses and go. The sooner we find more, the better. Don't worry about us."

"Let me take that bit off first," Dante said. He left the room with the bridle, and they waited for several minutes for him to come back. When he did, the bridle was bitless, and he put it on Oriflamme's majestic head. The golden stallion moved his head around a little. "Better?" Dante asked.

"Yes. Thank you." Oriflamme tipped his head to the side, as if considering something. "The magic is still here with it."

"All right, let's get going, then." Black led his group out to the foyer. "Dress warm." They pulled on boots and coats and hats. Opening the front door, he staggered back when a gust of wind punched him in the stomach, almost bending him over.

"Nice day out," Jared said, grimacing.

"Ah, don't be a pansy," Dante said and stepped out onto the porch – where he was knocked off his feet by another violent gust of wind. Jared laughed and stepped over him, his head bent against the weather. The sleet had turned back to rain, and now it was lime green, falling from orange and red clouds.

Black stopped Charlotte before she could step out. "Stay close to me," he said. "I know your magic is getting stronger, but there will be Desolates out here, and this weather is dangerous." It was even more than that, he suspected. It was unbalanced, because the magic was off. The Flying Ponies were not united.

"I will," she said, nodding, her blue-grey eyes serious. They moved out together, with the three horses right behind them. Thunder rumbled and Black glanced up, noting that the brief lightning was brilliant blue, contrasting sharply with the reds and oranges of the thunderheads.

"So how far do we go? How does this work?" Jared asked, glancing back at the house.

"Could you focus instead of thinking about Symphony?" Charlotte said, her voice cutting like a whip.

Jared's eyes widened and he pointed at her. "I am focused! It's nasty out here and I don't want to run around in the rain for hours!"

"Children." Dante shook his head at them. He'd recovered from his fall and was composed as usual. "Let Oriflamme have a moment."

The palomino charger stood with his nose lifted into the air. Black had tied the reins in a knot and pulled them over his head so they didn't trip him up. The horse turned his head to the left, and then to the right, as if scenting the air. The green rain soaked them and ran down their coats in thick rivulets, while thunder grew closer, shaking the ground.

Charlotte shivered, and Black drew her close, putting an arm around her. He knew she didn't need him to, but he wanted to make sure she was warm if not dry. *Come on, Oriflamme. Find at least one of them.* He noticed that Jared's attention was wandering back to the house, and he hoped that Symph wasn't toying with the eldest Flynn. She had a magnetic personality, but as he'd found many years ago, she could polarize you with it.

The charger suddenly whinnied and said, "Penumbra approaches!"

Compatriot and Hawker grew still, their heads turned in the direction Oriflamme was indicating. "Not again," Charlotte murmured.

"We need to get the horses in the house!" Dante ordered. "Oriflamme, Compatriot, Hawker – go! Get inside!"

But the horses were so still they appeared frozen. Black heard the dapple grey stallion before he saw him. Penumbra was alone this time, though, and Black's heart dropped. This wasn't good. It meant the magic was strong enough with the lead horse he didn't need a human to anchor him to it anymore. He subtly tried to ease Charlotte behind him, but she refused and instead pulled away and marched toward the dapple grey.

"Did you come to join me?" she asked, hands on her hips, her tone icy.

Penumbra stopped and looked down his nose at her. "Look who thinks she's still the Capall," he said. His tone was sarcastic and curt, and he looked over her head at the Flying Ponies. "You know I've come for them. They belong to me." He whinnied, a long loud note, and the other three echoed it.

"No!" Charlotte threw her hands up. "You are **not** taking them!"

The grey stallion gave her an amused look. "You think you can stop me?" He started to walk past her, and she put herself in his path. Black quickly moved to stand next to her.

"They're not going with you," he told the lead horse. "They belong to the Flynns."

Penumbra breathed out a long sigh. "For many years you served us well, Sullivan. It is a shame that now, when the Flying Ponies need you most, you have deserted us." The disappointment in his eyes and voice only made Black see red.

"You're the one who deserted them," he snapped. "You betrayed their magic into Baron's hands. Why? Don't you realize that once he has what he wants, he'll cast you aside like the hunk of wood you are?" The words hurt to say, because Black knew they were so much more than that.

Penumbra almost seemed to smile. "You really believe that Baron holds any power over me?" The words drifted in the cold air, and a sense of horror slithered through Black's veins. "Oliver knew better. He knew what we were when he brought us to life. Baron thinks we are toys, playthings for children. He only covets us because of our magic." The grey took a step closer, and this time Black pulled Charlotte behind him. "Do you dare make that same mistake, Sullivan Midnight?"

"You have to answer to your Capall," Dante cut in, moving closer to the grey. "You made Baron your master."

"The only master is me," Penumbra told him, tossing his head. "That's why these three will go with me, because they are mine to command." He struck the ground with a hoof, and a dozen red and green sparkles leapt into the air. "Come, my fellow Flying Ponies."

Charlotte spun around to face them. "No! You *do not* answer to him! You answer to the Flynn family!" Desperation clouded her voice. Jared came to stand beside her, his face set with deep determination.

"Charlotte is right: you belong to the Flynns," he told the three. "You are staying with *us*!"

Black kept his eyes pinned to Penumbra. The stallion was watching Charlotte and Jared, and Black noticed him tensing. A moment before the grey horse charged, he yelled and grabbed Charlotte, yanking her out of the grey's path. Penumbra hit Jared hard enough to knock him down, and then reared up, slashing through the green rain with razor-sharp hooves. Dante ran to Jared, jerked him to his feet and pushed him away. He then took a stance between the rampaging stallion and Jared.

"**Enough**!" Oriflamme's deep voice boomed through the woods. Penumbra dropped to all fours and locked his gaze on the charger. "That is *enough*, Penumbra! The children mean no harm to you or to us. You will not treat them this way!" He stomped a large hoof into the ground. His magic, swirling particles of rose, blue and silver, cascaded over him.

"Oriflamme speaks the truth," Compatriot said, backing up the palomino. "These children are not your enemy."

"You have no enemies, Penumbra," Hawker added.

The dapple grey stallion snorted and lifted his head high. "You really think these children will protect you?" He shook his head. "They want to enslave you, as Oliver did. They think we are nothing but wooden *toys*, nothing but whimsical *hobby* horses!" His voice rose in anger. "I will no longer tolerate these humans who think they own us!" A ringing neigh erupted from him.

At his cry, the other Flying Ponies under his control stepped from the trees and Black knew there was no choice but to run. He gave a sharp whistle and Hawker raced over to them. Before Charlotte could react, Black tossed her onto the light grey stallion's back.

"Go! Back to the house!" he yelled. Hawker whirled around and bolted. Penumbra yelled something, and three of his Flying Ponies took off after them.

"Dante!" Black shouted. Dante was already on the move; he'd been watching, and now he shoved Jared toward Compatriot. The shiny black stallion stamped his feet as Jared mounted.

"Go, get away!" Dante ordered, giving the stallion a slap on his rump. Jared was in the middle of protesting when

Compatriot spun around and ran back the way they'd come. Dante looked at Black. "What now?"

"Now *we* go!" Black said and moved toward Oriflamme. The charger was static, his gaze on Penumbra, and his magic roiled in the air around him. But Penumbra's magic was blooming too, filling the air with glittering red and green particles. Black reached the palomino and mounted, waving at Dante. "Let's go! Come on!" What was he waiting for?

Dante looked at him, and there was resignation in his brown eyes. "I don't think that's going to happen." As he spoke, Bedlam and Warpaint closed in on him, and Black's heart sank. The two stallions bared their teeth and backed Dante away from Oriflamme. "Easy now, ponies, easy," Dante coaxed, holding his hands out in front of him. "Let's talk about this."

"We are done talking," Penumbra said, glancing at Dante. "We will no longer be slaves to humanity!" He lunged at Oriflamme, and the charger darted to the side, nearly throwing Black. He settled deeper into the saddle and tried to help the stallion by not getting off-balance. Penumbra charged again, and this time Oriflamme met him in a clash of wooden bodies. Black jerked his legs back so as not to get crushed, and realized if the palomino meant to stay and fight, then he needed to get off him.

Dante was being forced further into the dark woods by the two stallions. Black leapt off Oriflamme and got out of his way as he fought with Penumbra. The rest of the Flying Ponies stood in a semi-circle, watching the two fight. Black started for Bedlam and Warpaint. He wasn't sure how he was supposed to back the stallions down, but he had to. He wouldn't let them hurt his old friend.

"You betrayed us," Bedlam said to Dante. He snaked his neck out low.

"You wanted to use us," Warpaint added. His eyes glittered.

"Now, now, that's not the way it is," Dante said. He was trying to be nonchalant, but Black heard the slight tremor of dread in his voice. The carousel horses were no longer under the control of a Capall, which begged the question: what had they done to Baron?

And if Oliver had known what the horses would be like, as Penumbra had said, why had he done it? Why bring to life something that wanted to hurt you? Black moved out to the side of Warpaint, and watching the chestnut tobiano stallion, eased his ratchet out. He hated the idea of hurting any of the ponies, but if it meant saving Dante, so be it.

Chimerical and Moxie were coming at him now, teeth showing, both mares oozing with animosity. Black held the ratchet up. "I'd rather not use this," he warned them, "but I will if you force me."

Moxie tossed her head, her black and white hide gleaming under the low light from the storm clouds. "You can't hurt us, Sullivan."

"Try me," he said through gritted teeth. He swung his right arm in a few circles, loosening the muscles.

"You are weak and pathetic," Chimerical taunted. Her pale blue body was streaked with green rain.

"Whoa!" Dante shouted, drawing Black's attention for just a second.

It was enough. The mares charged. Black brought his arms up but it wasn't fast enough. They hit him hard, knocking him flat on his back as they leapt over him. He turned his head, saw Moxie swap directions, and rolled to the left, out of the way of her hooves. Chimerical whinnied, an angry sound, and struck out at him. Black pushed himself upright and turned to face her. Moxie circled around behind him.

He hoped Dante was holding his own, because there was no way Black could help him now. Penumbra and Oriflamme were still fighting, but it didn't look like either stallion was landing any significant blows. The other ponies were gone; he thought they'd pursued Compatriot and Hawker.

"You know this is wrong, Chimerical," Black told the blue mare. "Penumbra's lying to you. You were brought to life to bring joy with your magic, not this." Whatever this was, whatever end game the dapple grey stallion was playing at.

She tossed her white mane. "I know the truth. You made us slaves. All we did was stand on a machine while children assaulted us!"

Black coughed out a laugh of shock. "Is that what Penumbra's been telling you? Don't you remember Coney Island? Those children, *all* of those people, **loved** you!" He couldn't believe what the mare was saying. They'd been *assaulted*? This was insane!

"Enough talking," Moxie said from behind him. He glanced back at her. The pinto mare, her turquoise and red magic floating around her, was standing with her head lowered, like she was ready to charge. His skin prickled.

This was not good.

$\mathcal{H}$awker wove through the trees ahead of his pursuers. The green rain stung Charlotte's face and she ducked her head low next to the stallion's powerful neck. Behind them, running hard, were Bathos, Tomahawk and Harmony. Charlotte wanted to go back to Black. She wanted to try and talk Penumbra down. But she understood why Black had sent her off. If Penumbra were to gain three more ponies, he would be much harder to stop.

"Charlotte!"

She pulled her head up and looked to her left. Jared was riding Compatriot. The black stallion's white legs flashed in vivid contrast to the green of the rain and the brown of the earth. They rode closer and she saw the fury in her older brother's eyes, fury that coursed through her as well.

How could Penumbra do this? And what had he done with Uncle Baron? She sucked in a sharp breath. *He wouldn't have...killed him, would he?* No. Her uncle was too powerful for the grey stallion to do that. Wasn't he? But he hadn't been strong enough to keep Penumbra from running off and taking the Flying Ponies with him.

Tomahawk, the bay splash pinto stallion, rushed past them and cut hard to the left, forcing Hawker and Compatriot to slide to a stop. They slipped on the soaked grass, and Charlotte had to scramble to stay on. Hawker tried to dodge right, but Bathos, the bay Appaloosa stallion, and Harmony, the grey mare with the turquoise and yellow tack, were right there. They had nowhere to go.

"Stop this now," Tomahawk ordered. "You belong to the carousel, and the carousel is Penumbra's." His voice was clear and cold.

"He does not own us," Hawker told him, his voice haughty. He snapped his teeth at Harmony when the mare got too close.

"We are meant for happiness," Compatriot added. "Not this evil Penumbra is bringing upon us."

Charlotte could feel Hawker gathering himself, and wrapped her hands up as best she could in the stallion's stiff upright mane. She glanced at Jared; he was doing the same thing, twining his hands in the black stallion's white mane. Hawker slid a hind hoof back, and then a front one, slowly easing backward.

"Oh, no," Harmony said. She moved closer and nipped at Hawker's neck. "You're going back to the herd."

Hawker went still for a moment. "Make me," he snorted and leapt forward. Harmony squealed and darted away, and Hawker launched into a gallop. Charlotte leaned over his neck as the stallion zipped between trees. Soon, the mansion came into view, and he jumped and cleared the steps, landing just in front of the door.

The door whipped open and Rory stood there. "What is going on?" he demanded as Gavin and Danny peeked out under his arms.

Charlotte slid off the horse just as Compatriot landed next to her. "Get in the house!" Jared ordered and gave Charlotte a firm push toward the door. Rory stepped back, at the same time shoving his younger brothers backward. Jared followed them in and then the two horses clattered in as well. Jared slammed the door.

"What happened? Where're Black and Dante?" Symphony asked, her eyes glued to Jared.

"And Oriflamme?" Marta asked, her eyes wide behind her glasses.

"Penumbra," Compatriot said. "He came with the Flying Ponies."

"And Uncle Baron too?" Rory asked, looking between Jared and Charlotte.

"No. All by himself," Charlotte said. "And we need to go back, because the boys are in trouble." Her pulse pounded thinking about what Penumbra might do to them. *To Black. We can't leave him alone.*

"I know," Jared said. "But we're taking Dreadful with us. And I'm grabbing my bat." He darted off to the left and ran up the stairs. The others turned their attention to Charlotte.

"So the ponies aren't listening to Uncle Baron

anymore?" Gavin asked, confusion on his face. "But I thought they had to listen to the Capall."

"Penumbra said they're strong enough they don't need to now," Charlotte said. "Where are Dreadful and the mares?"

"In the basement," Rory said, shrugging. "They wanted to go down there, and I couldn't stop them." The shrug said he hadn't tried that hard.

"Go get them," Charlotte told Danny, who nodded and raced off, eager to help. She put her hands in her coat pockets and tried to shove away the panicky feeling eating at her. Black and Dante could handle themselves; well, she knew for a fact Black could, and Dante had been in plenty of fights on the Island, so he should be all right. As for Oriflamme, she didn't think he'd yield to Penumbra unless forced. They had to hurry. They had to go back.

Jared arrived the same time the other three horses came thundering down the hall. Dreadful slid to a stop next to Symphony, who said, "I'm going with you. I know those ponies, too. I can help."

Jared opened his mouth, but Charlotte said, "Fine. We don't have time to argue. Let's go."

"Wait." Jared barred the door. "We need a plan of attack. We can't go charging in – we're outnumbered."

"I'm going," Rory said.

"Me too," Gavin echoed. Danny added his assent.

"We can't all go," Jared said, shaking his head. "That's too many to keep track of." Immediately the other three boys started arguing, and Charlotte caught Dreadful's eye and jerked her head toward the door. Enough was enough. They'd wasted too much time.

She flung the door open and ran down the stairs, the bay horse right behind her. She heard Jared shouting as she threw herself up on the stallion and they raced off into the woods. There were no signs of Tomahawk, Harmony and Bathos, and she suspected they'd gone back to the herd. Dreadful rocketed through the trees, and she held on for dear life. As much as she already loved riding Hawker, she knew she needed the cavalry horse for this.

It didn't take long for Dreadful to find the herd. Penumbra and Oriflamme were in a standoff, and as Dreadful came into Penumbra's view, the dapple grey sent out a warning whinny. All the other Flying Ponies turned toward them, and Charlotte saw no sign of Black or Dante.

"Get off," Dreadful ordered. "I fight better alone."

Charlotte dismounted, and Dreadful gave his mane a shake and put himself between her and the others. Tomahawk moved toward him, and Charlotte wished she'd grabbed something to defend herself. As much as she would detest striking the carousel horses, she would if it meant staying safe.

"You know you belong with us," the bay splash pinto stallion told Dreadful. He lifted a front hoof and jabbed it toward Charlotte. "She is not your owner. She only holds you back."

Dreadful was silent and still. His orange magic blossomed in the air around him, tangling in little sparks with the rain that continued to fall from the drenched heavens.

Tomahawk pawed at the ground, his gaze never leaving the bay cavalry horse.

"You shouldn't be here," Sirocco said to Charlotte as the mare came at her from the side. "This isn't about you."

Anger flooded Charlotte's system. She narrowed her eyes and retorted, "And *you* should know this is **not** what Oliver intended for you! Why would you do this? Why do you want to hurt people?"

The pretty palomino mare lowered her head. "We don't wish to hurt anyone, Charlotte. We only wish to be free."

Charlotte tossed her hands in the air. She kept one eye on Dreadful; he was just standing there, a frightening statue, and she wondered when he would attack – *if* he would attack. "Free? How free do you want to be? You're a *living carousel horse!* And I've never asked much from you – just help finding the missing Flying Ponies!" She couldn't stop the outrage that shook her voice, nor did she want to – Sirocco needed to know none of this was okay. The mare refused to look at her, and Charlotte wondered if this was Penumbra's chink in his arrogant armor, this beautiful mare that radiated gentleness.

"Don't listen to her, Sirocco," Harmony said, stalking over. The grey mare's magic, turquoise and yellow mixed together, billowed in the air. "You know Penumbra only wants what's best for us."

"That's not the truth," Charlotte argued. It struck her for a second that this was funny, her fighting with two wooden horses out in the midst of the rain-soaked woods, but it passed. This was her reality now. "Harmony, how can you think this is good? Black and Mr. Coal were never anything but kind to you! And Dante was probably nice, too." She hoped he'd been, anyway. Black had never said anything about him mistreating the horses.

Harmony made a loud laughing noise. "Kind. They kept us trapped on that machine! You call that kindness?"

Abruptly, before Charlotte could defend Black and his grandfather, Dreadful reared up. A wave of orange magic shot out and enveloped Tomahawk. The bay pinto whinnied and sprang sideways, shaking his whole body. Dreadful charged him. Tomahawk turned and met him in a crash of wood that reverberated throughout the forest. Squealing and lashing out, the two stallions circled one another.

Charlotte, stunned by what was happening, failed to see Harmony as the grey mare struck her, knocking her to the ground. Surprised, she pushed herself to her knees only to have the mare push her back down with her front hoof. "Get off me!" Charlotte yelled, but the mare laughed, a diabolical sound that brought fear rolling through Charlotte.

"Stop!" Sirocco's voice was loud. Charlotte turned her head to see the palomino strike out and nail Harmony in the side. The grey mare lost her balance, allowing Charlotte to scramble to her feet, her boots slipping on the wet leaves.

"Hey!" Jared's voice cut through the air moments before he came into view riding Compatriot. The black stallion was galloping hard, and came to a wild sliding stop in-between the two feuding mares. "Get on!" Jared reached down to grab Charlotte's hand, but she backed away from him.

"We can't leave!" she said. Not when Dreadful was fighting like a demon, never giving Tomahawk an inch. Not when Oriflamme was bravely trying to keep Penumbra from interfering with the fight. She thought her older brother might grab her anyway, but he gave a quick nod and slid off his mount. Compatriot whirled to face Harmony, and the grey mare lunged at him, snapping her teeth at his face.

"Get out of our way," Compatriot ordered, throwing the two Flynns a look. They moved at once, trying to get out of the path of all the furious horses.

"You're okay?" Jared asked, keeping her behind him.

"Yes. And stop that," she said. "I'm not breakable."

He scowled at her. "Where are Black and Dante?"

"I don't know." But she wasn't leaving without them. She took a couple of deep breaths, surveying everything going on. She counted the assembled ponies and noted four of them were missing: Moxie, Chimerical, Warpaint and Bedlam. Where had they gone? Were they with the two missing boys? Flintlock, Crescendo, Pageantry, Bathos, Charade, Fanfare, and Lucida were watching Penumbra and Oriflamme.

"We can't stay here, Char. It's not safe," Jared said, putting a hand on her shoulder. "It's not fair to ask our horses to try and protect us from all the others."

She knew that. Compatriot was scuffling with

Harmony, and Bathos had nudged Sirocco back into the small group of ponies not fighting. Penumbra was half-heartedly sparring with Oriflamme, his attention mostly on Dreadful, who was giving it to Tomahawk. The two stallions spun and danced around one another. Tomahawk's magic, turquoise and red, surrounded him as he came around hard and kicked out, his back hooves finding purchase on Dreadful's chest. The bay stallion staggered and he gave a sharp whinny. His magic exploded, the orange particles buzzing as they swarmed the pinto.

"Get down!" Jared yelled as the magic scattered and came at them. He and Charlotte stooped; she wasn't sure what it would do to them, but didn't want to find out. "We need to go," Jared told her, but how could they?

"We can't leave our ponies here with them," she said, shaking her head. She saw Penumbra from the corner of her eye come charging toward the two fighting stallions, and screamed. "Dreadful! Look out!"

The bay cavalry horse swiveled his head as Penumbra smashed into him. Dreadful fell on his side and thrashed as he tried to get up. "No!" Charlotte shrieked and ducking her brother's grab, ran to the horse. Penumbra was rearing and striking out with his front hooves, and she dropped next to Dreadful. "Get up!" she ordered him. "Dreadful, get *up*!"

Penumbra plunged back to the earth and planted one hoof on Dreadful's side. "He is finished," he said, his tone haughty and hot. "And you two are our prisoners!"

Charlotte's skin tingled and her breath caught in her

chest as the dapple grey lowered his head until he was nose-to-nose with her. She inhaled a short breath and sputtered, "Get away from us."

He snorted in her face and said, "Now *you* belong to *me*."

20

"*I* will admit I never thought I'd be held prisoner by a bunch of psychotic carousel horses." Dante gave a disparate chuckle and put his head back against the couch.

Black didn't even bother to answer him. He was pacing back and forth in the small living room in the apartment inside the carousel. Was Charlotte all right? Had Hawker made it back to the mansion? Had Penumbra managed to overtake Oriflamme? *We have to get out of here. I need to know she's all right.* He'd checked his cell phone for service, but the phone was out of order. He attributed it to the growing magic.

"Well? Nothing, Sully?"

"What do you want me to say?" Black glanced at him. "That this sucks? Because yeah – it does." Fury vibrated in his voice.

The four horses had driven them back to the carousel

and made no effort to hide their disgust with the two young men. Dante had taken a nasty nip on the back of the arm from Warpaint when he'd tried to stop and reason with them. He was rubbing it now, a sour expression on his face. They knew the four ponies were guarding them; Black had stuck his head out the door and almost gotten it bitten off by Bedlam. Four maniacal guards, no phones, and no discernible way out.

Yeah, this **sucked**. He wasn't fond of that word, but there it was. As he was turning to pace back the other way, the door was thrown open and Jared and Charlotte tumbled in.

"Charlotte!" Black raced to her and pulled her to him, hugging her close. He glimpsed Bedlam's fierce face before the door was slammed shut, and turned his attention to the trembling girl in his arms. "Shh, it's all right," he murmured. "It's okay." It wasn't, of course, but he wanted to soothe her. At least she was safe, and he would keep her that way.

But he soon realized her trembles were not from fear. She was *infuriated*. She jerked away from him and the blazing fire in her pretty eyes made his spine stiffen. Something bad had happened. Something catastrophic.

"What happened to the two of you?" Dante asked, gingerly getting up off the couch.

Jared, eyes full of seething anger, said, "What does it look like? We got captured, same as you two!" He looked like he wanted to punch somebody.

218

"Charlotte?" Black reached out and touched her chin. "What happened?"

"Penumbra has Dreadful, Oriflamme and Compatriot," she spat. She whirled away and stalked around in a circle, shaking her head. "Dreadful was fighting Tomahawk, and winning, and then Penumbra barreled into him and knocked him down, and he didn't get up." She stopped abruptly, her breath catching. "It wasn't even that he didn't get up," she whispered. She turned her head to look at Black, and his heart splintered at the sorrow in her eyes. "He *gave* up. Why would he do that?"

He moved to her and settled his hands on her slender shoulders, giving them a gentle squeeze. "I don't know. Did Penumbra hurt him?"

She dropped her gaze to the floor. "I don't think so," she said, her voice low. "Like I said, he was beating Tomahawk."

Black looked to Jared for confirmation, and he nodded. "Like she said. He was struggling and then Penumbra put a hoof down on his side, and that was it. He went quiet." Jared heaved out a sigh and bent over, putting his hands on his knees. "I feel sick."

"Don't throw up in here," Black told him, his voice sharp.

"I'm not that kind of sick," Jared informed him, straightening and meeting his gaze. "What do we do now? We've got the two mares and Hawker, but how long before Penumbra goes after them at the house? He'll be able to find the rest of the missing horses, too, right?"

Black took a moment to steady his heartbeats. "Yes, without any guidance from Baron."

"Is Uncle Baron here?" Charlotte's head snapped up.

"No," he said, his voice soft. "We don't know where he is."

She seemed to wilt, and he took her hand and led her over to the couch. "Sit," he said. "Are you two hungry or thirsty?"

Jared gave him an incredulous look. "Are you crazy? Of course not!"

"Hey." Dante's tone was harsh. "It's a reasonable question. No need to take his head off."

Black appreciated the concern, but he knew where Jared was coming from. His stomach was full of sandpaper and rocks, too, and he saw the desperation in the other boy's eyes. "We'll figure this out. We have to."

"So, figure it out," Jared snapped.

Displeasure welled in Black, and he told him, "Let's you and me take a walk." He pointed down the hall to the kitchen, and with a roll of his eyes, Jared strode to the other room. Black shot Dante a look and followed him.

"I'm not a kid," Jared grumbled when Black stepped into the kitchen.

"I didn't say you were," Black pointed out, his voice low but steely. "But you getting up in arms isn't helping. I know what we're up against. Believe me. Dante and I know these horses." He kept his tone level, but he wanted to make sure Jared knew he meant business.

"Why are they doing this? Why is Penumbra determined to wreck us?" Jared leaned back against the counter.

Black ran a hand through his hair. It was getting shaggy; one of these days, when they'd set the world right again, he'd have to get it cut. "I'm not sure."

Jared blew out an exasperated breath. "You just said you know these horses."

"And I do," Black said, nodding. "But remember: the magic affected all of them in different ways, and they've had the magic now for decades. Maybe it's warping some of them, messing with their minds, that kind of thing." He couldn't come up with another reason for why Penumbra was going the way of darkness.

Jared took that in, and crossed his arms over his chest. "If that's the case, what do we do with them once we've got them all together again? We can't put them back on the carousel. They might hurt somebody."

Black had been considering that. "I know. First things, though: we need to get our ponies back, and we need to find the missing ones before Penumbra does. Agreed?"

"Yes." Jared rubbed the back of his neck. "How, though? We're trapped here."

There was that. They'd never make it past the four horses guarding them. "Black!" Dante's yell from the living room broke his line of thought and he ran down the hallway, Jared on his heels.

Charlotte was standing in the center of the room amongst a cyclone of spinning purple magic. Dante was watching her, and he looked at Black with fear on his face. "She's tapping into some deep magic, Sully."

The walls of the apartment were shaking, and the lights flickered on and off. Jared made to move closer to her, and Dante caught his arm. "I wouldn't," he warned. He held out his hand, and there was a slight burn mark on it. "That magic of hers means business," he added.

"We can't let her bring the place down," Jared argued.

Black was studying her. Charlotte seemed to be in a trance. He took a step closer. "Charlotte," he said, raising his voice when she didn't respond. Repeating her name, however, only made the magic darken and glow, until it looked like sparkling black gold. *Not good.* His stomach tightened and he looked at Dante.

"I know," Dante said. "This is Oliver all over again." His voice was thick and constricted.

"What do you mean?" Jared asked. When neither acknowledged him, he reached out and shoved Black. "What's going on with her?"

Black had hoped it wouldn't come to this. He and Dante had gone through this with Oliver, back in the day, and it hadn't been pretty. And Oliver had had much more finesse with his magic than Charlotte could possibly have at the moment.

"She's collecting her magic," Dante said. The magic stuttered in the air, and fell into a pool of writhing black and purple sparkles before leaping into the air again and surrounding Charlotte. "Which is to say that she's summoning it, from deep inside herself."

"And that's bad, right?" Jared stared at his younger sister.

Black exhaled slowly. "Not bad, per se, but it does mean she's going to be a little unstable."

"Like Uncle Baron?" Panic edged Jared's voice.

"Let's hope not," Dante said, taking a step back as the magic formed itself into tendrils and reached out toward him. "We've already got uncontrollable carousel horses running amok."

"How do we wake her?" Jared asked, worry etched into his voice and face.

"We don't," Black told him. "She has to finish the process. As Dante found out, the magic will protect her until she's done." But what had happened to trigger the gathering? Had her emotions gotten enough ahead of her that her body had done it on its own? There was so much that wasn't understood about the magic, so much he knew they'd never understand.

It lasted a few more minutes, with the three of them tense and worried. When the magic collapsed to the floor again and then slithered off into the crevices in the old wooden floor, he rushed forward to catch her when she fainted. Easing her up into his arms, he carried her over to the couch and gently set her down.

"Charlotte." Jared knelt next to her and Black stepped back, letting him have the space. Dante came around and stood behind the couch, a grim look on his face. He reached down and touched Charlotte's hair.

"We'll have to be careful when she comes to," he said.

Jared looked up at him. "What I mean to say is she's likely to be disoriented for a bit, and her emotions might be out of line." He took a deep breath. "Just as your great-great-grandfather's were after his gathering."

They need to know Oliver is alive, Black thought. He hadn't wanted to bring it up when they'd talked about Symphony; one new person added to their group had been enough. But now, with Charlotte going through this, he needed to. It was time.

"Dante." Black's voice was solemn, and Dante stood straight. "Oliver is alive," he added, his voice quiet. When Dante's mouth dropped open and he tried to say something, Black said, "I know it's true. My grandfather has been in contact with him ever since the Island. He told me he hasn't heard from him in a couple of months, though."

"But we went to his funeral. We saw him in the casket." Dante's eyes were wide with disbelief. "Midnight, we *saw him in the casket!*"

Jared slowly got to his feet and Black watched him with concern as he sat down in Cornelius's old wooden rocker. "My great-great-grandfather is *alive?*" He put his head in his hands. "Why didn't he stop Uncle Baron? Why didn't he ever come see us?" The instant despair in his voice was disheartening.

"I don't know." Black felt he was repeating the same words over and over. "I don't know why he's letting this go on. He has to know by now the magic is back."

Dante started pacing. "I don't believe it. I really, honestly don't."

"You have to," Black told him. "And we need to find him. Penumbra has seventeen of the ponies under his control now, plus himself. Even if we were to find Orrick's horses, it might not be enough to stop him." He thought of the speech he'd given Charlotte, about how they would persevere and win the fight, but after witnessing Penumbra's booming power, he knew that was no longer the truth. They needed something much stronger. Some*one* much stronger.

They needed an archimage who was decades old and unstoppable.

21

*W*hen Charlotte came back to herself, dragging her way up through the dark magic that filled her soul, she found the three boys silent and sullen. Swallowing hard, her throat and mouth dry as dust, she pushed herself upright. Dante was brooding in the far corner, one hand at his chin, his eyes downcast. Jared was slumped in the old rocking chair, his eyes closed. And Black—

"Charlotte." Black turned away from the door and jogged over to her. Jared and Dante both gave her their attention as he sat next to her on the couch. "How do you feel?"

"Um." She wasn't sure she wanted to tell him. The magic was surging throughout her body, and she felt she could lose control of it at any moment. She wasn't sure what had even happened. "I feel stronger," she finally said, her voice low and hoarse.

Black looked over her head at Dante, and she could sense they wanted to say something to her and were choosing not to. Black took her hand and gave it a squeeze. "You collected your magic to you," he said. "You summoned it, in other words."

"My head feels fuzzy," she told him. A few sparkles of purple wafted into the air when she pulled her hand from his, and she watched them float out into the apartment. The floor trembled beneath their feet. She closed her eyes and willed the magic to recoil.

"It will take some time to get used to all of the magic you have now," Black told her.

"Right, but I think perhaps you should try it out on those four beasties holding us prisoner," Dante said. Charlotte looked up at him and saw how serious he was. "I don't think they can hold you now."

But she wasn't sure she wanted to use it. Turning her attention back to Black, she said, "What if I can't control it? I don't want to hurt anyone, including the ponies." They were against her now, but that didn't mean she wanted to harm them.

"I think Dante's right," Jared said. His voice was low and he looked shell-shocked. "We need to get out of here, Char. Do what you have to."

"Jared, what's wrong?" she asked. Something had happened while she'd been out; she could sense the despondency in him.

He raised his head to look her in the eyes. Black shifted

on the seat next to her. "Oliver is alive," Jared said, his voice low and gloomy.

She took that in, rolled it around her mind a little bit. Everything she'd learned about magic made his news feasible. This archimage power was incredible, and she didn't even know how to really use it yet. "Why aren't you happy about that?"

"Happy?" He gave her an unbelieving look. "If he's been alive this whole time, why didn't he ever visit us? Why didn't he try to stop Uncle Baron?"

She had no answer for that. But the fact that there was someone else who knew how this felt, this great storm of magic inside her, could be nothing but good, especially if he wasn't running with Uncle Baron. "How do we find him?" she asked Black.

"We don't know," he said, shrugging. "But we have to, because Penumbra has gone too dark, and has too many of the Flying Ponies for us to beat with just who Orrick has." He sat back against the couch. "My grandfather has kept in contact with him, but hasn't heard from Oliver in two months."

"Someone must know how to find him," Dante said. He gestured to the door. "If you will, sweetheart. I want to get away from these horses."

Charlotte nodded and got to her feet. The magic blossomed through her, and purple sparkles fell from her hands. She clenched them into fists and took a deep breath. *You don't control me,* she whispered to the magic. *I control you.*

"Are you sure about this?" Black asked her, rising to his feet. "I don't want you to do this if you don't want to."

And that was the humorous thing – she *did* want to. Or, at least, her magic wanted to. It was bubbling and brewing and itching for her to turn it loose. She turned her gaze toward the door. Beyond it were four carousel horses who meant to keep her locked away, helpless to stop their lead horse. That didn't work for her.

She walked to the door, knowing the three boys were at her back, *had* her back if she needed them, and put her hand on the old bronzed handle. It wasn't locked; she pulled down on it and swung the door inward.

Bedlam stuck his head in, his reddish eyes glittering. "You are not leaving," he told her.

"I am," she said. She held up her hands; magic dripped from them and puddled on the floor. Bedlam's ears flickered forward, and he snorted.

"Strong magic," he told her. But then his lips curled back over his teeth and he snapped at her. She slapped his muzzle and he reared back. Purple magic swarmed over his head, and he whinnied in agitation and backed further away.

"What are you doing? Don't let them out!" Moxie said, prancing up beside him. But her eyes widened, and she stepped away.

"That's right," Charlotte told the two. "We're leaving. I don't want any problems." She kept her voice as even as she could. Black slid out around her and waved his arms at the two horses.

"Back off," he ordered. "We don't answer to you, or to Penumbra." He stayed between them and Charlotte and she wondered where the other two were, if they had gone back to the herd.

They climbed the short set of stairs to the carousel platform, and then she saw Warpaint and Chimerical. The pinto stallion and blue mare turned toward them, and she paused, watching them as they approached.

"You aren't leaving," Chimerical told the group. "Penumbra wants you here."

"We don't care what he says," Jared told her. "We're going." He stepped down off the platform and Chimerical charged him. Charlotte threw up a cyclone of magic, and it zipped in-between the mare and Jared, blocking him.

Chimerical squealed and spun, lashing out with both hind feet at it. Warpaint lunged around the side at Dante, who kicked out at the horse. Warpaint drew up and snorted. "This is pointless," he said. "Even if you escape, Penumbra will find you."

"And you no longer have Dreadful, Oriflamme or Compatriot to protect you," Chimerical chimed in, tossing her white mane.

"They have me." Charlotte walked past Jared, using the magic to force the blue mare back. "Come on," she said over her shoulder. She was shaking, afraid if she let too much of the magic go it would cost her, but they needed to get away from the horses and back to the house to regroup. Black and Dante stepped to either side of her, and it bothered her that Jared lagged behind. Why wasn't he his normal overprotective self? *I'll have to worry about that later.*

Bedlam and Moxie raced out to meet the other two horses, and the four stood watching Charlotte and the boys walk toward the path beneath the trees. The air was sharp as needles, and the brisk wind brought rushes of yellow and orange with it. The rain had at least stopped, and the clouds above were royal blue, like Baron's battered briefcase.

Once they reached the trail and started down it, Charlotte tried to withdraw the magic. It flew around inside her, ranting and wild. She stopped and closed her eyes, wishing that her uncle was here, that he could help her learn how to control it.

"Deep breaths," Black said, his hand on her shoulder, keeping her grounded. "We're safe. Try to relax."

It wasn't that easy. Now that she'd collected her magic, she wasn't sure what to do with it. She needed help. But she listened to his soft, even voice, and finally the magic receded, slithering back into wherever it kept itself when she didn't need it. She opened her eyes and looked up at him.

"Better?" he asked, studying her eyes.

"Better," she said, wondering what he saw and afraid to ask. "We should keep moving."

"After you," Dante told her. He was more serious than she'd ever seen him, and it frightened her a little. If Dante was this upset and worried, they had to be in big trouble.

"Stay close together. There will be a lot of Desolates out

now," Black warned, staying at Charlotte's side. She noticed he had his ratchet in hand. Jared and Dante walked behind them, and again, she wished she knew why her older brother was so upset. Was it because Oliver was alive? Wasn't that a good thing, as long as he wasn't evil?

As they walked, the sky above turned darker. The trees had long since lost their leaves, and their branches hung over them like skeletal arms. The trunks of the trees shimmered in dark purples and reds, no longer their ordinary brown. Little bits of random colors floated by on the breeze.

"Was this how it was on the Island?" she asked Black, her voice low. She didn't want the other two to hear.

"No," he said. "Actually, the magic made more sense then. This," he waved his free hand around, "is what happens when it gets out of balance."

"Is that because the ponies aren't working together?"

"Yes." He had his head turned away from her, and she knew he was watching for Desolates. She wondered if the magic was freaking out too because she couldn't control her archimage powers yet.

Her thoughts traveled to Uncle Baron. What had Penumbra done with him? Or worse, *to him*? She still had a hard time reconciling who he'd become with the man who'd taken them in after their father passed away. Baron had been nothing but patient and kind. In those first months of living in the city with their uncle, Danny had cried himself to sleep every night. Marta and Gavin had withdrawn from everyone but themselves, and Rory had grown more sullen and defiant. Only Jared seemed capable of continuing on; she herself had dived into her make-believe worlds, wishing she could run away with her beloved characters.

But the Doctor hadn't whisked her away in the TARDIS, and the *Millennium Falcon* had never shown up. Eventually, she'd made her way out of the fantasies and into her new world where a doting uncle and stern, but kind housekeeper lived. Her siblings had pieced themselves back together with Uncle Baron's help, and they'd moved on as much as anyone who'd lost their parents could.

And now he's been taken from us, too. The thought flooded her eyes with unexpected tears, and she reached up and dashed them away. No one needed her tears. Black glanced at her and started to stop, but she gave a quick shake of her head and sped up. She didn't want to talk about her uncle now. She wanted to get home and see her siblings and the others.

They made it back to the house without any mishaps. Rory was on the porch waiting; his face fell as he realized that they were missing the three ponies. "What happened to them? Are you guys okay?" he asked.

"We're all right," Black told him as Jared barreled by and went inside. Rory cast a confused look after his older brother.

"What's with him?" he asked, looking at Charlotte.

"I don't know," she said. "Penumbra captured the ponies." Her voice faltered and Black put his hand on her shoulder, giving it a squeeze.

"Well that's great," Rory said, irritated. "How did that happen? I thought Dreadful was supposed to be super powerful."

"He is," Dante said, pushing past him. "But Penumbra is strong enough now that he no longer needs a Capall."

"Yeah I know that," Rory retorted, following them into the house. "But I thought Dreadful could take him down."

"Dreadful can take who down?" Helen turned toward them and bustled over. "Jared said the ponies were captured? How on earth did that happen?"

Black sighed and ran a hand through his hair, pushing his bangs back. "Penumbra's strength is growing."

"Dreadful gave up," Charlotte said, shaking her head. "He let Penumbra win." She couldn't fathom why he'd done it. Oriflamme and Compatriot would've backed him if he'd fought – she knew they would've. But with Dreadful gone, and the other two stallions with him, they only had Hawker, Czarina and Ranee. It wasn't much of a force.

"Oriflamme is gone, too?" Symphony had been standing with Jared, but now walked over, looking stricken. "I thought you would get him back. We just rescued him!"

Charlotte's eyes narrowed. "Black and I found him, not you," she told the older blonde girl. She turned to Dante, ignoring Symphony's indignant gasp. "Please tell me you know someone in the magic world who can find Oliver for us."

"Oliver?" Helen's voice was uncertain. "Not Oliver Flynn."

"Yes, him," Charlotte said. "Well?" she demanded,

keeping her eyes on Dante. He took a deep breath and settled his hands on his hips.

"Why do you assume I'd know someone?" he asked.

"Because you deal with magic," Charlotte retorted. "And if Oliver can get Dreadful back then we need to find him."

"I think we all need to take a step back and regroup," Black said, his calm voice annoying her. She turned to face him and he pulled back a little at the look on her face. "We need to be rational," he added.

"I *am* being rational. Penumbra has more magic than all of us, and we have to stop him before it's too late," Charlotte said, trying not to sound upset. Why wasn't Black more gung ho about finding Oliver?

"Why do you want to find Oliver?" Jared asked. His voice was loud and cut through the murmurings of everyone else. They turned to stare at him.

"Why *don't* you want to?" Charlotte argued. "He's an archimage. He can help us!"

"Sure, like he helped us when Dad died? Like he helped us when Uncle Baron went crazy?" Jared's voice was on the verge of shaking. "We don't need him!" Gavin reached out to touch his arm, but Jared shook him off. "Don't," he warned.

"What's up with you?" Charlotte asked, crossing her arms over her chest. "Why are you being so weird?"

"Weird?" Jared's face started turning red. "Am I the only one who thinks finding our great-great-grandfather isn't the best thing to do? We don't know him! What if he's worse than Uncle Baron? What if he agrees with Penumbra?" His voice rose until he was shouting, and the three remaining carousel horses flinched away from him, their eyes rolling. He stopped and took several deep breaths.

Charlotte's anger with him faded. He was hurting. How could she not have noticed it before? *He's always the protector, that's why. He never lets us see how much he's hurting, how much things are affecting him.* She went to him, wrapping her arms around his waist and putting her head on his chest. "I'm sorry," she said, feeling his heart beating hard beneath her ear. "It's going to be okay." She pulled her head back and looked at him. "I don't know how, but it will." She tried to put as much feeling and hope into her words as she could, because she *needed* her older brother to be all right.

"I know." His voice was gruff, but he forced a tiny smile for her.

She let go of him and stepped away to give him space. A few purple bits drifted from her fingertips, and she reached into herself to force the magic back. It wasn't time for that yet. It was building though, a pressure that would need to be released at some point. She only hoped that she'd be able to direct its energy and not hurt anyone with it.

"Okay then," Dante said, clapping his hands. "I suggest we get something to eat and sit down to figure out our next move."

"To the kitchen," Helen commanded, and everyone started trooping down the hallway. Charlotte waited to walk with the three remaining horses. They needed her to be strong and tough, and that's what she was going to be. She would get Dreadful and the others back.

22

"*B*lack, can we talk?"

He turned to face Symphony and nodded. After lunch everyone had agreed to split up a while for space, and he'd gone into Baron's study, but left one of the doors ajar. "What do you need?" he asked her.

She shut the doors and walked closer to the desk. "I don't need anything," she said. "I wanted to tell you something."

He gestured. "Go ahead."

"If you didn't want me here, why did you let me come?"

"Is that really what you wanted to say?" Irritation crept into his voice.

Instead of answering him, she paced down the length of the study and then back, glancing at him every so often. He shoved his hands into his back pockets. What angle was she trying to work? Had she thought he'd fawn all over her? "Symph," he said, causing her to jump. "Spit it out."

She turned to face him. The low lighting of the office caught on the strand of black pearls she wore around her neck, and he turned his head away. He didn't need that reminder of their time together on Coney.

"I haven't been honest with you, Sullivan," she said, bringing his head back around. She stood tall, arms at her sides. "The real reason I'm here is because I'm working for Oliver."

He would reflect later that maybe he should've expected it. After all, with everything else falling apart, why not? He squeezed his hands into fists. "Are you spying on us, then? Is that it?"

"He wanted to make sure his family was secure," she told him. With a dry chuckle, she added, "I'll have to tell him they are not."

She was baiting him, and he was amazed at how he fell prey to it again when it had been so long. "Why does he care? My grandfather says Oliver walked away from the Flying Ponies after his fake funeral. What's the point?"

"The point, Sullivan, is that the carousel is important. He trusted that his great grandson would be the one to see the magic back into the world. Unfortunately, he couldn't handle both the ponies and his own archimage powers." Symphony shrugged. "So now here we are, with Penumbra planning to terrorize humanity, Baron gone, and Charlotte unable to get the job done."

Agitation rolled through Black, but he refused to chase it. Symph meant for him to get mad. He shrugged at her.

"What's your plan, then? Are you going to take over getting the ponies back?"

She smiled, and it struck him that she was so much more than the Songbird now. This was a woman who knew her way in the world, and never bowed to anyone. "I think you know better than that, don't you? The carousel is the Flynn legacy. Charlotte no longer has the Capall power, but she is an archimage like Oliver and Baron. She must complete this quest."

His skin prickled at her tone. There was finality in it, and he couldn't help but wonder what would happen if Charlotte were unable to rein Penumbra in and unite the Flying Ponies again. "Why doesn't Oliver help her? Why is he just spying on her through you?"

"He's waiting to see if she needs help."

"Sounds like you think she does."

Symphony arched an eyebrow and strode toward the door. "She's young. She's been sheltered. We'll see if she can make things right."

Sheltered? Black couldn't let that one go. "She hasn't been sheltered. Her parents are dead. Her uncle has abandoned her and her siblings. Penumbra stripped her of the Capall title." His words were taut. "And she just lost Dreadful."

Symphony got to the doors and glanced back at him. "This is the time for her to step up, Sullivan, and prove she is the right one for the job." She left the study, and Black sat down on the massive desk.

So all that flirting with Jared, all the giggling and teasing, that's all a ruse. She's just here to make sure Charlotte doesn't mess up. He closed his eyes. What could he do to help Charlotte? It was clear, at least to him now, that Oliver didn't want to be found. Symphony wasn't going to reveal his location. Without the help of the powerful archimage, how were they going to win?

And it was definitely *they*. Even though Symphony made it clear Oliver wanted to see Charlotte win the day, Black fully intended to help her, any way he could. Someone rapped on the door, and he said, "Yeah."

Dante stuck his head in. "Just you?"

Black nodded and Dante came in and locked the doors. Black raised an eyebrow.

"I have an idea, but you're not going to like it," Dante told him.

"What else is new?"

Dante's gaze narrowed. "Don't know as I've seen you this mad in a while. Symphony say something you didn't like?"

"Get on with it." Black wasn't explaining himself to Romano.

"You need to let Charlotte use her archimage powers." Dante held up his hands, as if expecting Black to argue. When he didn't, Dante lowered them and added, "I don't see how we're winning this war without them."

"Me either." Not at this juncture, anyway. Not after finding out Oliver was letting Charlotte struggle through things on her own.

"I expected you to fight me on this."

"Me too." Black pushed himself off the desk. "Look, Symphony told me she's working for Oliver. She's here to spy on us and see if Charlotte can beat Penumbra."

"Of course she can, *if* we let her be who she's meant to be."

Black gave him an appraising look. "You're not surprised by my news."

"No." Dante turned away. "The Songbird is all kinds of things, Sully. You're just seeing this side of her for the first time. I saw it years ago."

Black had nothing to say that as he followed Dante out of the room. They crossed the foyer to the living room, where everyone else was hanging out. Apparently they hadn't needed as much space as he had. The three horses were standing in the back, and he wondered how long Penumbra would wait before coming for them.

"What's the plan?" Jared asked. He seemed back to his old confident self, but Black wasn't sure how much he was hiding, either. A person could only take so much before they buckled.

"We need to challenge Penumbra head-on," Dante said. He started to say something else, stopped, and pointed at the TV screen. "Turn that up," he ordered.

Gavin grabbed the remote and did as asked. Everyone turned their attention to the screen, where a reporter was standing in a park. Behind her, trees whipped in the wind and a swing set was rocking back and forth, the swings bucking and tossing.

"...you can see, the weather has grown steadily worse in

the last hour. Two old trees have already been uprooted by the wind, and we've all noticed the wild colors. Storm trackers from around the world are weighing in on this freak tempest, but no one seems to know what we're dealing with here in Smoke City. " The scene cut to two old oaks lying on their sides, their roots exposed to the driving wind.

Dante muttered beneath his breath and turned to look at Black. "Penumbra's not wasting time, is he?"

"I'm not sure that's his doing, actually." Black moved closer to the TV. "I think the weather is off because the magic balance is off."

"So we need to set it straight before something majorly gets wrecked," Rory piped up.

"I think you guys are all missing the point," Marta said, her authoritative voice drawing attention. "People can see the magic now." She waved a hand toward the TV.

"She's right," Dante said. "If Penumbra and the others start showing themselves, people are going to get jumpy."

"When Dreadful and I flew home from the amusement park, some school kids saw us," Charlotte chimed in.

Black walked away from the group, thinking. If they were going to throw down with Penumbra and his ponies, they would need to do it away from people. *We need to do it here, or at the carousel.*

"So, are we forgetting about finding the Tyranny's ponies then? And what about Uncle Baron?" Charlotte asked. "Are we assuming the worst?" There was a crack in her voice that belied the casual tone she used.

"The worst?" Danny's voice was high. "Why the worst? You think Penumbra hurt him?"

They were all quiet then. What *were* they to assume, Black wondered. Could Penumbra hurt the archimage? He'd never tried to challenge Oliver, or even Adara. Not even Symphony or Helen had anything to say to that.

"I think we need to go after the Tyranny," Charlotte said a few moments later. "If we can find their ponies, we'll have more power to bring against Penumbra."

"You don't think he'll have found them by now?" Rory asked. "If he can come and go as he pleases, I bet he's looking for the missing ones right now."

"That's a safe assumption," Black said, turning back to the group. He sought Charlotte's eyes for a moment. Hers were full of determined anger, and he realized how much she'd grown since she'd first stumbled upon the carousel a few weeks ago. Maybe a month ago, he mused. Time didn't seem relative anymore. All that mattered was stopping the dapple grey stallion and saving the missing ponies.

"We need to find them first," Jared said.

"No." Charlotte's voice was calm and lined with tenacity. "I'm going to confront Orrick. I have the archimage power, just like Uncle Baron. I'll make the Tyranny tell us where those horses are."

No one said anything. Black mused that this was probably the first time her siblings had heard her speak with such defiance and fury. "She's right. She's capable enough to force Orrick's hand."

"You don't think Penumbra could've stolen the ponies

already?" Rory argued. "What's the point of going after them if he has them? We can't beat *him*."

"We don't know that," Marta said. "We have three Flying Ponies and Charlotte's power."

"Ask the horses what they think," Gavin suggested.

Dante called out, "Hawker, what do you think? Can you three fight back against Penumbra?"

The light grey warrior horse walked over to them. The two mares followed, and it was Ranee who spoke. "We are as skilled as any of those Penumbra leads," she said.

"You only have to turn us loose," Czarina added, tossing her head.

"Hawker?" Black wanted to hear it from all three.

"They are right." He lifted his head. "We are as tough as any of the others. We will fight Penumbra."

"There, see? We've got an archimage and three carousel horses," Danny said. He walked over to pat Hawker on the neck. "That should be enough to scare Orrick into giving up his horses."

"What are we waiting for then?" Charlotte said. "We need to go now."

Dante shifted on his feet and looked at Black. "I don't know. That sounds like a plan for failure."

"It's all we've got," Charlotte told him. "So let's go. I'm tired of standing around. I want those missing horses."

"Go with what we've got," Black agreed. "And this is what we've got."

"Yeah, but this time, we're *all* going," Jared said, his

voice hard. "We take the three horses and we show Orrick we're not afraid of him anymore."

"I'm in," Rory said.

"Me too," Danny said, nodding.

Black looked at Dante. "You know how to find him, I assume?"

Dante nodded, but his eyes glinted with unease. "I don't suppose I can sit this one out."

"No." Charlotte pointed at him. "You need to confront them, too. It will be good for you."

"Good." Dante snorted. "Yes, and while I'm at it, I'll have them rip out my toenails." He made a face at her.

She smiled. There was no humor in it, and she told him, "You did it to yourself. Now you'll undo it. Let's go." She left the room, and her siblings followed her. Helen and Symphony, who had stayed silent, looked at Dante and Black.

"You're really all right with this, Sullivan?" Helen asked, tapping her fingers against her hip.

Aware of Symphony studying him, he nodded. "Yes. Charlotte can do this."

Helen turned to go. "Then we shall all go and support her."

Symphony offered Black a smile laced with barbed wire. "We'll see how she does against the Tyranny."

Black watched her walk out of the room, and Dante let out a low whistle. "Makes you wonder what will happen if Charlotte can't seal the deal, doesn't it?" He started to leave, paused, and added, "I'd keep my eyes on her, Sully."

He'd already been planning to. This side of Symphony was unknown to him, and he wondered when she'd lost her softness, when she'd become this cold woman who only seemed interested in the failure of the Flynns. Was it jealousy over Charlotte? He didn't think Symph was really that kind of person, but he hadn't thought she'd be *this* kind, either.

Charlotte, Black, and the twins took the ponies, Gavin and Marta doubling on Hawker. Everyone else piled into the Cadillac and Dante drove toward Orrick's place. The ponies' magic kept their riders from getting cold, and Black tried to enjoy the flight on Ranee. But his mind churned with everything going on, and he wondered where and when it would all end, *if* it ended. What if they couldn't stop Penumbra? What if the magic grew too wild?

"You okay?" Charlotte asked from her seat on Czarina. The brown mare looked like she was having a ball flying. Charlotte looked like she wanted to hit something. Or someone.

"I'm all right," he said, knowing he wasn't. It wasn't the time to get caught up in whether he was okay or not, though.

Charlotte didn't say anything else. The twins were clinging to Hawker, the big grey stallion moving effortlessly through the orange sky. Black drew in a breath. Was this to be their new normal? At Coney, the magic had been thick and wonderful, and at times it had strayed into the atmosphere. But never like this, with weirdly-colored clouds and rain.

The black Cadillac turned onto a winding dirt road that Black realized was a driveway. It ended in a circle drive in front of a beautiful old white house with dark green shutters and a wide veranda porch. The three carousel horses landed, and Black slid off Ranee, giving the mare's neck a rub. Dante and the others stepped out of the SUV, and Dante waved toward the front door.

"There you go," he said to Charlotte. "You wanted to confront them – go right ahead."

"Coward," she chided him and strode toward the wide front steps. Her family followed, and Dante turned his head to look at Black.

"She can call me anything she wants at this point," he said. "But I'm not ringing that doorbell."

Black scowled at him and followed the family. Symphony and Helen were hanging back, too, but he figured that was all right. Helen was an observer and Symph wasn't planning on being any help.

Charlotte rang the doorbell and then knocked on the big green front door. Jared and Rory were right behind her, trying to look intimidating, Black supposed. The younger three stood just behind them. When no one answered, Charlotte tried again.

"So now what? No one's home," Rory said, flinging his hands into the air.

"Patience," Jared told him. "They might be slow getting to the door."

"They are old," Gavin pointed out.

Charlotte gave the door another hard rap with her

knuckles. This time, they could hear muttering and talking going on behind the closed door. There was a click, and it slowly swung in. Orrick stood there, his eyes narrowed behind a pair of reading glasses.

"I thought we were done, young lady," he told Charlotte.

"No. I want those ponies back, and you're going to give them to me." Her voice was hard and she leaned toward him. "So, we're all coming in, and we're going to have a little chat about that, and at the end of our talk, you're going to hand the horses over."

He laughed, a really genuine one. "You certainly are spunky," he said. "Go ahead then, come right on in. And bring those three beauties with you."

23

*C*harlotte glanced over her shoulder. She didn't like the idea of bringing the three horses into Orrick's home, but neither did she want them left outside. "Okay, fine. But one wrong move toward them and, well, you'll be sorry." Her bravado seemed to be failing now that they were here, and she hated that. This wasn't the time to back down or back off. Things were getting serious, and she needed the power to bring Penumbra to heel.

Orrick led them further into the house, through a long hallway that ended in a glorious parlor room. The furniture was antique and dark wood, and the carpet a rich old turquoise blue. The horses crowded together near the big windows, while the humans found places to sit.

Settling himself down on an old claw foot couch, Orrick angled his body toward Charlotte. "I suppose you've decided to be brave and come see me because something happened. You lost some of your confidence in beating Baron."

"Baron's lost the Flying Ponies," Charlotte said, her voice flat. "Penumbra is strong enough now he doesn't need a Capall. He's also taken control of Dreadful, Oriflamme and Compatriot." It burned that she'd lost them. It hurt that Dreadful hadn't been willing to fight.

"Oh." This seemed to set Orrick back. He dropped his gaze to his hands for a moment or two. "You think by taking my ponies you have a chance of beating him."

"I do." Charlotte's heart was starting to pound a little; she glimpsed Roswald and Ignace slipping into the room. That put her on edge.

"You have my whistle, don't you?" Orrick asked.

"Yes, but Dante doesn't think it works that well," Charlotte told him.

"Don't you have the bridle?" Ignace asked, moving further into the room.

"We lost it. Oriflamme was wearing it when Penumbra captured him," Black said.

The three men of the Tyranny shared an incredulous look. None of them said anything, and unease moved through Charlotte. The bridle couldn't be that important, could it? Maybe it hadn't had as much magic as they'd thought, and that was why it hadn't helped Oriflamme.

"Well that's interesting," Orrick finally said. He rubbed his chin. "I guess it didn't have the power we thought it did."

"No, it didn't," Black agreed. Everyone in the room was

poker-faced, except Danny, who was staring around at all the oddities and curiosities in the room with unabashed wonder. "But with your ponies we should be able to beat Penumbra."

"You're so sure about that," Orrick said, shaking his head. "I don't know. And besides, why would we want to help you? We offered help, and you shot us down." He directed his gaze to Charlotte.

"I know. But these are desperate times," she told him. "You had to have noticed the weather and all the craziness going on in Smoke City. We *need* to bring him down."

Orrick sat back against the couch. Charlotte glanced over at Black; he didn't appear worried, so she figured they weren't out of luck yet, but what if Orrick just flat-out refused to give them the ponies? Could she really use her magic against anyone like that, enough to hurt someone? Because it might come down to that. She knew it.

"If you go down that path, it can only end badly," Ignace said, his voice low.

"What do you mean?" Jared asked, engaging for the first time. "We have to stop him. That isn't a question."

"He means the ponies could destroy themselves in battle," Orrick said. "You have to consider that. If Penumbra is as crazy as you think he is, he won't stop. He'll risk wrecking everything to keep his freedom." He heaved a heavy breath. "Oliver was a fool to bring them to life."

Everyone was quiet then, absorbing that. Charlotte couldn't stand the thought of losing the Flying Ponies, but what was the alternative? Let Penumbra run uninhibited and spread his dangerous magic to the whole world? What if he was already? They had no idea where the ponies were.

"Where is Baron now?" Roswald asked. His voice was cold and it slithered through the room.

"We don't know," Black said.

"Really. That's interesting." Roswald turned his eyes to Symphony. She and Helen had come in behind everyone else, and stood along the wall, looking cool and composed. Charlotte kind of hated the singer at that moment. "Why didn't you think to ask the Songbird? After all, she knows many more secrets than she's probably admitted."

"Symphony?" Black's voice was hard. "Do you know where Baron is?"

"Wouldn't I have told you, Sullivan, if I did?" She tipped her head, looking coy and smug.

Charlotte wished Black would roll his eyes and tell her off, but he didn't. He was too sweet for that. He did call her out though.

"You're working for Oliver, Symph. Is it too much to assume that you'd know where Baron was? I should've thought to ask you before." Black's tone was curt.

"Oliver's *alive?*" Orrick's voice was filled with shock.

"It makes sense – he absorbed a great deal of the Flying Ponies' magic," Ignace said, shrugging, "just as all of us who were around them did."

"Wait. You're working for our great-great-grandfather?" Danny's voice pitched. "Why didn't he come to see us?"

"Because he doesn't want to interfere." Symphony

pushed herself away from the wall and began to meander around the room. She knew she'd draw everyone's eyes, and Charlotte *really* wished she'd fall over in those ridiculously tall heels. Why did the blonde have to be so sophisticated? And perfect-looking?

"So you're just what, babysitting us?" Rory asked in disgust. "That's stupid. We don't need him or you."

"Yeah," Danny concurred, glowering.

Symphony laughed. "You really are too cute," she told the boys. "Oliver wants an appropriate heir to the carousel. If Charlotte can prove herself worthy, which she hasn't yet done, then she will be allowed to keep the carousel." She turned on her heel to stare at Charlotte. "If not, then the Flying Ponies will be taken back to Oliver, and he will decide their fate."

"Like what, putting them in some boring old museum?" Danny asked. "That's stupid!"

"They'll only go to Oliver if Penumbra can't be beaten," Charlotte retorted, her voice hot. She got to her feet. She was still a couple inches shorter than Symphony, but she tried not to let that bother her. Fisting a hand on her hip, she added, "If I can't beat him, why should Oliver think he can?"

"Because he brought them to life," Orrick told her. Charlotte turned to look at him.

"You have to give us those horses you took," she said. "We need them. The longer we wait, the longer Penumbra has to run amok."

"I don't like your tone," Orrick said. He gazed up at her

from his slouched position, his eyes calculating and cold. "I think we should go after the dapple grey by ourselves and bring him down."

"Try it," Charlotte said, scoffing. "I'd like to see that."

"All right, everyone settle down," Dante commanded. He moved into the middle of the room. "Charlotte, Orrick, you're going to have to work together to do this. There's no alternative, not now. Penumbra is too strong."

"You shut up." Orrick jumped to his feet, quicker than anyone his age should have the right to be. He stepped in close to Dante, who to his credit didn't flinch. "Your opinion means nothing here."

"Easy, old boy," Dante said, smiling through his teeth. "I've more friends here than you."

"Are you so sure about that?" Orrick swept a hand around the room. "I don't see anyone backing you up, son."

"Don't call me that!" Dante shoved a finger into Orrick's chest.

"Guys." Charlotte rubbed her forehead. "Just stop. Orrick, we need those ponies. If Penumbra brings down the world, then there's nothing left for you, either. And you've run with magic for a long time. You know the damage it can do."

He appraised her, and she lifted her chin a little, determined to look tough. "Yes, that is true," he conceded. "You know you still won't have the numbers on your side. I only have eleven."

"And Penumbra has eighteen, counting himself. I know. But I'm getting better with my magic. I think we can beat him." They had to. What other choice was there? And yeah, she wasn't brilliant with her magic yet, but it was raw and surging, and if she had the guts to unleash it, she knew it would do damage.

"Where are they?" Black asked, getting to his feet. His face was devoid of emotion.

"You think you can order us around?" Ignace asked. "You do remember how it was on the Island, Mr. Midnight."

"Yeah, I remember the three of you skulking in the shadows, waiting to steal the Flying Ponies," Black said, nodding. "Give them back."

Orrick cleared his throat. "They aren't here."

"So where are they?" Charlotte asked. She glanced toward their three ponies, and noticed it was starting to rain again. Vibrant drops of orange struck the pane, causing the three horses to shy away from it.

"Hidden, so that no one could find them all at once," Orrick said.

Charlotte looked at him. "In different locations, then."

"Yes." He nodded. "Clearly we thought ourselves clever at the time."

"And they're still where you left them? You've checked on them recently?" Dante asked.

"Not recently. They are quite secure, though," Orrick told him.

"Penumbra will seek them out," Charlotte said. "We need to go get them." Anxiety was starting to grow in her stomach; at that moment, the dapple-grey stallion could be finding the missing ponies.

"If you'll excuse us for a few moments," Orrick said, and he left the room followed by Ignace and Roswald, who cast a furtive glance back at the three carousel horses.

Charlotte looked at Black. "Well? Do you think they're going to help us?"

"I think we might have to force their hand," he told her. "I know you don't want to use your magic that way, but you might have to." There was indecision in his voice, though, and that wasn't reassuring.

She looked at her siblings. They were quiet, and she wondered what was going through their heads. They hadn't asked for this craziness, this wild adventure that their uncle had given them. That they hadn't all run screaming back to Smoke City meant something, however. They were family, and they weren't going to desert one another.

The Tyranny walked back in, and Orrick said, "There are stipulations to this agreement."

"You're going to give them to us," Charlotte said.

"Now, now, not so fast." Ignace's voice was slow, as if the rest of them couldn't keep up with him. "We agree to let you use them to bring Penumbra down, but then they must be returned to us."

"You don't own them!" Marta interjected. She got up from the ivory-topped piano bench she'd been sitting on with Gavin. "They were never yours."

"You either agree to this, or you don't," Orrick told

Charlotte, locking gazes with her. "We will offer you all of our assistance to bring that devil down, but you must honor us by letting us keep those ponies that are currently in our possession."

Charlotte could hear the murmured outrage from her friends and family. Of course that was a crazy idea! Why on earth should she allow them to keep the horses they'd *stolen*? "No. I won't agree to that. They belong to my family." Her voice was strong and hard, and she knew there was no negotiating anymore. She would take the horses if they wouldn't give them up.

Orrick smiled. "I figured as much. You tell me you want to defeat Penumbra, but you are unwilling to do everything to accomplish it. You will all see yourselves out now."

Dante and Black both moved toward him, but Charlotte held up her hand. She'd had all she could take of Orrick's condescension. "No, Mr. Fowler. You misunderstood me," she said. "I was merely doing you a favor by *asking* for my horses back." She took a step forward, readying herself. The magic crept through her veins, and purple sparkles fell from her fingers. Orrick's eyes widened.

"Don't you dare unleash that here," he chided, his face paling. "These are irreplaceable antiques!"

"We don't have to do this at all," Charlotte told him. "Tell me where the horses are and we walk out and don't come back. Refuse, and I can level this place." She could, too. The strength of her magic was mesmerizing and heavy. With it she could crush this house.

The men of the Tyranny glanced at each other, and

Charlotte knew they were caving. She concentrated on reining in the magic, though a few more sparkles fell to the floor and glittered at her feet. The rush of the magic was insane, and she knew why her uncle loved it so much. Why hadn't he shown her more of his own? She was sure there was a lot he could've taught her. They needed to find him. She refused to entertain any thoughts of his demise – even Penumbra couldn't be that cruel.

"You really give us no choice, then," Orrick said, his voice heavy. "But understand that we are only giving them to you out of duress – I would not work with you under any other circumstances."

"Fine by me," Charlotte told him. She considered something. "And I want the magical items that you use on the ponies, like the whip and that old rag."

"Now listen here, young lady, we're already giving you—"

"I know." She nodded, stopping Orrick's rant. "I don't care. The only things that matter to me are stopping Penumbra, uniting the Flying Ponies, and finding my uncle." Venom laced through her words. "Now tell me where the horses and items are."

24

*B*lack approached the old barn with caution. After eating and a long night of not much rest, he'd volunteered to go get Eidolon by himself; the bay pinto mare was unpredictable, and she didn't like Dante. He pushed open the doors and the hair on the back of his neck stood up. "Easy, girl," he said, his voice soft and cajoling. "It's me, Sully," he added.

"Sullivan." The word was nothing but a whisper, and it made his heart pump harder. Eidolon was not only touched in the head, but she was wild. When the ponies would run around after the park shut down, and only the glowing lights of the carousel illuminated the darkness, she was the hardest to convince to get back on the platform.

"Yeah, Eidolon, it's me. Come on out," he said. Gone was the sweetness in his voice. "I'm taking you to some of the other ponies." He had Hawker outside, waiting. The grey war horse had wanted to come inside, but Black had thought meeting the mare alone would be better. *I should've listened to him,* he thought.

The shadows moved, and the mare stepped out from them. She was across the barn, against the far wall, but even at that distance, he could feel the anger rolling off her. He started toward her. There was no time to be afraid.

As he drew closer to the mare, he could see the whites of her eyes, and the way she pawed the ground, her elegant head and neck tense. "I'm not here to hurt you," he said. There was no telling what sorts of things the Tyranny had done to the horses in their possession, given Roswald's proclivity toward abuse. "See?" He held out his hand.

Eidolon was suddenly motionless, one foreleg suspended in air. Without warning, she attacked.

Black threw up his hands and jumped to the side. The mare barely missed him. She swapped directions and charged again. This time, stumbling over a pitchfork hidden beneath some old hay, he wasn't quick enough to avoid a blow from one of her hind feet as she dashed past. Grunting with pain, his right knee blazing with heat, he reached down for the tool and hefted it.

Eidolon stopped, ears swept forward, watching him as he watched her. "Come on, girl," he said. "Don't do this. I want to take you to the other Flying Ponies."

"Flying Ponies?" She tipped her head, a stray sunbeam shining through a crack in the wall behind her, bathing her in yellow.

She doesn't know what she is. She doesn't remember. An unexpected swell of sympathy swept through him. "Do you remember Coney Island?" he asked. "Or the carousel?" Hopefully something he said would jog her memory. She remembered him, at least.

The mare paced away from him, and he let her go. His knee was throbbing now, and bending down, he rubbed it but kept his eyes on the horse. She was muttering to herself, and he frowned. She was as off her rocker as Dreadful was. A sharp pang went through him. How was the bay stallion holding up with Penumbra? Was the dapple grey being nice to his three captives?

Eidolon whipped around and raced back to him. Drawing up close to him with a toss of her head, she said, "I remember. I was part of the Flying Ponies!"

"And you still are," he said, his voice gentle. He held out his hand. "I'm going to take you to Hawker, Czarina and Ranee. They'll be glad to see you." Or not; Ranee had made it clear she disliked the high-strung bay pinto.

She snorted. "Ranee does not like me."

"No, but the other two do. Come on." He was hoping she wouldn't be temperamental about leaving. The mare followed him to the doors, but when he stepped outside, she refused. "Eidolon, come on," he said, trying not to be irritated with her. After all, he had to remember that the horses had only lately been able to access their full magic, too. The barrier had kept them from using all of it.

A thought occurred to him, and he paused while waiting for the pinto to follow him out. Was that why Penumbra had gone dark? *All that stored magical energy, and no way to fully use it for all those years...* The thought trailed off. Perhaps the magic had driven them to a point of madness. *But only some of them are acting that way, not the whole herd. So why is that?* Would the journal his grandfather had given them offer any clues? He'd meant to look at it earlier, but they'd been busy.

The mare stuck her head out, and Hawker whinnied to her and trotted over. The stallion lowered his head to touch his nose to Eidolon's, and she jerked away with a squeal. "You don't recognize me, Eidolon?" Hawker asked.

She snorted. "You are a Flying Pony," she said.

"Hawker," he told her.

She stepped out of the barn, and Black swung the door shut behind her. Now, if she would follow him and Hawker back to the house in the woods, he'd be all set. "Eidolon, I need you to follow us," he told her. He mounted the grey stallion and the mare pawed at the ground.

"I will trust you," she said, but there was a thread of doubt in her voice, and Black wondered what harm the Tyranny had done to her. It would've been easy – the ponies hadn't been fully alive until the barrier was lifted, and they couldn't have defended themselves. The thought made him see hazy red, and he blinked it away. Now was the not the time for anger. It was the time for finding and reuniting the Flying Ponies.

"Thank you," he said. He turned Hawker. The grey took four long running strides and leapt into the air. It was such a bizarre sensation; the air was chilled, yet Black was warm due to the pony's magic. Eidolon watched them go for a moment, and then jumped into the air, and he could see her delight as she bucked and whirled before coming up beside Hawker.

He hoped the others were having good luck finding their horses, too. The decision to split up into different teams had been Charlotte's; she and Jared had ridden off on Czarina, leaving Dante and Rory to take Ranee. The first three horses they'd decided to retrieve were Eidolon, Chevalier, and Contessa. Czarina was friends with Contessa, who was a sweet palomino mare. Chevalier and Dante had always gotten along, so it made sense that he volunteered to find the other charger.

As they flew through the lavender sky, Black tried to enjoy the magic. He wished he could access it so he could help out more, but that wasn't in his wheel house like it was Dante's. The best he could do was support Charlotte and her family in their quest to find the ponies.

Hawker dove down, and Black could make out a small town. The wind was coming up, and it was driving flecks of orange through the sky around him. Beautiful, and yet dangerous. Eidolon stayed right beside them, and he was happy that they were getting some of the herd back together.

Two hours later the horses swooped down low over the forest, and he saw the mansion. Relief spread through him; it had been a long time since he'd ridden this much, and never so long on a wooden horse. He'd be glad to stretch his legs. They landed in the yard, and the door opened.

"You got her." Danny's eyes lit up as he stepped out onto the porch. "Can I ride her?"

"Not just yet," Black said, and when Danny's face fell, added, "She didn't remember that she was a Flying Pony. I want her to have some time with the others before anyone gets on her."

"She didn't remember? Is that weird?"

"Not really. Most of their magic was locked away too, because of the barrier. She wasn't really alive until your sister lifted it, and her memories are fuzzy." Black watched the pinto mare prance around the yard, sniffing and snorting. "And she's a little touched in the head, even on a good day."

"Great, another Dreadful," Danny said, rolling his eyes. "Just what we need."

"You sound a lot like Rory," Black told him. "That's not necessarily a good thing, you know?"

Danny scowled. "I'm not – well, okay maybe a little." He shrugged. "I'm okay with that. But I like to read, and he doesn't, so that's something."

Black grinned. "Yeah, that is something. I like to read, too, mostly mysteries."

"I like those too." Danny came down the steps. "Do you really think we can beat Penumbra? I mean, it doesn't seem like it should be hard. He's a wooden horse. But he's pretty strong."

"He is strong." And wild and unstable and dangerous. Black wasn't sure what to tell the younger boy. That he wanted to keep up the Flynn family's spirits was obvious. But could he, with them knowing what they were up against? "I just don't know," he added. "We can't give up yet, though. Charlotte is learning to use her magic, and that will help."

"You don't want her to use it, though." Danny was staring off toward the two horses, who were talking to one another across the yard. "Why?"

"If she can't control it, she could give in to it," Black said, feeling heavy in his chest. "She could turn to the darker side of it, like your uncle did."

"True." Danny was silent for a few moments. "But she's tough. I know people don't think so. I know how they treated her at school, like she was some weird geeky girl." He exhaled a breath. "She loves the horses. She's going to get them all back."

"I think so, too." *And she'll have all of us to back her up.*

Charlotte swung down off Czarina and approached the large shed. Rust bled down the white sides, but the hinges on the door were shiny. She slipped the key from her pocket and slid it into the lock on the chain. Jared came up next to her, but remained quiet. He'd been quiet the entire ride here. Pocketing the key again, she pulled the door open.

In the faint light she could make out the shape of a horse. "Contessa? Hi," she said, keeping her voice low. "I'm Charlotte. I'm here to take to take you back to the Flying Ponies."

The horse didn't speak, so she moved closer to her. In an instant, the mare charged at her. Charlotte threw her hands out on instinct, and purple magic exploded around her. The mare drew up short. "I'm here to help you," Charlotte said. Why was the mare reacting this way? Didn't she know who she was? What she was? *Maybe she doesn't. She's been locked away, all alone, for decades. The five the mob had were together, so they had someone to talk to.* She thought about people who were kept in solitary confinement, and how lonely they became. *And look at Dreadful – he was certifiably nuts! He still is.* She was just used to his brand of crazy now.

She turned back to the door. "Czarina, come here," she said. The brown mare trotted over. "Talk to Contessa. She doesn't seem to remember who she is."

Czarina walked into the shed, and Charlotte glanced at Jared. He seemed uncomfortable with this whole thing; did she confront him now, or wait? The two mares were murmuring quietly, so she said, "What's going on with you?"

He started. "Nothing."

"Right." She kept her gaze on the mares.

"I'm worried," he said. "What if Penumbra takes these horses, too?"

"We fight to get them back and beat him."

"The bridle was a joke."

"Does that matter?"

"It was supposed to make whichever horse wore it stronger." His jaw was clenched.

She could feel anger sliding through her. "So it didn't work. Dante said there was a chance it wouldn't. Maybe Penumbra was too tough for Oriflamme to beat. I don't know. But I *do* know that once we have the other Flying Ponies together, we have a chance of winning. And I'm going with that."

He said nothing, and she walked into the shed. "How's it going?"

Czarina turned her head to look at her. "She remembers, but she is afraid."

Charlotte stepped close to the palomino mare and touched the side of her face. "It's okay to be afraid, Contessa. I'm afraid, too. But we have to be tough. We have to be brave, because Penumbra is going to try and wreck the world if we don't stop him." Thunder pealed overhead, as if punctuating the point.

The golden mare nodded her head. She was pretty; her bridle was blue and her saddle brown, with red and pink trappings. "Penumbra is a good horse," she said. "We have much magic in us, and it has been locked away for so long. He has lost himself to it."

"That's what I think, too," Charlotte told her. "We need to go. You can meet up with the other horses we have." She left the shed and the two mares followed. Charlotte swung up onto Contessa, leaving Czarina for Jared. Her brother mounted without a word, and the two mares took off into the pink and gold sky.

They were now one horse stronger, and she assumed Black and Dante would come through with the ones they'd been sent to retrieve. They still had more to find after that, and then they'd have enough to seek out Penumbra and confront him. She rubbed Contessa's neck, glad the mare had trusted Czarina enough to come with them. She didn't understand Jared's reticence, and that bothered her, but at least they were working together.

Once they landed in the yard at the house, and their mares were greeted by Hawker and Eidolon, Charlotte and Jared hurried into the house. Gavin greeted them; he'd been keeping an eye on the other two horses from a window in the living room.

"Is it safe for them to be out there?" she asked her younger brother.

"I think so. I've been watching for Desolates," he said. "Was Contessa easy to find and convince?"

"She was. Dante isn't back yet?"

"No."

That worried her. "Where's Black?"

"I don't know. He might be in the kitchen."

Charlotte nodded and headed that way. She met him as he was coming from the dining room and stopped. He smiled at her, but she didn't smile back. "Was Eidolon easy to work with?" she asked as he stopped in front of her.

"She didn't remember who she was at first," he said. "She can be wild, but she seemed okay once she saw Hawker. How about Contessa?"

"Same thing. Czarina had to talk to her, and then she was okay. Contessa told me she thinks Penumbra has gone nuts because the magic was locked away in them for so long. He's losing himself to it."

"I think so, too. I think the horses that were kept away by themselves forgot things, too, because there was no one else there to keep them sane." Black frowned. "Are you okay? You're tense."

"Jared is uptight about something."

269

"Think he's still angry about Oliver?"

"I don't know. I don't care. We're not going looking for Oliver, anyway. We can take Penumbra down by ourselves." Courage bubbled through her. "I know we can."

He grinned, but it looked like he was hiding something behind it. "Once Dante gets back, we'll split up again and go get the others."

"Then we'll get some rest and go look for the ponies Penumbra's leading." She was certain Dreadful, Oriflamme and Compatriot weren't going along with him.

They heard the front door open, and then the noise of multiple hooves on the marble floor. Charlotte turned and ran down the long hallway. Dante was shutting the door; when he turned around, he flashed a grin at her. "And another one," he announced. "I brought them all in; I spotted seven Desolates about a half-mile from here. Don't need to serve up Flying Ponies to them."

Charlotte focused on the newest horse. Chevalier was a beautiful black stallion covered with shining silver chain mail. A single unicorn horn marked his headpiece like Oriflamme's. He was speaking with Hawker while the mares stood in their own group. Again, they had six; soon, they would add eight to that number and could throw down against Penumbra.

"What now? We going after the others?" Rory asked her.

"We will, but I think we should rest first. I'm tired, and I'm sure you guys are, too. Plus I could stand to eat." She wished she had unlimited endurance, but that wasn't the case.

Helen gave a brisk nod. "Follow me to the kitchen, everyone." She put her arm around Danny's shoulder and steered him toward the hall when he didn't seem keen to move. "Even you," she told him.

"Aw, I just wanna hang with the horses," he said, but let himself be guided down the hall.

Charlotte watched her family, Dante, and Symphony follow them, and then walked over to the horses. Chevalier dipped his head to touch her outstretched hand. "Hi," she said, admiring the way his armor shone under the chandelier.

"Hello," he said. "Hawker tells me you were the Capall, until Penumbra stripped you of its title."

"Yeah," she said, nodding. "He's running berserk now. That's why I need you guys to help me stop him."

"We will do our best," Chevalier told her. Charlotte nodded and walked over to the mares, keeping her eyes on the bay pinto. Eidolon was talking with the others, tossing her head for emphasis. She stopped when she noticed Charlotte watching her.

"So you're the one who lifted the barrier," Eidolon said, moving closer to her. She had grey eyes that gave Charlotte an unsettled feeling. The mare reached out her nose and sniffed at her jeans and sweatshirt, drawing back with a snort. "You possess magic, too."

"I do. I'm an archimage."

The mare rolled her eyes. "So was Oliver, for all the good it did him." Before Charlotte could ask what she meant, the pinto turned away and went back to speaking with the other horses.

Black was waiting in the hallway for her. "I think it would be wise to—"

The house let out a roar, and the entire structure shook. A couple of framed pictures fell to the floor, their glass shattering. Charlotte and Black exchanged wide-eyed looks and ran back to the foyer. She noticed he was limping. They could hear the others coming behind them. The horses were huddled together in the center of the foyer, their heads up and ears alert. Something pounded on the front door, and the house growled.

Charlotte went the windows and looked out. "Oh no," she breathed, her heart rate picking up. "Those Desolates Dante saw are here already."

"Time to show them who the boss is," Rory said.

"Not so fast." Helen's voice rang out above the din of the house. "There's no reason to go out there unless we have to."

"I'm with her," Black said, nodding. The house shook and the chandelier swung above them, casting weird shadows across the walls.

"Why are they drawn here, when there's magic all over the place now?" Marta asked. She stood beside Hawker, one hand on his neck.

"They're drawn to the ponies and this house because their magic is so pure," Dante told her. He came to stand next to her, his eyes on the windows. "These creatures, the ones in this forest, fed on the wisps of magic the ponies and house gave off. They were people who could still see smidgens of magic here and there, but they were unable to handle the pure magic. At some point, it overwhelmed them, and turned them." His voice was soft, and his gaze flicked to Black for an instant. "There were others that became consumed by the magic as well. We had a few that turned on the Island, and had to be taken somewhere else."

"Like where?" Gavin asked.

"Anywhere away from people," Dante said. He strode forward to look out the windows. "Symphony, darling, I don't suppose you could sing them to sleep."

"Would that work?" Jared asked.

"No," Symphony said. "We tried it on the Island, on – well, it doesn't matter." There was a small hesitation in her voice that caught Charlotte's attention.

"Who did you try to use it on?" she asked, turning around to face the singer. When Symphony started to shrug, she added, "No, I want to know." She suspected there had been someone close to Black who had been turned into one, and now had to wonder if that person was who they tried to pacify with the Songbird's voice.

"I don't think that's relevant now," Dante told her, his voice firm.

"My grandmother," Black cut in before Charlotte could repeat her request. Charlotte looked at him, and saw sorrow in his eyes. "Her name was Greta."

"Oh, Black," Charlotte whispered. She wanted to offer some kind of comfort, but he'd already turned his shoulder to her and was staring out at the lost creatures. "I'm so sorry."

He nodded. "It is what it is," he said.

That was true, but still. She wasn't sure how else to offer sympathy, if he would even want it. One of the creatures thumped on the door, and the house went dark. No one moved. The house was silent, the only noise coming from outside, where the seven Desolates had gathered on the porch and were beating their fists against the siding.

"Do we fight them now?" Jared asked.

"We may have to drive them back from the house," Dante said. "Sully? What do you think?"

Before Black could answer, they heard thumps on the roof, drawing their attention overhead. The roof creaked and the house let out a pathetic groan. Charlotte's magic swelled through her, and she forced herself to stay calm. She walked to the front door and put her hand on the handle. Everyone was still looking up at the ceiling; she wasn't sure anyone had even noticed her movement.

She opened the door and stepped out.

The monsters stared at her, hands suspended in the air, inches from the walls of the mansion. Resolve welled through her, and she called forth the purple magic. It came at once, exploding in a cloud of sparkles and power, and the two creatures closest to her wailed and fell back, one of them falling down the stairs. A wave of her hand (she'd seen Uncle Baron twisting his hands in intricate designs, but didn't know how to copy them or what they did) sent another ball of magic at the two to her left, and they screeched and clawed at their faces.

She ran past the two on the stairs and into the yard. Three Desolates stood on top of the lowest part of the roof and were ripping up pieces of it. "Hey!" she yelled. She sent a wave of magic spilling out toward them, furious that these things would attempt to harm her home. The house was starting to shake; she could see ripples in the glass of the windows, and thrust her hands up at the monsters.

The magic tore into them and they fell down. Charlotte grimaced; one of them had put a leg through the roof. She heard shouting from inside the house but didn't give pause to it. One of the creatures got to its feet and shoved a hunk of tile into its mouth. Another burst of magic smashed into the three. She hoped to knock them off.

As she concentrated on her pulsing magic, something grabbed her left arm. She screamed as bitter cold swept through her body, and looked down at the pasty hand of one of the Desolates. Jerking her arm away, she watched the monster's face twist while its body started to glow with a purplish cast. *My magic,* she thought, remembering. *It absorbed some of my magic!* It lunged for her and she thrust her right hand out. A mini cyclone of magic hit it square in the chest and it stumbled backward. From what Dante had said, all of them were drawing from the house's magic and probably hers, too, but this one had taken directly from her by touch. Her left arm was turning numb, and she moved away from the Desolate. Throwing a wild look up at the roof, she saw the other three had commenced tearing into it again. Was her magic making them stronger? But how else was she going to stop them? The magic was her only weapon.

Hawker burst into the yard from around the house, the other five horses charging along behind him. He slid to a stop by the Desolate who had touched her, whirled around, and kicked it with all his might using his hind feet. The monster careened off its feet and fell to the wet earth.

"Take the ones on the roof!" Ranee yelled as she swept

by. The big grey mare leapt into the air and took down another of the monsters.

Charlotte turned her attention back to the roof. *Should I climb up there?* Her left arm was now dead weight, and she realized she wouldn't be able to. But she could still direct her magic, and she let fly another purple cyclone. It swirled up over the house and wrapped itself around the Desolates. One of them toppled forward, and fell off the porch roof. The other two were jumping up and down on the house, and with a crash, fell through. Terror seized her and for a moment, she couldn't move.

The front door opened and her family spilled onto the porch. She ran for them, only to have the monster that had fallen off the roof leap in front of her. Furious, she yelled and slammed into it with her magic, forcing it to its knees. The magic swarmed over the creature and it howled and writhed. For a second, she thought to let it consume the beast. *You are not your uncle.* The words came unbidden and she reached out with her soul, pulling the magic away from the Desolate.

Running past it, she jumped up the steps until she reached her siblings. "Are you guys okay?" she asked.

"Did you see them fall into the house?" Marta's voice was shrill.

"I did." Charlotte looked at Jared. "We can't let them destroy it!" She glanced at everyone, and added, "Where are the others?"

"Black sent us out here, said it was safer," Gavin said. "He stayed in there with Dante, Helen, and Symphony." His fists were clenched, and there was steel resolution in his eyes. "We have to get the monsters out."

Czarina ran up to the porch, her brown mane wind-blown. "Stay out of the house!"

They could hear crashes coming from inside, and Charlotte pushed past Rory and Danny to get to the door. She glanced back once; the ponies had the other Desolates on the run. She shoved the door open and went in.

One of the Desolates immediately lunged at her, a stark craving look on its ashen, sunken face. She hit it hard with a blast of magic. A surge of arctic pain shot down her left arm and she forced herself to pay attention to the two large creatures in the foyer. Dante and Black were using a baseball bat and broom to drive the other one toward the door. Symphony and Helen were nowhere to be seen.

The creature closest to her leapt up and grabbed the chandelier. Charlotte ducked away as it came crashing down, glass shattering and spilling across the floor in a flash flood of broken shards. Black glanced her way for a mere second before resuming his attack on the Desolate he was helping Dante with. Why were these two stronger than the ones outside? Were they sucking magic from the house? Black had told her the creatures were starving for more magic to sustain themselves; the mansion was rife with ancient magic just like the Flying Ponies. She grabbed an umbrella from the stand in the corner and whacked the monster near her with it, no longer wanting to use her archimage power in case she was only making them tougher.

"Get the door!" Dante yelled. Charlotte sidestepped her creature and reached for the handle. The monster swiped at her, narrowly missing her right arm. She flung the door open.

"Look out!" she hollered at her family. Jared shooed everyone off the porch as she sprung the umbrella open in the creature's face and it stumbled backward, toward the doorway. She kicked out, hitting it in the groin, and it bellowed and fell back further. "Get out!" she yelled and kicked it again, adrenaline mixing with the magic in her veins and giving her an eruption of strength. The Desolate flew backward, landing on the steps on its back.

"Move!" Black shouted a moment before he grabbed her around the waist and hauled her out of the path of the other monster. It crashed right through the windows to the right of the door, splintering the wood casings around them and showering them with debris. It fell to its knees on the porch before lurching upright again and turning around.

"Back, beastie," Dante warned, clutching a bat as he moved to confront it again. The house let out a great long sigh, and shook hard. Pictures along the hallway leading toward the back of the house fell off the walls. A hissing noise rose from under the marble floor.

Charlotte tore herself from Black's arms and raced into Baron's study. Rounding the desk, she yanked open the drawers until she found Oliver's journal. She snatched it up and sprinted from the room even as the house sent undulating waves through the floor beneath her. Three Desolates were in the house now, and she realized the mansion was trying to fend for itself. It heaved the floor upward under the monsters and they flew into the air only to come crashing back down. One went through the floor, and they could hear it wailing as it fell into the darkness of the basement.

As she watched, horrorstruck, two more of the creatures shambled through the gaping hole in the outside wall. *Where are the ponies? I thought they were driving the Desolates away?* Sharp pains shot through her arm, and she gritted her teeth. She couldn't think about that now. Her home was at stake. She saw the umbrella on the other side of the room and ran for it.

A shriek echoed through the old house as she reached the umbrella. The floor tipped beneath her and sent her sprawling across it. She hit her chin on the marble and tasted the bitter iron of blood in her mouth. Twisting onto her side, she reached out and snagged the umbrella and journal. A Desolate loomed over her, leaning down with its grotesque hands grasping at her hair.

"Get back!" Contessa charged in, the golden mare rearing and striking the creature in its face. Charlotte scrambled out of the way, clutching her weapon and the book. Czarina and Chevalier came leaping into the room, the black charger lowering his head and gouging the Desolate in the back. The monster squealed and tried to turn on him. Chevalier spun and kicked out, and the creature sailed through the air, landing hard and cracking the floor beneath it. It too disappeared into the black hole.

"Get on!" Contessa commanded, turning her head to look at Charlotte. "We have to go!"

"We can't!" she said. "They'll destroy the house!" Blood dripped from the scrape on her chin and her left arm was spasming, but they couldn't run. Not now. Not when the house needed them.

Chevalier nipped at her arm. "She said *get on*! The house is going to come down on top of you!" The charger jabbed his horned head at her when she didn't mount the palomino.

"He's right, the house is losing!" Black said from behind her. She turned and saw the resolute dejection on his face.

"There're more Desolates coming!" Ranee yelled as she thundered up onto the porch. "Everyone out!"

Charlotte's heart was breaking. No, they hadn't been in this house long. But this was *home* now. How could they leave it? The house would be torn apart. It was already breaking at the corners of the walls as another Desolate stepped through the door. She tucked the journal into the front pocket of her hoodie and went to the staircase that led up to the left. If they had to leave, if this was it, there was one other thing she needed.

The picture of the carousel was hanging by one corner when she reached it. She took it carefully into her hands, the crook of the umbrella hanging from her arm, and turned to go back downstairs.

A bright light shot past her and circled back. "Sunny!" she cried. She hadn't seen the little bug since that night in the basement. Sunny zipped around her head and darted down the stairs. Charlotte took the stairs in twos as she raced after her little friend.

Contessa was waiting for her; everyone else except the creatures had left. Charlotte mounted the mare and the palomino galloped toward the hole in the wall. With a leap she was through and clattered down the porch. Sunny buzzed in the air ahead of them.

"Wait!" Charlotte yelled and Contessa spun around to face the old house. Charlotte pressed the carousel picture to her chest as she let the umbrella fall to the ground. All of the Desolates were inside now, and she could see four more stalking out of the woods to the left of the yard. The windows in the living room burst outward, glass catching in the purple grass.

"It's going to collapse in on itself," Contessa told her, her voice soft. "I'm sorry."

There was nothing they could do now but watch. The house gave a loud moan and they could see it buckling. The Desolates were keening as the place folded in on itself. Charlotte wanted to look away, to look anywhere else, but the terrible sight held her, and she stared as the structure gave way and fell to its demise.

They reconvened at Whimsies. The four Desolates from the woods had turned on them, and they'd taken the ponies and the Cadillac and run. Black leaned his head back against the wall and closed his eyes. Not since losing his grandmother to the devastation of the magic had he felt this lost. The house was gone. The Desolates there would suck every last bit of the magic from the wreck and feed off it for months. And on top of that, his right knee was throbbing.

"Question."

Marta's sharp voice rang through his head and he forced his eyes open. "What?"

"If the barrier hid most of the magic, why didn't those Desolates just die? They had nothing to live on," she said. The left pane of her glasses was cracked, giving her a mad scientist glamour.

Black rolled his head to the right. "Romano? You tell her." He didn't want to talk about magic.

Dante was dour-faced. "Once they'd turned, there was just enough to keep them going. There haven't been any new Desolates since the barrier went up. What you've seen, the ones in the woods, have existed since before that." He grunted and added, "Now, what with all the magic unleashed, and strong enough for people to see it and believe in it, if they choose to, any number of people could succumb to it. All it takes is someone with a penchant for it, an inkling of magic in their blood, and a desire to play around with it, for them to go that way."

"What about Charlotte, Uncle Baron, Symphony and Helen? And you?" Jared asked. He was skulking around by a display of miniature dolls that gave Black the creeps. "Why haven't any of you turned then?"

"Oh, we could," Dante said, his voice low. "If we were to give into the magic enough, let it fill us all the way up and let it control us, it would." He shrugged. "It's a struggle." His eyes drifted to Charlotte for a moment.

"Where did Symphony and Helen go?" Charlotte asked. She was rubbing her left arm in a dispassionate way that drew Black's attention. Had she hurt herself? She'd had blood on her chin from her fall in the house, but that had been wiped away.

"They went to the basement," Jared said. "They were leaving, taking one of the doors. I don't know where."

"Why? Why did they run?" Rory was fiddling with a display of strange flat discs.

Black had an idea of where the two had gone, but it wouldn't be a popular assumption, and he said nothing, instead waiting for Dante to speak. But Romano seemed as reluctant as he was, and finally Black muttered, "They went to Oliver."

The air in the room went cold and still. Dante looked over at him, unease in his eyes, and Black exhaled a long breath.

"Are you serious? You think they went to *him*? What would be the point?" Jared asked. Anger strained his voice.

"I don't believe it. Mrs. Trudeau wouldn't desert us," Danny said.

"That doesn't matter." Charlotte's voice was piercing. "We still need to go get those other horses from the Tyranny."

"You honestly think Orrick gave us the right locations." Gavin's voice was threaded with unbelief. "Just because he gave up three of them doesn't mean he did the rest. The Tyranny probably went and took them."

"I'm with him," Dante said, nodding. "Orrick knew he only had to give you enough to get out of the house, without you coming back right away. So three locations were right, and the rest are false. I'd bet on it."

Charlotte's eyes narrowed. "You're wrong. How would Orrick have known which three we'd choose first? We chose them at random." She crossed her arms. "The locations are right." Unfolding her arms, she went to Hawker, who bent his head to nudge her shoulder. "I'm going to find the others. The rest of you can stay here and fret over Helen and Symphony!"

"Wait." Black pushed away from the wall. Enough was enough. "Charlotte's right. The Tyranny had no idea what horses we'd go after first. We need to concentrate on the locations they gave us and go get the others. Once we have them, we confront Penumbra." Command and ire rang through his voice. This was no time for self-doubts.

"What about our house?" Rory's question halted all conversation. "I mean, we let that go? Where are we gonna live now?"

"The townhouse," Charlotte said. She turned away from Hawker to face them. "It's our house as much as it is Uncle Baron's."

"I agree," Jared said. He was frowning at Rory, who was still fiddling with the discs.

"Is there anything here we can use?" Gavin asked, looking over at Dante. "You said this place has lots of magic in it."

Dante barked out a short laugh. "It did once, yes. Now?" He waved a hand around. "Not everything here is magical; most of it's just tricks and shams. One had to know what they were looking for to see the *real* thing."

Orrick had cleaned him out; Black could see the truth of that in his old friend's eyes. It was of his own doing, though – if Dante hadn't sided with Orrick against Charlotte, he might've been able to keep all his magic objects. It wasn't *just* the store his friend was referencing, Black knew. Dante Romano was mostly tricks and shams, too.

"We should go to the house, get some food and rest, and find the missing horses." Charlotte put a hand on Hawker's neck. The light grey stallion bobbed his head in agreement.

"Good a plan as anything else," Black agreed. Once outside the store, he mounted Eidolon, wanting to keep a closer tab on the bay pinto mare since they were headed into the city. Charlotte was on Czarina. Dante elected to drive the Caddy; Jared went with him. Marta chose Contessa, Gavin got on Ranee, and Danny was trying to choose between Chevalier and Hawker when Rory simply climbed into Hawker's saddle and grinned at him.

The Flying Ponies took to the sky. Protected by their magic, their riders didn't feel the changing wind currents or the blue rain drops that were starting to fall. October was usually set aflame by reds and oranges and yellows; this year, it was brimming with every color beneath the sun. Black tried to enjoy it. Magic on Coney Island had never been threatening. It had simply existed everywhere back then, and people had appreciated it. *People were the threat, not the magic.* What was true then was true now too, except for the horses. The magic had corrupted some of them; he had to wonder how long before it corrupted the rest, if it did. What would they do then? Could they destroy the Flying Ponies if needed?

He glanced at Charlotte. She was leaning over Czarina's neck, grim determination making her face brittle. Why had things gone this way? What he would give to have met her under different circumstances! He turned his gaze away and concentrated on riding Eidolon. There was no sense in wishing for things that could never happen. This was their reality, and he'd have to make do. It was what he'd done his whole life, trying to make the best out of situations that left him reeling.

They reached the townhouse in fifteen minutes. It sat atop a small hill, along a winding road leading up out of the bowels of the city. The horses set down just outside the garage, and Charlotte ran around back to grab the hidden key to let them in. Black had never visited the house; any time he'd been called to the city, he met Baron in one of his warehouses filled with crates of things that were never explained. It was another mystery in a long line of them surrounding the man and his industry.

An antique black and yellow BMW sat in the cavernous garage. They left the horses there and proceeded into the house and down the hall to the kitchen. Black watched the family rummage around in the fridge and cupboards. Charlotte was favoring her left arm; she attempted to reach up and open a door, but winced and turned away. His concern piqued, he walked over to her and touched her shoulder.

When her eyes met his, his heart fell. Something had happened, all right. Without a word, he took her hand and led her out into the big dining room. "Tell me what happened," he said once they were alone.

She grimaced. "I don't want to."

Worry started to bleed into his system. "Did a Desolate touch you?" When she didn't answer, his breath caught in his lungs and he couldn't breathe for a few seconds. Her skin wasn't turning ashy yet. Her eyes were still blue flavored with purple. "Does your arm hurt?" he asked once he could speak.

"It's numb." She wandered away from him and over to a huge cabinet with glass doors embossed with flowers. "These tea sets belonged to my great-great-grandmother," she said. Her voice was low and raw, like she was trying not to cry. Black didn't go to her, though – she wouldn't want his sympathy. "I wish I could meet her." She glanced out the window. "Was she nice?"

"She was lovely," he said. "And I know what you're thinking, but she died a long time ago."

"You thought that about Oliver."

She had him there. He wished she could meet Adara too. The chances of both of them being alive were probably nil, but he did have to wonder. A gust of wind slammed into the house, but the structure didn't move. It was as unyielding as Baron himself was. *What did Penumbra do with him? Is he still alive?* He knew the Flynns thought the carousel horses wouldn't be that cruel. After all, they were objects made for amusement. His time in the world, however, had shown him that even things built for enjoyment could become instruments of death. With primal magic raging through their wooden bodies, there was no telling what the horses were capable of now.

"Am I going to turn?"

He wasn't sure how to answer. "I don't know." His voice was heavy with things that they needed to talk about, yet couldn't. Not now, not when the magic was rampaging and uncontrolled, and she'd been marked by a monster. "Do you feel different?"

She considered. "My magic is cold now," she said.

That wasn't good. He didn't say that, though. It was her magic; of course she knew it wasn't good.

"If we can't find the other horses, we still need to make a stand against Penumbra." Her voice was a whisper.

"I know."

The house around them was quiet. There was so much Black wanted to say to her, but nothing that would make it better. There was no sense in trying to convince her things would be okay, that they would be all right. She knew they wouldn't. She drifted toward the kitchen. He let her go, and stayed in the dining room.

When it was all over, and he knew which way things had gone, there would be time to talk to Charlotte about where their relationship was going, if it was going anywhere. He hoped it was. He hoped she could fend off the creature trying to take over her. There was nothing he could do about it, nothing Romano could do. They'd tried before and failed.

*T*wo hours later, Charlotte sat in the library on a dark leather couch and stared at the bookcases that lined the room. Her siblings were all upstairs, presumably sleeping. She should've been too, but the growing numbness in her body kept her awake. Black hadn't said anything about it; that struck her as odd, because he was normally protective, but she hadn't wanted to bring it up either. If Dante knew he was keeping silent.

The magic lay coiled in her veins, but little tendrils snaked here and there through her body. With each breath she took, they spread a little further. At least it wasn't painful. It was just cold. Her eyes roved over the titles of the books on the shelves, nothing drawing her immediate attention. Uncle Baron had quite the collection, though. He was interested in all kinds of literature, from the macabre to historical, but a lot of his books were nonfiction.

She got up off the couch and wandered over to the

furthest case. The books on this one were old, some of their covers worn enough the titles were unreadable. She traced the tips of her fingers over them, not really paying attention to what she was doing.

The door opened and Black stepped in. He didn't see her right away; he shut the door and sat down on the couch. She watched him for a few seconds before clearing her throat. He jerked and turned toward her.

"I didn't realize you were downstairs," he said, frowning. "You should be resting."

"I know. I can't sleep."

"Your arm?" Concern spread across his face, but he remained seated.

"A little," she said. "I'm worried we won't get the other horses in time and we'll have to face Penumbra with who we have." There was no sense in trying to hide her worry from him. She didn't want to be anything like Uncle Baron, who never let anyone in.

Black nodded but was quiet. What was he thinking? Was he worried about that too, or was he worried that she would turn into a Desolate in front of him? She could feel the magic squirming in her veins, pushing back against the cold that was trickling through her muscles in her left shoulder.

"Why haven't I turned yet?"

His eyes snapped to her, and she saw fear in them, but didn't take the question back. He took a breath and said, "You're an archimage – your magic is holding it at bay, I guess." His voice was low and washed out with melancholy, and she pursed her lips.

"What's wrong?" she asked. She didn't move closer to him; if he was choosing to keep his distance from her, she wasn't going to invade his space.

"Wrong?" He sighed and sat back. "A Desolate touched you, we lost the mansion, we don't know if we'll get to the horses first before Penumbra does, and we have to somehow stop him and his herd." He made a gesture in the air. "That about sums up *what's wrong*." There was no irritation or anger in his voice, though – only weariness.

"We're going to beat him." If he wasn't going to bolster her spirits, then she had to.

He glanced at her. "You should try to get some rest."

Anger started to simmer in her heart. "You can't give up hope, Black. If we can turn Penumbra, convince him to be good again—"

"I know. I know it's still possible, but you do realize what we're up against, yeah?" He pushed himself up and walked over to her. He kept a few feet in between them, though, probably for his safety.

"I do. But I'm not afraid."

He smiled. It didn't reflect in his eyes. "I know. You're one of the bravest people I know."

Not *girl*, but people. She smiled back. "I'm not going to turn into one of those things. I can feel my magic fighting the cold. And we'll find the horses first. I have faith."

"In what?" He crossed his arms over his chest.

She took a step closer to him, and he parried with one back. "You, Dante, my siblings, our horses, and myself. I can use my magic to fight Penumbra, to make him see he can turn back to the good." She'd said it so many times internally that she believed what she was telling him, even though worry ate at the edges of her confidence.

He wanted to believe, too. She could see the struggle in his eyes. He wanted to support her, but didn't want to raise her hopes. "We both need some sleep if we're going horse hunting tomorrow." He turned away.

"There're rooms upstairs you can sleep in."

He shook his head. "I'd rather be on the first floor." He went back to the couch and lay down. "I'll see you in the morning."

Irritated with his dismissal but unwilling to argue, she left the library and shut the door. The house was stalwart and silent. She missed the mutterings and murmurings of her home in the woods. Funny, what you could get used to. She had been scared of that house at first. *I was scared of a lot of things.*

The door behind her opened and she turned to face Black as he stepped out. "I thought you were resting," she said.

"I thought you were going upstairs." His voice was low.

"I was headed that way." She bit her lip. "Black, what's really wrong? I know what we're up against. But you're being weird."

He chuckled with no warmth. "Weird?"

"With me." She rubbed her hand up and down her numb arm. "Is it because of this? Because I might turn into a Desolate?" She wasn't sure she wanted him to answer. Maybe she shouldn't have asked.

He put his head back against the door, his hands jammed into his front jean pockets. "There's nothing I can do to stop it," he said. "I want to. I don't want you to get hurt during all this. But Dante and I, when my grandmother started turning, we couldn't stop it. Even with all Dante's magic tricks it still happened." His voice was hoarse.

"You don't have to protect me from everything," she said, taking a step toward him. "I mean, I know you want to, and I admire that." She wasn't sure what to say to make him feel better. "Distancing yourself isn't helping, you know? No one should probably touch me now – I get that. But you can still talk to me."

He straightened and looked at her. "We have been talking."

That wasn't what she had meant, and she knew he knew it. Before she could say anything else there was a loud noise from the garage. She rushed to open the door that led out into it, and saw Hawker standing with his head bowed. Three large paint containers were lying on the floor on their sides.

"What happened?" Charlotte asked, stepping down into the garage and walking over to the horse.

"I backed into that shelf," he told her. "I am sorry."

"It's okay." She patted his neck, noticing that Black hadn't followed her. She wasn't sure she was disappointed or annoyed, and forced herself not to dwell on it. If he felt he couldn't be close to her, then it was better to find that out now instead of later. "I'm going upstairs to sleep. You guys all right in here until morning?"

"We are," Czarina said, nodding. She stood close to Hawker. "Get some rest. You will need it."

Wasn't that the truth. Charlotte left the horses and headed upstairs, noting that Black had disappeared. She went to her old room, turned on the light, and shut the door. It seemed like years since she'd last been here. Uncle Baron had bought them new furniture for the mansion in the woods, so her bed and dresser were still here, but the bookshelves were devoid of her treasure trove of books. With a sigh she sat down on the bed. Those books were long gone now, along with everything else in the mansion.

The one thing she hadn't taken, because it was a duplicate, was an old picture of her and her siblings with their father, Baxter Flynn. Taken a year before he'd died, before her family had fallen apart, it showed them all happy and smiling. Danny had behaved for once. She took the picture off her nightstand and held it with careful fingertips. Tears clouded her vision as she stared at her father's face.

Things had been off-kilter, tilted, since the day he'd died in his car. Uncle Baron had come at once to their house to take them home with him. It had been a rushed day that ended with the twins pale and silent, Danny sobbing in Jared's arms, and she and Rory quiet and withdrawn.

"Hey."

She flinched and looked up to see Jared standing there. "Hi."

"Couldn't sleep either, huh?" He leaned against the doorframe.

She set the picture down on the bed next to her, drawing his attention to it. He moved closer and grimaced.

"That was a long time ago."

"Not so long." She touched the picture. "Do you think about him?"

"Of course."

She glanced up at him and smiled. Of course he did. "I miss him. I wonder how different things would be if he were still here."

"We wouldn't have the carousel," Jared told her.

"You don't think so?"

"No. Well, I don't know. I know Dad wouldn't have let Uncle Baron bring you out to the woods to see it."

"Why not?" She gave him her full attention now.

"He didn't trust Uncle Baron." Jared sat down on the bed next to her.

"I never knew that." She folded her hands in her lap. Her nails were starting to get long; she hadn't been chewing on them as much since finding the Flying Ponies.

"Dad didn't talk about him much, but when he did, it was never that nice," Jared said. "I wonder where Uncle Baron is."

"Penumbra wouldn't have hurt him." She couldn't believe that. As much damage as the stallion had done and was planning to do, she still couldn't think that he would hurt their uncle. "Maybe he went to see Oliver."

"That's where Helen and Symphony went, too." A tinge of bitterness laced his words, and she wondered how much her brother had fallen for the Songbird.

"You like her."

"I did." He got to his feet and walked to the door. Turning to look at her, he offered a small smile. "I know better now. Get some rest." He left and shut her door, and she flopped backward on the bed.

Her thoughts turned to Penumbra. She missed him, even though he'd turned on her. *The magic is corrupting them. It's not just affecting Penumbra; Bedlam, Flintlock, and Sirocco are even willing to do bad things now.* Bedlam was ornery, but he hadn't struck her as mean when she'd met him. And Flintlock and Sirocco had been gentle and willing to help her. There had to be something she could do to fix the magic dwelling in them.

Maybe with my magic I can fix theirs. That was at least an idea. She was not going to entertain any thoughts of having to destroy them. Yawning, she got up and shut her light off, crawled into bed and drew the heavy comforter up. Five minutes later, she drifted off to sleep.

*A*fter breakfast the next morning, Charlotte split up the horse locations among them. Black looked at the piece of paper in his hand. The others were talking, but he tuned them out. He had asked to go find Phantasm, a red spotted mare who had not been easy to deal with on the carousel. If the magic had warped some of the calm horses, he could only imagine how it had distorted her.

"Everyone set?" Charlotte asked, glancing around the group. She didn't appear to be in pain, and acted like nothing was wrong, but he wished she would tell the others. There was no sense in hiding the fact she'd been touched by a Desolate. It was a wonder she hadn't changed into one yet.

And I can't do a thing about it. His gut churned with anxiety and dread, and he turned away. Getting Phantasm was his job for the day. He was taking Hawker with him;

the big stallion would hopefully have a calming effect on her. As he started to leave the kitchen, Charlotte called to him and he stopped, gritting his teeth. Didn't she understand that he didn't want to talk? That there was nothing he could do to help her?

She waited until the others had filed out before saying, "We can't avoid each other." She wasn't looking at him, though. She was staring out the window over the sink.

"I can't help you." It hurt to say it. No matter the amount of magic floating around in their world, there was nothing strong enough to reverse what had begun inside her.

She turned to face him. "I didn't ask you to. It's something I have to fix."

That was probably true, but it didn't stop him from feeling terrible about it. "I know. You have to understand, though, that I *want* to help you, but I don't know how."

Her expression softened. "I get that. But saving me isn't your job." She motioned toward the sticky note in his hand. "Getting back that horse is. Whatever happens with this," she swept a hand down her body, "is my responsibility."

"Then I better get on with it." He turned his back and strode through the kitchen, shoving through the door. If she called out to him, he didn't hear her. Hawker was in the garage; he led the big horse outside and mounted, and they took to the blood-red sky.

Two hours later, Hawker touched down on the Upper Peninsula outside an old cabin. Black stepped down, marveling at the speed at which the carousel horses could fly. It would've taken at least seven hours to drive here, if not more. He peered in one of the windows; it was streaked with grime, but he could make out a horsey shape across the main room.

He tried the door. It was locked, so he walked around back, checking the various windows to see if any were open. He wasn't in the mood to use magic to open up the cabin. But after five minutes, he conceded Hawker would have to break into the place.

The grey stallion's blue and red magic wafted through the air and swarmed over the old lock. In seconds there was a click, and Black pushed the door open.

"Who are you?" a low voice asked.

"Sullivan Midnight," Black said. He watched as the mare stepped from the shadows. She was a red chestnut, with light orange dapples over her whole body and green, blue and yellow tack. Her yellowish eyes glittered. She walked over and sniffed his outstretched hand. Drawing back with a snort, she looked him up and down.

"I remember you."

"Good. I'm taking you away from here," he told her. His voice was strong. This one respected firmness. She was one of the few who didn't listen to Adara because she hadn't commanded enough authority in her voice.

"They tried to hurt me," Phantasm said. "Those men, the ones who smell like cigars and the sea. I couldn't move then, but I resisted with my magic."

She was surprisingly lucid, and much more in control of herself than he'd imagined she might be. Good. At least this one thing was going his way. "No one is going to hurt you now," he said, his voice still holding that strong ring. "Hawker is with me. Let's go."

Phantasm followed him outside, and Hawker stepped forward to sniff noses with her. Black let them have a few moments to get reacquainted. The air was alive with a strong wind coming from the west, out toward Lake Michigan. With it came currents of air swirled with blues and greens that looked odd against the red sky. Phantasm lifted her head and studied it.

"The magic is growing wild," she said.

"It is," Black agreed. "We need to go." He went to Hawker and mounted, and as he settled deeper into the saddle, a piercing whinny erupted from the woods behind the cabin. Hawker tensed, and Phantasm whinnied back in greeting.

Penumbra stepped from the woods, his head high as he surveyed them. Behind him were Bedlam, Flintlock, and Tomahawk. The dapple grey stopped and Black swore he was smiling when he looked at Hawker.

"So nice to see you all again," Penumbra said. He laid one ear back. "Well, Sullivan, not you perhaps. I see you've been busy, stealing the missing horses."

Black let the anger roll through him and kept his voice under control when he said, "I'm not stealing anything. The Flying Ponies, which includes *you*, belong to the Flynn family. I'm just returning what's theirs."

"We belong to no one," Bedlam snapped. The blue dappled horse watched them with his head lifted high, staring down his nose at them.

"We belong to the family of Oliver Flynn," Hawker said. Black could feel the tension in the horse's back and reached down to stroke his silky wooden skin.

"You are coming with me." Penumbra's eyes narrowed and his green and red magic began drifting in the air. Tomahawk and Flintlock moved out to the sides of him, while Bedlam stood beside him. Wind barreled through the trees, their bare branches whistling as they rubbed against one another.

Hawker turned his head. "Please dismount," he said.

"No." Black had witnessed once what Penumbra could do; he wasn't going to let Hawker and Phantasm fall into his hooves. "We're leaving. Let's fly!"

But as Hawker started to turn away so he could get airborne, Penumbra leapt in front of them and reared. His magic shot out toward them, and Hawker jumped sideways. Black clung to his short mane as best he could and gripped tight with his legs. Bedlam rushed at them, teeth bared, his own blueberry-colored magic swirling around them. Hawker spun and lashed out at him with his hind legs, and then jumped forward into a run.

Phantasm was already in the air; she circled around them as Penumbra and Tomahawk met them with cyclones of magic. A blast of blue magic from below caught Hawker in the belly, knocking him around as he fought to maintain his speed. Black pitched to his right, almost going off.

Tomahawk dashed by them, close enough his chestnut mane snapped Black in the face. He swerved in front of Hawker, forcing the big grey to dodge to the left to avoid colliding with him.

Bedlam and Flintlock were chasing Phantasm, but the spotted mare was fleeter than they were. She circled them, around and around, her eyes flashing as she called them names. Penumbra dove at her from above, and she finally broke her circle and sprinted through the air. He gave chase, gaining on her with long strides.

"Help her," Black called to Hawker, and the stallion galloped faster. But Flintlock doubled back and rushed at them, her front hooves slicing as she tried to knock Black off. He bent low over Hawker's neck, and she overflew them, her nose scrunched in anger. Hawker pulled into a climb as Black kept his eyes on the dark palomino mare. She was already heading for them again, and he wished there was some way he could get through to her. This wasn't her true nature. It wasn't the true nature of *any* of them.

Phantasm let out a loud squeal and he looked down to see her diving in a spiral, chasing Bedlam. The blue stallion was flying as fast as he could, but the red dappled mare easily caught him. She bashed his hindquarters with her front hooves and bit his flank. He whipped around, trying to attack, but she jumped up, clearing him and leaving him in her wake.

Penumbra came shooting toward Hawker, and this time the big Trojan horse couldn't get away. The two greys met in a clash of wood. Black pulled his left leg out of the way as Penumbra smacked Hawker's left side with his hoof, throwing Hawker off balance. Penumbra rushed him, hitting him hard, and Hawker fell away, losing his airspeed and dipping back toward the ground that was rapidly rising to meet them.

"Hawker!" Black yelled as the grey keeled over to his right, dropping his shoulder and scrambling to come around in a climb away from the earth. The trees were reaching up with thick bare boughs as the big grey scraped over top of them, Penumbra hot on his heels. Black leaned forward over Hawker's neck, hoping to lend him some sort of speed or strength or anything to gain ground.

"It's useless to run!" Penumbra yelled, flying past them and wheeling around to face Hawker.

"Says you!" Black yelled back as Hawker avoided him and launched into a sprint through the air. Penumbra spun around to give chase.

"Hawker!" Phantasm came galloping toward them, her chestnut mane flowing like a wave in the wind. Her yellow and green magic spun in loops around her, and she pulled up to fly beside them. "We must get away!"

It wasn't that easy. Already the other three were converging on them; Black gritted his teeth as Tomahawk smashed into them, causing Hawker to bash into Phantasm. The mare was able to jump ahead and recover her strides, but Hawker wasn't as quick, and he fell over on his left side, his legs flailing like windmills as he scrambled to right himself. Black tried to use his weight to help; he grabbed onto the horse's thick short mane and pulled with all his might, dropping his body almost off the right side of the horse to try and right him. Hawker whinnied, terror filling his cry, and Black knew then it was hopeless.

They were falling with no way to stop.

*T*he trees stretched toward them. Black closed his eyes, his thoughts jumping all over. Charlotte filled his mind until he couldn't see anything else. There was so much to tell her, so much he wanted to show her. She was going to beat the monster inside her. He knew she would. Hawker was jerking beneath him, bringing Black's mind back to their rapid descent, and he cringed and wrapped his arms around the stallion's solid neck.

Another twenty feet and they would crash into the silent sentinels waiting for them. Black rubbed a hand over the horse's neck, wishing they weren't going down like this. *This is my fault. I should've protected them better. I should've realized what the magic would do to them when they gained it all back, when they truly woke up.*

It was too late now.

As horse and rider braced for the impact, hearts thundering in unison, they jolted to a stop in midair. Black's breath whooshed out in a gust and he looked down to see Phantasm below them, holding them up. They lay across her saddle. She tossed her head.

"Well, go on and straighten yourself out, Hawker," she directed. "You're heavy!"

Hawker struggled for a moment. "I can't. You'll have to set us down."

Snorting in irritation, the mare swooped down to the ground and landed, and gave a short buck that heaved them off her back. Black jumped out of the saddle, avoiding getting crushed as Hawker fell to the ground. In a few moments the grey had regained his feet, and he shook himself before looking at Phantasm.

"Thank you," he said, his voice heavy with appreciation. He bowed his head to her.

"You're welcome. Sullivan, are you all right?" Phantasm asked, glancing at him.

"Yeah, and we need to go before they come back." He looked up, but the other four horses were gone from sight. "You two okay? Did they hurt you?"

Phantasm shook her head. "I don't believe so. Perhaps if we turned back to solid wood our paint would be damaged, though."

He moved closer and scrutinized their tack. There were definitely some marks on their saddles and breast collars. "I think so, too." He wondered though if that would ever happen now, what with magic loose in the world. Would they even want to get back on the carousel? He had to wonder, but he wasn't ready to ask that. It wasn't his place to ask that, anyway. "Come on. The others will wonder where we are."

Mounting Hawker, he was happy when the horses elected to gallop through the woods instead of taking flight right away. They had no idea where Penumbra had gone, and getting into the air might draw his attention, if he was hanging around. *I'm thankful he came after us, though, and not Charlotte or the others.* Charlotte had been going after Ringmaster with Contessa, who had always gotten on well with the buckskin circus horse. He hoped that the others had found success, that they'd gotten to the horses before Penumbra.

He almost got ahold of Phantasm. He looked at the red mare; she was flying along with no effort, her eyes gleaming with delight. Danny was right: it would be a disaster to place the carousel in a museum, where the horses couldn't fly around. He remembered the movies where things in museums came to life, but the magic in those movies was nothing compared to the Flying Ponies' power.

They touched down in the dark outside the townhouse, and he hurried to let them into the garage. Flipping on the lights, he stumbled back against the wall.

"Don't look so shocked, Sullivan," Baron said, a sardonic tilt to his mouth. "I do live here, you know." He was leaning against the back end of his flashy old BMW. Scorn sparkled in his eyes.

Black had no idea what to say to him. No one else was in the garage. "Where have you been?" he finally managed.

Baron studied one of his gloved hands. "Attending to business."

"Liar." Black waited until Baron looked at him. "Penumbra told us he no longer answers to you. You've been hiding."

"It's good to see Phantasm." Baron walked toward the red mare, but she backed away, shaking her head.

"You smell of smoke," she said.

Baron stopped to sniff at his jacket. "So?"

"I hate smoke." The mare moved further away from him.

"Where are the others?" Baron asked, turning his head to look at Black.

Black shrugged. "No idea." He waited for Baron to say something, but when he didn't, he added, "How did you know this was Phantasm? You've never seen her before."

"Ah, that. Well, someone left Oliver's journal on the couch in the library, and I thumbed through it. He has information on every single pony." Baron pointed at Phantasm. "She's an interesting little mare, isn't she?"

"Why are you here?" Black asked.

"To help."

"Help." Black frowned. "Forgive me if I don't think you mean helping *us*."

Baron laughed and went up the short steps to the house. "Helping myself, dear boy," he said before he went inside and shut the door.

Black moved away from the wall and toward the house. "Stay here," he told the two horses. "The others should be back soon." Hopefully, anyway, since it was now dark. He went into the house. Baron wasn't in sight, and he headed down the hall to the kitchen. His stomach had started growling the hour before, and there had to be something to eat in that gargantuan refrigerator.

As he stepped through the door into the kitchen, the back door opened and Helen walked in. They stopped short at the sight of one another, and then Helen laughed. "Sullivan, good to see you! I was hoping this was where the children had gone to stay."

"How was Oliver?" he asked, walking over to the fridge and opening it. He didn't really want to know but couldn't help but ask.

Helen sat down at the bar and said, her voice casual, "He is up to speed on everything that's happened so far."

"And?" Black turned away from the fridge with a plate of cold chicken. "Is he going to step in and do something?"

"Not yet." Helen watched him as he put a couple pieces of chicken on a plate and brought it over to the bar. Sitting, he began eating. "Everyone is all right? Have you found any more ponies?"

"I brought Phantasm back," he said. "And yes, everyone is okay." Should he tell her that Charlotte had been touched? Was that his business to tell Helen? "Well, not everyone." *Charlotte might not tell her, and she should know.* "When the Desolates attacked the house, and Charlotte was outside, she was touched by one of them." The words were bitter on his tongue. Helen's mouth dropped open, and only a squeak came out.

"What? How did that happen? You *let* that happen?" Anger boiled in her voice, and she jerked back from the table and got to her feet, tossing her hands in the air. "Is she changing? What's happening to her?"

"She's not changing, so far. Her arm that was touched is numb," he told her, ignoring the fact that she'd accused him of not protecting Charlotte. He couldn't acknowledge that without fury choking out rational thoughts.

Helen ran her hands over her hair. Fear brightened her eyes. "This is unacceptable, Sullivan. *How could you let it happen?*" She met his gaze and took a step backward, away from the table.

"*Let it happen*? Are you insane? You think I wanted it to happen!" Black yelled, jumping to his feet, his food forgotten. "I didn't know! I wasn't out there!" He'd been trying to keep the monsters from wrecking the inside of the house. Charlotte had bolted on them without a word; it had been several minutes before he'd even realized she was gone.

Helen's eyes narrowed into slits. "I expected you to take care of her. She is just sixteen."

He clenched his jaw to stop from blurting what he really wanted to say. "I know. But she's tough and brave. She doesn't need me to watch her all the time." And with that, he realized that was what Charlotte had been trying to tell him since the Desolate had tainted her. She liked his protection, but she didn't *need* it. *I'm such an idiot.*

"What is going on in here? I can hear you two upstairs!" Baron said as he walked in. He looked back and forth between them.

"Charlotte has been touched by a Desolate," Helen said, jabbing a finger toward Black. "He should've prevented it!"

Baron's face turned white and he rushed to the table to lean on it. When he turned his eyes to Black, they were turbulent with emotions. "Is this true? How did it happen?"

Black snorted. "If you care so much about her, why did you abandon her? And the others? You don't care about them. You only cared what they could do for you!" His voice rose in fury and he rushed at Baron and grabbed him by his silk shirt collar, hauling him upright. Pulling back a fist, he stopped shy of Baron's face. Breathing heavy, he shoved Baron away from him and turned, trying to collect himself.

"I care about them. They're all I have," Baron whispered. "Please, Black, you have to believe me. I never meant to hurt any of them, especially Charlotte."

"Like I believe that." Black waved a hand at him, disgust rolling through his voice. "Just shut up."

"Baron, pull yourself together," Helen ordered. "If you're going to help the children, then you can't be falling apart yourself."

Black turned to see Baron lift his head and pin Helen with an incredulous look. "How is it you know about the Desolates?"

Helen arched an eyebrow. "My dear, I know a lot more than that. Sit down, and I'll get you something to eat while I explain."

Baron sat while she went to the fridge to rummage around. Black, not needing a primer on what all had already gone down, left the room and headed to the garage to check on the horses. He looked at his cell phone but had no messages. Where could the others be? Why weren't they back yet? Hawker and Phantasm were talking when he opened the door and came down the steps.

"Is everything all right?" Hawker asked, his voice quiet and deep.

"I'm wondering where the others are," Black said.

"I'm sure they are fine," Hawker told him.

Before Black could answer, his phone rang, and he yanked it from his pocket. "Hello?"

"Sully, Dante here. Rory and I are having a bit of trouble with...hang on a minute, will you? We're having – yes, I know! Sully? Hang on just a minute!" Dante's voice was loud, and Black's brows wrinkled in concern as he waited for his friend. "There, now just hold it a second – I said *hold it*! Sully? Sully, can you hear me?"

"I'm here, Dante. What's going on? Where are you?"

"I'm – I'm with – **stop it**!"

The phone went quiet, and Black stared at it for a second before dialing Dante. It went to voicemail and he cursed, trying it again. He didn't have everyone's numbers, so he couldn't call the younger siblings. He tried Dante again, and then Charlotte and Jared. No one answered, and panic nibbled at the edges of his consciousness. Who had Dante and Rory gone after?

"They will be fine," Hawker said, watching him.

Black ignored him as he paced back and forth. Of course things weren't *fine*! It sounded like Dante and Rory were in trouble. Had Penumbra gone after them? If he had, could their three fight him off? Would they be stronger than Penumbra and his herd?

The smaller garage door burst open and Gavin ran in. He stopped and looked at Black. "Are you all right?" Black asked, running over to him. The younger boy's face was streaked with dirt and he was shaking.

"We were attacked by some of the horses," Gavin said, a tremor in his voice. "Warpaint and Moxie. They tried to take Czarina, but she fought them off."

"Is Marta with you? And Danny?"

"Danny went with Charlotte."

"What about Jared?" Black crossed his arms.

"I don't know where Jared went. He didn't want to go. Marta is outside with Czarina and Memento, who doesn't want to come in." Gavin's voice had quieted.

"Okay. Come on. I'll talk to her." Black followed him outside, where Marta stood with the brown mare and a dark dapple grey mare with yellow, turquoise and green tack. She eyed him with suspicion until he got closer and she could see him clearer in the lights from the garage.

"Sullivan!" Memento trotted over to him and nudged his shoulder. "I'm so happy to see you!"

"I'm glad to see you, too, old girl," he said, rubbing her nose and behind her ears. "Are you all right? Gavin said you were attacked by Moxie and Warpaint." He looked her over; she seemed okay, just rattled.

She sniffed. "Ruffians, the both of them! The magic has made them unruly!"

315

"It has," Marta agreed. She was rubbing Czarina's neck. "Are you okay, Black? You look upset."

"I'm…" he stopped. "I'm not fine," he said. There was no reason to lie to her. "Dante called, and something is going on with him and Rory. And Charlotte and Danny aren't back, and Baron and Helen are here."

"What? Are they okay?" Gavin asked. He and Marta exchanged a covert look that Black couldn't even begin to decipher. "Are they inside?"

"They are. You guys can head in. I'll take care of the horses."

"Thank you," Marta said, and unexpectedly hugged him. "I'm glad you're okay," she whispered, pulling back and looking up at him. "We need you." She followed Gavin into the house, leaving him alone with his thoughts and the two mares.

*C*harlotte tried to breathe as softly as she could. Behind her, pressing up close, was Danny. She inched forward a little and he shoved her, trying to see around her. "Would you stop?" she whispered, whipping her head around to glare at him. "We're trying not to get caught!"

Danny glowered at her. "I want to see!"

"Shush." She turned her attention back to the barn yard in front of them. They were hiding out in some thick bushes behind a rotting log fence. Behind Danny was Contessa. The three were watching the two horses standing between them and the barn. Chimerical was pacing and Bathos stood at attention, his eyes riveted to the spot Charlotte was occupying. Had he heard them? And how were they supposed to get Ringmaster out when Penumbra had guards here?

Moonlight filtered down through the lilac clouds,

helping the motion lights on the barn brighten the yard. Little swirls of magic floated around, causing Chimerical to snort and stomp her hooves.

"This is ridiculous! Why don't we go in there and get Ringmaster?" the blue mare asked.

"Penumbra wants us to wait. He knows the Flynns will be coming for him soon," Bathos told her. The big bay Appaloosa kept his eyes on the bushes.

"And he expects us to what? Hurt them?" She scoffed.

"I don't think you'd have a hard time doing that," Bathos said, shooting her a look.

Chimerical spun to face him. "Believe what you want," she snapped. "I'm starting to think this plan for world domination is ludicrous. We're carousel horses! He really thinks the world will bow to us?"

Bathos pawed at the ground. "Why not? The world bows to the preposterous every day. Look at those phones the children have! If something inanimate can hold them captive, why can't we?"

She tipped her head to the side. "You have a good point."

Charlotte heard Danny sputter behind her and elbowed him.

"Did you hear that?" Bathos asked, again looking toward their clump of bushes. Chimerical trotted toward them, and Charlotte knew the jig was up. She waved to Danny and Contessa to stay hidden, and jumped out, waving her arms. Chimerical spooked and half-reared.

"It's just me," Charlotte said, her eyes on the two horses.

"Really. You expect us to believe you came alone?" Chimerical asked, looking her up and down.

"Believe or not, it's the truth." Charlotte climbed through the fence and moved toward the barn. "If you don't mind, I'm going to step inside and talk to Ringmaster."

"Oh, we mind, all right," Bathos told her, stepping into her path and lowering his head. "But if you care to try and get by us, please proceed."

Charlotte's heart hammered but she didn't slow down. She refused to let fear of what might happen stop her from the goal of retrieving the circus horse. As she hurried her strides, Bathos snaked his neck out at her. "You don't frighten me," she called.

"Yes we do." Chimerical lunged at her. Charlotte tried to jump out of the way and stumbled. Chimerical pushed her, knocking her to the ground. "Stay down!" the blue mare ordered. "You belong in the dirt!"

Bathos trotted over and sniffed at Charlotte. "She is weak, as Penumbra said. She isn't fit to run the carousel."

Charlotte eased herself up only to have Chimerical knock her back down. "Stop it!" Charlotte yelled. "You belong to **me**! Not the other way around!"

"Leave her alone!" Danny burst into the yard, screaming like a devil and waving his arms in the air.

Bathos charged him. Danny cut to the left, avoiding the Appaloosa. Bathos swapped ends and went racing after him. Charlotte shoved herself up from the ground and ran toward the barn as Chimerical took off in pursuit of

Danny. She slid the bolt back and pushed one of the doors open.

Bits of moonlight filtered inside, and she reached out and flipped a light switch, the overhead lights coming on and illuminating the entirety of the building. "Ringmaster?" Charlotte said, taking a few more steps inside. Black had told her the buckskin stallion had been stable and reliable on the Island, and she prayed that was the case now. "Where are you?"

"Aha!" Chimerical erupted into the barn and whinnied. "Ringmaster! My old friend, I'm here!"

"Chimerical?" a booming voice called. "Is it really you?"

"Come into the light and see for yourself," the mare said.

Charlotte swallowed as a tall stallion stepped out from behind an old tractor. He wore light blue and yellow tack, and a yellow feather jutted from the brow band of his bridle. "Ringmaster, don't listen to her! She's not right in the head!"

"And who are you?" he asked, moving closer to them. His dark tan hide glowed in the lights.

"Charlotte Flynn, great-great-granddaughter of Oliver," she told him, holding out a hand toward him. "Please, listen to me. You can't go with Chimerical. You'll only get hurt if you do." She took a breath. "Penumbra wants the world to bow to him! He's gone completely crazy!"

Ringmaster stopped, his body taut. "Chimerical, is the child telling the truth? Is she of Oliver's blood?"

"What of it?" Chimerical pranced over to him and he

lowered his head to rub it against hers. "Penumbra wants you to come see him."

"Charlotte!" Danny's cry made her run to the door. He was riding Contessa now, who was trying to avoid getting beat on by Bathos. "Come on!"

Charlotte whirled to face Ringmaster. "You have a choice to make tonight, big guy," she said. "Either you trust me and help take down Penumbra and save the world, save it for the children, or you go with Chimerical and abuse the magic Oliver gave you."

He stood still, and she could only hope her words were playing on his good nature and love of children. Dante and Black had both spoken with fondness for the buckskin; would he decide to use his magic for good? She could barely concentrate over the rush of her heartbeats in her ears. *Please, please choose me. You have to.* Contessa wouldn't be enough to stop the other two from taking Ringmaster. She was positive of that.

"Ringmaster, come," Chimerical said, rubbing her nose along his arched neck. "You know you belong to Penumbra – he is our lead horse."

The buckskin shuddered and stepped sideways, away from her. "He is, yes, but if he is asking us to ruin the world, to torment children, then I refuse." He looked her in the eye. "And you should refuse, as well. We were created, brought to life, for the pleasure of people. We were brought to life for the children."

She reared back, striking out with a foreleg. "Listen to

yourself! Who cares about the kids? Penumbra has set us free! We never have to return to the carousel!"

Ringmaster snapped his teeth at her. "Away with you!" he ordered. "I am not helping Penumbra tear down the world!" He galloped toward Charlotte, who wasn't sure what he was doing until he slid to a stop on some loose hay next to her. "Get on!" he said. She mounted and he bolted through the open door.

"Yes!" Danny shouted. "You got him!" He was clutching Contessa's mane as she danced and spun around the yard, keeping them away from Bathos.

"Let's fly!" Charlotte yelled, and Ringmaster leapt up, his powerful legs driving them higher and higher into the midnight sky. Contessa followed, and they could hear Bathos screaming in frustration, yelling to Chimerical to come. Charlotte looked down toward the barnyard.

Chimerical was leaving the barn, head hung, ignoring her comrade. Bathos kept yelling at her, though his words were lost into the air as Ringmaster and Contessa galloped faster and faster, leaving them behind.

Charlotte tried not to feel bad for the blue mare. She'd tried to steal Ringmaster from them, after all. But there had been genuine affection between them, and she could understand the pain of losing someone close to you. *I'm losing Black.* The thought tore through her, like dynamite obliterating a mine, and she squeezed her eyes shut before tears could collect. This wasn't the time, and it sure wasn't the place.

But there was no denying the truth of the thought. The

numbness was spreading up into her left shoulder now, rendering that arm almost useless. She could still move it of course, but without any feeling in that hand, it was harder to do anything with it. Black was pulling away because he couldn't stop it from spreading, and he couldn't save her from the monster itching to climb into her soul and claim her body as its own.

He doesn't have to, though. This is my fight, not his. He said he understood that, but did he really? He was from another time, where men were always the protectors and women were expected to let them do it. She loved that he wanted to take care of her, but she was finding out her own strengths and didn't need to be guarded all the time.

Jared was finding that out the hard way, too. He had refused to come with her, refused to go with any of them, and had slunk off to the library to sulk. They hadn't waited around for him to come out of his funk, either. If he was over helping her find the missing horses and beating Penumbra, then fine. She would do it without him.

Bathos and Chimerical didn't give chase, and a couple hours later, Contessa and Ringmaster touched down outside the townhouse. Charlotte and Danny swung off and led the horses into the darkened garage, the outside motion lights casting eerie morphing shadows on the pavement.

Charlotte saw Hawker and Czarina along with two mares she didn't know, but that was it. She figured they were Phantasm and Memento, the ones Black and the twins had gone after. "Hawker, where are all the others?"

"They have yet to return," he told her. He sniffed noses with Contessa and Ringmaster. "It is good to see you, Ringmaster."

"You as well, Hawker." Ringmaster looked past him. "Memento, Czarina and Phantasm – I am pleased to see you all, as well."

Charlotte frowned. Why hadn't Rory and Dante gotten back yet? Had something happened to them? They had taken Chevalier, Ranee and Eidolon with them – had they been attacked? Anger at Penumbra began slow-burning in her system, but she forced it away. Dante was smart. If something had gone down, he would be able to handle it. They'd had the furthest to fly, too – all the way to the tip of the Upper Peninsula, which jutted out into Lake Superior.

"Let's go in and eat and get some sleep," she said, turning for the short steps.

"Can I stay out here with them for a while?" Danny was stroking Contessa's neck. "I just want to hang with them."

A soft smile stole over Charlotte's lips, and she nodded. "Sure. Come in when you're ready." She left him there, surrounded by the living wooden ponies.

The house was quiet when she stepped into the foyer from the garage. Shadows swayed on the wall from the outside lights, and she made her way down the hall to the kitchen. No one was about, to her relief, and she flipped on the light above the granite sink and opened the fridge. She wanted to call Dante and Rory and find out what was happening but wanted to trust that they could deal with whatever came up. Taking a bowl of leftover pasta out of the fridge, she shut the door and lifted the lid on the bowl, sniffing it. Even though Helen hadn't been at the town-house in days, this still seemed fresh enough to eat.

"Hello, darling."

Charlotte almost dropped the bowl. She set it down on the counter and turned to face Baron. He wasn't smiling. The light above the sink touched his face, and she could make out the sallowness of it. He came closer. : His eyes were dull, and stubble peppered his jaw.

"What are you doing here? I won't let you have my horses!" Charlotte's anger at Penumbra, at the entire situation, erupted against him, and he flinched, stepping backward.

"I don't want them," he said. He held out his hands in a pleading manner. "Please, you must believe me. I-I heard from Helen what happened to you." He pointed at her arm.

Clenching her fists, she said, "I don't believe you!"

Baron stared at her, as if there were no words he could say. She rubbed at her numb arm. Helen was back, then? And how had *she* known about the Desolate's touch? *Maybe Black told her. I know he's here, because Hawker and Phantasm are, too.* She turned back to the bowl of pasta salad and getting out a smaller bowl and spoon, scooped some pasta into it.

"I know you must hate me," Baron tried again. "I know I've done some bad things—"

"***Bad?***" She set her spoon down in the pasta and braced her palms on the counter on either side of it. "You honestly think that's all it is, *bad*? You've unleashed a herd of magic-

325

possessed horses with a leader fixated on controlling the *entire* world!" The look she shot him echoed with venom. "That's more than bad, Uncle Baron!"

"At least you're still calling me that," he said. His pointed toward her arm again. "I really am concerned about you. How do you feel? Can you feel it inside you?"

The eagerness in his voice, even that small amount, turned her stomach. "Yes, I can feel it," she said. "My magic is holding it off for now." And yes, she was still calling him Uncle. Though he was a madman, he was still family. He always would be, despite the outcome of their battle with Penumbra.

"Good." He offered her a genuine smile, but she looked away. She wasn't buying that. "You're strong, Charlotte," he added. "I know you can beat the creature."

"Are you referring to Penumbra, or the Desolate?" She knew what he meant. His niece was changing into a monster even as she was fighting one.

"You know what I mean." Of course he wasn't going to say it. Why did she think he'd be any less enamored with magic, even after he'd lost Penumbra?

"I'm going to bed," she told him and put the unfinished bowl of pasta in the sink, and then placed the larger bowl back in the fridge.

"I really am glad to see you again," he said.

"Where were you?" She couldn't resist finding that out before leaving the room. "Did Penumbra actually do something, or did you run away from him?"

Ire flashed in his eyes. "I did *not* run away. I simply removed myself from a situation that was deteriorating."

"Yeah." She rolled her eyes, stalked out of the room and headed down the hall. He'd run away, all right, because he'd discovered, as they all had, that Penumbra was no longer controllable. He was full of rampaging ancient magic that was unstable.

The only way to control him was to defeat him.

32

*W*hen Black walked into the kitchen the next morning, he found the Family Flynn standing in a tight little circle. No one looked at him as he made his way to the coffee pot and poured himself some. Their voices were hushed, and he realized that Rory was not in the circle.

"Didn't Dante and Rory get back yet?" His voice was loud in the space around them, and Charlotte shook her head.

"No. We've been calling them, but they aren't picking up." Her eyes had purple circles underneath them, and Black resisted the sudden urge to give her a hug.

"We think Penumbra did something," Gavin added. "Charlotte and Danny were attacked by a couple of the horses, too."

Black frowned and sat down at the table. "They had three of our horses with them. Even if they were attacked, they should've been able to fight them off." He considered. "Dante did call me last night, but he got cut off." Had Penumbra set up attacks at each of the remaining missing horses? Why wouldn't he take them for his own instead of waiting for the Flynns to show up? "Maybe Penumbra was there. I don't know."

"Maybe that's not what happened." Marta pulled out a chair and sat down across from him.

"Then what?" Jared asked. "You think they ran away with four carousel horses?"

Black studied the other boy over the rim of his coffee mug. Jared's face was wan; he looked like he hadn't slept in days. Was he still hung up on the fact that Oliver was alive? Why did that bother him so much? Black wasn't much on psychology and trying to figure out people's minds, but Jared's attitude was going to weigh heavy on the others, and they had enough to deal with.

"I don't know," Marta said. She adjusted her glasses. "Anyone else have ideas?"

"They can take care of themselves," Charlotte said. She walked over and poured some orange juice into a glass.

"You really think that," Jared said.

"We all have to. What else can we do? We have to keep going." Charlotte sipped her juice, her eyes cast down.

They were quiet then. She was right – what else was there to do? They had found most of the horses the Tyranny had been hiding. *It's not enough, though. Penumbra still controls most of the Flying Ponies, and his magic is going to be too strong for us to overcome.* Doubt whispered over and over in his mind.

"So, we're going to assume they're fine, and forget about them?" Jared's voice was loud in the hush. "Great plan!"

Before anyone else could confront him, Baron walked in from the backyard. He shut the door and stared at them, his eyes unfocused. "What is going on?"

"Nothing you need to know," Gavin said. He was drawn and pale, and kept glancing at Charlotte every few seconds.

"Rory and Dante didn't come back," Danny volunteered, flinching when Gavin shot him a look.

Baron's brows drew together and he said, "We must go look for them. There's no telling what that devil horse has done!"

"'Devil horse'? You mean the one you *sided* with?" Jared shot back. "What do you care what he does?"

In the seconds surrounding his venomous words, Baron had the audacity to look wounded. Hurt. He let out a long sigh. "I am your uncle. I care about all of you. It might not feel like that at times, but—"

"But nothing," Gavin retorted. "If you did care, you wouldn't have run off with a herd of wild carousel horses. You would've stayed with us. We don't need you." Gone was the quiet boy; in his stead had come this furious personality, as if he were taking up the mantle oft-times worn by Rory.

Charlotte remained silent during the argument, and Black wondered why. Why was she so lackadaisical about

Rory and Dante's whereabouts? Didn't she care? Didn't she want the horses back? She was rubbing that affected arm, and he couldn't stop the swell of fury that rose inside at being helpless. Even Baron couldn't do anything, and he was an archimage.

"We *must* do something." Baron walked through the room, ignoring the others, and disappeared through the door to the dining room.

"How do we find Penumbra?" Marta asked. The question was meant for anyone, but no one answered.

Charlotte set her cup down. Everyone looked at her, and when she met their gazes, Black saw the reality with which she was living.

The monster was taking hold.

He left the room, unable to stay. That he was being a coward wasn't lost on him, and he didn't want to think of how it looked to the others. Did they even know yet? Had she been strong enough to tell them the truth? Or was she trying to spare them that burden? It didn't matter anymore, because he saw it in her eyes, the creature that was becoming her.

Baron was in the garage, speaking with the horses when Black found him. He paused on the top step, watching. The horses were gathered around Baron like he was some kind of leader, a beacon in this weird world they inhabited. Baron saw him and said nothing, only beckoned him to join.

Hawker and Contessa nosed Black's shoulder as he stood between them. The gesture was appreciated, but it wasn't their comfort he sought. "You can heal her, right?" he asked, his breath hard in his chest as he stared at Baron.

Baron tipped his head back to stare up at the ceiling. The horses were motionless. Their magic was welling in the spaces around them though, and Black wished to be far away from it once their job was done. Magic had always been in his life; did a life exist anywhere, especially now, that magic wouldn't taint?

"There is no healing to be done, as far as I understand," Baron said. "Perhaps if I possessed all the knowledge of the magical world I could find something, but I do not. It is a cross she must bear alone, and either consume it or succumb to it." He let his head tip down, and he rested a hand on Czarina's saddle. "You and I both know how this all works."

That wasn't enough. For all the knowledge Black had gained in his years, it wasn't enough. "Maybe Oliver could do it."

Baron laughed. "You would stake her life on a great-great-grandfather who has never once shown himself?" The laugh turned into something cold.

"Is that any worse than you betraying her?" He was tired of holding back, tired of pretending this man was still that boy who used to visit the carousel and spend hours with it. That was what he'd been doing, he realized now, hoping that his friend was inside this man.

That quelled the laughter. Baron replaced it with haughtiness. "Oliver is nothing. The carousel has passed on to different hands, and I'm going to take it back from that crazy grey horse."

"With what? These guys? You should know better." Black rubbed Hawker's neck. If the horses were offended they showed no sign.

"If Charlotte can't fight, then we must," Baron countered. "And yes, I will fight with just these few if it means getting into battle."

He talked a great game, Black admitted. It sounded pure and true, like Baron was a superhero. What would the battle even look like? How did they find Penumbra? The smaller garage door opened and Helen stepped in. Bits of chalky color clung to her overcoat and shoes. She gave the collar of the coat a shake.

"It's getting worse out there," she told them as she drew closer. "I saw two cars run together in an intersection because the magic just swallowed one and shut it off."

"Are you sure it wasn't because their drivers are imbeciles?" Baron asked.

She stilled. "There were young children in both vehicles, Baron."

His lips thinned into tight lines. "That is a shame, then, and why we must find Penumbra and attack him."

"You expect us to believe you're on our side," Black said.

"I am on your side. Believe it or not. It doesn't matter." Baron turned back to the ponies, leaving both Black and Helen out of the continuing conversation.

"Step outside with me, Sullivan," she murmured and left the garage. Black followed. The morning sky was dewy with yellows and pinks, reminding him of the lemonade sold on Coney back in his time. It also brought up memories of Symphony; she loved the little parasols the vendor would stick in the drink before handing it over to her. Her green eyes would light up like fireworks, and she'd tuck her arm through his as they strolled the Bowery.

He gave himself a mental shake. *Enough of that*, he chastised himself. Those days were long gone. He waited for Helen to speak. When she didn't right away, his mind returned to the Island, and he momentarily wished to be back in that era, doing what he loved and happy with life. What he had now, of course, was great. He had strong feelings for Charlotte. What they would turn into later, *if* there was a later, he didn't know. *I should be with her right now, instead of hiding.* His chest tightened with that truth, yet he stayed rooted in place, waiting for Helen.

"You can't save her, Sullivan," she said. Her voice was soft, and she was facing away from him. "But you *can* be supportive." There was no condemnation, merely a simple statement.

"How? I can't watch her turn. I won't."

"Perhaps she will fight it off. She has a strong heart." Now she turned to face him, and the kindness in her eyes about did him in. "Your lack of support is a lack of faith in her, you know."

He kept his mouth closed, because he knew it was true. How could he be expected to stand there and watch her wilt, though? How could he watch her change into a creature with nothing in its soul and eyes but vacancy and the desire for magic?

Helen gave his forearm a gentle squeeze and moved past him toward the house. "Take some time out here and think things over," she whispered. Then she left him, and he sat down on the red grass and turned head-on into his sorrows.

33

*C*harlotte stared out the window in the large living room at the red grass and yellow sky. It looked like a grand billboard for McDonalds, and this at least gave her a small thing to smile at. There hadn't been much since Baron had deserted her and the others, and she'd realized how much he'd used her. Now he was back, claiming that he was going to help bring Penumbra down. How much could she believe, though? Did she even want to try?

Jared was still out-of-sorts, and that also weighed on her. It wasn't fair to expect him to be stable all the time; at some point, they needed to step up and take their own actions. A sudden pain shot through her left shoulder and raced down her side, and she clutched at it. The monster was growing, stretching its limbs to inhabit hers and pushing its dark self into her soul. Her magic was struggling to fight it off. The purple sparkles that had fallen so easily from her fingertips a few days ago were now gone, drawn deep into her body to fend off the desolation inside her.

Black had left the kitchen two hours ago. He'd gone outside, according to Helen, who was as sympathetic to Charlotte as she'd ever been. That wasn't saying a lot; the housekeeper wasn't known for her warm fuzzy personality. She was a rock, though, in the storm of magic that surrounded them now, and for that, Charlotte would be ever grateful.

She turned from the window and swept her gaze through the room. The house was quiet, almost eerily so, and a pang of longing pricked her heart for the home they'd lost to the monsters. Thinking of Sunny, her little winged friend, she wondered where the bug was now. Had she been possessed of magic, too, like the house? Charlotte sat down in Baron's favorite recliner and rested her head back.

They should be looking for Rory and Dante. They should be confronting Penumbra with the horses they had. Instead, all she wanted to do was sleep. Her body was exhausted from fighting against the creature inside, and in turn, her mind was mush. She closed her eyes. What would a couple minutes hurt?

"Charlotte!"

Jared yelled her name as the house shook with the impact of something heavy. Her eyes snapped open as her older brother rushed into the room. He stopped and his mouth fell open. "You're *sleeping*?"

"No." She jumped up as another blast rocked the house.

"What's going on?"

"Penumbra and his herd are here," Jared said as they ran down the hallway, turned the corner and raced to the front door. He yanked it open and they burst out onto the flaming red grass.

The grey stallion stood in the air above them, his red and green magic swirling around him like the tails of a whip. He struck a hoof into the air and the magic threw itself against the house, shaking it to its foundation.

"Penumbra!" Charlotte yelled, drawing his attention. He touched down on the grass, neck arched, his nostrils flaring.

"You wanted to know where I was, so here I am," he told her. His magic shifted and slid all around his body, causing it to glow. "I've come to relieve you of your horses."

She jabbed a finger at him. "They all belong to *me*, like you do! You're not taking them!"

He tossed his head and laughed. "Foolish child," he said. He whinnied and immediately, from above and behind the townhouse, his group of Flying Ponies appeared. "We are stronger than you. We will beat you." Again, his magic slashed at the house. This time windows shattered and glass cluttered the air. Jared and Charlotte ran further into the yard to escape it as it rained down.

Charlotte looked up at the flying horses and her heart seized with dismay. Ranee, Chevalier and Eidolon were among his numbers, all looking as possessed as the rest of the herd. A black and white pinto mare with a brown saddle stood next to Eidolon. The upper half of a knight was carved at the back of her saddle, his one arm outstretched and his other holding a shield. *Is that Banshee? Isn't that who Dante was going after?* Her breathing grew raggedy in her chest. What had Penumbra done with Dante and Rory?

Danny, Marta and Gavin ran around from the back of the house, followed by Baron and Helen. Where had Black gone? Why wasn't he out here, trying to stop Penumbra? Well, she wasn't waiting for him. Charlotte marched toward the grey.

"This ends now, Penumbra," she said. Her voice rose on the chilled air. The stallion turned his head to look at her, and she almost stopped at the madness shining in his eyes. Almost. But she'd faced down madness before, when she'd confronted Dreadful at the amusement park. She would do so again.

Flintlock and Compatriot dropped down in front of her, shielding her from the grey. "Flintlock, please," Charlotte pleaded. "Don't do this! Don't help him ruin the world." The dark palomino mare's ears flickered forward, like she was listening, but at a sharp neigh from Penumbra, her ears swept back against her skull. She lunged.

"No!" Charlotte threw up her hands and purple magic swarmed from her into the air between them. Flintlock drew up short, snorting, her eyes dark with anger. The purple magic glittered heavy in the air before sweeping forward and surging over the palomino. She reared, shaking her head, trying to toss the magic from her body, but the more she plunged and danced, the more the magic clung. It coalesced into a blanket that wrapped itself around her, and she fell to the ground.

"Enough!" Compatriot stomped his hooves and his blue and red magic hit Charlotte hard. She fell backward, feeling Jared catch her even as the wave of magic engulfed him as well. They both fell to the grass, and she struggled to her feet, turning to face the crazy horses.

The whole herd had landed in the lush side yard now, and her breathing labored at the sight of them all, manes whipping in the wind coming up. The trees at the side of the yard rattled their bare bone branches, and she saw that the horses had all the humans rounded up in a neat circle. *No*, she thought. They were not going out like this.

She summoned the magic, calling it up from the deep well inside herself. The Desolate growing within her roared and stretched its limbs, and she cried out as the monster yanked at her magic, trying to devour it. Staggering from the forces swirling inside her, she tried to send her power toward the Flying Ponies.

Penumbra strode into the circle to face her. He watched as her magic sputtered from her fingers and fell to the ground, disappearing as soon as it touched the red grass. "You are losing, dear Charlotte," he said. "Give up your horses now, and I will spare you and yours."

Several nasty thoughts rose inside her mind, but she was better than that. "We are ending this now, Penumbra," she said. Her throat clogged with those thick words, yet they did nothing to the grey stallion. He lifted his nose into the air.

Her siblings came to her sides. She wished she could call upon the Flying Ponies in the garage, but was unwilling to risk them. Penumbra's lips twitched.

"You think you are strong enough now, don't you?" he taunted. "I know your ponies are locked inside the garage. Rest assured, they will be joining us shortly." He flicked his tail, and Harmony and Moxie trotted over to the big garage door. They bowed their heads, their magic rising and combining and then attacking the door.

"No!" Marta screamed, but it was already happening. The magic twisted the metal with loud screeches until it was nothing but a ball on the ground at their hooves. They used their magic to hurl it into the Cadillac, wrecking the big vehicle. Hawker stepped from the garage, followed by the mares and Ringmaster, and when Penumbra turned to face him, the light grey war horse stopped and dipped his head.

Charlotte's heart tumbled. They *needed* their horses to stand up to the dappled lead horse, not give in to him! "Hawker!" she yelled. "Don't!"

The war horse lifted his head and called, "I am not giving in!"

As he said this, the others behind him rushed toward Penumbra, teeth bared and magic flashing as they converged on him. The dapple grey leapt into the air as his herd lifted off with him. Hawker's small group stopped and looked up, waiting his command.

"Come with me," Penumbra said, floating in the air above them. "You know you yearn to rejoin the herd. We are right here waiting." His voice was soft and melodic, and for a moment, Charlotte thought they might go.

"Stay and fight, coward," Hawker said, voice rumbling deep in his chest. "You speak as a lead horse, yet your actions are contrary to one. Stay and show what you are made of!"

"Yeah, that's tellin' him!" Danny cheered from beside Charlotte, and she let out a harsh laugh, the air in her tight lungs finally loosening.

"Get him, Hawker!" Gavin yelled.

"Bring him down!" Marta cried.

Helen and Baron stood off to Charlotte's right, and she glanced at them. Would Baron cheer too, or was his heart still with Penumbra? Neither adult said anything.

Hawker shot into the air, followed by Ringmaster. The two stallions met Penumbra in the air with loud furious whinnies. The dapple grey struck out at them and whirled, planting his hind feet in Ringmaster's chest. The buckskin fell back but surged forward with a ringing neigh. Contessa, Czarina, Phantasm, and Memento joined the fight, the mares quickly breaking off to go after members of Penumbra's herd.

Charlotte groaned when Flintlock bit Contessa's neck, leaving a gash in the bright palomino's wooden hide. "Fight back!" she yelled. "Keep fighting!"

"Help them," Jared said, and she realized he wasn't speaking to her – he was urging Baron. Baron's face was turned upward as he watched the sky battle happening overhead. "Uncle Baron do something!" Jared said.

If he did do something, would it help or hinder Hawker? Charlotte reached for her magic. The Desolate inside was pulling against her, trying to bind her magic to itself. She closed her eyes, seeking, pulling, the magic scraping deep within. Her hands clenched into fists. Her mouth twisted into a grim scowl, and she fought for her magic.

"Fight with me, Charlotte," Baron whispered a second before his hand was holding hers. She panted as purple magic erupted from her mouth, flying into the air. It hit Flintlock square in the hindquarters, sending the big mare sprawling. She fell to the earth, and the twins pounced on her, straddling her neck and side.

"Danny! Jared!" Marta yelled, and the two brothers raced to them, adding their weight and holding the mare down.

"Focus," Baron said, tightening his grip on Charlotte's hand. She tried, her eyes glued to the horses fighting above them.

Penumbra dashed at Memento, and the dapple grey mare had to break off her pursuit of Moxie and Chimerical. They escaped while she turned head-on into Penumbra's attack. The two dappled horses crashed in a deafening collision of old wood and lacquer, and Charlotte nearly lost her concentration.

"*Focus*," Baron ordered. "Focus on Penumbra. If we take him down like Flintlock, we can deter the others."

Was it that easy, though? Thoughts raced through her mind as the carousel horses reeled and spun and whirled in a macabre dance. The monster inside her was tearing at her chest. Her lungs were hot, searing pain scorching through them. This was how Black's grandma had felt as she changed. This was how all those poor souls had felt.

"Flintlock!" Tomahawk and Warpaint flew to their fallen comrade and landed. Warpaint, his red, blue and yellow magic swarming over him, struck out with a front hoof and caught Gavin in the side. He shouted and fell off Flintlock.

"Stop it!" Marta screamed from her seat across the mare's neck. "Leave us alone!"

Jared got to his feet and took off his brown belt. He whipped Warpaint in the face with it. The brown pinto jerked backward, stunned. Tomahawk, the feathers tied in his mane and tail flying, let out a war cry and reared. His front hooves slashed at Jared, who stumbled backward. His foot slid on Flintlock's shiny side and he crashed down.

Charlotte started to pull away from Baron, but her uncle kept a firm hold on her hand. "Don't worry about them," he said. "Concentrate on Penumbra. He controls them all."

She knew that. This wasn't what her great-great-grand-parents had wanted for their beloved carousel horses. This was madness.

And then *true* madness dropped from the sky onto the lawn in front of them. Dreadful bowed his head to her and then met her gaze.

"Hello," he said. Orange lightning rolled through the depths of his eyes, crackling with insanity. His black mane and tail billowed in the increasing roar of wind.

"Dreadful." His name was a prayer on her lips and she stepped forward. Baron let her go. There was no use trying to tether her any longer – she and Dreadful were meant for one another. "I've missed you."

*H*e said nothing. The bay cavalry horse was within reach of her. Charlotte tried to grasp his bridle. With a battle cry, he surged forward and snapped his teeth at her, causing her to yelp and drop to the ground. Baron tried to intervene, but Dreadful drove him back, stalking the man until he too stumbled and fell. Dreadful turned his head, his elegant neck curved, and looked right into her.

"You are diseased," he said. His voice, that dry rustle of air through parched grass, was familiar in her ears. He turned all the way to her and lowered his head. His red and orange magic floated around him, tiny particles of power arcing and chasing one another. "You are failing."

"Not as much as **you**," she retorted. Her chest rose and fell in great gasping waves. "You're working with Penumbra! You hated him!"

"Well done, old boy," Penumbra called as he landed

behind the bay stallion. "I knew she couldn't resist you." There was snark in the grey's voice. "He saw how right I was, Charlotte. He sees that the world needs rebuilding, and to do that, it must first bow."

Charlotte reached up and placed her trembling hand on Dreadful's muzzle. "No," she whispered, never letting her eyes leave his. "He's wrong. Help me. Stay with me." There was nothing to be done for the tears in her eyes or the shaking of her voice. This was it.

"Finish her," Penumbra ordered. "And we will be on our way."

Dreadful moved in close. His breath tickled her cheeks and blew wild caresses through her crazy hair. She tipped her face sideways to rest against his. "Do it, then," she whispered. Her hands knotted into fists in the thick grass and she tried not to remember how she'd thought she could win. Her magic was no match for these horses. The monster inside roared in approval as it gathered it all to itself.

When nothing happened seconds later, she drew back, leaving a small gap between them. Her wide eyes saw Penumbra waiting behind him, pawing at the ground. When she aligned her sight with Dreadful's again, he winked.

And whipping around, collided with the grey.

Time could not stand still. As much as she had heard the phrase, had watched it used in TV and movies, it wasn't possible. And yet, here, now – it did.

The two stallions, a bay and a grey, fought and clashed

and warred against one another as everyone else ceased moving. Baron helped the younger siblings and Jared up and wrapped his arms around Gavin and Marta while Danny stood in shock beside Jared. Charlotte got to her feet, knees threatening to send her twirling back down. All the horses landed and as one watched the stallions fight.

There was no sound save for the crash of wood on wood. Again and again they struck one another. Legs tangled and manes flowed and magic coalesced and disintegrated only to waft into sight a half second later. Neither horse got the advantage. It was a bizarre two-step, danced by antique carousel horses possessing terrible magic.

The Desolate inside Charlotte was spreading through her now that she was weakened and not paying attention. She could feel and smell its reeking breath inside her lungs. Choking and coughing, she went down on one knee, still trying to watch the battle even as she lost the one inside her.

Her family was instantly beside her. Jared was holding her, his voice loud but unintelligible to her. Danny and Gavin were crying, while Marta watched in silence, her glasses hanging at the tip of her nose. Baron's face was wiped of emotion, but his lips were moving, repeating something she couldn't understand.

Jared was saying, "stay" over and over and over, and she wanted to. She really did. But she had lost that last thread of magic she'd been grasping. The monster had torn it from her. It was binding itself to her now. The numbness was sprinting through her body, and a wail crawled up her throat and launched from her mouth in a frightening keen.

They all jumped. Baron's face crumpled and tears coursed down his cheeks. Maybe he really had cared. Maybe he'd only been blinded by Penumbra's dazzling array of magic and lunacy. Dreadful hadn't been the mad one after all. She shoved them away, desperate for one last glimpse of her bay horse.

He was on his hind legs, swaying, his front legs locked in mortal combat with Penumbra's. Wind tumbled their manes and tails and their magic, their colors, wound around them like sparkling ribbons of devastation. She reached down deep, tunneling through the darkness, searching for her last shred of humanity. Finding it, she shot to her feet like a spring.

"Dreadful!" His name ripped from her and was promptly tossed to the frigid gale. The two stallions kept fighting.

They didn't see her fall, writhing, to the grass, the ash overtaking her skin as her body warped and buckled and twisted, becoming something it was never meant to be.

They didn't see the monster where the girl used to be.

Hurry. Hurry. Hurry. The word repeated over in his head as Black drove the BMW down the road. Something was wrong. The sky had turned black. Charlotte wasn't answering her phone. His skin prickled with apprehension.

I shouldn't have left. He hadn't been able to stay, either. Everything they were going through had taken its toll, and he'd fled like the coward he'd claimed Baron to be. *But he stayed. Maybe he was telling the truth. Maybe he was trying to help.*

He'd been at the park in Smoke City, watching a few teenagers throw a football around, when the wind whistled through the air and the sky had gone dark. This black wasn't the work of an approaching storm, though – it was something far more sinister. He shoved his boot down on the accelerator and the antique sportscar ate the road in front of it.

Black whipped the car into the drive and gunned it up the hill. Throwing it into park and shutting it off, he climbed out and slammed the door shut. All around him it was silent. A stray leaf blew past, drawing his eyes to the sky. And he saw them.

The Flying Ponies, magnificent in their carnival paint, thundering through the obsidian sky in a continuous flow of bright colors and whirling magic. They were headed away from the city, back toward the carousel deep in the woods. He tried to count them, but they were too fleet. Once they had gone, he released his breath and realized a Desolate was standing in the side yard.

"No." The word was a grimace, a flash of suffering. He stumbled toward the creature.

"Black!" Marta sprinted to him and flung her arms around his waist. He embraced her even though his focus was on the monster. "Black," Marta said, and reached up to touch his shoulder. He looked down at her, down into a face drowning with misery, and knew.

"Sullivan." Helen was marching toward him, her arms wrapped around Danny and Gavin. They were crying. Behind them was Jared. Dried tears streaked his face. Black sucked in a breath as they reached him and Marta. He didn't want to know for sure, didn't want that confirmation.

"She has gone," Helen said. There was no waver in her voice, but her eyes were deep pools of anguish.

He would later tell the family it was like his spirit had left his body. It hovered over them all, watching while his

351

body, stripped down to nothing, fell to the earth. Everything, in those seconds, was muffled by despair. Tears coursed down from his eyes and he pounded the grass with closed fists. She had gone, and he had not been here.

The creature had won, and he had lost.

When he came back to himself, and was able to rally enough to stand, to climb up with the help of Jared, he forced his eyes to the monster. "When?" Had it been minutes ago? An hour? And why was it standing there, swaying, its hands clenching and unclenching?

"Only minutes before you arrived," Helen said.

"Why hasn't it attacked?" He could not think of it as "she" or "her." The girl he'd fallen for was gone.

"Dreadful is keeping her stable," Marta said. She looked like she wanted to hug him again but kept still at Jared's side. "Penumbra came, and they fought. Dreadful turned on him and stayed to help us when they all left."

"All? Even the ones we had?" Hope crumbled within him.

"Yes." Jared was staring at the ground. Marta wrapped her arm around his and squeezed, but he made no notice of it.

"Why? Why didn't Hawker and his herd fight?" Why had they given in?

"Penumbra was going to destroy us all if they resisted any further," Gavin said. He wiped an arm over his face, smearing his tears. "We tried to convince them to stay, but Hawker said we were too important, and they weren't."

"He said we could win without them," Danny added, sniffling. He gave up and blew his nose into his shirt.

"Where is Baron?" Black asked, turning his eyes from the family. His stomach was too sick to watch them falling apart. *Coward*, his mind whispered.

"With Dreadful," Helen said. "Children, you must go inside. The weather is turning bad, and I don't want you near the Desolate in case Dreadful can't hold it."

Not a single one resisted. They trooped into the house and shut the door. Black glanced at the monster again. "Why did Penumbra leave Dreadful here?"

Helen had the nerve to chuckle. "He knew better than to take him. Dreadful has a deep connection with Charlotte. Even as that creature, it's still there. Penumbra knows he can't control him."

"He couldn't have controlled Hawker, either. Or the others." His voice was flat. "It doesn't make sense why they left."

"It does, dear boy, but you're too worked up and run down to see it." She moved close and put an arm around him. "Come along. You need to rest, too."

He wanted to fight her. He wanted that with all his heart, but it was too far gone to function true, and in the end, he let her guide him inside. Sitting in the living room alone, he sobbed.

"This isn't right." Gavin's voice was low and full of sorrow.

"Well, we can't leave her outside. We have to finish what she started," Jared said as he shut the door that led down to the basement.

They had all agreed, more or less, to lock the Desolate in one of the rooms in the basement. Dreadful had used his power to get it down there, and Baron had locked it in himself. Now they stood in the hallway, clustered together in resolute sadness. Everyone waited for someone else to say something brilliant, to ease their anguish, but nothing would come. Nothing *could* come.

Finally, they meandered down the hall to the kitchen, a room in which suffering people often found themselves. There they pulled out chairs to sit, or in Danny's case, jumped up on the counter to perch. Baron sat down last, his tall frame settling heavily into his chair.

"We need a plan," Marta announced. When no one volunteered any ideas, she added, "We have to do it for Charlotte."

Black winced. He wasn't ready to hear that, not yet, not when she'd only been a Desolate for a few hours. Dreadful was standing in the corner, his head lowered, his muzzle almost rubbing the floor. Black saw him wince, too. In this pain they were united.

"So, there's *really*, honestly, nothing you can do Uncle Baron?" Danny asked.

Baron raised his head to study him, and Danny ducked down, biting his lip. The motion plucked at the threads of Black's soul. That had been something Charlotte would do.

"Marta's right, guys. We can't sit around and waste time. We have to find Dante and Rory, and stop Penumbra," Gavin said.

"What I don't get is why he left at all. He had us right where he wanted us," Jared said. "Why not take out all the Flynns?"

"You think he hurt Rory?" Danny's eyes widened.

"What do you think?" Jared fired back. Gone was the overprotective brother; he was barely able to protect himself any more.

"Boys." Helen's voice was hard. "That is enough. Penumbra left because there is nothing, to his mind, that we can do now to stop him. I do not see him as a killer."

"He told Dreadful to finish Charlotte," Jared pointed out. He managed to say her name without choking up. Mostly.

"Yes, he did. He told *Dreadful* to do it," Helen said. "He wasn't going to do it himself."

"We've got one Flying Pony, and we know the locations of the others the Tyranny has," Gavin said. "Unless Penumbra goes and gets them."

"Well, he has all four of the ones Dante was supposed to have," Baron said. He sighed and looked down at the table. "I honestly have no idea where we should go now, what we should do. Even my archimage power is nothing compared to what the Ponies wield."

That sat heavy and looming over them all. Dreadful's ears flopped and he let loose a lingering horsey sigh. Everyone else was silent. Black drummed his fingers on the table, the action at least giving him something to do. But at Jared's clearing of his throat twice, he stopped. There was no sense aggravating the other boy.

"Hey, what about Symphony and Oliver?" Danny said, sitting up straight on the counter. "I mean, why don't we ask them for help?"

"And where has *your* grandfather been?" Jared asked, looking at Black, who shrugged.

"I don't know. He left after giving me Oliver's journal."

At that, Marta got up and ran from the room. Within a minute, she was back with the leather journal and sat down, laying it flat in front of her and opening it.

"No help there, darling," Baron told her. He propped his chin in his hand.

"Don't call me that." She lifted her chin and glared at

him. Venom filled the space between them. "That's Charlotte's nickname."

"Yes, you're right," he said, nodding. His voice was soft. "I'll think of something for you."

She waved her hand like she was shooing away his thoughts. "I don't need one. There has to be *something* in here that will help us." She started thumbing through the pages.

Black watched her, but his focus was somewhere else. In his mind's eye, he was seeing himself say goodbye to Symphony on that late autumn day, a day not unlike this. She had fragmented his heart, too. He had left Coney Island believing he would never find another girl as amazing as her. A spectre intruded in the scene, and he shut it down before the tears had a chance to build again.

"There's nothing in there I haven't already read," Baron was saying as Black settled back into the present. "I discarded all of it. It's just background on the ponies."

Marta ignored him. Gavin had moved in closer and was watching carefully as she flipped pages and murmured to herself. Jared got up and walked over to the fridge. He opened it, rummaged around, sighed, and shut it.

"Wait, what's that?" Gavin asked, reaching over to stop Marta from turning the page. He ran his finger down the seam between the old pages. "Look, there's a pocket in there." A small rise in his voice brought Jared's head up and he came back to the table.

Marta used her slender fingers to pry the aged paper apart, and slid out a little note, along with a small photo. She read the note and passed it to Gavin, and then studied the antique photo. "Okay, if you know about all the Flying Ponies, then who is *this*?" She held the photo outward toward Baron.

He squinted and frowned and reached for it. "I don't know," he muttered. "What does the note say?"

"It doesn't say his name," Gavin told him. "But listen to this: it says he's more powerful than any of the Flying Ponies, because," he gulped and swept his eyes around the table, "he is the true lead horse of the carousel!"

Stunned. That was the only word Black could later use to describe what they were feeling. Dreadful shuffled out of his corner and walked around to stand behind Baron.

"You recognize him?" Baron asked the bay.

Dreadful bobbed his head. Wisps of orange flitted through his dark eyes. "He is Chieftain."

Black frowned, thinking back to that time. He had never heard of this horse, but he'd never been to the warehouse where Oliver had stored the carousel before bringing it to the Island. He held his hand out for the picture, and Baron handed it over. Chieftain was a copper chestnut with a dark flaxen mane and tail, and wore military tack, much like Dreadful's. He had four white stockings, and was carved in a standing pose, with his left front leg raised off the ground. He was outstanding.

"Did you know about him?" Baron asked, watching Black's reaction.

"No. Never heard of him, until now." Black reached into his memories, but there was nothing of this stallion.

"Maybe Oliver thought he would be too hard to control if he's really the most powerful."

"Yeah, thank goodness we only have *Penumbra* to deal with," Jared said, groaning. "This doesn't help us."

"Sure it does," Gavin told him. "According to the note, all the horses have to answer to him. So, if we can find him, we can beat Penumbra!" Excitement filtered through the haunting sadness in his voice.

"Gav's right," Marta said, nodding.

"Nothing there about where he is, though?" Black asked, gesturing toward the note.

Gavin's face fell a little. "No, but Oliver would know. Or maybe your grandfather!"

"If I knew where he was, maybe. Either of them," Black said. But he didn't, and Cornelius hadn't contacted his grandson since he'd dropped off the notebook.

"Well, can't you call him? He has a phone, right?" Danny said.

Baron chortled. "I've never seen Cornelius use a cell phone. A telephone, yes, but nothing so modern as a mobile phone."

"Grandfather isn't big on modern technology," Black added. "So no, I can't just call him."

"Dreadful, do you think you could find Chieftain?" Marta asked. She was studying the note Gavin had handed back to her. "I know supposedly only Penumbra can do that, but maybe you can try."

"He did, remember? With the so-called magical bridle?"

Jared asked. "And then Oriflamme said he could use it, and then we lost him to Penumbra."

She narrowed her eyes into a fierce look. "I **know** that, but maybe he can *try again*."

Dreadful gave his head a shake. "I can't," he said. He shrugged one of his powerful shoulders.

"Hey, so if you know about Chieftain, then what are the chances that Penumbra and the others do, too?" Danny asked. "Won't Penumbra go after him?"

"Not if he knows Chieftain is stronger," Gavin told him. "I mean, that wouldn't make sense."

"They don't know," Dreadful said before any more speculating could occur. "Oliver let me meet Chieftain after the others were taken to the Island." He tipped his head to the side. "He told me not to tell them."

Black inhaled a sharp breath. Either Oliver had figured the chestnut would be too hard to control, or he'd suspected Penumbra of treachery at some point, and held Chieftain back as a defense against him. Either way, this worked to their advantage. Penumbra had no idea there was a fail-safe out there.

"I say we go find ourselves this chestnut military horse," Gavin said.

"What about Charlotte?" Jared asked. "We're going to leave her locked up? Alone?"

"You know you can't get near her," Baron told him.

Jared rubbed a hand over his head. "I know. But I think one of us should stay here and watch over her."

"That will be my job." Helen got to her feet.

"How do we find Chieftain?" Marta asked. "Anyone have any ideas, at all?"

They had none. They had no connections to Cornelius at the moment, and he was the only one who knew where Oliver had been. Black thought about things, and with a silent groan, brought up something they hadn't discussed.

"What if Chieftain isn't around anymore? What if Oliver had him destroyed? Or lost him to someone else?"

"Like the Tyranny?" Danny said.

"No, because if they had him, Orrick would've gone after Penumbra and brought him down by now, so he could have all the Flying Ponies to himself," Black said. The thought had crossed his mind that Orrick might have Chieftain, but he figured he was right in what he said.

"Let's get back to how we find him," Marta said, redirecting the conversation. "Is it possible we could use those doors in the mansion's basement? Maybe Chieftain is around Coney Island."

"What if they don't work now?" Danny asked.

She pointed at Baron. "He's an archimage. He can access them. Probably has in the past." She kept her eyes on her uncle, and he finally nodded.

"Yes, I've used them, several times." He switched his gaze to Black. "She's right, it's worth a look."

"Then let's go." Black got to his feet and walked over to Helen. "Keep it safe," he said, his voice low.

She lifted her chin. "*It* is Charlotte, Sullivan. You must keep telling yourself that."

He couldn't, so he didn't acknowledge that. He walked

out to the garage, the family trailing him. The wind was howling now, and as he stepped outside he noticed the green swirling snowflakes. Marta stopped next to him, stuck her tongue out, and then reconsidered.

"We don't know what they would do to us," she told him.

"Good thinking," he said and looked at Baron. "How do we do this? We have your BMW two-seater and Dreadful. That's not enough room." And he wasn't staying behind.

Baron studied the sky for several moments, trepidation on his face. "Four of us can go," he finally said. "Dreadful can take two, the car two. So who is going?"

"I'm staying," Jared said. "If Charlotte gets rambunctious or something, I can help Helen."

No one else said a word. The wind blew in hollow freezing whirls, blowing around the odd snowflakes. Gavin and Danny glanced at one another. Marta stared resolutely at Dreadful, who was bobbing his head and muttering to himself.

"Well," Baron said, "we need one more to stay behind." He eyed each of them. Black too stared ahead, not giving Baron an answer. "Fine. I will decide, since none of you can. Danny, you are staying here."

"What? No! That's not fair! It's because I'm the youngest, isn't it?" he ranted, scowling. "Not cool, Uncle B!"

Baron walked over and placed his hands gently on the boy's shoulders. "You are strong, Daniel, stronger than you know. But you are young, and you are emotional, too much so for this journey. Gavin and Marta both get along well with Dreadful, and Black needs to go. This is as much his quest now as it was Charlotte's." He stopped, bowed his head. "*Is* Charlotte's," he corrected. "Please, no arguing. Stay here with Jared and Helen and protect your sister, if she needs it."

Danny opened his mouth, closed it, opened it and said, "Okay. I'm still not cool with it, but I get it." He sighed and headed back toward the door.

"Be careful," Jared said, putting his hand out for Black to shake. Black nodded as they shook.

"We will be, as much as we can." He knew it had to be hard for Jared, staying behind, yet he was willing to do it. He nodded at the other three and Dreadful. "We better get moving."

The twins mounted Dreadful and the bay horse rose into the knifing wind, his mane and tail blowing about. Baron hopped into the car and started it, revving the engine as Black got in. They backed down the drive, Baron eased the car into drive, and the BMW bolted down the road.

*D*arkness. Reaching up, feeling around. Did it know this place? It was in a box of some sort, and there was no magic. None it could sense or taste.

It rubbed at its head. Something was odd, there, too. Didn't it used to have hair? It whined. The noise rose until it filled the space.

"Charlotte. It's me, Jared."

It paused, cocked its head. Did it know that voice?

"I don't know if you can tell its me, or even if you can hear me." A pause, a thud against the door. "There has to be a way to save you. I don't know how. Maybe Oliver will, or Chieftain. Yeah, so there's another lead horse, only this one is truly the big gun, the one who's in charge of the whole carousel. Black, Uncle Baron, and the twins went to find them." Another quiet thud, and then a sniffle. "I'm sorry. I'm so sorry. If this had to happen, it should've been me.

Not you." More sniffles, and then a small sob. "I have to go. I won't be far."

Footsteps sounded and receded. It could hear them overhead, and then they were gone.

Darkness, and no magic.

38

When they pulled up in the car, Baron slammed a hand down on the steering wheel. "You didn't tell me the *entire house was gone*!"

"Oh, yeah," Black said, wincing. "We knew it was gone before we left."

"Then why would Marta even suggest this!" Baron shut the car off and got out, throwing the door closed. Dreadful landed in front of the car, and he stalked over to the horse. Black got out and carefully shut his door.

"Marta, why would you suggest coming back? And why on earth did *no one* tell me the house was gone? What on earth happened to it?"

"Desolates," Gavin said, jumping off the horse. "That's when Charlotte got touched, when they attacked." He put his hands on his hips and studied the area where the house had once stood. "Do you think we can find a way down to the basement?"

Baron choked out a desperate laugh. "That's *all* you're honestly thinking about? The house is **gone**! There's nothing left but some old shingles and wood! How on earth do you think we can find the basement!"

The other three cringed at his voice level. Black walked over to the remains of the house. The roof had come down flat on the ground, squashing everything. It was certainly a magical collapse; houses didn't fall straight down like this. "Any chance you might be able to find the basement?"

Baron rubbed a hand down his face. "No. No, there is not. It's all gone. The magic has even gone, probably consumed by those devil creatures."

"Hey," Gavin snapped. "Our sister is one of them now! Don't call them that."

"Forgive me." Baron motioned toward the house. "This is a lot for me to take in. You realize how old this house was, and who built it." He rubbed a hand down Dreadful's neck.

The twins were quiet. Black walked around the whole of the house, studying the roof's edges, but Baron was right – there really was nothing there. That was it. What else could they do? "The horses were headed in this direction when I got back to the townhouse," Black said, musing. "Would they have gone back to the carousel?" he asked Baron.

"Likely yes, though the machine itself has little magic as you know, just enough for that small apartment inside." Baron walked back over to the car. "We may as well go. There is nothing else for us to see here."

Dreadful suddenly stiffened and swung to face something from the woods. Baron motioned for the twins to get into the car, but they stood their ground beside one another and the bay stallion. Snowflakes drifted on the breeze here, too, but they were black and brown, and disappeared once they lit on the earth. Black walked over to stand beside Marta, and she glanced up at him. In that look he saw fear, but unyielding determination, too.

Orange and red magic bloomed in the air around them, and Dreadful paced forward, his head up and ears pricked forward. Seconds later he let out a glad whinny and bolted.

"Dreadful!" Marta yelled and chased after him. Gavin and Black ran behind her, with Baron bringing up the rear. The bay horse disappeared around a bend in the trees, and when they found him, moments later, they all stopped and stared.

Black's heart crashed around inside, battering its walls, threatening to leap up his throat and out into the cold. A man stood there. A liver chestnut horse stood beside him. Dreadful touched noses with the horse and the man reached out to rub his neck.

"I don't believe it," Black murmured. They'd told him it was true, that he was still alive, that he had another carousel horse who could truly take down Penumbra, but he realized he hadn't believed it, not really, not until this *very moment*.

"Hello, Sully," said Oliver Flynn as he walked toward them. "It's been a while, hasn't it?"

39

Black put his hand out for the older man to shake. Oliver shook it and then turned to Baron, who's jaw was slack. Gavin and Marta stared at Oliver. He smiled at them.

"You must be some of my great-great-grandchildren," he said. "The twins, no doubt."

"Gavin, sir," Gavin said, keeping a neutral tone as he put his hand out. Oliver flashed a smile and shook it.

"No need for the 'sir' part, young man," he said. "And Marta? I thought so," he said when she nodded. He turned back to Baron. "And my great-grandson, Baron." He tilted his head, like he was giving Baron the once-over. "Surprised to see me, are you? Didn't really believe I was alive?"

"No," Baron said. He didn't seem capable of any longer words.

"This is Chieftain, who is the *true* lead horse of the

Flying Ponies," Oliver said. "We've come to set things right, so to speak."

"How?" Marta asked, crossing her arms. "And why didn't you tell us Penumbra wasn't the one? And for that matter, we thought Dreadful was supposed to be stronger than Penumbra. So why believe what you're telling us now?" A black snowflake landed on her glasses and she reached up to wipe it off. "Well?"

A smile twitched in the corners of Oliver's mouth. "You are a brave little one, aren't you? Questioning me as if you know me?" He took a step closer to her, and Black moved to her side. Oliver huffed out a laugh. "Still protective of the ladies, Sullivan? But then you know the score, don't you?"

"I do." Black's voice was low and taciturn. "Answer her questions, Oliver."

Chieftain tossed his head, and when he spoke, it was in a commanding voice that shook the ground beneath their feet. "I am Chieftain, crown king of the Flying Ponies! They will all bow to me!"

Black and Baron exchanged looks. *And I thought Penumbra was tiresome.* But Dreadful seemed okay with him, so he couldn't be all bad, Black supposed.

"That doesn't answer any questions," Gavin said, shrugging when the chestnut bared his teeth at him. "That doesn't scare me. I've seen worse."

Chieftain's eyes slimmed down to slits, but Oliver held up his hand and the stallion stayed quiet. "I had the Flying Ponies created. I endowed them with magic from the bridle of Pegasus. They will do as they are told, by myself and my chosen lead horse." He indicated Chieftain.

"You waited long enough to show up," Black said. "Where were you when the house fell?"

"That is a pity, but it shall be restored once the horses are back on the carousel," Oliver told him.

"Our sister is a Desolate now!" Gavin said, balling his fists up. "You weren't here to stop that, either!"

"Oh, I am sorry. I did not realize that keeping you children safe was my responsibility." He shot a look at Baron. "I would think that to be your guardian's duty."

Baron blanched and looked down at the ground. It was one of the few times Black could remember seeing his old friend cowed by someone.

"Don't worry about your dear sister," Oliver said, flicking his fingers. "She will be dealt with soon enough." Before anyone could ask what that meant, he pointed at Black. "You and Dreadful will come with me, and we will set things right in this world."

"By stopping Penumbra? Getting the horses under control? What exactly are you planning to do?" Black had wanted to find Oliver. He'd wanted to believe that this man, with so much archimage power it was practically arcing off him, could be trusted to do the right thing. Now, he wasn't so sure. Had Oliver's magic driven him mad, as it had so many of the horses?

"You will see." Oliver mounted Chieftain and pointed at Dreadful. "Mount up, old friend."

"No." Black straightened to his full height. "I want you

to change Charlotte back. I know you have the capacity to do it. If not alone, then with Chieftain's help. And maybe Baron's." He honestly didn't know if Oliver could do it but had to try. He couldn't leave Charlotte as one of those *creatures.*

Oliver began to applaud. "You have, in the many years since we've last seen another, finally grown a backbone, my boy." Chieftain stamped his front hooves in time with the clapping, and his dark eyes bore into Black's blue ones. "Well *done.* It's a shame, though, that you can't refuse me."

Before Black could ask what he meant, Oliver pointed at him and an arrow made of black magic erupted from his finger and hit Black square in the chest. It knocked him down and he sprawled on his back. Dreadful whinnied and trotted over to him as Marta and Gavin rushed to him as well. Black pushed himself up, shaking his head. His chest ached with each breath he drew.

"There's stronger magic than that, boy, if you don't come along. We have work to do, and I have no time to acquiesce to your puny requests. *Mount* **up.**" Oliver held his gaze with one of stone, and Black pushed himself to his feet.

"Black, no," Marta said, grabbing his coat sleeve. "Don't go with him! We need you!" Her glasses were askew, and he smiled half-heartedly and set them right before turning to mount Dreadful. The bay cavalry horse snorted and tossed his head.

"Go back to the townhouse," Black said, his tone firm. "The others need you, and you have to tell them what happened." He shifted his eyes to Baron, who stood there like he'd been beaten with a whip. "Baron," he said. "Baron!" The other man's head snapped up and he stared at Black. "Go with them. They *need* you now. Be the uncle I know you can be. Protect them!"

"A-all right," Baron muttered. He cast a side glance at Oliver, who sighed and made a motion in the air. A buffeting wind came and shoved Baron toward the car. "B-but we won't all fit," he murmured.

"Really, it's hard to believe that you are any relation of mine, particularly since you're an archimage." With another great gusting sigh Oliver sent a spiral of black magic over the BMW, and it transformed into a pearl white Mercedes sedan. "Now get out of here before I decide you're wasting my time," he ordered.

Baron scurried to the car and got in, but not before shooting Black a pleading look. There was nothing Black could do, though. It was true: Oliver held too much magic, and none of them could do anything against it. Not even Baron.

Gavin shook Black's hand. "Be careful. Come back."

"I will. Try to find Rory and Dante – you're going to need them," Black told him in a low tone. "Watch out for one another." Gavin nodded and climbed into the front seat of the car.

Marta stood there, arms folded tight across her chest, expression stolid. For all purposes, Black thought she looked like a Weeping Angel from *Doctor Who*. The thought almost made him shudder. "Marta," he said, his voice gentle. "You have to go with them." It wasn't going to be safe with him, and he wasn't risking another member of the Flynn family.

She responded by hugging Dreadful's neck. The stallion lowered his head until he was hugging her, too, and soft noises emanated from his throat. When she was able, she stepped back and met Black's eyes.

"Take Penumbra down," she said. For a moment, he thought she might hug him, too, but then her spine stiffened, she turned, and climbed into the back seat of the car.

Baron spun the car around and roared off down the road. Black watched it until he could no longer see it, and then gave his attention to Oliver. "What now?" he asked.

"Now," Oliver said, smiling, "we ride. We conquer."

Banshee – (according to Irish folklore) a spirit in the form of a wailing woman who appears to or is heard by members of a family as a sign that one of them is about to die.

Bathos – a ludicrous descent from the exalted or lofty to the commonplace.

Bedlam – a scene or state of wild uproar and confusion.

Charade – a blatant pretense or deception, especially something so full of pretense as to be a travesty.

Chevalier – a member of certain orders of honor or merit; a knight.

Chieftain – the chief of a clan or tribe.

Chimerical – wildly fanciful or imaginary.

Compatriot – a native or inhabitant of one's own country.

Contessa – a countess.

Crescendo – a gradual, steady increase in loudness or force.

Czarina – a Russian empress.

Dreadful – causing great dread, fear or terror.

Eidolon – a phantom or apparition.

Falconer – a person who trains or hunts with falcons.

Fanfare – an ostentatious display or flourish.

Flintlock – an outmoded gunlock in which a piece of flint striking against steel produces sparks that ignite the priming.

Harmony – agreement or accord.

Hawker – one who hunts with hawks or other birds of prey.

Imperator – an absolute or supreme ruler.

Lucida – the brightest star in a constellation.

Melody – musical sounds in agreeable succession or arrangement.

Memento – a keepsake or souvenir.

Militia – a body of citizen soldiers as opposed to professional soldiers.

Moxie – courage and aggressiveness.

Oriflamme – any ensign, banner or standard, especially one that serves as a rallying point or symbol.

Pageantry – a spectacular display

Penumbra – a shadowy or indefinite area.

Phantasm – an apparition or specter.

Ranee – a reigning queen or princess.

Ringmaster – a person in charge of the performances in a circus ring.

Sirocco – a hot, oppressive wind, especially one in the warm sector of a cyclone.

Tomahawk – a light ax used by the Native Americans as a weapon and tool.

Warpaint – paint applied by Native Americans to themselves and their horses before going to war.

ACKNOWLEDGMENTS

Once upon a time, there was a little girl who dearly loved horses. Her parents, Don and Cathy, supported her horsey habit with horses, 4-H, and showing (and lots and lots of books). She rode horses with her sister Julie and their younger sister Kristen even showed for a little while. There were shows and trail rides and an amazing 4-H club called Equine Menagerie.

The little girl eventually grew up and headed off to college, where she met a boy named Ryan. Some years later, she married him and they had two wonderful kids, Jasper and Kiera. There were some horsey adventures sprinkled in among all of that, but the girl didn't own a horse.

Even though she didn't have a horse, she had a family she loved very much, which had grown. Now she was part of the Ransom clan, along with Gary, Sharon, Brett,

Michelle, Brianna, Jonathan, Carissa, Lance, and Sarah. Her sisters got married, too, Julie to Derek and Kristen to David. Don and Cathy had four more grandkids: Jackson, Ashlynn, Lincoln and Della. There were many family adventures, including a recent trip to Cedar Point Amusement Park, where the girl got to meet the infamous Haunted Carousel Horse.

But the girl longed for another real horse, and in December 2013, found the perfect one: Blackjack, a black Missouri Foxtrotter pony with a nefarious attitude. BJ was joined by Mina, a Haflinger mare, in the spring of 2017, who belongs to Kiera. The girl and her daughter have had many riding adventures along with Julie and her horses, and look forward to many more.

That's the short story of my life so far. I love all the people mentioned in it. They have been supportive and encouraging, two things authors need a lot of in their life. I also have a wonderful library work family who keeps me laughing and loves books just like I do.

My stories would not have come to life without the work of K. R. Conway of Wicked Whale Publishing and Kat Szmit of One Wicked Wordsmith. You two fabulous women made the Flying Ponies more extraordinary than I'd ever imagined they could be. You guys make them soar!

To everyone who bought LIFT, read it, and let me know how much they enjoyed it, thank you. Hearing how much you like the Flying Ponies, Charlotte and Black truly makes my day and puts a big smile on my face. The Flying Ponies started with me, but they really belong to all of you.

And finally, an epilogue to that short story: When the girl decided to share her stories with the world, she knew that her Lord, Jesus, would bless each and every one – and so far, He has.

L. M. Ransom lives in West Michigan with her husband, son, daughter, and a beloved Jeep named Bernadette. She also shares her home with two crazy Dachsunds, and her heart with two naughty ponies. L.M. is a librarian by trade, and an author by passion. She draws from her lifelong love and obsession with all things equine to spin tales about nefarious carousel horses.

A self-professed geek girl, L.M.'s fandoms span the galaxy from Tatooine to Gallifrey, and back down to the seedy streets of Gotham City. As a Christian, she feels a calling to tell clean, intriguing stories for readers to escape into. You can find L. M. on Facebook, Instagram, Twitter, and lmransom.com.

Made in the USA
Middletown, DE
22 November 2019

79184729R00219